A HEARTLESS DESIGN

ALSO BY ELIZABETH COLE

Honor & Roses

Choose the Sky

Raven's Rise

Peregrine's Call

A Heartless Design

A Reckless Soul

A Shameless Angel

The Lady Dauntless

Beneath Sleepless Stars

A Mad and Mindless Night

Daisy and the Duke

Heather and the Highlander

Rose and the Rogue

Poppy and the Pirate

A HEARTLESS DESIGN

ELIZABETH COLE

SKYSPARK BOOKS

PHILADELPHIA, PENNSYLVANIA

↗

THE FIRST TIME IT APPEARED, *the ship gleamed silver in the bright marine sunlight, flashing brilliant, even over the sea's own brilliance. It was like staring into the depths of a diamond. And, like a diamond, the ship itself was nearly indestructible.*

She stood upon the deck, her face turned to the brisk wind. Above her, the sails snapped, white as a summer cloud—an age-old technology that caught age-old winds. But beneath her feet and under the new, gleaming deck was another innovation: steam. The combination of a metal hull and a steam-powered propeller made this ship unique. Her ship. Her invention.

What could defeat such a ship? Cannon fire could not sink it, weather could not slow it. It would be a new queen of the waves. Such a beauty of the high seas deserved a name worthy of it, the name of a warrior goddess: Andraste.

Yes, it was glorious and glittering to behold. But as her proud inventor looked to the horizon, she saw dark clouds gathering, pushing toward the ship with unnatural speed and fury. A storm shouldn't frighten her, for had she not conceived of the Andraste *to counter exactly this challenge? But a shiver rippled through her as distant thunder rumbled.*

Then, a glance behind her, at the still-blue part of the world, revealed that her ship was not alone on the water. A ragged fleet approached in defiance of the wind, and she knew in her bones that their intent was not friendly. Privateers? An enemy navy? Did it matter?

She shouted an alarm, but no one responded. Where was the ship's crew? She surely had not boarded alone! She raced to the main mast and began to tug at lines, but she was only one person, and this ship required far more hands to sail. She looked at the billowing black clouds ahead, then at the fleet approaching at speed.

She would be trapped. Her ship would be taken from her. And her fate would be decided for her...

* * * *

In the study of 42 Quince Street, her landlocked London home, Cordelia Bering woke up suddenly, and shivered in the wake of the vision. She was still sitting at her desk, where she must have dozed off and fallen into a dream of her ship again. As an engineer, she'd designed several ships in her life, but none captured her imagination like this one. If only it could one day actually be built!

She shook her head, willing herself to come back to the present moment. The breeze coming in through the open window of the study hinted at an unusually cool night for late spring. Ah, yes. She must have felt the cold and her mind spun it into a disturbing dream to wake her body up. Her dreams were rarely so frightening, or so vivid. Clearly, she was working too much.

Especially because she was supposed to be getting ready for the evening. She briefly considered not going out, but her aunt Leona did enjoy the parties of the Season, and Cordelia hated to disappoint her. The two women were all that remained of the close-knit Bering family, though they had many friends, like those who'd invited them to the party tonight.

As she rose from her chair and left the study to go to her bedroom on the floor above, she wished she could feel more excitement about the coming evening. But the truth was that Cordelia herself had little interest in such events anymore—at twenty-five years old, she was now considered to be on the shelf by most of society, and had been for at least two years. But lately she did not relish staying home every night, when the time stretched out too long and lonely, and a vague disquiet had begun to take hold of her spirit.

Her days were full. Her nights were not.

In her bedroom, the chosen gown had already been laid out, and Cordelia changed into it with the help of her maid, who kept glancing at the clock. The high-waisted silk dress she wore would scarcely keep her warm even on a balmy night. The thin, fashionable fabric, dyed a deep golden yellow, would be useless this evening. So Cordelia twirled a cashmere shawl around her shoulders, casting a look in the large mirror above the vanity.

"Bond, can you fetch the pearl drops for my ears?" she asked her maid as she considered her reflection. "I think they'll go best with this gown."

"What? Oh, yea." The young woman was still adjusting to being called by her last name, instead of the name she used most often: Lucy. She did look the part of lady's maid in her starched blue gown, and she was taller than many her age, which gave her a natural air of confidence.

She hurried to the jewelry case and extracted a pair of earrings for her mistress. Then she hastened back, her brown curls bouncing as she walked. "Here they are, ma'rm." Bond offered the earrings with a slight bob of her head.

"Madam," Cordelia corrected her gently. "Or ma'am."

The girl flushed. "Madam," she repeated carefully, in an accent now much closer to Cordelia's own. "Here are the pearls, *madam*."

"Perfect." Cordelia took the earrings from Bond. "You're doing very well."

Bond had been Cordelia's lady's maid for only a few weeks, but she was a fast learner. Her hazel eyes lit up at Cordelia's praise. "Thank you, madam."

"And, Bond, lady's maids don't say *yea*. They say—"

"They say *yes*, madam," Bond replied quickly. She paused, then confessed, "It's hard to keep it all in mind. Move like so, talk like so, *not* talk like so…I'll never catch on."

"It's just a matter of practice. You've come a long way. Soon, I'd be able to put you in any home in London." Cordelia smiled at the girl as she put on the earrings.

"Oh, ma'am! I wouldn't want to work for anyone but you. Just think if I worked in another house and someone found out about me, where I'd been!" Bond shuddered. "I'd die of shame, ma'am. That's all there is to it." Lucy Bond wasn't exaggerating. Her past was rather more colorful than that of most servants. She grew up in a rough part of the city, and fell into working for a local criminal. It was a risky way to live. Only a few months ago, she'd been in Bridewell, a hideous place even compared to other prisons. Many women would die of shame before admitting that they'd seen the inside of it. Many more would die because of the stigma alone. No reputable household in England would hire a former criminal, leaving the convicts who managed to complete their sentences little choice but to return to a life of crime simply to survive.

So what kind of household is mine? Cordelia wondered for the thousandth time. But she didn't let her thoughts show. The young woman standing in front of her had enough burdens.

"Nonsense, Bond." Cordelia turned back to the mirror, casting a final look over her appearance. She said, "In a little while, you'll be able to put aside your memories. And rest assured that I have no intention of shipping you off anytime soon. Besides, I imagine you'd miss Jem." She looked archly at the girl, whose blush deepened.

"Yes, ma'am. I would at that." Bond's attraction to Cordelia's footman had been almost instantaneous, and it was definitely mutual. Cordelia, who kept a close eye on her household, saw it at once. Unlike many other ladies, however, she didn't discourage the match. Nothing about her household or her servants was traditional.

"Enough of this talk. It's for another day. Now, in your opinion as a lady's maid, how do I look?"

"Perfect," Bond said, casting an admiring look over Cordelia's ensemble. "Shall I call for the carriage?"

"Yes, I'll be down in a few moments. Let my aunt know as well."

Drawing a deep breath, Cordelia rose and turned toward her window. It looked out over the grounds behind the house, where lush gardens and a carefully maintained lawn made the property appear much larger than it was. The last hints of twilight were fading in the sky, leaving most of the grounds in deep shadow. The lights from the windows of nearby houses occasionally twinkled through new leaves, reminding her that she was not as alone as she sometimes felt.

So why did this melancholy come upon her so often of late? Cordelia tried to ignore it when it surfaced. She had a number of good friends to visit, and she normally relished time spent alone in her study, where she worked both for business and pleasure. In addition to her ship-building work with various clients—under a male pseudonym, of course, because who would work with a female engineer?—she also created speculative designs for her own amusement. The ship *Andraste* was one such design, and she enjoyed tackling the various practical issues it presented. She even occasionally penned scholarly articles describing some of her innovations, but she had never mentioned this new ship idea, except to her own father and to one dear friend and colleague. It was too close to her heart to offer it up to the greater world.

But despite all the things that should occupy her mind, something had come over her with the advent of spring. A slight sadness, coupled with a restlessness…and a sense of foreboding. She watched the quiet scene below her window and tried to shake the feeling. She had a calm, well-ordered life, she told herself. Nothing was going to change it.

Cordelia headed down the stairs a moment later, the hem of her gown trailing along the steps behind her. The deep gold fabric set off her black hair to perfection, and the cream-colored wrap accented the dress without showing it up. Once she'd have been ecstatic to think of the looks that would be cast her way tonight. But it had been years since the attentions of men had been anything but a burden.

Cordelia's aunt, Leona Wharton, stood in the foyer, looking up at her niece with a gentle smile. She had moved in with her brother—Cordelia's father—after the death of her husband, although Cordelia's father passed soon after. No matter what tragedies life brought her—large or small—the delicately built woman maintained a cheerful, calm disposition. She had been a rock to her niece, and Cordelia couldn't imagine life without her.

"Aunt Leona, you look lovely tonight."

"Do I?" Leona replied in delight. Her now-silver hair was held up with delicate silver combs, showing off the fine bones of her face and neck. She was dressed in a trim, dark blue frock covered with a cropped spencer jacket in a lighter shade. Leona stopped wearing mourning years ago, but she rarely wore light colors anymore.

"Did Ivy tailor that coat?" Cordelia asked. Ivy was officially a parlormaid, but she also performed many duties for Leona, who didn't feel she required a dedicated lady's maid herself.

"Yes. She is clever with a needle. But look at you! I expect no less than two proposals tonight."

Cordelia rolled her eyes. "Are you counting Mr Hayden's proposal in that prediction?"

"Oh, heavens. Has he asked yet?" Her aunt clucked indulgently.

"He has not," Cordelia noted, with considerably less indulgence, thinking of her latest admirer. That Mr Hayden hadn't formally proposed yet actually surprised her a little. Yes, the man was charming, polite, and very attentive. But he was a little too insistent in his protectiveness of her around other gentlemen, particularly considering that she had met him only about four months ago, and that he hadn't ever raised the topic of marriage. She hoped he wouldn't be at tonight's event.

"Well, I expect it will not be long," Leona said. "One can't blame a man for trying to win you. I have always thought that you were, and are, the finest prize in

London."

At that moment, the butler stepped into the foyer. "The carriage is ready," he informed Cordelia in his gravelly, low-pitched voice. He wasn't a tall man, but he had a certain presence due to his sharp blue eyes, bald pate, and the noticeable scar on one cheek—the last being evidence of a misspent youth. He stood out, even in the uniform of a servant, which too often rendered people invisible. *Oh, but my servants* want *to be invisible* , she reminded herself.

"Thank you, Stiles." Cordelia nodded to him. "You should not expect us before three. Lord Gough's events tend to be lengthy."

"That's very true," Leona agreed. "Once, years ago, he held a ball on a Tuesday, and Mr Wharton and I didn't come back home 'til Friday."

Cordelia laughed. "I pray tonight won't be a repeat of that!"

"Ah, every Season seems to be brighter than the last," Leona said. "I will never tire of the spectacle and the giddiness of the crowds. It keeps one young."

Cordelia murmured an agreement, though she didn't quite share her aunt's enthusiasm lately. She'd never minded the London Season before, but this year's was different. Practically since the beginning of the Season, she had the odd sense that she was being watched…and not just by admirers.

"We shall await your return," Stiles rumbled. He held the front door open for the women to pass through. The moment he did so, a large ginger cat glided in, as though the butler had opened the door for him especially.

"Get out of the ladies' way, you impudent thing," Stiles growled at the cat.

His order was about as effective as one might expect,

and the plump cat merely leaned against Stiles's legs as he passed, purring loudly.

"I see Nero is in for the evening," Cordelia commented, smiling at the house cat. "See that he gets a bit of supper, Stiles, please."

"Aye, we wouldn't want the poor thing to waste away," the butler muttered.

Cordelia took her aunt's hand as they stepped out into the night. Resuming their previous conversation, she said, "It's too bad for the contestants, then, that I have chosen not to marry."

"But someday, dear child..." It was a discussion they'd had many times before. Stiles inclined his head almost reverentially as they passed, and if he was listening to the rather personal conversation, he gave no outward sign of it.

"Aunt, I have no need of a husband, and no wish for one. I have explained that." They walked down the short flight of steps to the stone-paved drive, and Cordelia glanced behind her in time to see Stiles scoop up the cat as he closed the door. The butler pretended to be annoyed with Nero all the time, but somehow always had a treat in his pocket for the animal.

She faced front again. A young man, angular and lanky, with dark hair and eyes, stood at attention by the carriage. His lips curved into an approving smile when he saw the ladies in their finery. His given name was James, but he'd always gone by Jem. He acted as both footman and driver. He offered a hand into the coach, first to Leona, then Cordelia. A moment later, he sprang onto the driver's seat. The women settled back as the coach began to move forward down the white gravel drive.

Evidently, Leona didn't feel she had been convincing enough. "My child, marriage can be a partnership. Your parents were very happy together, and even though Walter and I did not marry for love, we found ourselves to be well-suited. He made me happy."

"I understand what you're saying, Aunt," she said patiently. "But I am afraid that marriage is not in my future." She was grateful for the darkness inside the carriage. The shadows concealed her expression, and she didn't want to upset her aunt. For Cordelia, marriage was more than just unlikely; it was impossible. She had a host of secrets to keep. Her household servants' pasts, her unconventional and clandestine occupation, and her method of paying for it all. What man would allow such activities to continue, if he learned of them? A husband would eventually know all her secrets. That was a danger she could not risk.

Leona, though unaware of her niece's turmoil, gave up the argument gracefully, and turned to lighter subjects. The carriage clattered onward, away from Quince Street and toward the heart of London.

When they arrived in Mayfair, the ladies saw a line of carriages stretching for an eternity before the townhouse that Lord Gough maintained during the Season. Cordelia looked at the line in resignation, then called up, "Jem, just pull around the parked carriages and let us out where you can. We can both walk that distance."

"With pleasure!" Jem called back. He muttered a few choice curses at some of the less alert drivers as he guided the vehicle down the street, but soon pulled the horses to a halt. A second later, the carriage door opened and Jem's dark head appeared. "Ladies, if you please." He helped them both out. "Shall I wait?" he asked, his expression betraying his distaste for the notion.

"Heavens no, Jem," Cordelia told him. "Go on home. We'll hire a cab when we leave."

"Very good, my lady." Jem couldn't suppress a grin as he remounted the carriage seat and grabbed the reins, driving out as quickly as possible.

"Shall we?" Leona asked, gesturing down the street.

"We may as well." Cordelia straightened her shoulders. The ladies turned toward the townhouse where candlelight flooded outward into the cool spring night. They joined the stream of glittering people entering the wide open doors, a crowd that was almost entirely exactly what it seemed to be.

Except for those few attendees who were not.

↗

Lord Gough's party was a legitimate crush. The heat of the packed bodies welled up into the air, mingling with the scents of wine and hothouse lilies. Dozens of couples waltzed to the strains of the very latest music, performed by musicians who'd been imported from Vienna for the occasion. Everywhere one looked, there was a fashionable lady dressed to the nines and blooming like a flower. The only flaw in the picture was the predatory look each one wore. With narrowed eyes, Sebastien Thorne surveyed the scene from a doorway. He had seen battlefields less menacing than this place.

As he stepped into the room proper, he felt eyes from every direction settle on him. At over six feet, with broad shoulders, there was plenty on which to settle, and not a few ladies smiled at what they saw. Lord Thorne, the newest Earl of Thornebury, had nearly all the makings of a prize catch on the marriage mart. Handsome, titled, and decorated with military honors…the only question was why he hadn't already been ensnared.

"My lord," one matron purred as she stepped into his path. "It's so marvelous to see you back in town. You remember my daughter, Rose." The simpering miss beside her inexpertly batted her eyelashes at him. The mother went on, "You are never about in London, sir. It's quite criminal the way you avoid us all."

"How kind of you to say it," Sebastien returned. "Of course, I would spend more time in London if my finances permitted, but Cheshire is lovely for those who like a simple life, as I do."

He didn't have to add anything more. The matron was already pulling back at the intimation that London was too expensive for him. Earldom or no, she would never let her daughter marry a pauper. With a secret smile, he continued on, secure in the knowledge that he could still fend off the worst of the marriage-obsessed ladies of the *ton*.

In this manner, Sebastien Thorne waded past the scores of ladies and their mothers, as well as other gentlemen he knew. He paused to exchange pleasantries when he had to, but he kept moving, always aiming for a particular alcove on the upper floor. Damn Neville for arranging this rendezvous at a ball. He was used to unconventional meeting places, but a *ton* ball was a trap for a bachelor like himself.

Finally, he reached the upper alcove, where an unremarkable-looking man stood watching the crowd below.

"Have I offended you in some way, Neville?" Thorne wondered aloud, when he came within earshot of his comrade.

The man threw an amused glance at him. "I assure you, Lord Thorne, I have nothing but the greatest respect for you."

"Then why have you forced me to walk this gauntlet of marriageable women?"

The other man's mouth twitched. Julian Neville held the military rank of captain, but no one would picture him as one. Rather short and lightly built, with sandy-colored hair and a face most often set with a mild expression, Neville didn't look like the image of a heroic officer.

Looks were deceiving. Neville had saved more lives than nearly anyone Thorne could name. His affable expression also hid a mind like a steel trap.

"It's good to see you, Sagittarius," Neville muttered as Thorne came abreast of him and leaned against the balcony rail.

"You too, Aries," Thorne responded in the same tone. They knew each other well, but habit and ritual compelled them both to use their code names. For the two men were more than just fellow officers. They were members of a unique circle of spies, one so secret that even most members of Parliament had no idea it existed.

"When did you get back from abroad?" Neville asked, not referring to France by name. Thorne looked more closely at the other man. Under his customary calm demeanor, Neville was tense. Lines showed around his eyes, as if he slept little these days.

"Two nights ago. Something tells me my reprieve won't last long. You have some information for me?"

"I am afraid so." Neville paused, managing to examine the immediate area for eavesdroppers without actually moving a muscle. His voice dropped to a lower tone that didn't carry past Thorne's ears. He said, "We have word that an unfriendly person is keenly interested in some engineering plans. It's something to do with shipbuilding. A vessel or a weapon or a war machine…we just don't know. Ever since his fleet was routed at Trafalgar last autumn, Bonaparte has been mad to rebuild his navy with ships that can challenge England at sea."

"He's got his work cut out for him, then," Thorne noted. The British Royal Navy was the dominant force in the Atlantic. No other power could come close to matching their fleet strength, in either the number of ships or the guns they carried.

"True," Neville agreed. "Necessity is the mother of invention, though, and we got word that someone has developed some sort of…innovation that could change everything."

Thorne inhaled. "Where did we hear this?"

"One of our agents overheard a conversation while he was on another mission, but unfortunately was unable to identify or apprehend the speakers."

"But it's trustworthy?"

"Most certainly. We do know the code name of the endeavor: Andraste."

"Have I heard that before? Is that a proper name?" asked Thorne, thinking back to his schooldays.

"A deity, I think?" Neville shrugged, annoyed at his own lack of knowledge. "Some ancient name. And before you ask, we don't know if it means anything specific to the project, or if it was chosen randomly."

Thorne nodded, catching the urgency under Neville's words. "So. Give me the details. Where am I going? What nation is behind it?"

"That's where it gets interesting. The plans are *not* with a government. The owner is a private citizen. And judging from a few other points our agent overheard, it seems highly likely that this person is actually in London."

"That narrows it down," Thorne muttered sarcastically. "You can be sure, by the way, that the French will try to buy these plans."

"Not just the French," said Neville. "Every government in Europe would try for them. Prussia, Spain, the Dutch…not to mention that upstart nation across the sea. *Especially* them. Considering the length of coastline they have to defend, the United States' navy is laughable."

"Forgive me for not laughing at the moment. Very

well. We'll just have to find whoever has these plans and get them first." Thorne didn't like that their side had just learned about the plans when the French already knew they existed. Staying one step ahead of Bonaparte's spies was hard enough. Now it sounded like they were two steps behind.

"I was just going to order you to do that," Neville noted in his mild voice. "You're taking all the fun out of things."

"Apologies. Is this my assignment, then?"

"The Astronomer says so." As always, Neville avoided mentioning any detail about their superior's identity. "Of course, others from the Circle are available to aid you should you need it. But we have great confidence in you."

Thorne nodded. "I hope I live up to it." Like a dog on the scent, he was eager to get out of this place and start his work. "I'll begin straightaway."

"Thorne, don't you dare leave this party for at least an hour."

"Why, for God's sake?" His eyes flickered around the vast house. The din alone was enough to drive him outside. With the clashing scents and all too observant guests, he grew conscious of a strong desire to hide behind a curtain, as if he were still a child in the nursery. "Events like this give me hives."

"You just arrived," his friend explained patiently. "Everyone knows you're here. And since you rarely attend such events, people will note it. As, indeed, they already have. So linger. Play the carefree aristocrat."

"So that's why you had this meeting here." Thorne felt rather tricked, but also had to admit a grudging admiration for his colleague's cunning.

"Partly. You do have a reputation to maintain, and your work for the Astronomer kept you so busy you haven't been in town much. Also, the meeting place was convenient for me," Neville said. His tone was still agreeable, but his eyes had hardened.

"I wasn't thinking," Thorne said quietly in apology. "I expect you have a lot on your mind." As the Astronomer's right-hand man and the First Sign of the Zodiac, Neville was privy to secrets and threats to the country that would make most men insomniacs. He once confided to Thorne that the only reason he could sleep at all was because he had been given some power to respond to those threats.

Neville nodded slightly, accepting the apology. "We live in interesting times." Then he took a breath, deliberately relaxing. "When you do leave, go out through the gardens. There's a package concealed by the statue of Diana, in the third grotto on the south side of the lawn. Just look for your mark. All the details I can give you will be there. Encoded, as usual."

Thorne nodded. His eyes flicked once more around the ballroom, committing it to memory. Most of London's polite society were there, all decked out with jewels and silk, as if there were no world beyond this room. It was all so dull.

Then, he saw something new. Thorne glanced down at a vision before his eyes. A woman in a golden-yellow gown swept across the floor below, the dress throwing her creamy flesh and raven hair into sharp relief. Even from a distance, it was obvious that she was a beauty. A retinue of gentlemen followed at her heels, drawn to her like magnets to iron. He said, "I suppose I could stay a *little* while."

Neville saw the object of his attention and laughed. "Enjoy the view, Thorne. Just keep your head about you."

"When have I not?"

Neville said, "I remember how we met, Thorne. You

weren't always so aloof."

Maybe not. Thorne's gaze lingered on the woman below for a moment. Lingered on the smooth white skin, the way it contrasted with the black-as-night hair so artfully curled and twined about her head, just begging him to loosen it, to let it fall over that skin, fall down to her narrow waist, hidden by the lines of the ballroom dress. He could picture her without that proper attire. The alternative made his lips curve.

Then he took hold of himself. He had work to do. Saying goodbye to Neville, Sebastien turned and walked away. He wasn't in London to pursue a woman, lovely as she might be. He had an assignment, and the beauty below could have nothing to do with it.

UNLIKE THE EXTRAVAGANT TOWNHOME WHERE Cordelia Bering and Sebastien Thorne both lingered so unwillingly, the Bering house on Quince Street was quiet. Stiles and the other servants had completed most of their daily tasks, and nearly all of them were in the kitchen after the late meal, enjoying an hour of relaxation.

Outside, a shadowy figure watched for any sign of stragglers. The house was located at the end of a twisting, tree-lined drive, rather isolated from other homes in the area. Secluded and quiet, the garden was filled with hiding places, and only a few lights were on inside. The shadow noticed that the ground floor windows were set low, and in addition to the main entrance at least three doors opened to the outside.

As a burglar, the shadow was delighted with the place. Moving cautiously, he approached one of the long windows on the ground floor. (Clumsy thieves tended to have very short careers.)

He reached the window and pulled out some specialized implements. These tools were not intended for any honest purpose. Slender lengths of metal, they were meant to shimmy open a window sash, or to slip a lock open in place of a key. Despite the burglar's skill, the window nevertheless gave him some trouble. He cursed softly once. The house was not as easy to break into as it seemed. But he kept at it, wondering if he would have to go so far as to break the glass to gain entry. Breaking glass was noisy, a last resort.

Just then, the window lock gave with a snap. He slid the pane up and slipped through the casement, a tight fit even for a man of his slight size. Once inside, the burglar held still as a statue, hoping the minor sounds he made hadn't been heard by anyone.

After a few moments, all remained calm.

He began to methodically cover the room, searching in drawers and on shelves for something very particular. Beautiful ivory statuettes were ignored. A silver cup was passed over. Finding a locked cabinet, the thief took out another tool and worked at the lock until it gave. He extracted a large object from the lowest depths of the cabinet.

"There you are," the burglar muttered. "Right where he said you'd be."

He carried the object a few steps, then placed it on a table and pulled out another tool designed to pry the box open, working it into a narrow gap. The heavy metal at the hasp suddenly snapped off. He pulled out a stack of papers, and held them close to his chest. Sliding the box back onto its shelf, he silently closed the cabinet door. With luck, no one would even notice the broken box and missing papers for at least a few days.

Smirking, he moved back to the window to leave. All went well until the burglar felt something move under his foot, and a yowl shattered the quiet.

A huge cat leapt into sight, and the man instinctively leaned back, crashing into a bookcase. The clatter echoed through the house, and a woman's voice shrieked from a nearby room.

The thief cursed as the papers spilled out of his hands.

Frantically, he gathered them up.

"Hey! Stop there!" a voice called out, just as a door was flung open, spilling light onto the thief.

An angry maidservant stood in the doorway of the room, shouting again. The cat hissed, circling the man as if it were determined to arrest him.

The burglar grimaced. But he had the papers again, so he wriggled through the window, then hurtled out onto the lawn.

* * * *

"Jem! Mr Stiles!" the maid continued to sound the alarm. "Hurry! Someone's broken in! And he's getting away!"

In that moment, Jem burst out from a door on the other side of the house, where the kitchen lay, and charged after the fleeing shape. The thief had a long head start, and Jem knew he'd have to catch him before he reached the main road. He followed the crashing sounds, since it was too dark to see anyone in the heavy undergrowth.

Jem gained on the thief, but just as he lunged forward—actually touching the edge of the man's coat—they reached the road. Turning suddenly, the man shoved Jem roughly, knocking him backward. Then he sprinted along the roadside, vanishing around a curve further ahead.

Breathing hard, Jem scrambled up from the ground and began to run again. But it was no use. He'd never get the thief now. Sighing painfully, he slowed to a halt, then turned back toward the house to report his failure.

He found the study a blaze of light, with the furious housemaid Ivy, Stiles, and now Lucy Bond as well. They were all surveying the damage.

"Jem!" Lucy cried when she saw him. "Did you get

hurt?"

"No, I'm all right," he said, leaning on the doorjamb. "Afraid I didn't catch him, though, sir," he added, looking at Stiles.

"Too bad," Stiles growled, his face red. "I had a few things to say to him." His hands clenched into fists.

"Was anything taken?" Lucy asked anxiously. She swallowed, obviously thinking the same thing as everyone else. If a constable or detective came to the house, they would question everyone, looking for an easy suspect. That was something that struck fear in any servant's heart. For these particular servants, such an event would be tantamount to a second trial…an inevitable conviction.

"He was holding something," Ivy declared. "But I'm afraid I couldn't see what it was. Maybe he dropped it outside?"

Jem shook his head. "I didn't see anything, but it was dark. I think he was startled before he could get further into the house. He couldn't have wanted something from this room." He looked at Stiles for confirmation. "There's nothing worth much money here. It's just Miss Bering's study."

Stiles agreed. "He probably just broke in here because it was the furthest room from where we were."

"But Nero sounded the alarm," Lucy said proudly, now holding the cat in question tightly in her arms. "I'll find an extra piece of fish for you, sir."

Nero purred loudly, his previous rage forgotten.

"We ought to be grateful for the cat's alertness," Stiles said, nodding to Nero. "And there's no need to consult the authorities. But I will inform Miss Bering when she returns. Jem," he added, "I'll have to ask you to stay awake tonight, lad. We may have scared him off, but…"

Jem nodded. "I'll stay up, and I'll walk the house

every hour. If something happens, I'll hear it."

"Good. Ivy, ask Cook to make up a bit of soup for the lad," Stiles ordered. "He looks in need of a bite, after all that running."

"Sure I will, and Bond will bring it to you," Ivy said, already moving toward the kitchen.

"I'm going to check the rest of the windows and doors," Stiles said grimly. "And we'll have to take steps to improve the locks. Imagine! Breaking into *this* house!" he added in astonishment.

Jem chuckled. "Well, they don't know who or what we are, do they?"

Lucy gasped. "But what if they do? Perhaps that's why they chose this house! They knew we wouldn't want to make a fuss!" Nero, riled by her tension, leapt free and disappeared out of the room.

"You worry too much, Lucy," Jem said, putting his arm around her in a comforting hug. "I've been in this house for years now. No one knows what little secrets we have, aside from our own families. It's just a coincidence." He looked at Stiles over her head, warning him not to disagree and upset Lucy further.

Whether or not Lucy believed Jem, she relaxed slightly in his embrace, and certainly didn't mind his closeness.

"A coincidence," Stiles said strongly, whether he believed it or not. "And if they do come back, we'll make sure they know we're not to be trifled with."

THE PARTY QUICKLY BECAME TOO much for Cordelia to tolerate, and that nagging feeling of being watched continued. But of course she was being watched, she told herself. That's what these parties were for—to allow the glittering crowds of London to gaze at and gossip about everyone else. *It's nothing more than that,* Cordelia thought. Still, the urge to escape persisted, so she left her aunt with their mutual friend Mr Edward Dunham, who was so charming that her own momentary absence would not be missed.

Pacing through the gardens, Cordelia sighed restlessly, until she found a hidden grotto. A white marble statue of Diana stood in the middle of it, looking elegant in the moonlight. Her nakedness would be scandalous if she weren't a goddess. But Cordelia admired the goddess's coy expression and the bow she held in one white hand.

This was the sort of place trysting lovers might hide in. But it suited her purpose as well. More than anything else, she wished to be alone. The usual crowd of men had clung to her tonight, all polite and all attentive. Too attentive.

She sat on a stone bench, lost in thought. Perversely, as soon as she was truly alone, she felt a sense of melancholy wash over her. Something about the evening reminded her too much of a particular evening in the past.

In a flash, she realized what memory had been teasing her all night. She had been nineteen. On a night just like this, she received the proposal that her heart had been aching for. Her childhood sweetheart, Vincent Jay, had asked her father for permission, then asked Cordelia to marry him. Overjoyed at the proposal, she had erased the nervousness in his eyes with a happy, innocent kiss. That spring night was the beginning of an all-too-brief period of happiness, one that abruptly ended with Vincent's untimely death. Years later, the pain still lingered.

"Stop it, you goose," she muttered to herself. She didn't need anyone to comfort her. She had endured years of solitude; she could endure one more night. She continued to sit quietly as the sounds of party guests rose and faded. A couple walked by, speaking in low tones. Though Cordelia could not discern any words, the intimacy of the conversation needled her, making her oddly jealous of the pair.

A gaggle of voices suddenly became louder, and a rustling of leaves brought her to her feet. It sounded as if someone had found her grotto. Then a huge shadow loomed over her.

Had she been followed by someone after all?

"Leave me alone!" she warned the huge shape. Cordelia stepped away, nearly tripping on the bench behind her, and found herself staring at a tall—and devastatingly attractive—gentleman. "Oh. I mean…I thought you were…looking for me…never mind." She tried to calm her racing heart.

"Pardon me." The man bowed slightly, looking just as surprised to see her. "I assure you I didn't know this hiding place was occupied."

"I didn't mean to be rude. It's just that sometimes

there are conversations I'd rather avoid. Are you in need of a hiding place?" she asked, while finding her footing.

He smiled faintly. "I do indeed. I fear I am being stalked by the…mothers." As if to emphasize his predicament, he kept his voice low. But his dark eyes gleamed with amusement, not fear.

Cordelia hesitated for a second, then decided that for once, propriety could be ignored. She was old enough to sit with a man in a secluded spot if she chose. And she was suddenly curious about this newcomer. "Please join me, then. I can sympathize with the need to avoid match-makers." She sank slowly back onto the bench.

"May I?" He sat next to her after she nodded. "I'm sorry to have intruded on your privacy," he said.

"It's quite all right. I was a little out of sorts," she said, putting out her hand, startlingly white in the dappled moonlight. He took it, bowing his head just a bit in a po-lite gesture. Then they caught the voices of the matrons every bachelor in London most dreaded, much closer this time. Putting a finger to his lips, he held her to silence while they passed by.

When it was safe to speak again, Cordelia couldn't suppress a soft laugh. "You *are* being stalked, aren't you?"

"It's a curse, I'm afraid." He looked at her, his gaze intense. "I think you must understand the feeling of being pursued."

Cordelia nodded, thinking not of the dozen marriage proposals she'd received recently, but of the strangely intense dream she'd had earlier, the one about her ship.

He had not released her hand yet, and when Cordelia shivered, he must have felt it. She withdrew her hand, not even aware that he'd exceeded the bounds of politeness by keeping hold of her so long.

"I wish they'd leave me alone," she muttered, half to herself. He heard her comment, though, saw her rub her arms to rid herself of the goosebumps that had arisen.

"Are you cold?" he asked, looking concerned.

"No," she said. "Well, yes. A little. It's nothing."

But he had already shrugged out of his jacket and draped it around her. Cordelia was cocooned in a comforting warmth, along with a masculine smell like leather, and perhaps sandalwood. The gesture was as intimate as it was chivalrous, and she was suddenly conscious of how much of a stranger he was to her. He hadn't even offered his name.

Casting for a safe topic, she said, "I haven't met you at these events before." She waved her hand to indicate the Season in general. "Do you live in London?" She tried not to notice the lines of his body under his linen shirt, more obvious now that his coat was off. She hoped the darkness hid her involuntary glance. He was worthy of a second look, which she was determined *not* to indulge in.

He laughed to himself, at some private joke. "I have a house here in London, but circumstances force me to travel." He paused, perhaps considering how much to tell her. "My family estate is in Cheshire. I don't get to spend as much time there as I'd like either. Too much time abroad."

"I have never been out of England," Cordelia admitted. "My father once told me he took me to Scotland when I was three, but I don't think that counts, do you?"

"Not if you don't remember it." The man smiled. "You live with your father?"

Cordelia stilled. "He has passed away."

He apologized instantly. "Forgive me. I shouldn't have asked."

"How could you know? Anyway, it happened some

years ago." She didn't need to mention that her mother was gone as well; something in his expression told her he'd guessed.

"I suppose I should return to the house," Cordelia said after a moment.

"Don't go," the gentleman said suddenly, a new tone in his voice.

She looked at him, searching. "Why not?"

"It's too pleasant out here to go in that hot box again. And I barely know anyone in there, aside from Lord Gough…and all the mothers."

"Then why did you come?"

Again, he smiled as if he had a secret. "I have to attend some functions. It's expected of me."

"You don't seem the type to endure the dictates of polite society," she noted, thinking that he only played at being a gentleman. There was something rather rebellious about him.

"Perhaps not." He looked at her again, and Cordelia suddenly felt the hiding place had somehow become a lair. *His* lair. He managed to corner her without moving at all. "But tell me something. Why are you here? You come to a party only to hide in the garden? I noticed you inside before, in that lovely gold gown. You were surrounded by admirers."

"I suppose. But I was tired of being around people," Cordelia said, leaning back against the stone wall behind them.

He murmured, "Yet you invited me to join you." His words seemed to wrap themselves around her, warmer than the coat he'd already lent.

"I should not have done so," breathed Cordelia.

"But you did anyway." He reached toward her, slowly enough that she could object to the move. "I may have to take advantage of that."

Cordelia's brain was swirling in the scent of him, now stronger than before, and strangely exciting. She asked, "What sort of advantage?"

"Just a kiss," he returned.

Oh, why did he have to be so flirtatious? "I do not kiss," she said primly. Or she *tried* to be prim about it. It was difficult when she was so curious about what a kiss with him might be like. Deliberately, she leaned away from him. "By your own admission, you are not familiar with London society, sir, so let me tell you what they call me. *Heartless*. It's a true description. And you'll forgive me if I leave you now."

He stopped her with a look. "You may leave when you return my jacket." Was he laughing at her?

"Here, take it." Cordelia stood up and almost flung the jacket off. He stood as well, preventing her flight. "Thank you," she added. Her breeding would not let her be too impolite.

"I've offended you. Is it so unbelievable that I want to kiss you?" he asked, real curiosity in his voice.

"Not at all," she retorted. "For years, I've put up with this kind of thing, men wanting a kiss, or more, just because they think me pretty. God grant I get old and ugly quickly so it will stop."

"God forbid. You've never once found a man you've wanted to kiss?" he continued, as if truly interested in the answer.

She paused. In truth, there were few she could remember who had stirred her even a little. The man in front of her now, though, certainly commanded her attention. "Why should you care?"

"Because you're too lovely to be put on a shelf. You're made for living."

"I suppose you are the judge of such things," she said sourly.

"I have some experience," he drawled. "And I can tell one thing about you already. You want to prove me wrong. So here's your chance. One kiss, and you may flee back into the ballroom, secure in the knowledge that I am as disappointing as all the others." His absurdly self-assured tone belied his words.

Cordelia stood stock-still. She'd never heard an offer like that before. It wasn't veiled in a proposal, and it had a kind of honesty about it. "All right."

If the man was surprised at her acquiescence, he didn't show it. "You're game? Have a seat, then."

"No. One does not need to sit for a single kiss." She was very determined on that point.

"Have it your way." He shrugged. He cupped her face in his hand, looking at her with a sensual curve to his own lip.

"Is this a necessary step?" she asked, warming under his examination.

"I have only one kiss to give you. I must make sure it's well planned."

Cordelia caught the teasing in his voice, and felt compelled to return it. "Well? How long do you intend to plan for a simple kiss?"

"Impatient, aren't we?" He bent down and laid his lips on hers. He moved his hand to the back of her neck to better control the kiss, and let his mouth linger.

Cordelia's resolve to be unmoved slipped when he touched her, and when his tongue teased her lower lip, she gasped at the sensation.

He continued to brush her mouth lightly, using even his breath to titillate her. He seemed to sense her relative inexperience, but also her interest. He deepened the kiss, parting her mouth to dart inside with his tongue. She fluttered beneath him, her heartbeat surging.

Cordelia had never connected the word *kiss* with what was happening to her now. This was far beyond anything she'd expected. And she didn't want it to stop.

But when she felt the man's arm slip around her waist, drawing her closer, she knew she had to end this madness. Her hands were somehow laid flat against his chest, so she pushed him a bit. He released her, but didn't step away. A pleased, insolent, very intriguing smile hovered on his lips. "Heartless, you said?"

"Yes," Cordelia said shakily. She wasn't sure her legs would work properly to let her walk away. "Don't think you've changed my opinions."

"You've changed a few of mine," he said, watching her back away. "Perhaps I was mistaken in not attending more society functions."

"So you could seduce women in dark corners?" she asked sharply.

"So I could meet you."

Cordelia frowned. "You haven't met me. We don't even know each other's names. And it doesn't matter, because I assure you that we'll never see each other again."

"Don't place too high a wager on that, beauty. I know we will."

Unsettled by his confident prediction, Cordelia rushed out the grotto without looking to see who might be around. Fortunately, this part of the garden was quiet at the moment. She hurried back to the house to find her aunt. She wasn't sure what had just happened, but her whole body was singing with unfamiliar sensations. Whoever that man was, he was dangerous. She was lucky she had escaped with no more damage than bee-stung lips and an admittedly speeding heartbeat. It was high time to leave, before she could encounter him again.

* * * *

Sebastien waited for the goddess to disappear, then took a long breath.

He wasn't fooled by her nonchalance earlier, when he first stepped into the grotto and surprised her. He knew fear when he saw it. That woman wasn't heartless. She was frightened.

Of what? Him? No. She never would have let him get so close. But *something* had been on her mind, something that made her edgy and wary.

Sebastien felt a familiar growl boiling up, a need to strike out at whatever was threatening him. But nothing was threatening *him*. He wondered why that protective urge was uncurling now. Lovely as she was, the gold-gowned lady wasn't his responsibility.

But the woman had affected him far more than she ought to have. Despite her willingness to linger with him, she was obviously innocent…although her reactions to his kiss hinted at her being a very quick learner. And he'd be more than happy to teach her.

No. He had to stop that line of thought. She was a lady, albeit one daring enough to risk a kiss from a stranger. He did not dally with ladies…it was not his style, nor did he relish the idea of being trapped into marriage after an indiscreet encounter. Widows, courtesans, Cyprians…those were his sort. Practical, delightful women who didn't entangle a man in drama.

The gold-gowned, black-haired lady seemed quite capable of entanglement. Possibly in a literal way. He wondered what she thought of ropes and knots.

"Get a hold of yourself, Thorne," he muttered. He scolded himself for getting carried away by a beautiful face.

Then his eyes narrowed as a new thought seized him. Why was such a beautiful, supposedly innocent woman hiding in exactly the place where he was supposed to pick up the hidden information? He looked at the statue of Diana, the one Neville told him stood here in this grotto.

Thorne suddenly lunged toward the statue. At her stone feet, he found a tiny folded letter marked with a barred arrow, the astronomical symbol for Sagittarius. The lady hadn't taken it. But could she have read it? The letter was still sealed, and it would be written in code, but there were ways around that. And it had been almost an hour since he last saw the woman in the ballroom, surrounded by her admirers.

He reassured himself that it was probably just coincidence. He should have learned her name. Tucking the folded letter in his pocket, Sebastien sauntered back out into the main gardens, looking for all the world like a slightly drunk gentleman getting a breath of air.

Why was he unable to get the thought of the goddess out of his head? Was the woman a spy? Was she after the plans too? Or was she just in the wrong place at the wrong time? Or the right time! He smiled, remembering the kiss.

Shaking his head, Sebastien paused and took out the letter. Standing under a lantern, he unfolded it and read the cramped and cryptic handwriting. Neville, using a coded language known only to the Zodiac, related every detail that he knew of the assignment. Sebastien read the letter carefully, then read it again.

"Kingston China Company, on Dock Street." He muttered the name of the front the other agent had overheard, too quietly for anyone but himself to hear…not that there was anyone nearby.

After the third reading, he nodded to himself, confident that he had memorized everything in the letter. He reached up to the lantern, opened the glass door, and thrust the paper into the flame. It flared for a moment, then turned to ashes. He headed back to the house. He'd walk straight through the ballroom. He wouldn't even *look* for the gold-gowned, green-eyed beauty.

He had work to do.

AUNT LEONA WAS NOT WRONG about the length of Lord Gough's balls. As the hours wore on, more and more people arrived. Despite the fact that the house seemed unable to hold any more bodies, more appeared anyway.

Thankfully, Leona didn't notice Cordelia's preoccupation, since she was being entertained by Mr Dunham. Dunham was a regular fixture in society due to his charming manner. A widower for years, he was a sought-after companion among older ladies at these events.

Of late, Dunham seemed to know when Leona Wharton would be attending something, and he was frequently at her side. The development had not gone unnoticed among the *ton*, and Leona was getting some jealous looks.

Cordelia rejoined her aunt and stood alongside Dunham. She sipped some punch, hoping that the drink would cool her. The stifling heat in the house had only increased. Even if it were freezing, though, she would still be heated from the kiss of the mysterious gentleman. What had she been thinking, to allow him such a liberty?

"Bonaparte is no longer a threat," one of the gentlemen standing in their group asserted. "We routed him at Trafalgar."

"Oh, did *we*? I thought it was Lord Nelson and the brave Royal Navy who routed the French and Spanish fleets," Dunham noted. His dry wit was renowned, and he could wield it like a scalpel when he chose.

"By we, I meant England, of course," the man amended.

"Of course," Cordelia echoed. The man was really insufferable. She was glad Dunham was there to take the brunt of his boorishness.

"My point," the other man went on, "is that we don't have to worry about an invasion. The French advance is over."

"Perhaps we are safe from an invasion—perhaps—but I've heard that Bonaparte is considering keeping British ships from trading at European ports, which will pinch in the coming months. We need a real peace, not a stalemate," Dunham argued.

The voices of the men blurred as the talk turned political. Distracted, Cordelia looked around, feeling prickles on the back of her neck. She was certain that someone was watching her, very intently too. Was it the man from the garden?

To escape the feeling, she headed for one of the small rooms set aside off the ballroom for ladies to rearrange their hair or fix a ripped hem. Although she didn't need to do either, she was grateful to slip into a room limited to women.

Of course, it was crowded, just like the rest of the house. Two young ladies in striped silk gowns chattered away near the door. One of them was picking at the diaphanous fabric of her dress, but it was clear that she was far more interested in what her friend was saying.

"Mama told me everything. He's just returned to London, and he's *here* tonight. He never attends balls, says Mama. Not for years! But he's got the title now. So he must be looking for a wife at last."

"But Belle said he was absolutely penniless!" the first girl insisted passionately. "He gambled it all away, and there's nothing left but some moldering ancestral home miles from anywhere, so entailed that it's nearly worthless."

"He's an earl," her friend noted. "That's all I need to know, should he glance my way."

"A title won't keep you warm in winter. I'd rather have an income to buy decent clothes."

"If I were married to him, I wouldn't need any clothes. I'll point him out to you, darling, and it will all become very clear."

"Oh, you're wicked!" Her friend giggled and blushed at the same time. The two made their way back out to the ballroom, leaving Cordelia to shake her head over their conversation. She had no idea who they were talking about, and she tried to be grateful she would never need to worry about such things. A pulse at her temples warned her that a headache was coming on.

"Cordelia," a voice broke in, "are you not well?" It was Aunt Leona, looking lovely in the soft light of the room, save for her concerned expression.

"I'm well enough." Cordelia rubbed her temples, hoping to thwart the headache. "It's just so warm in there."

"Yes," Leona agreed. "But that's not all that's bothering you."

"I have been worried lately, for some reason," Cordelia admitted. "And tonight…I felt like I was being watched." She, of course, couldn't say she'd also been kissed by a complete stranger, or that she had enjoyed it far more than she ought to…which was to say, at all.

Her aunt took her hand. "Darling, you are undoubtedly being watched, but I am sure only by admirers."

"They are too admiring, then." Cordelia shrugged. "I wish I could explain that their attentions are unwanted." But she had wanted the kiss. Oh, Lord, she needed to stop thinking about that!

"My dear." Leona said nothing more than that, instead providing the only support she could—simply being there for her niece.

"I am sorry, Aunt. I don't mean to spoil your fun."

"Not at all." Leona leaned in closer. "To be honest, this crowd is rather dull tonight."

"Politics is on everyone's lips," Cordelia agreed. "Even Mr Dunham can't stop himself from guessing Bonaparte's next move."

"Ah, those discussions are for larger heads than ours. Let's go home," her aunt urged.

"Yes, Aunt." Cordelia tried to shake off her uneasiness. She was no one special, after all. She wasn't important to the *ton*, or influential in any way. True, engineering was an odd profession for any woman. But virtually no one knew she did it, so why would anyone be watching her? Still, she was grateful that they were leaving.

Leona led her niece through the throng, but before they could mount the great staircase to the entry hall, a cultured voice halted them.

"My ladies, surely you are not running away!" Dunham emerged from the crowd, his twinkling eyes surveying them both.

Leona answered, "I fear that the heat has quite overwhelmed me, and my niece is taking pity on an old woman by accompanying me home."

"Old?" Dunham put on a shocked expression. "Never say so! You outshine half the ladies here tonight, Mrs Wharton."

"You have a flattering tongue." Leona smiled.

"You spare me the difficulty of lying, madam. The words are sweet because the subject is."

"Such gallantry. You make me sad to leave, and Cordelia as well, I'm sure." Leona frowned slightly, seeing that Cordelia was distracted, staring off into space. "Darling? Will you not bid Mr Dunham good night?"

"What?" Cordelia suddenly recalled herself to the conversation. "Oh, yes! Mr Dunham, you are always a gentleman. And you deflected that popinjay before, whatever his name was."

"I am perpetually pleased to puncture the ego of a puffed-up popinjay, Miss Bering."

Both women laughed at his words, just as they were meant to. Cordelia felt herself relax again. Humor was always good medicine.

He bowed slightly. "But now you must take your charming chaperone home. I wish you a speedy recovery, madam."

Leona smiled winsomely, and Cordelia thought she detected a slight blush, over and above what could be blamed on the heat. The ladies left the party, grateful to step into the cooler outside air. One of Gough's footmen hailed them a hired coach.

Except for the rattling of the vehicle on the London streets, the drive back to the house was a quiet one. Cordelia sat lost in thought, and her aunt was too gracious to interrupt with idle conversation. The carriage turned up the long drive to the house itself, the gravel crunching under the wheels.

Whoever had first designed the property clearly enjoyed the idea of privacy. The drive twisted in a way that concealed the house from the street, so arriving in front of the home was always a bit of a surprise. When the horses halted at the front steps, the driver leapt down to open the carriage doors.

As they walked toward the door, Cordelia saw a grim-faced Stiles waiting there, and she knew something was terribly wrong.

Cordelia saw Stiles standing at the door, his posture giving no hint if he was weary from waiting up until the ladies returned. (Considering he'd been awake since dawn, it was likely, but he would never let such a thing show on his face.) One would think he'd trained from the cradle for his position. The idea made Cordelia smile, since she knew that his past had been quite different.

"I see you have endured the evening unscathed, my lady," Stiles rumbled.

Stiles was a perfect butler in nearly all respects. The only obvious deviation he made from proper address was to call the mistress of the house *Lady* Cordelia. In fact, she held no title at all, and so she ought to be called simply Miss Bering. Stiles ignored this rule entirely. To him, she was and always would be *Lady* Cordelia, and the rest of the household staff took their cue from him.

"We are none the worse for wear," Cordelia assured him, still concerned by the man's expression and the way he glanced toward Leona. Catching his silent request, she added, "But I shall retire now. Can you tell Mrs Landry to send up some chamomile tea? Aunt Leona?" She looked over toward her aunt. "Do you want chocolate?"

Chocolate was typically a morning drink, but Leona never let a thing like custom get in the way of modest enjoyments. "The day I don't want chocolate is the day you'll call the undertakers, dear. And I too shall go up to my room. Good night, Mr Stiles."

"Good night, madam." He bowed.

Leona headed off to her own chambers, which were located in a separate wing on the ground floor, unlike the rest of the bedrooms. She loved the gardens in the back of the house, and spent most of her free time working in them. She always said the upper floor was too far from the scent of flowers.

After waiting to ensure the older woman would not overhear anything, Stiles looked back at Cordelia.

"What happened?" she asked in a low voice.

"Someone tried to break into the house tonight," he said. "*Did* break in, in fact. He opened a window in your study. Fortunately, a maid was in the hall and heard the noise. She yelled for us. Jem tried to chase the man down, but he lost him."

Cordelia went white at the news. "They were in my study?" she whispered.

"Yes, my lady. He didn't have time to get further into the house. But do you think he could have been after something there?"

Cordelia didn't answer his question for the moment. Instead, she confided, "Stiles, tonight at Lord Gough's party…I felt like someone was watching me."

"Are you sure?" From his tone, she knew he did not disbelieve her, and for that she was profoundly grateful.

"It was just a feeling," she said. "I have no proof."

"Still, on the same night someone breaks into your home…" Stiles frowned, assessing this new bit of information. "If I wanted to steal something, I'd watch the owner too."

"It could be coincidence," she argued with no hope

that it was.

"If this were a random theft, it's possible," said Stiles. "But I get the impression, my lady, that you do not think this was random." His keen blue eyes were sympathetic.

"I must check the study," she said. "If he took—"

She was interrupted in her thoughts by the arrival of the maid Ivy, bearing a tray to take to Leona's room. "Did you tell her, sir?" she asked.

"Ivy," Stiles said wearily. "How does one greet one's mistress when she returns to the house?"

"Oh!" The girl's eyes widened when she realized her lapse. Then she pasted a smile on her face and bobbed a curtsey. "Welcome back, madam."

"Thank you, Ivy," Cordelia said, relieved the events of the night had not thrown the servants off too much. "And don't worry about what happened. I won't let anything disrupt my household."

Stiles added, "Now take that to Mrs Wharton or it will get cold."

Ivy nodded and hurried off.

"Come with me to the study," Cordelia instructed Stiles. "I'll explain everything there."

"I will be there in a moment, my lady." Stiles turned to lock the great front doors with the large key on the ring he held.

Cordelia picked up her skirts and walked quickly down the hall to her study. Opening the door, she viewed the small space, lit only by the moon filtering in through the windows facing the back garden. When she lit the lamp on the table, the signs of the burglary attempt became obvious. The furniture had been pushed out of place, and a few books still lay on the floor where they had been knocked down.

Knowing what the most valuable thing in the room

was, she hurried to a cabinet which was normally locked at all times. Now, however, she pulled it open with no resistance. With a sinking feeling, Cordelia saw the wooden box on the lowest shelf. The lid sat slightly askew. It had been pried open.

Even before she looked, she knew the contents were gone.

Someone had stolen the plans for the *Andraste*.

Cordelia sat down on the floor, too stunned to think further.

She looked around the study where she spent so many hours. It was not merely a room to her. It was a place of memories. The fact that someone had stolen from her was bad enough. The fact that they took something from *this* room felt like a gross violation.

This was where her father had spent his days, poring over books or encouraging his young daughter to help him as he pictured a new idea on paper. So many of them didn't work—would never work—but that didn't matter.

Cordelia remembered some of the more ridiculous notions they'd devised together. *Anyone can make a boat that floats*, her father would say. *Let's design a boat that can sink!* And little Cordelia would join him to craft a mad design like that.

As she grew older, she learned the methods behind his apparent madness, and found out why scholars and tradesmen from all over the country—even across the Continent—corresponded with him. Alfred Bering was a self-taught engineer, and he had a gift for finding ways to make small changes in a design that ended up profoundly altering its effectiveness. Ships were his prime interest. He had sailed in his youth, before marrying and settling into a new career as an engineer. Unfortunately, Cordelia's mother had passed away when she was still quite young, leaving her and her father on their own. So it was no surprise that her father taught her to love the sea and ships as much as he did. Until his death, they had spent summers at their cottage in Bristol, where her father took young Cordelia to watch the ships come in and talk to the captains.

After his death, Cordelia could not bear to live in the little seaside house in Bristol; it felt so different without him. So she and Leona remained in their London home year-round. Cordelia made his study into her own, continuing to create plans and plot ideas, many of them based on their earlier wild dreams.

Naturally, she didn't get rid of a single page of her father's work. Every time she looked at one of his designs, she felt like he was speaking to her again. But now someone had taken their most valued design, the one for the ship she'd named *Andraste*. The one item that she swore she'd keep safe.

A sound behind her broke her reverie. "Your tea, my lady," Stiles announced, bearing a small tray. "I thought you'd probably stay in the study for a while."

"It's gone, Stiles," she said, distracted. "It's gone! I don't know how they knew where it was. I should have destroyed it…"

"My lady." The butler put the tray down on a clear spot, and turned to his mistress. Seeing her glassy eyes, he produced a handkerchief out of nowhere. "You must remain calm." He poured the tea himself and handed her the cup.

"Thank you." Cordelia tried to smile at her longtime servant, but it wobbled.

"You are certain the burglars took something?"

"That box is empty." She pointed, and hated the way her finger wavered. "It contained a number of papers which my father and I had been working on when he died, and which I'd continued to work on. I fear that they may be quite valuable to certain people."

Stiles looked around, probably wondering how old books and papers could possibly interest a thief. "I am no scholar, my lady," Stiles admitted with his gift for under-statement. "You'll have to tell me what is so important about old notebooks that someone would want to steal some."

"Not some. A very specific set of plans. Papa and I talked about a new ship I began to design. Perhaps he mentioned it to someone he shouldn't have. He corre-sponded with a number of other gentlemen. They ex-changed ideas and discussed problems they encountered. So it's likely that he said something to one of his col-leagues, and the idea circulated." Cordelia frowned, re-membering. "If someone thought Papa had plans for something important like this, they might go quite far to get the details." She started to shiver. The vision of a ship floated in front of her eyes, a ship of the future, ironclad, beautiful…and valuable.

"The plans really could be that important?"

She nodded. "In truth, they are…were…the most valuable thing in this house. To the right person, that is." She looked up at the butler. "Stiles, I must tell you some-thing else. The thief will return."

"And why is that?"

"Because once the thief—or whoever he works for—examines those papers, he or they will realize that they are incomplete. A vital part of those plans are with my own work, in a different part of the study."

The butler considered this. "You could destroy them."

"I will not do so unless it can't be avoided," Cordelia said. "The ship could be very important…if used well.

But now that someone has taken part of the plans, I must watch over the rest of them."

"If your papers cannot be destroyed or removed from the house, we will have to make the house harder to get into," Stiles said decisively. "I will oversee certain improvements to the house to deter thieves."

"I suppose I should have done that years ago." She balled her hands into fists, angry at her own naiveté. "I knew some of the work we'd done might interest certain people, but I never thought…"

"They won't get them," Stiles promised. "There won't be a way for anyone to sneak in when I'm done."

"Please do whatever is necessary. Don't worry about cost."

Stiles paused, then said, "My lady, I don't believe the papers are the most valuable thing in this house. You are. And you will find your household will do everything we can to keep you safe."

Cordelia was touched. "Thank you, Stiles. And you're right, of course. We must make some changes to the house."

"Put it out of your mind tonight, my lady," Stiles urged. He walked out of the room, leaving Cordelia alone with her thoughts.

She didn't know how long she remained there when Bond appeared in the doorway. "My lady, may I see you to bed? It's very late."

"I doubt I can sleep," Cordelia said, putting down her long-empty teacup.

"You should try, ma'am. There's nothing more you can do tonight. Jem will stay awake to be sure no one returns. Tomorrow we'll all get to work to protect the house and you."

Cordelia let Bond walk her up to her room and prepare

her for bed. But as she lay with her eyes wide open, staring into the darkness, she could see only a phantom ship, gleaming in imagined moonlight.

She whispered, "Who else knows about *Andraste*? Who did Papa tell? And why?"

THAT SAME NIGHT, IN THE small hours, Sebastien Thorne pursued his own hunt for the information the Zodiac charged him to find.

From Gough's party, a carriage took him to a house in a neighborhood that no one would associate with a titled gentleman. The place was sturdy enough, though outwardly run-down. Notably, it was not far from St James Street, where there were several gaming hells and other houses of dubious repute. Thorne sometimes found it very useful to be close to those places.

The front of the house was rather grimy, and the windows were always blocked by heavy curtains. Everything about it discouraged curiosity. Thorne liked it that way. He let himself in with his own key; there were no servants here. He had purchased the property almost as soon as he joined the Zodiac, knowing that he needed to keep one part of his life secret from his family.

Inside, he lit a candle and headed up the narrow staircase. He'd made improvements to the rooms, particularly the ones that he used as a bedroom and a study. A large clothes press held an array of items—most of them had no place in a gentleman's wardrobe. Rough trousers, carefully scuffed boots, mud-stained jackets…even a selection of hats and wigs, in case Thorne really wanted to be unrecognized.

He wouldn't need anything so drastic tonight. He selected a few pieces of clothing, plain but not worn, and all in black. He laid aside his fine apparel from the party and pulled on the new items, amused by the knowledge that many men of his station would never even contemplate changing their cravat without a valet.

He traded his smooth leather shoes for a worn pair of work boots that he'd commandeered from one of his servants a few years ago. The long greatcoat he donned was dark grey, made of rough fabric with artfully placed stains along the bottom, as if he could not afford to have it cleaned. He tousled his brown hair, and then grabbed an ill-fitting, battered hat.

Glancing in the mirror, he grinned at his reflection. Clothes did indeed make the man. No one would mistake him for an earl now. Dress like an earl, and people treated him like an earl. Dress like a pauper, and he'd be lucky if he could get a carriage to stop in the street.

Satisfied with his appearance, he left the house again, eager to begin his hunt for the documents. Truth to tell, he was glad of the assignment. He hated the idle time between missions. He had never cared for the usual aristocratic diversions, and he was in no mood to be chased by silly ladies seeking a titled gentleman.

No, give him a life-or-death mission every time. What woman could compare to that? He tried to push away the image of the woman who *did* threaten to compare to that…the lovely vision in the garden. She was a novelty, that was all. He'd forget her within a day or two.

According to Neville's now-destroyed letter, the people after the mysterious plans had a front called the Kingston China Company. It was in the shipping district, close to the docks.

He hired a carriage to take him as far as the district's

main thoroughfare, then he began to walk, covering the distance quickly with his long stride. He passed through streets that became narrower and darker, the buildings looking more workaday and worn. As he moved toward the smell of the river, he considered everything that had brought him to this point.

Fifteen years ago, he'd never imagined that he'd be an honored peer, let alone a trusted agent of the government. No, fifteen years ago he'd been a rowdy, frustrated younger son—the "Honorable" Sebastien Thorne—whose only goal was to cause his family as much aggravation as possible.

With no expectations for him to live up to, he'd sunk to ever lower levels of behavior, daring his parents and older brother to call him on his debauchery. At first it was a bit of gaming and a lot of women. But he'd quickly fallen deeper and deeper into debt, seduced by the excitement of gambling, always ready to convince himself that his bad luck would turn.

It wasn't until the day that he'd woken up on Hampstead Heath outside the city, still drunk from the night before, with nothing more than the clothes on his back— his money and watch long gone—that he admitted he might have a problem.

His father was not sympathetic when Sebastien had returned home to beg for more money. The elder Lord Thorne had heard similar speeches many times before. This time, he agreed to settle Sebastien's debts on one condition—he would purchase a commission and Sebastien would serve as an army officer. It seemed the only way to prevent his dissolute son from falling back into his old ways.

And, by pure good luck, it did the trick. The army proved to be the perfect place for Sebastien. It demanded an order and discipline that he'd never been asked to give, but—after a few humiliating encounters—he found that he craved. He learned there was a vast difference between the respect men gave to a title and the respect he could earn with his actions. All at once, he was not only part of something greater than himself, he was directly responsible for the lives of others.

He wasn't long in the army before he gained the notice of a few particular people. As a commissioned officer, he was given tasks somewhat different than the enlisted men. When he proved he could be trusted to perform those tasks, he was given other, more mysterious jobs, and he quickly found his strength.

Sebastien Thorne was a good soldier.

But he was an exceptional spy.

Thorne didn't know exactly what attracted the attention of the group he now worked with. But one day, he met another young officer named Julian Neville. Neville told him the story of the Zodiac, a small group of agents dedicated to protecting the Crown of England against all enemies. The history of the group stretched back many decades, but there were never more than twelve agents active at any time, each one taking a sign as a code name. If anything happened to make a certain sign available—as it inevitably did, since espionage was a dangerous profession—a new agent was selected after careful consideration. Thorne had been recruited as Sagittarius. He was wise enough to never ask what happened to his predecessor. He was also wise enough to never ask what would have happened to him if he'd refused to join the Zodiac.

To say that the group was secretive was an understatement. Thorne didn't even know everyone else who was in the Zodiac. The agents generally worked alone, with only a few trusted contacts.

Neville was Thorne's superior, and he couldn't imagine a man better suited to be an agent. It was Neville who trained Thorne in the finer points of espionage, and Neville who gave him the assignments. In turn, Neville reported to the "Astronomer," the one who truly ran the Zodiac. Thorne had no idea who the Astronomer was, and he would probably never find out.

It had been over a decade since that first meeting with Neville, but Thorne hadn't lost his zeal. Now, in the dreary and silent shipping district, he found the place he was looking for, the Kingston China Company. He found a hiding spot across the street from the main doors and hunkered down to survey the warehouse.

As Thorne waited for any sign of life, his mind drifted back to earlier that evening at Lord Gough's, to the gorgeous woman in the brilliantly golden gown. She had been a sight to behold, even if she was, as she claimed, heartless. Sebastien smiled into the dark. He wondered if he could change her perspective, given the chance. All that fine skin couldn't be so cold, even if her heart was.

Then he shook his head. "Stop it," he warned himself in a mutter. It had been a while since he'd been with a woman. He must remedy that situation, before he found an excuse to see the heartless beauty again.

Suddenly, he heard talking from around the corner. He strained his ears to catch any hint that these were the men he was hoping to find. The thickening mist from the river distorted sound, but he heard two distinct voices. A pair of men approached the door of the warehouse. He heard the rattle of a key in the lock, and then the groan of the hinges.

Thorne moved like a cat, reaching the door just as it swung closed again. He was lucky—the men didn't check to see if the latch caught on the door. They were not being careful. Without a sound, Thorne eased the door open, slipping into the musty-smelling warehouse. He heard footsteps fading away, but he paused to take in his surroundings.

It was definitely a warehouse, but it did not appear to be a well-used one. Wooden crates were stacked in piles, and sawdust and wood shavings, probably once packing material for china, lay scattered across the floor. He narrowed his eyes, seeing where the feet of the men he followed left their mark on the floor. He'd have to be careful not to give away his own presence by disturbing the sawdust. That meant either keeping well into the shadows, by the wall…or by stepping exactly where his quarry had.

He chose to stay near the wall, and he kept his ears open as he crept through the darkness. He'd covered several yards when he heard a noise behind him. The door had opened again. Thorne slid between two large crates, hardly daring to breathe. He heard more footsteps, but they passed his hiding spot without slowing. He exhaled.

The latecomer rounded a corner, and a rough voice greeted him. Thorne used the sounds to cover his own approach. He desperately wanted to hear the conversation, hoping it would relate to the plans he was seeking.

"You got it?" a voice asked.

"Barely. I got into the house, but some little git of a maid heard me and raised the alarm." The newcomer's voice was both defiant and nervous. "One of them chased me all the way to the road! I was nearly caught."

"You deserved to be, if you couldn't slip in under the noses of a bunch of drowsy chambermaids!"

"More than you can say, since you couldn't be bothered to do it yourself. Here." The sound of something hitting the surface of the table echoed through the warehouse.

Thorne wormed his way forward until he could catch a glimpse of the newest arrival through a gap in the boxes. By his profile, he was a middle-aged man, thin and wiry from rough living. Candlelight revealed the sheen of sweat on his face.

The mostly hidden man at the desk opened the package eagerly and began to sift through the stack of papers. He unfolded several, putting them aside. As he worked his way through, he said, "Something is missing."

"I got everything in the box," the thin man protested. "Every scrap of paper!"

"So you say. How do I know you haven't hidden what I need?"

"I wouldn't know what to hide! Those scribbles all look the same to me. If you need more, they must be somewhere else in that house. Just tell me where the rest of the papers are, and I'll go back."

"It's too late," said the other unseen man. "They'll be alert now."

"Look, I can get what you're looking for," the thin man begged. "Let me try. I need the money!"

"Too bad." There was a scraping sound as one of the men stood up.

The thief's eyes widened in fear, and Thorne had a moment of premonition. Although he couldn't see it, he knew the other man was drawing a pistol.

The thief snapped out of his momentary shock and turned to run back to the door of the warehouse. As he did, a shot echoed through the building, but it went wide of its mark. The thief was still running. Thorne waited as the two other shapes dashed by his hiding spot and left him behind.

He moved to the table where the men had been, but the surface was empty. One of them must have taken the papers along. He swore in frustration.

There was little more Thorne could do here. He trailed the others out of the building, moving as fast as he dared. Fortunately, he remembered the streets immediately around the warehouse, and he knew where the thief was likely to run. Once he got outside, he slipped into the alley where he had hidden before, and watched. The thief was nowhere to be seen, but the first two men he'd seen now chased up and down the street, casting about for their quarry. One ran in the opposite direction from the alley, toward the main thoroughfare. The other moved more slowly, walking toward the riverfront. As he went, he peered down the alleys and into the various doorways. Thorne noticed the gleam of a knife blade in the man's hand.

Picking up a small stone, Thorne hurled it so it clattered at the far end of one alley. The man heard the sound and moved toward it, not knowing he'd pass Thorne on the way. His eyes flicked from right to left, but even so, he was very surprised when Thorne stepped out of the shadows and delivered a quick blow to his head.

The man grunted, stumbling backward. Thorne easily grabbed the arm holding the knife and twisted it so that the blade fell to the ground. He kicked it, sending it sliding into the dark shadows of the alley. Then he turned to the man, memorizing his face.

"What do you want?" the man asked. His voice came out in a sharp whine. "I don't have any money." He squinted, trying to see Thorne's features in the darkness.

"I don't want your money," said Thorne. "I want you to be quiet." He hit the man once more, and this time he crumpled to the ground. A quick check revealed he didn't have the papers on him. *Too bad*, thought Thorne. He turned around and headed back out to the street, moving at an easy pace, but keeping a sharp eye out for either of the other men. One of them had the papers, and the other knew about them.

He hadn't gone far when he caught sight of the thin man scuttling down the further end of the street, almost at the river. The thief saw him coming and halted for a moment. Although Thorne was a stranger and not one of his sometime employers, his natural instinct was still to run when he saw a large, unsmiling man coming toward him. By that point, however, it was too late. The thief turned tail, but got only a few paces when Thorne caught up and seized him.

"What're you doing? There's a mistake..." the thief sputtered.

"Shut up," Thorne said quietly. The menace in his tone was enough to stop the thief cold. He even forgot to try to wiggle free of that iron grasp. "You robbed a house tonight."

The man began to deny it, but the words died on his lips when he saw Thorne's expression. "Are you..." He frowned. "You're not with Dodd's gang."

"Dodd hired you to rob the house?"

"Aye. Gerald Dodd. He was going to pay me to take a box from this one house. Said it would be an easy job!"

"We'll talk about this on the way," Thorne said, prodding the man forward. "Move."

"Where are we going?"

"You're taking me to the house you broke into."

"Are you working against Dodd? Because I don't want to be in the middle of this..."

"You're already in the middle of this, friend," Thorne said. "Stop worrying about Dodd. He's not here right now, but I am. And if I decide that you're not being helpful, I've no reason to keep you around. Understand?"

The man nodded quickly.

"Now, where was the house?"

"Pretty far out. On Quince Street. It'll take till dawn to walk there."

Thorne looked up the street. "Walk along the river until we get to the next street. Then we'll pick up a ride. What's your name?"

"Um, John. John Bailey," he stuttered nervously.

As they walked, Thorne kept a close eye on his prisoner. They reached the main street without seeing any sign of Bailey's former employers. Thorne hailed a cab by holding a silver coin up where the driver could see it, and after Bailey was encouraged to give the directions, they were on their way.

In the carriage, Thorne leveled his gaze on the unfortunate thief. "Tell me exactly what you were stealing."

"Dodd told me to go to this particular house, break in, and take a box out of a study on the ground floor. He said tonight the owners of the house would be gone and only servants would be there. He said it would be easy, and it did look easy. But a maid heard me when I made a noise. Then one of the other servants chased me all the way off the property."

"What was in this box?" Thorne asked.

"Just papers. It was a heavy wooden strongbox with a lock. I knew I wouldn't be able to run with the whole thing, so I pried it open and took the papers out."

"Why would Dodd want a strongbox of papers?" Thorne had a guess, and didn't like it. Dodd, whoever he was, must have somehow learned about the plans and decided to steal them so he could sell them to the highest bidder.

Bailey must have thought along similar lines. "He's got his fingers in a lot of pies. He probably wants to sell what's inside. He'll sell anything for a profit."

"Suppose I'll have to have a word with Gerald Dodd soon," Thorne noted. Bailey paled at his tone. "Who were you stealing them from? Who's the owner of the house?"

Bailey shrugged helplessly. "I wasn't told any name. Just where the house was and what window to break into. Said I didn't need to know more than that."

Thorne grunted, thinking. "Why'd he hire you? Why not just do it himself, if he knew where it was?"

"Dodd doesn't get his hands dirty like that. He's a boss." Then Bailey added, spitefully, "Not to mention, he's too fat to be a good thief nowadays."

The coach jerked to a stop. Thorne put one hand on the door. "I'm stepping out first. No tricks."

Bailey nodded. He climbed out after Thorne and looked nervously at his surroundings. Quince Street was in a neighborhood of quiet, stately homes. It was not the most fashionable district of London, being a little too far from the heart of things. But it was thoroughly respectable, and Bailey clearly felt out of place.

"All right," Thorne said as the coach clattered away. "Show me."

Bailey took the lead, walking up Quince Street with a shuffling gait. It was shortly before dawn now, and the silence of the neighborhood at that hour was almost deafening.

They reached a driveway flanked by two gateposts. On top of each one, instead of the usual eagle or lion, there was a sailing ship wrought in iron.

"This is the place?" Thorne asked Bailey.

"Yes, sir." If Bailey hoped that was all his captor wanted, he was mistaken.

Thorne dragged him forward. "Come on, then. I want to see the house itself, and exactly where you broke in."

His shoulders slumped, Bailey led Thorne up the drive. He looked like he expected to be attacked by a vengeful butler or footman at any moment, but the stillness was not broken. Soon enough, after they had made their way through a copse of trees that hid the house from the road, Bailey halted. "The study is at the back of the west wing, just round the corner there."

"I want to see it." Thorne noted every detail of the grounds as they crept forward, keeping to the shadows on the edge of the deep green lawn that surrounded the house like a moat.

They stopped again as Bailey pointed. "That's the window I used. I'd have got out easy if I hadn't tripped over the blasted housecat. Look! They've left a light burning!"

"They were worried you'd come back," Thorne muttered. That was interesting. The people in the house either knew or suspected that the thief had not fully succeeded.

"The box'll be gone now," Bailey guessed aloud. "They'll have moved it."

Thorne withdrew into the deeper green of the trees bordering the lawn. "I'll be staying here for a while."

"You plan on getting the other papers so Dodd can't?" Bailey asked.

"Is that any concern of yours?" Thorne asked.

"No," Bailey assured him hurriedly. "But Dodd will come for me, and what am I supposed to tell him about you?"

"Nothing," Thorne said, looking Bailey full in the face. "In fact, if you're smart, you'll disappear altogether."

"What do you mean?" Bailey began to back away, looking even more nervous when Thorne reached into his coat. But he only pulled out a small bag that made a distinctive jingling sound. He took out several coins. "Your accent. You're not from London," he noted as Bailey stared at the money.

"I was born in Dorset," he admitted.

"Go back there," Thorne advised. "And don't stop anywhere you usually go to pack anything. The further away you get, the more likely you'll live."

"What's this all about?" Bailey asked, staring at Thorne as if unsure he was human.

"Something much bigger than you, friend. Now go." He dropped the money—probably more than the thief would have earned from five jobs like this one—into Bailey's palm. "Godspeed."

Bailey lost no time in disappearing. Thorne was relatively confident that Bailey would live. The man was a weasel, but weasels were usually interested in self-preservation. In any case, he had to concentrate on getting the papers out of this house and to the Zodiac, where they would be safe. He noticed the sky lightening in the east. He would stay only long enough to learn the layout of the house. One circuit around, and then he'd vanish.

* * * *

Up in her room, Cordelia stood at her window in the cool hour before dawn. She had a nightmare featuring the *Andraste*. Unlike her usual mental image of it, where the sides shone silver like a knight's armor, in this dream the ship was the blue-black of a folded blade.

The sea it sailed over was dark, the waves tinged red by sunset. The sails were filthy with salt and grime, and the shouts of men—sailors? soldiers?—echoed over the water. She stood gazing at the ship from a headland, watching in despair as her beautiful creation, the bright ship *Andraste*, became bloodstained in battle.

At the window, Cordelia bowed her head. What had she been thinking? She imagined her design would save lives, not help destroy them. She'd been a child when she first dreamed up the *Andraste*, with a child's naiveté.

Outside, something caught her eye. Cordelia watched a shape drift over the lawn. Something—someone—was on her property. The figure was scarcely noticeable in the dim light, and she stared hard for a minute to make sure she was not mistaken. But then it moved again. Yes, it was a man. A man watching the house.

The thief returned! She knew she should pull the bell to summon help. Jem could try to chase the man down again. But something held her in place. She tried to see the outline of the man on the lawn. Was he old? Young? Big? Small? Was he the same man who had broken in before? Cordelia kept to the side of her window, hoping that she was invisible to the watcher. Who was he?

Suddenly, the shape moved again. Walking parallel to the edge of the lawn, the man made his way to the gravel drive, where he halted for a moment. Then he turned and disappeared. But right before he did, Cordelia caught the shape of his silhouette against the white gravel. She had no reason to believe that she had seen this man before, but the impression was seared onto her overactive brain. The shape of the head, the set of the broad shoulders. Even under the greatcoat that covered his frame, she knew who it was. It was the man who had kissed her in the gardens last night.

She could not forget the shape of him.

She trembled, remembering how close he had been to her…but why had he followed her, if not to force her to give him the papers?

His kiss must have been part of a cold-hearted seduction plan. Did he really think seduction would work? Hadn't it, almost? Only she had left him, and that's when he must have decided to go for the more direct method of breaking into her house.

If she had let him kiss her even a little more, who knew what might have happened? She couldn't pretend she hadn't been extremely affected by his attention. But even worse was that little pull in her heart. She had *liked* him, even before he kissed her. He seemed…fascinating. Part of her wondered what it would be like to have someone like him at her side. If they could be allies.

Now she knew the answer. He was just another enemy.

Cordelia turned away from the window. "I know what you want," she said, though no one could hear her. "But I'll never let you get it."

↗

THE MORNING DAWNED BRIGHT AND glorious, but no one in the house on Quince Street was in a mood to appreciate it. A few servants, led by Stiles, paced around the yard, discussing the house in a professional manner.

"Those windows are so low to the ground, you can practically call them doors," Jem noted critically. He'd been a pickpocket in a former life and, as a member of a gang, had also stolen from several houses of the gentry. "We can't keep watch all night, every night, so we'll have to secure them somehow."

"And locks alone won't do," Bond added. "Any decent thief knows how to muffle the sound of broken glass."

"Towel," said Jem.

"Or cut a pane out with a jeweler's knife," Bond suggested.

"You did that?" Jem asked, looking at her with a certain respect.

"Not to a window," she explained. "I cut out a bit of glass on a locked cabinet. Just enough to turn the latch from inside."

"And what was inside?"

"A jewel case. Most of the stuff was paste, but there were these pearls..." Bond's eyes grew dreamy. "Ludd only gave me one tenth of what he got for 'em. Stingy bastard…considering I did all the work for 'em. I ate like a queen for three months, though."

Stiles grunted, interrupting her reverie. "That is not the sort of story you should be proud of, Miss Bond."

She shrugged. "No sense denying the past. We've all done things we shouldn't to fill our bellies."

"Well, put your talents to better use now."

Bond said, "Many homes bar the ground floor windows."

"Ugly," noted Jem. "Miss Bering won't like it."

Bond considered the side of the house. "You could plant something nasty and thorny in front of the windows…but that takes time to grow, and Mrs Wharton might take issue if we alter her gardens."

Jem laughed. "*Might* take issue? We'd be run out of town if we touched a single plant!"

"Bars it must be, then," Stiles said. "Jem, could you get into the upper windows?"

"I could," Jem admitted. "But I'm not sure how many would try. It wouldn't be a quick job, that's for sure. If it were me, I'd climb that vine-covered trellis over there, then scramble over to the window that opens at the end of the hallway."

Bond gasped. "That's too far. You'd fall and break your back!"

"I've made further leaps," he said, grinning. "Don't you worry about me. Though if I did get hurt, would you kiss it to make it better?"

"Enough," Stiles rumbled. He frowned at the young couple, who seemed to be having entirely too much fun. "We'll put a sash lock on the window by the trellis. No one could pry it open while hanging from the sill." Satisfied that they could secure the house against most intruders, the butler directed his underlings to return inside, where they had other duties. Whatever they'd been be-fore, they were respectable servants now. Well, mostly respectable.

* * * *

After seeing the stranger in her garden, Cordelia had lain on her bed, staring at the walls, her mind consumed with memories of her father and the awful days following his death. When daylight finally crept into the room, she fell into an exhausted, dreamless sleep, though she felt no better when Bond woke her several hours later.

"It's eleven, ma'am," Bond said after she'd shaken Cordelia awake. "You said I should never let you sleep past eleven."

"No," she agreed groggily. "I should be up and about."

"Shall I bring your tea up?"

"I'll take breakfast downstairs," Cordelia insisted.

Bond helped Cordelia dress with a minimum of fuss. She'd chosen a filmy Grecian-style gown in white lawn. With its high waist and tiny sleeves, it was the height of fashion, though Cordelia privately found the style a bit scandalous. She couldn't deny how comfortable it was to wear, however, particularly in warm weather.

"It will be hot today, ma'am," Bond said as she but-toned up the back of the gown. "It's already hot on the east side of the house. Here." She handed Cordelia a fan, the thin wooden spine covered with silk dyed a rich shade of green. Cordelia idly snapped it open and fanned herself experimentally.

"Very pretty, ma'am. Brings out your eyes. Do you want the jade necklace?"

Cordelia shook her head. "A good thought. Not at the moment, though. If I go out, I'll wear it."

"I'll put it aside, then," the maid replied easily. She was clearly retaining everything she'd been taught about clothing and jewelry, Cordelia noted as she watched Bond gather up the gold gown from last night to take downstairs to press, and repair it if necessary.

Cordelia went downstairs, where she found her appetite revived by the smell of baked bread and fresh jam. When she was nearly done eating, Stiles appeared in the dining room. After a perfunctory greeting, he related his plans to add bars to the windows. Then he added, "I talked it over with Mrs Landry. We decided that it may have nothing to do with your father's work. Rather, it may have to do with…one of us."

Cordelia looked at him with a newfound concern. "One of the servants? Oh, no. That's impossible."

"Nothing is impossible, my lady. You know our pasts, and so do a few others—not all of them friendly. I won't surprise you by admitting that I made many enemies in my time."

"But that was years ago," she insisted, as if that could ward away the logic of his argument. "You even changed your name."

"A grudge can last a lifetime, my lady. And people talk. Maybe someone finally discovered that I'm not as dead as they thought. My name is different now, but I can't do much about my face. It may be best that we leave this house in order to protect you."

"No!" Cordelia said. "Absolutely not. Where would you go? What would I do without you?"

Ivy appeared in the hall, bearing a tray holding a small teapot and cup. The scent of tea drifted in the air. She halted when she saw her mistress arguing with Stiles.

"Ivy, take that to Mrs Wharton in the garden," Stiles ordered.

"Have you told her, then?" Ivy asked, ignoring the order. "We'll leave if that's best, ma'am. Don't know where I can go, but I'll be damned if my old boss takes what I done out on you."

"Ivy!" Stiles growled. "Language!"

The maid looked abashed. "I meant that I'd be quite distraught," she corrected herself.

"No one is going anywhere," Cordelia said firmly. "If anyone is to blame, it is me. I should have destroyed those papers long ago. I didn't. But I will decide how to…extract this household from any future entanglement. I promise."

Though how she could do that when she didn't know who her enemies were would be quite a challenge.

* * * *

Despite his late night, Sebastien slept for only a few hours after returning to his family's townhome, once again dressed as the gentleman everyone knew him to be. In his dreams, he chased a thousand threads throughout the city, looking for the elusive papers. Not knowing what exactly they were for made everything worse. He feared he would look right at them and not recognize what he was seeking.

Groaning at the sunlight, he summoned his valet to help him dress, then went down to the breakfast room.

The townhouse that the Thorne family had purchased several years ago was located in a quiet, well-to-do neighborhood. The building itself was not large, nor was it particularly ornate. Sebastien was glad of that, because he knew what other families of his class spent on maintaining their homes in town, and the idea of squandering funds on that sort of thing made him furious.

The walls were painted rather than papered, and ornamentation was restrained compared to earlier eras. The molding was inspired by Classic art. Sebastien's eyes followed the flow of one design that marched around the room just below the ceiling. The repeating curves looked simple, but a trick of the eye made it hard to decide exactly what the pattern was. Not unlike his life, he reflected ruefully.

He poured coffee into two separate cups. He had no intention of sharing—he merely wanted to avoid getting up to refill anything. He carried those to the table, then pulled together a plate of cold meats and bread off the sideboard. Sitting down at last, he decided to forget his assignment just until he finished eating. There was nothing he could do at the table to solve this mystery.

However, his mother sought him out before his coffee had a chance to cool. She appeared in the doorway, dressed in powder-blue damask that set off her fair complexion and still-golden hair. Sebastien had inherited his father's coloring, not his mother's. But he did have her stubbornness.

She surveyed him with narrowed eyes. "Are you slipping back into your dissolute ways, Sebastien? I am told that you didn't get home until well after dawn."

"Gough's ball," he explained shortly, hoping to put her off. He lifted the first coffee cup to his lips and drained it. His mother looked on in frank disapproval.

"You hate those things." She sat down across the table from him, her back ramrod straight. The woman had been born with perfect posture.

"I met an old friend there. Another officer."

"And then went carousing all night, I'll warrant. Sebastien, when will you admit that you cannot live like a young lad first off in the world? You are thirty-five, and the heir now. You need to take responsibility!"

Sebastien bit his tongue. The facade he had to keep up in front of his family was by far the worst part of his role for the Zodiac. Of course they knew nothing of his work as an agent, and his best screen to fool everyone was to pretend that he hadn't changed much from his callow youth—that he remained an inveterate drinker and gambler. It worked, but it wasn't without consequences.

"I was being responsible," he said, now trying to think of a way to soothe her. He took a sip of coffee from the next cup to give him a moment to come up with something.

"Oh, indeed. How exactly?"

Inspiration struck. "I was auditioning young ladies for the part of countess."

Her expression softened a bit. "And did you find any to your liking this time?"

"One," he said honestly, and smiled, remembering the kiss.

His mother looked delighted. "Well, well. Who is she?"

"Sadly, I didn't get her name."

"What? You were not introduced? How do you know that she would be suitable?"

He remembered her figure as being perfectly suitable, not that he could tell his mother that. "The sight of her across the room was enough to get my interest. Fate dictated that I wasn't to get her name last night. But she intrigued me, Mother. Trust me…I'm going to find out more about her." Such as her name, where she lived, and if she was a spy.

Unaware of the particular direction of his interest, she said, "I suppose that's the best I can hope for. Sebastien, the continuation of the line is crucial. Knowing that you were settled would be a great comfort to me in my final days."

"Final days? You're at the peak of health!"

"We thought the same of your father, remember. And his heart gave out with no warning. And Fate took your brother too. You must promise me that you will pursue a proper marriage, dear."

"Don't rush me, Mother. I'm still getting used to the title. It weighs more than you'd expect."

"You miss George. So do I." She bent her head. Sebastien knew she was fighting off tears.

In a proper world, his older brother, George, would have been the one to carry on the glory of the Thorne line. He had been the one with the training and the attitude to be a proper heir.

But only a short while after he became earl, he didn't come back from a ride. The household was sent out to look for him; they found him on a disused path, his back broken and his horse gone. He died within days.

So Sebastien, once the carefree younger son, found himself elevated to the lesser title of viscount with the death of his father, and then, all too soon, to earl after George's passing.

He looked at the woman across from him, her face fragile in the morning light. He said, "I know I disappointed you."

"No, Sebastien. Don't ever think that. You worried me, you enraged me. But you never disappointed me. You were a wild young man, and I should have begged your father to take you in hand long before events took over. The army did seem to help you. I know you would have liked to stay. But you are needed here. I'm only sorry it took the death of your brother to bring you back home."

He reached over and took her hand. "At least I am

back home." Giving his mother a reassuring smile, he added, "And I'll try to live up to your expectations."

After placating his mother, Sebastien went to his office to dispatch some legitimate business for a few hours. The running of the family estate was not really burdensome, since the family's retainers were all old hands who were thoroughly competent. But Sebastien knew familiarity was key if he was ever to truly step into the role his brother left. He also wanted to make sure that the men running the estates didn't get too enthusiastic. The finances of the Thorne family had been troubled until very recently. His father's gambling habit had not been as rampant as his second son's, but he had debts too.

In the short time that George had been at the head of the family, he wisely spent money on restoring the Cheshire estate, Thorne Hall. He had planned to make it his permanent home after finding a wife. Unfortunately, George's death meant that the estate was still underused, though his mother and younger sister, Adele, would go there after the Season ended.

The accounts were newly fattened from a few seasons of good management, but Sebastien intended to spend money slowly. The last thing he needed was to alert society that the Thorne fortunes were restored. He caught himself wondering if the gold-gowned temptress would care about his income.

Sebastien knew that the plan was for him to marry and take his wife back to Thorne Hall so they could raise the next generation. But he had another commitment, to the Zodiac…which his family knew nothing of. He considered the safety of the nation to be far more important than his own marriage, at least while the war continued. But he couldn't tell anyone without compromising himself and his fellow agents.

After dispatching with family business, he turned his mind to the assignment he'd been given. Energized now, he started to make notes, detailing all he knew so far, and all the items yet to be discovered. He wrote his notes in a sort of coded shorthand, so no secrets could be revealed by accident.

The work would be difficult, but he already had a short list of things to find out as soon as possible. First: learn who lived in the house Bailey broke into. He had to know if the owner was to be trusted or not. Second: find Gerald Dodd, the man who hired Bailey to steal the plans. Dodd was only a middleman, but he would lead to the next level, where things might get interesting. Third: find out, and quickly, what precisely the Andraste plans *were*. Learning either of the first two items would help him with the last.

The first was easy. With a few inquiries into the various social directories his mother kept, he learned who the inhabitants of 42 Quince were: the head of the house, a Miss Cordelia Bering, daughter of the late Alfred Bering, and also a Mrs Walter Wharton.

Wait. *Mrs Walter Wharton.* Sebastien laughed out loud when he realized that he knew her. He had met her when he was much younger. Searching his memory, he summoned an image of a very kind woman. Leona Wharton had taken an interest in the young Thorne boys. Sebastien realized now that it was probably because she had no children of her own. It shouldn't be too difficult to beg a renewal of acquaintance. He hoped she was not involved in the problem of the papers.

Of course, she and the other lady, this Miss Bering, might not even know what was in the house. If so, they were innocent, and didn't realize what they had lost. Yes, that possibility made far more sense. Perhaps the late Mr

Bering had left something behind, and that's what the thieves were after. Thorne decided this only made his job more important. He had to get those papers before anyone else did…and before either woman could do something foolish.

THAT AFTERNOON, CORDELIA WAS HARD at work in her study. The windows had been opened to allow the fresh air in, and the result was a constant, soft rustling of papers on the large desk.

Cordelia was still worried about the theft, but she tried to dismiss the issue from her mind until she could take some decisive action, rather than dither about possible scenarios. Less easy to banish was the memory of the man in the gardens at Gough's party. The rationality of daytime made Cordelia doubt what she thought she'd seen through her window in the predawn light. She had to have imagined that the same gentleman had somehow appeared on her lawn a short time after kissing her at the party. She had been so entranced by his kiss that she kept seeing him in her mind, and simply mistook a dream for reality.

The memory was seductive enough to make her lose concentration. She stared outside at nothing in particular while she savored the memory of his mouth on hers, and the way his fingers teased her skin so lightly…

She flushed, suddenly realizing that her muscles had grown warm and languid, and that she was unconsciously wetting her lips. What was wrong with her? She must forget that it *ever* happened. There were other problems at hand, ones that she could solve. Shuffling through a small stack of recent correspondence, she selected one letter, scanning the enclosure with a thoroughly professional air.

"Cannot adjust capacity of intake in new design," she murmured aloud. "May have omitted element in early version. Please see enclosed sketch. Can you offer any advice, Mr Lear?"

She smiled to herself. "Yes, I think I can, sir." She reviewed the sketch for a few moments, and the issue became obvious. She began to draw an altered plan that would work properly. Her worries of the past few days fell away as she worked.

Unfortunately, as a woman, she would never be taken seriously as an engineer. Her father had been respected because he was intelligent, but also because, as a man, he could meet with other colleagues, prove his worth, and earn their trust. She could not. While he was alive, she didn't mind using her father's name on her own work. She owed him everything, after all, and they privately laughed at their secret: that many of Alfred Bering's later projects were not his at all, but those of his daughter. He was supremely proud of her, and often took the opportunity to mention her work to colleagues, though he wisely withheld the fact that they were the brainchild of a young woman—most men not being terribly open to the idea of women having brains at all.

After her father's death, she could no longer hide behind his name. However, that didn't prevent her from inventing someone *else* to hide behind. Thus, Mr Lear was born. Cordelia dreamed up the eccentric professor and gave him a personality and history. He was precise and neat, and lived in London after being exiled from his native village following a private disagreement, an *affaire du coeur* that threatened to end in a duel. (Cordelia had been considerably more romantic when she was younger.)

A shy gentleman, Lear never went out. He hired a secretary to record his works. And all his mail eventually ended up at the residence of his sole confidante, the now late Alfred Bering.

Cordelia had successfully maintained this facade for a few years now. The work that "Lear" did provided much of Cordelia's income. Lear only corresponded via letter, and he regretfully declined all invitations to conferences and meetings on the basis of his extreme shyness and frequent poor health. Cordelia saw no reason why she couldn't keep the pretense up indefinitely.

A knock at the door broke Cordelia's concentration. Ivy stepped in, saying, "Mr Jay is here, my lady. Shall I show him in?"

Cordelia blinked. "What time is it?"

"Just after three."

Visiting hours already? Cordelia hadn't realized how much time had passed. She put the pen down on the desk. "Please show him in."

Ivy nodded, then paused. "I should ask Mrs Wharton to chaperone, should I not?"

Cordelia sighed. Despite her age, she was still expected to act like a flighty girl in her coming-out Season. She told the maid, "She's probably in the gardens. Tell her she need not rush inside. After all, Mr Jay is practically family."

In fact, William Jay was the only person in the world besides Cordelia and her servants who knew that Mr Lear was a complete fabrication. Cordelia had taken him into her confidence as she invented Lear. Cordelia trusted him fully. Jay had been an occasional student of her father's, but more than that, he was the younger brother of her beloved Vincent, to whom she had been engaged for such a short time. When Vincent died, Cordelia and William had grieved together. They became true friends.

He also served a vital purpose, since he could deliver "Lear's" work to various conferences and institutions. More importantly, he was a man who could claim that he had met Lear, thus providing a necessary support for the otherwise invisible engineer.

Moments later, Ivy returned with a young man at her heels. William Jay was only twenty-three, and his lanky frame and unselfconscious smile made him appear even more youthful. His clothing was perfectly correct for an English gentleman, a brown broadcloth coat worn over a spotless white shirt and buff pantaloons that were tailored precisely to eliminate the merest possibility of a wrinkle. He kept his light brown hair as short as possible, having found that any longer style just vexed him. He was, above all, practical, and Cordelia admired this trait.

"Miss Bering, how are you this afternoon?" he asked as he entered. He carried a thin leather case with him. At Cordelia's invitation, he sat in a chair opposite her.

"Well enough," she said, smiling at him. "And you?"

"Extremely busy. But I had to visit for a moment to pass on my best wishes to you, and my congratulations to Mr Lear. Sadly, I expect that he is enjoying his afternoon nap right now." The last part came out with a sly smile and twinkle in his blue eyes.

"The professor has been ill again," Cordelia replied, keeping a straight face. "But I shall be pleased to pass along any message to him for you."

"You may tell him that the design created for the Scottish firm worked perfectly."

"It's just a matter of seeing what's there," she said. She appreciated that William played along in this little game. Indeed, he seemed to enjoy it.

"If it were that simple," he responded, "the firm would

not have paid for outside help. It's just as well Lear doesn't care to be social. I suspect that smaller minds resent how his work illuminates their own failings."

"How cynical, Mr Jay. I'm sure they know such aid is never meant to show off or belittle their own efforts."

Jay shook his head. "You think far too highly of people, Miss Bering. You'd be appalled if you knew what men say about each other."

Yes, that was undoubtably true. She briefly wondered what that man in the garden last night would say about *her* . She needed to think of something else! "Tell me, what have you been working on?" she asked.

Excited to share, Jay started to explain his latest project, and Cordelia felt the last of her worries about the previous evening slide away. She was in her element, working with a friend who understood her. Everything would sort itself out.

* * * *

Sebastien Thorne continued to work on his assignment from the Zodiac. Fortunately, this next foray did not require him to dress in carefully fatigued clothes and pretend to be someone else. No, this time he strove to look exactly like what he was, a peer of the realm with every expectation that the world functioned to serve him. He called for his carriage, which was brought round immediately. "Forty-two Quince Street," he directed. It was time to meet the ladies who called that place home.

The house, unsurprisingly, looked less sinister in the daytime. Part of the building was older, with narrow windows and fretwork done in stone. On either side of the original house, though, more modern wings had been built. These boasted larger multipane windows and cleaner lines. The house was not massive, but was still extremely generous for two women and the small household they would require.

The grounds were lush with greenery and thousands of flowers in various linked gardens. Further on, Thorne glimpsed the corner of a building that served as a mews and stable and carriage house. A narrow-framed young man was just brushing down a horse, and he paused in his work to look at Thorne. Thorne caught something odd in the man's gaze…a certain kind of insolence. Then he shrugged off the feeling. There was no reason to suspect the servants of anything. The property showed every sign of being well cared for.

He walked up the wide stone steps. He had barely touched the brass knocker when the door swung open. A petite maid appeared, saying, "Good afternoon, sir."

"Is Mrs Wharton at home?" he asked, presenting his card. "I am a friend of hers."

"I will find out, my lord," the girl curtseyed, very precisely.

"It's been quite a while, but I hope she will remember me."

"Please step inside, my lord." Holding the card, the maid disappeared through a set of heavy doors, one left open slightly.

He waited. It was, of course, perfectly acceptable for someone to decide to whom they were "at home," but Thorne had long ago decided that it was a stupid custom. Though the maid's voice was pitched low, he caught her words through the open door.

"My lady, there's a Lord Thorne to see Mrs Wharton. He says he is a friend."

My lady? Thorne wondered at the address. He thought he'd learned the names of everyone in the house, and there was no mention of anyone with a title. So who was the maid talking to? There was a period of silence, but Thorne wasn't sure if he simply could not hear the lady's reply.

Then the maid came back, and told him, "Mrs Wharton is not in the house, my lord. But Miss Bering is, and she said that if you would not mind joining her and her guest for a moment, Mrs Wharton will be here shortly." The longer speech gave Sebastien a chance to better hear the maid's speech, and he was momentarily confused. Her voice had no traces of a lower-class accent. She sounded like a lady herself.

"I do not mind at all," he said, smiling. Inwardly, he was still puzzling over the *my lady*. Perhaps the maid was new, and misspoke out of nervousness. She took his hat and bore it away to some cloakroom. A certain mechanical air about her movements attracted his attention. It was just slightly off, not quite natural. Yes, she must be new to the job.

"This way, my lord," the parlormaid said, and led him down the hallway through the doors to a small study in the new wing, where two people were sitting.

Seeing them, he stopped short, dumbfounded, although part of him should have expected this. Miss Bering was the woman from the gardens. The same gorgeous woman who nearly seduced him without any effort...the one he had suspected of being a spy.

$$\nearrow$$

CORDELIA WAS STUNNED BY THE appearance of the man she knew only as a devastatingly handsome mystery, and the one she thought had been watching her house earlier. She'd convinced herself she was wrong, but perhaps she shouldn't be so quick to absolve him.

"Lord Thorne, ma'am," Ivy announced. Having seen Cordelia's expression, Ivy lifted her hand and casually touched her ear as she spoke. It looked like she was merely brushing a curl away, but in fact Ivy was silently asking if she needed help.

"Thank you, Ivy," she said, tapping her finger twice on the desk to indicate she was fine. "And please find Aunt Leona—Mrs Wharton, that is—in the gardens and let her know she has a guest. Now." She nodded to her maid, and gave her a little smile to reassure her.

Ivy curtseyed and left the room.

Cordelia glanced once at William, and then at the designs spread on the table between them. Although there was no reason for the papers to be hidden—after all, they weren't even hers—she was uncomfortable with this particular man perusing such work in her house. If only she had learned his name last night when he found her in the garden! She would not have been surprised today.

Her friend caught her look and moved to put the papers away. Before he could, Lord Thorne stepped right up to look at the papers as if he had every right in the world to do so.

"Miss Bering, I am sorry I have no one else here to offer a formal introduction," he began to say, though his attention was on the desk.

He didn't look the least bit sorry to her. "It is too bad that my aunt is still on her way inside," Cordelia replied.

Fortunately, Jay redirected Thorne's attention by standing up and bowing. "Good afternoon, my lord. I am William Jay," he said. "How do you do?"

Thorne acknowledged him with a brief, almost mocking bow. "How do you do. I do hope I'm not interrupting anything important."

Cordelia did not like the idea of Lord Thorne and Jay in the same room. She cleared her throat, and then said lightly, "Certainly not. In fact, Mr Jay was just on his way out. He has a number of other calls to make."

"But you both look to be hard at work on those…what are these?" Thorne leaned over the designs and made a show of examining them. "Is this for a boat of some type?"

She took a breath, then said, "Yes, it is for a boat of some type. My dear friend Mr Jay is an engineer." She stressed the *dear friend*.

"Is the boat for you?"

"For me?" Cordelia asked, puzzled.

Thorne fixed his eyes on her now, asking more pointedly, "Why is he showing you plans for a boat?"

"That is none of your business," Jay said, affronted.

"It's all right," Cordelia said, smiling at Jay to reassure him. She turned to Thorne, losing the smile. "Mr Jay was one of my father's students. He was showing off his latest work to me. It's very kind of him to remember his teacher's family, isn't it?"

Thorne appeared taken aback. "Of course," he managed. "Most thoughtful."

"But alas, he does need to be going," Cordelia went on, throwing Jay an encouraging glance.

"I could stay until Mrs Wharton returns," Jay offered, even as he began to put the plans back into his leather case.

"That's sweet, but not necessary," Cordelia said. "Thank you so much for calling, and I hope you call again soon."

"Of course, Miss Bering," Jay said, though he was clearly unhappy at leaving her alone with Lord Thorne. "I am glad to leave you in good health. Oh, and please convey my message to Mr Lear, and do let me know if there is *anything* at all I can do to aid him."

"I will," Cordelia assured him. She noted that, like Ivy, he was sending her a silent signal in case she needed help. She merely shook her head once and gave him an especially bright smile as she said goodbye.

Still with misgivings, Jay left, followed by Thorne's cool gaze. "Mr William Jay," Thorne said quietly. Cordelia didn't like his tone at all.

She stood up, watching Thorne as though he were a panther about to strike. "So you are the Earl of Thornebury, according to your card. Shouldn't I be addressing you as Lord Thornebury?"

"A quirk of history," he explained in the tone of a man who has explained it many times before. "Long ago, the first earl insisted on continuing being called Thorne even after the king recognized the earldom. Some joke about being a thorn in the king's side, I gather. Tradition has kept up the convention. Thornebury is the honor, Thorne is the head of it."

"I see. And I am to believe you actually do know my aunt?" Cordelia asked skeptically.

"Yes, although I think the last time I saw her I was about thirteen years old." He smiled in a way that almost made him look harmless. Almost. "I'll be honest, Miss Bering. I did not expect to meet you again. And certainly not here, nor in this capacity."

"What capacity are you referring to?" she asked.

"Since I've been elevated to my father's title, I am most interested in renewing some old acquaintances."

"Such as my aunt," she said. *You show up to renew your acquaintance with an elderly woman of little social influence, immediately after someone robbed me and you tried to seduce me?*

Thorne nodded, acting as if his explanation was believable. "I am just back from abroad, and I find the adjustment to London rather jarring. I like to have people I can trust about me."

"Yes, last night you said you traveled." Cordelia kept her voice even. "Are you back from France?"

"Yes, in fact," he replied, his expression becoming far more guarded.

"Is it very difficult to come and go, considering the tensions between our governments?" Cordelia knew she shouldn't goad him, but she couldn't resist. There was something very wrong about his appearance at her house.

"I've never been one to let obstacles get in my way," he said.

"Of that I have no doubt, my lord." Cordelia looked him directly in the eyes. Before he could respond, Leona stepped into the room.

"Cordelia, darling, Ivy told me we had a guest..." Leona's face lit up. "My Heavens! It can't possibly be... Sebastien Thorne!"

"Mrs Wharton. How do you do." He bowed, and smiled a bit smugly. He plainly enjoyed the look of surprise on Cordelia's face.

"So you do know each other," she said.

"Oh, yes!" Leona laughed, the silvery sound temporarily disarming them both. "Sebastien Thorne. Except you're not just Thorne anymore, are you? I'd heard something…"

"He is Earl of Thornebury," Cordelia said.

Leona raised an eyebrow. "Is that so, my lord? You must be introduced to my niece, Miss Cordelia Bering."

"We are acquainted already," Cordelia said, then bit her tongue. Oh, how could she ever explain the manner in which they'd actually met?

Thorne looked amused at Cordelia's discomfort. "So we are. Meeting your niece was a most charming discovery. But I didn't know until just now that she was related to you. And it is you I hoped to see, as I have very fond memories of you."

"Heavens, you were just a boy when I saw you last. In Cheshire, it must have been, when my Walter and I stayed at your family's home."

"You have a good memory. You were very kind to me and my brother. Even when we came into the dining room dripping wet from the rainstorm."

Leona laughed again. "Your mother was most concerned about the carpet. Did it survive?"

"It was forever changed," he admitted. "But tell me how you have been. Clearly you live in London now."

Cordelia explained, "My aunt came to stay with us several years ago, not long before my father died."

"I was only recently widowed at the time," Leona added.

"So Alfred Bering was your brother?"

"Exactly so." Leona smiled at him. "And now you must be married with children of your own."

"No." Thorne laughed a little. "I expect I shall remain a bachelor until I die."

"Not if you're the Earl of Thornebury," Leona said with meaning. Then she frowned. "But if I recall, you are the younger son."

"Yes. My older brother, George, died just over a year ago," he explained, his expression now sober. "An accident while riding. I was in France at the time, and I could not return for many weeks."

Cordelia sensed that his brother's death still hurt. She suddenly felt cheap for attacking him about his motives in calling. "I am sorry for your loss, sir. We did not mean to summon bad memories."

"I don't need any aid to summon them, Miss Bering," he admitted, his eyes dark.

"Let us not dwell on the past," Leona said hastily. "And certainly not when we can do nothing to alter it."

"As you wish, Mrs Wharton," he said, turning his attention back to the older woman. "How can I brighten your present, then?"

"You might start by telling me how you know my niece. I don't remember Cordelia mentioning she was acquainted with you."

Cordelia interjected, "I cannot remember who introduced us." She didn't want her aunt to have an inkling of the real events surrounding their meeting. She hated that her subterfuge meant trusting Lord Thorne to go along with her lie, but he appeared to be game, judging by his tiny wink at her.

He said, "I can't remember either. Once I saw Miss Bering, I forgot everything else."

"Pretty words, sir," Leona said, a smile lighting her

face. "You'd best watch yourself if you wish to remain a bachelor."

"I shall remember your advice, Mrs Wharton," he replied easily.

Thorne continued to charm Leona by explaining that he hoped to widen his circle of acquaintances, and wished specifically to cultivate those people he had known before he became earl, since those were people he could be confident were not scraping acquaintance merely for access to his title. Cordelia, though still suspicious of him in general, had to admit his logic made perfect sense.

After a few more moments of inconsequential banter, Leona turned to her niece. "But Cordelia, my dear, are we keeping you? Don't you have to attend the Alberts' dinner tonight?"

"That's tomorrow evening, Aunt," she corrected her.

"Is it really? I could have sworn…" She looked rather flustered. Watching them both, Thorne wore a slight, satisfied smile.

Cordelia didn't like it. "Does something amuse you, sir?"

"Only the fact that you once told me that you were not a social butterfly. Yet it seems you're about all of London. Gough's ball last night, a dinner party tomorrow. You underrate your appeal, Miss Bering."

"Exactly what I have always said!" Leona chimed in. "Perhaps you can talk some sense into her. My niece would shut herself away from the world."

"That would be a crime and a great deprivation to society."

Cordelia marveled at how sincere he sounded. "Your *words* are very kind, sir," she said, keeping her tone as neutral as possible.

"He only speaks the truth, Cordelia. You should not

hide away here. I know the unpleasantness last night upset you, but—"

"Unpleasantness? In what way?" Thorne asked, interest in his eyes.

Leona lost no time in relating the drama of the previous night—at least, the version that Stiles and Cordelia had given her. Thorne listened with every appearance of surprise and concern. Cordelia tried to see a chink in his facade. But she only began to doubt herself. She hadn't seen the man outside her window clearly, and what would an earl be doing in her yard at dawn anyway? Perhaps he was just an ordinary earl…whatever that meant.

But then, why was he here now? Whether he was the thief or not, it was too coincidental that he would show up on Cordelia's doorstep the day after he met her in a dark garden and kissed her insensible.

"…don't you think, Cordelia?" Leona asked.

She blinked. "Excuse me? My mind wandered."

"Lord Thorne was asking about the stolen items. Of your father's. He has very generously offered to help in their recovery."

"Indeed?" She focused on Thorne. "That *is* generous."

Leona said, "You can tell him the particulars. Lord knows I never understood what Alfred and Cordelia chattered on about!" Her aunt then stood up and began to walk toward the door.

"You're leaving?" Cordelia asked, alarmed.

"Mr Dunham is escorting me to the opera tonight. Don't you remember?"

"Oh, of course. You'll want to be ready when he calls for you."

Leona turned back to Thorne and bestowed a motherly smile on him. "I am sorry I cannot stay to chat. But will you call again, my lord? It would be lovely to hear about your family and how they are doing."

"You may depend on it, Mrs Wharton," he said, smiling slowly.

Leona departed. Cordelia almost called her back, seeing as her aunt's role was to chaperone her in just this kind of situation. But Cordelia had often railed against the need for anyone to chaperone her at all, seeing as she was an old maid. She could hardly protest now. If Thorne noticed the older woman's lapse, he said nothing.

Cordelia regarded the man. She said, "You were speaking of my father's work. Go on."

"Tell me something about what went missing. I have some useful connections, and if there is a way to recover what was lost, I would be most happy to assist."

"My father's work interests you?"

"Er, yes. Of course."

"Was there a particular aspect of his work that intrigued you?" She went on, in no mood to coddle this interloper. "His improvements to hull valves? Or the mast fortifications he devised? I happen to know that other engineers have taken his advances further in the past several years. It may be that my father's work is quite out of date now."

He paused. "You're protective of your father's work?" he noted mildly.

"Someone has to be," Cordelia responded.

"I'm surprised you kept everything. The scribblings of scholars are rarely of value to anyone but the scholars themselves."

"My father was a genius," Cordelia said defensively. "His *scribblings* often saved lives!"

"How so?"

"Well, he used to look at the crippled ships pulled into harbor after a storm, and he saw that the masts nearly always broke at the same point near the base. So he designed a new base that was reinforced twice over. The captains who sailed on ships using his design swore that it got them through storms that would have destroyed another ship."

Thorne nodded. "What else did he think of?"

"Many things. Little improvements to make life easier at sea, or to build stronger ships. Even lifeboats can be improved. My father sailed for years, and he gathered a lot of practical knowledge. Just because there is a traditional way to make ships doesn't mean it's the best way." She was proud of her father's accomplishments, and she didn't think Lord Thorne appreciated it at all.

"You're extremely knowledgeable about his work."

"For a mere woman?" she asked archly.

"I am only noting your unusual interest."

"He was my father. Forgive me if I find *your* interest in it rather unusual, my lord."

"I like to be useful," he said easily. "Your aunt was alarmed by the break-in, but she was clearly relieved that the papers were the only thing taken. Your reaction is rather different. You think those papers are valuable."

Cordelia stared at him in chagrin. He was far more observant than he first appeared. So she hedged, "I was told that the contents of the box were unique."

His expression softened. "Told by your father?"

"Yes," she said. "He asked me to keep them safe. Obviously I failed."

"I would like to help you recover them."

"I would like to believe you."

He frowned. "But you don't."

"Your appearance here is very well timed."

"You don't trust me."

Cordelia actually laughed out loud at that. "Why

should I?"

He allowed the point with a slight nod. "I wish I had the time to convince you that I am acting in your interest."

"Alas, I do not have the rest of our lives."

"A pity," he said, his eyes flashing. "Miss Bering, why do you refuse my help?"

"It's a bit late for help, sir. The papers are *gone*, and I don't think the thief will return simply to nip the silver."

"For your sake, I hope no one returns." He sounded truly concerned. Lord Thorne confused her more every time he spoke.

"If someone does," she said finally, "he'll regret it. I will not stand by passively while someone tries to take more of my family's legacy."

Thorne smiled. "Well said, Miss Bering." If he thought her words were a threat aimed at him, he gave no sign.

A FEW MINUTES LATER, THORNE took his leave. A courtesy call should not last more than twenty minutes, and he already passed that mark. Besides, Cordelia Bering was dangerous. She had an answer for everything.

He met the maid at the door, where she already had his things ready. She opened the door for him, and stood almost at attention as he passed.

"Good day, my lord," the little maid murmured with her perfect curtsey. She closed the door softly behind him. He noticed, yet again, a slight strangeness in her manner, but he couldn't put his finger on what bothered him about it.

He walked back outside, glad to be in the fresh air and away from the distracting Miss Bering. Something was terribly wrong in that house.

Perturbed, Thorne headed for his favorite club, a haven for gentlemen trying to escape the life of the *ton*, and the likely location of a friend he needed to speak to. The building itself was set back from the street, and even the neighbors seemed to forget that it was not a private residence. Thorne walked up to the massive door in the front, and a liveried footman opened it for him.

The interior was cool and relatively dim, since the old stone walls of the mansion were thick, and the few windows in the front hall had their shades drawn. Another man saw him and said, "Good afternoon, Lord

Thorne." He was the club's equivalent of a butler. His name was Baxter, and he had a terrifyingly accurate memory.

Thorne nodded to him. "Do you happen to know if Lord Forester is here?" Which was a silly question. Baxter knew the precise location of every person in the building, and probably what they had all ordered to drink as well.

"He is in the library, I believe," Baxter murmured.

Thorne went up the stairs. He found the man he was looking for exactly where Baxter said he would be, sitting in a leather chair with a book his hand, although he wasn't reading it. Instead, he was sleeping.

"Wake up," Thorne said as he got closer.

Forester opened his eyes even as Thorne spoke, suggesting that he hadn't really been asleep. Bruce Allander, Lord Forester, was even taller than Thorne; his legs stuck out past the chair and under the one that sat opposite him. His jet-black hair was messy. An untouched glass of whiskey sat on the table by his side.

"Are you busy?"

"Do I look busy?" Forester laughed, spreading his arms to indicate the complete lack of activity surrounding him. In fact, they were the only two people in the small library at the moment, which suited them both very well.

"I have a question about astronomy," Thorne said.

"For that, I have to get some air," Forester said.

The two men walked back down to the ground floor, exchanging a few words with Baxter as they left. They strolled toward a park, not speaking until they were well away from any buildings, and no one was near them on the path.

"What's in the wind?" Forester finally asked. He didn't look at Thorne as he spoke, and anyone watching the pair would think the two men were chatting idly while heading someplace equally idle.

In truth, *idle* was a terrible word to describe Forester. He'd joined the army more out of curiosity than any need to prove himself. He was a big man, naturally athletic, and had a good mind for strategy. Like Thorne, he had been recruited into the Zodiac several years ago. When Neville first directed the two men to work together on a dangerous assignment in Paris, it had been the start of a camaraderie based on mutual respect. Whenever Thorne needed a second, Forester was the man he went to.

Thorne explained, "I'm looking for some plans for something called Andraste."

"What the hell is that?"

"I wish I knew."

"How can I help?"

"I ran into a name. Alfred Bering. Did you ever hear it?"

Forester considered it for a moment, then shook his head. "I don't think so. Who is he?"

"Who *was* he. He was an engineer. Primarily, he designed ships."

His friend nodded. "I think I begin to understand. So this man is dead?"

"Yes, unfortunately. But the work he did is still around, and a few people are very interested in it. Someone stole papers from his daughter's house last night. I've just come from there," Sebastien added.

"And you think they are *the* plans?"

"That's my theory," Thorne said. "My best guess is that the plans are for a new ship design. Something that the French think will help them defeat us at sea."

"Sounds like something we ought to prevent them from getting," Forester replied with his typical understatement. "So what now?"

"As I said, I just spoke with his daughter, who didn't tell me much. Actually, she told me as little as she possibly could."

Forester tipped his head. "Alfred Bering. Wait, is the daughter Miss Cordelia Bering?"

"Yes! Do you know her?"

Forester nodded. "I never met her personally. 'Heartless' Cordelia Bering is rather well-known for her eccentricity. She's refused every single proposal extended to her. Even one from a duke, if I recall, so at least you can't accuse her of holding out for something better."

"So she's rich," Thorne guessed. Marriage was usually an economic decision, and if she could choose to not marry, it suggested that she was a woman of independent means.

"Not that I know of. But…well, you met her. What did you think? Was she appealing?"

Sebastien tried not to think of Miss Bering's appeal and instantly failed, particularly when he remembered how the afternoon light in the study had—for one wonderful moment—suggested the shape of her figure under her white lawn dress. "I think some men might act very foolishly around her."

Forester's eyes narrowed as he guessed Thorne's meaning. "Is she involved with these plans going missing?"

Thorne hesitated, considering. "Miss Bering is an intelligent woman. She certainly isn't ignorant of her father's work, even though she first pretended she was. So this isn't a matter of someone tricking an innocent person into giving over a valuable document. She was wary of even discussing the nature of the stolen plans with me. I think someone may have approached her about buying the plans earlier, and she rebuffed them. Thus, the robbery."

"Or that's what she wants you to think," said Forester.

"But she was distressed about the burglary."

"She *appeared* distressed about the burglary," his skeptical friend corrected him. "A very different thing."

Thorne shook his head. "No. I already tracked down the man responsible. The robbery was real enough, and the household's reaction was strong. By his account, the servants nearly had him by the heels."

"All to make it look real."

Thorne shook his head. "A lot of drama for no obvious audience. She'd have to be playing several moves ahead. I don't know if she's capable of that."

"So you must find out more about her," his friend said.

"I plan to. But I can't investigate everyone at once. That's what I need you for."

"Just tell me what needs to be done," Forester said.

"Help me eliminate the obvious suspects and dead ends. Can you find out about the servants? Names, ages, where they've worked before? It's possible that one or more of them aren't what they seem. In fact, I'd bet on that."

"What do you mean?" Forester asked, curiosity in his eyes.

"I don't know. The maid I saw was decidedly odd."

"Lazy? Impertinent?"

"Not at all. Rather, she was *perfect*. As if she adores Miss Bering and lives to serve her. She actually called her *my lady*, or at least she did when she didn't know I could hear her. Miss Bering has no title."

"That's strange," Forester allowed. "If she's new, she might be nervous."

"That's what I first thought." Thorne sighed in frustration. "It was just a feeling I got when I was in the house. I got the sense that the maid and Miss Bering were acting in a play. As if one was playing at being a servant and one was playing at being served. I know that doesn't make sense."

"Not exactly, but if you sensed something strange, I'd cover a bet on your intuition. I'll find out who the servants are. You keep at Miss Bering. Gain her trust."

"She doesn't seem to be a trusting person," he said. Of course, there were several time-honored ways to gain a woman's trust. He could attempt a few of those. He smiled at the possibilities.

Thorne left Forester, and continued to turn over the options in his mind. He had a host of things to discover, but first he took what news he had to Neville. The officer was relieved to hear that Sagittarius had already made progress. Though some of the plans were gone, the intelligence that something remained was reassuring.

Thorne told him, "Remember the beauty we both saw at Gough's?"

Neville visibly searched his memory. Finally, he said, "Oh, yes. The woman in the yellow gown. What about her?"

How the hell could Neville forget that it was a golden gown, which practically made her the most glittering object in that whole ballroom? Thorne couldn't believe the image of Cordelia hadn't burned itself into the brain of every man who had seen her. Aloud, he simply said, "She has the remaining plans."

Neville couldn't hide his surprise. "A woman?"

"Miss Cordelia Bering, daughter of the late Alfred Bering. He was an engineer. His work remained in the house, making her the caretaker of them."

Neville groaned in frustration. "A *civilian*. Thorne, you have to convince her to trust you enough to give you the remaining plans. Do whatever you have to. Understand?"

"She's a lady."

"You're a soldier. And we are in the midst of a war." Neville paused. "I could assign someone else."

"No," Sebastien snapped. "I'll take care of it."

Leaving the Zodiac's headquarters, he reflected on his reaction. He loathed the idea of another agent, another man, getting close to Miss Bering. And wasn't he the best man to do it? He had a better claim to know Miss Bering than any other agent. Forester had encouraged him to get closer to her, and Neville all but ordered a seduction. It certainly wouldn't be the first time he'd slept with a woman solely to gain information. True, he never had to seduce a lady of his nation and class before, but the steps would be the same.

The stakes would not be.

The thought came unbidden and unwelcome. If something went wrong, she would be either compromised or ruined. And it would be his fault.

"But if she just gave me the papers, she wouldn't risk anything," he said to himself. She had already made it plain that she didn't trust him, and part of him did not want her to. Because seducing Cordelia Bering could be quite enjoyable. She said she was heartless. Thorne could be too.

He nodded to himself, having made his decision. He'd do whatever he had to, no matter how pleasant it ended up being.

* * * *

For Cordelia, the rest of the day was largely lost. Her thoughts drifted continually back to the gentleman called

Lord Thorne. Though she wasn't sure *gentleman* was the right word for him. He was more like a savage animal, playing at being civilized. The perfectly cut clothes didn't fool her; that man was used to rougher environments than London's social scene. And his sudden interest in her family, in her father's work, on the very day after someone tried to break into her home… Cordelia decided that the first thing she had to do was find out more about this man.

The next day, as soon as it was appropriate to begin visiting, she was in her carriage on her way to the home of her dearest friend. Eleanor Ramsay was one of the best-informed gossips in London. If Thorne had a past worth knowing about, Elly would know.

Elly was the wife of a wealthy tradesman who had invested shrewdly in shipping to India (which was indirectly responsible for the ladies meeting in the first place), and she lived in luxury in Park Lane. Elly always wore the latest gowns, and her hats were confections of the milliner's art. She cultivated a circle of friends based on her charity work, which also proved to be a rich ground for gossip.

But for all her outward appearances, she had troubles of her own. She was often separated from her busy husband, and in society she was snubbed by higher-class women who resented her for her wealth, particularly because the wealth had come from trade. Elly hid the unhappy side of her life from nearly everyone but Cordelia.

When Cordelia arrived at Elly's palatial home, the footman permitted himself a brief, respectful smile for the good friend of his mistress. "Mrs Ramsay is in the gardens. If you will follow me, Miss Bering?"

He led her through the marble foyer and the gracious rooms to the gardens at the back. They were a riot of spring color, the flowers competing for attention with the cloudless sky. Dressed in a spotless white lawn dress, Elly sat at a small table covered with tea things. She looked over as the footman's step crunched on the gravel path.

"Cordelia, my dear!" Elly stood up, her smile warm as the day. "How thoughtful of you to call. I have not seen you for ages."

"A week, I think," Cordelia corrected her with a wry smile. Elly was prone to fits of poetic exaggeration. The two ladies sat down at the table. The garden was beautiful, and Cordelia marveled at how peaceful it' seemed. Elly poured a cup of fresh tea, which Cordelia accepted gratefully.

"Do tell me what you've been up to," Elly practically ordered.

Cordelia got right to the point. "Have you ever heard of Lord Thorne?"

Elly sat up a little straighter. "Do you mean the new Earl of Thornebury?"

"Yes," Cordelia said. "The one with a family holding in Cheshire."

"Yes, of course that one! Cordelia, are you telling me you haven't heard of Sebastien Thorne?"

"Why should I have?"

"You ought to circulate in society more," Elly sighed. "Lord Thorne is *the* catch of the moment. All the women are wild about him."

Cordelia raised an eyebrow inquiringly, which was all the encouragement Elly needed.

"He is quite handsome, to begin with. Tall and dark and all that."

Cordelia couldn't disagree with that assessment, though she said nothing.

"He is the second son, and he seemed to embody all the worst tendencies of second sons. He drank, he wagered, he consorted with scandalous women." Elly paused, blushing a bit. "Not that you would know about that, dear. Suffice it to say he was a rakehell. Drove his family to despair. He has a younger sister who was convinced he was going to perdition, and she cried her heart out about it."

"He hardly sounds appealing as a marriage prospect," Cordelia observed.

"Well, I'm getting to that. One night…so the story goes…he was gambling all evening in one of the worst of the hells, drinking whiskey, with a woman on each arm… or something of that manner. He lost more and more money, but he wouldn't stop. Some men can't, you know. The thrill of cards or dice is a lure they can't resist.

"Anyway, he was enticed out of the gaming hell by the women, who turned out to be thieves. He was blind drunk, so they robbed him of everything he had on him and left him for dead in a gutter or a field somewhere.

"He woke up not knowing who or where he was. Utterly ashamed, he crawled back to his father, begging forgiveness. Vowed he'd start over. He made a name for himself in the army. Served gloriously and saved lives of innocents. The usual."

"I see," Cordelia murmured. "But he lost his family."

Elly nodded. "First, his father died of heart failure, making his older brother, George, the earl. Then the new earl was in an accident. So young Thorne sold his commission and came back to take on the duties of Earl of Thornebury. Thus he has gone from scandalous to sought-after."

"Certain women have always looked to marry wealth," Cordelia sniffed.

"But he's not wealthy. That's another sad part of the tale," Elly said, having evidently learned all of the man's history. "The estate was poorly managed, and there were gambling debts as well. I've heard Thorne Hall is little more than a ruin. But even so, he has the title, and great expectations of turning around his fortunes. But why do you ask about Thorne, dear?"

Cordelia had thought long and hard about how much she should say. Elly must not even suspect that Thorne had already done something as scandalous as kiss her. "Oh, I met him yesterday," she said.

"Did you?" Elly looked delighted. "How did that come about?"

Cordelia said, "It seems Lord Thorne knows my aunt. He paid a call on her—us—yesterday. Quite unexpected, since he last saw her when he was a boy."

"Is that so?" Elly asked speculatively. Her romantic brain was already turning. "And you just happened to be there! Did you charm him?"

"I seriously doubt it." Cordelia laughed in spite of herself, thinking of the real situation and the tension between them. "I hadn't heard of him, so I wondered if he was who he said he was. I had the notion that he might have been some unsavory character, using a false acquaintance to get something from me…from my aunt, that is."

"Oh, no. He's precisely what he claims to be! I think he is looking for a wife." Elly's excitement made Cordelia simultaneously amused and sad. Thorne had no interest in *her*, just the papers she possessed.

"He certainly wasn't looking for me to fill that role. And I am not interested in marrying anyone."

"Come now, dear. I've seen Lord Thorne. Are you telling me you don't think him handsome? Your heart didn't flutter just a little when you looked at him?"

Cordelia's whole body had reacted to him during their first encounter in the garden, but she couldn't confide that to Elly. Her sudden blush, however, couldn't be stopped.

"You turn pink just remembering his face! I knew it. You're not heartless at all."

Cordelia waved a hand self-consciously. "I assure you he did not express the slightest interest in marrying me. He is far above me in station, if not wealth. Why would he consider it?"

Indeed, why did Cordelia consider it, even for a moment? She didn't want to marry anyone, let alone the arrogant Lord Thorne. "Let's talk about something else."

Elly pouted briefly, but then brightened. "I did want to ask you if you had any recommendations for a footman. I had to let one of mine go."

"Why?"

Elly lowered her eyes. "He was impertinent." She didn't elaborate, but Cordelia guessed the story. As Elly's husband, Percival, was gone so often, it might have occurred to an ambitious young man that the wife was bored, and thus amenable to an illicit arrangement that would result in a promotion or gifts. It was not an uncommon thing to happen, though no lady ever talked about it directly.

Elly was no older than Cordelia, and just as attractive, with her plumper curves, limpid eyes, and very modish clothing. It wouldn't have been the first time Elly had to deal with unwanted attention. Fortunately, she had a friend in Cordelia, who seemed to always know how to find a good, reliable servant.

"A recommendation? I think I may," Cordelia said, smiling a bit. "Give me a few days and I shall have some names to give you." She often asked her own servants if they knew anyone trustworthy in need of a position. Then she interviewed every one of them herself to assess what role each one would excel at. The result was a pool of unlikely but talented people skilled enough to work any-where.

Elly said, "I don't know how you do it, dear. Your house is *so* well run, and here I am, with twice as many servants…and all the best ones have come from you!"

"I suppose that is my one gift."

"Not your only gift," Elly disagreed.

Before she could return to the topic of Sebastien Thorne, the footman reappeared, announcing another visi-tor. At Elly's approval, an older woman soon joined them. Dressed with more enthusiasm than elegance, the brash Mrs Smallhand exuded a kind of breathless energy.

"Afternoon, dear Mrs Ramsay. And you are…" She regarded Cordelia with a raised eyebrow.

"This is Miss Cordelia Bering," Elly said gently. "You may have seen her at one of my house parties." (They had, in fact, been introduced to each other at least twice before, a fact Cordelia politely refrained from mentioning.)

"Pleased to meet you, *Miss* Bering," the older woman said, looking Cordelia up and down. "A bit long in the tooth for a miss, are you not?"

"I am resigned to my state, Mrs Smallhand," Cordelia said. She was used to giving that sort of answer. This time, however, the words were more difficult to force out. The appearance of Sebastien Thorne had quite disturbed her equilibrium.

"We were just lamenting the difficulties of finding good servants," Elly explained, steering the conversation away from Cordelia's marital status.

"A perennial topic! My housekeeper dismissed a maid this very morning. Tea leaves going missing! And her with new shoes!" Her theatrically raised eyebrows filled in the rest of the story. Tea was fearsomely expensive, a pound of it costing a typical London laborer perhaps one third his weekly pay. Thus in most homes, it was guarded jealously by the housekeeper, kept under lock and key. Many servants did a lucrative side trade in drying once-used tea leaves and then reselling them. But theft was also common…and it was easy to blame a maid. Cordelia knew that it was just as likely that the one who kept the keys was responsible for the theft. But a lady didn't want to get rid of a housekeeper. Maids were cheaper to replace.

Elly made a sympathetic sound after hearing Mrs Smallhand's remark. "Miss Bering has uncommon luck with servants. Perhaps she could recommend one for you."

"Oh, Miss Bering, if you have somehow found the knack for hiring an honest servant, then you are a gifted woman indeed. The servant class, it seems, is almost entirely composed of thieves and ingrates."

"I have been quite satisfied with the moral fiber of my household," Cordelia said, carefully controlling her expression.

"And could you offer a name to another lady?"

"I'd be pleased to do so," Cordelia said. Her brain was already churning. She knew a former maid who had taken leave to care for a sick parent; the girl would soon need another post. "I shall send a name to your home within a day or two."

The trio discussed a few other items of gossip. A most eligible bachelor, Charles Wolverton, was suddenly no longer eligible. "Engaged to a bluestocking now," Mrs Smallhand said. "Good family, but the Brecknell girl isn't much of a catch to my mind. She is too tall for fashion, and quite…odd. Bookish, you know."

"I have a soft spot for odd girls," Elly said, smiling

sidelong at Cordelia. "When will the wedding be?"

"Not for a while," Mrs Smallhand said. "Wolverton plans to buy out his commission at some point next year. We may hope that England and France will declare a lasting peace soon. This Napoleon character must see reason. And where else will Britain engage in real war, if not France? Mark my words, soon there won't be a reason for a young man to join the army at all…at least not a man who joins for excitement. No, Europe will soon tire of war."

"Peace would be a wonderful thing," Cordelia murmured, not believing it for a moment. Mrs Smallhand had to be blind. Any reasonable person knew that Napoleon Bonaparte was *not* reasonable. This was a man who crowned himself emperor. Such a man did not agree to a peace treaty in good faith.

As soon as she thought of good faith, she saw Thorne in her mind. He was curious about the *Andraste* designs. But why? And was it in good faith…or something else?

Finally, Mrs Smallhand departed, and Elly took a breath. "Thank goodness that's over. She would shape the world to her own vision, wouldn't she?"

"What?" Cordelia asked. She had barely heard Elly's comment.

"Cordelia, you are miles away! What are you thinking of?"

She sighed. "Am I old, Elly?"

Elly looked at her. "Old? Did that harridan's remark sting you? You're not a debutante, dear, but you're not a crone yet. Why? Regrets?" she asked shrewdly.

"A few, perhaps." Cordelia fiddled with a spoon on the table. "I always chose to pursue the things that interested me, with little thought for what society might think. But perhaps I will pay for it soon. I have few friends, and barely any family. You heard what Mrs Smallhand said about Miss Brecknell: tall and odd! Dismissed with two words. That's my fate too, soon enough. An unmarried woman doesn't have many places to fit."

"Neither does a married woman," Elly pointed out. "Our paths are laid out for us, no matter who we are. But marriage does confer some privileges. You would get the protection and the wealth of your husband. You'd be sheltered, even as a widow. A good husband would take care of you."

"But I'd lose what few rights I do possess," Cordelia objected. That was the core of her fear of marriage. A husband would be able to stop her from designing ships. He could stop her from working as Lear. He would certainly stop her from hiring servants as she did now. If he so much as suspected the servants' histories, they'd all be punished severely, and Cordelia would be to blame. In fact, any man who knew even one of her secrets would be unlikely to consider her suitable for a wife at all. "You say a good husband would take care of me. But what if I chose badly? I couldn't function as a man's property."

"It's marriage, not slavery."

"That decision is the husband's to make," Cordelia said sourly.

"You're exaggerating. You have been cooped up too long. You are still attending the dinner at the Albert home tonight?" she asked. "You promised, and it's been planned for weeks."

"Yes, I agreed to go for your sake."

"Good. Mr Ramsay will escort us, but I know he'll talk business with Mr Albert all evening."

"We shall entertain ourselves," Cordelia assured her friend, little suspecting that the dinner would prove far more entertaining than she expected.

EVEN AFTER SUNSET, THE WARMTH of the day lingered. Cordelia dreaded a hot and stuffy dining room, but a promise was a promise. Bond selected a new gown for the evening, cut along the same lines as Cordelia's morning gown. This one, however, was of a finer weave, the white zephyr almost as smooth as silk, with a layer of shadow lace floating above it. Cordelia glanced at herself in the mirror. "It looks a bit low cut."

"It fits perfectly, madam."

"That's my concern," Cordelia muttered.

Bond tied a wide green ribbon at the high waist of the dress. The band of satin ran under Cordelia's chest, and the maid fluffed the bow at her back.

"The jade necklace and earrings, madam," Bond said next, presenting the items. "They will complement the green ribbon...and your eyes."

Cordelia put the jewelry on, and felt only slightly more comfortable with her appearance. The neckline was fashionably low, and Cordelia didn't remember her bust being quite so...

"Will people look at the necklace?" she asked nervously. "That is, I hope that's what they will look at."

The maid chuckled. "All the diamonds in the world won't distract some men! But the necklace is a lovely thing, ma'am," Bond noted professionally. "Never seen a jewel like it."

Cordelia touched the heavy, strangely twisted jade pendant that hung on the gold chain. "My father bought it on one of his voyages to the South Seas when he was a young man. It's a good luck charm, so he was told. He gave it to my mother on their first Christmas." Her vision grew misty. She had been barely more than a baby when her mother had taken sick, but she knew her parents had been happy together.

"I love it when a stone has a story to it," Bond said. With a critical eye, she checked her mistress over, then opened a small glass pot and applied the tiniest bit of color to Cordelia's cheeks. Young ladies of the upper classes never wore cosmetics, but Cordelia was just old enough that their judicious, subtle use would not be seen amiss. The maid declared, "Nothing too dramatic, but you have been a touch pale these past few days, ma'am. That's better. And look at your eyes now! You'll be the envy of all the ladies."

"Bring my shawl and fan." Cordelia stood up. "If I shall be the envy of all the ladies, I'd best get it over with."

Elly and her husband had arranged to take Cordelia to the dinner party, since Leona would not be accompanying them that evening. Elly cooed over Cordelia's ensemble, reassuring her, and Mr Ramsay seemed to be in a good mood. Their new landau was exquisitely appointed, and Cordelia allowed herself to hope that the dinner might be as comfortable as sitting on the vehicle's plush cushions.

Mrs Albert's home was fronted by tall Grecian columns in white painted wood. Behind the columns, the tall glass windows were all alight, even those on the upper stories, so that the whole house sparkled.

"Don't forget to compliment the columns," Mr Ramsay warned. "She just had them put in at great expense. I suspect this dinner is being given solely to garner praise for the house."

"Fortunately, they look quite impressive," Elly added. "I always feel so wretched when I have to say something kind about some garish ornament someone has insisted on."

Cordelia laughed, feeling that this conversation was proof that her life was heading back onto an even keel. Leaving the carriage, they avoided the mud in the streets and stepped up to the door, which was opened instantly by a footman.

As the hostess greeted them effusively, Cordelia caught a glimpse of someone she'd rather have avoided. Her frequent admirer Mr Hayden was there; he would no doubt be seated next to her at dinner. Yes, everything was *quite* back to normal, and she had to fend off her admirers as she had done for years.

Elly gave her no help. "Oh, there is Miss Brecknell! Come, Mr Ramsay, we must congratulate her on her engagement!"

Before Cordelia could evade Hayden, he saw her and lost no time in adhering himself to her side. The slim, dark-haired man was attractive, but he had no idea when to stop. He praised Cordelia, claiming ever more extravagant things about her beauty and grace. She suspected he got most of his compliments from volumes of poetry. She listened with half an ear while surveying the rest of the dinner guests.

"Miss Bering, your eyes are like jade butterflies," he was in the midst of saying.

"How pretty, Mr Hayden. But a butterfly made of jade would have a difficult job of actually flying, wouldn't you say?"

"How clever you are, Miss Bering," he said, his enthusiasm in no way dimmed. "Brains as well as beauty. You must have pity on me and accept my adoration at some point."

Cordelia summoned a polite smile. She was used to the praise of gentlemen, many of whom made marriage proposals to her. Theodore Hayden had not done so yet, though he laid broad hints of his deepening interest. She prayed he never would—she had grown nervous of the way he looked at her as if she were a meal to devour. But he never said anything outwardly offensive, or made any move so bold that she could feel justified in refusing his attentions completely.

She looked for Elly, hoping that her friend would rescue her from this conversation. But Elly was talking to another couple, clearly as ensnared by them as Cordelia was by Hayden. Before she could decide what to do, a different male voice echoed through the house, and something about the tone made a shiver run up her spine. It couldn't be...

A moment later, the all-too-familiar shape of Sebastien Thorne appeared. The hostess betrayed herself with an utterly panicked look before she bustled over to find out why the earl had appeared in her hallway before a dinner party. Elly, quick to notice any new person, also saw Thorne's entrance. She looked at Cordelia from across the room and raised her eyebrow significantly. Cordelia almost winced. It would never do for anyone, even her close friend, to think that Thorne was there on her account.

Snippets of the conversation that floated over to her made Cordelia more than suspicious. Thorne appeared to be convinced he had been invited to dinner, and the poor hostess could hardly tell an earl he was wrong. She suddenly remembered Aunt Leona's casual mention of the dinner party when he was at Quince Street yesterday. Did Thorne crash the party for the sole purpose of getting near her?

Within a few moments, an accommodation was apparently reached, for Thorne stepped into the room where the guests gathered and began to circulate among them, his manner easy and not in the least lordly. He seemed to know several people in passing, and the comments he made to ladies certainly had an effect. Every woman in the room, married or not, had an eye on him.

Cordelia was no exception. She couldn't stop herself from surveying his progress. He was dressed in the height of style, with a perfectly cut jacket in a rich chocolate shade, which only made the white lawn of his shirt look whiter. Buff-colored pantaloons hugged his legs like a second skin. Combined with his height and natural grace of movement, he was undeniably handsome.

When he caught her gaze, she looked away quickly. Her heart thumped, despite the fact that she hardly knew him. *Don't be foolish*, she told herself, trying not to stare at the figure, which was difficult considering how different he was from everyone else there. Taller, darker, much more vital than the dandy who hovered near her.

Hayden sniffed. "Look at him. Such a peacock. These highborn lords have never known what true hardship is."

Oddly, Cordelia bristled at the characterization. As a member of the gentry, Hayden couldn't have been terribly accustomed to the rough life himself. She said, "If I recall correctly, Lord Thorne served in the army for several years. Surely that entails some hardship."

"You are too kind, Miss Bering, too kind. He deserves no sympathy from you, and yet you give it freely. Your heart is too beautiful for this world."

"But I have heard that Miss Bering is quite heartless," a voice broke in. In the few moments during which Cordelia hadn't been riveted by his appearance, Lord Thorne managed to move right next to her.

Hayden looked affronted. "What a horrible thing to say to a lady."

"There is no need for offense," she interjected. "I myself told Lord Thorne that when we first met."

"So you know him," Hayden said, surprised.

"I wouldn't go that far," Cordelia said dryly. She turned to Thorne. "Good evening, my lord. I didn't know you would be in attendance tonight. What brings you here?" Driven by some perverse impulse, she offered him her hand.

"Why do you think I came, Miss Bering?" He took her hand and bowed elegantly, pausing for one aching moment before releasing her. Then he smiled. "Even a lord has to eat."

Unaccountably, she smiled at his evasion. Talking with Thorne kept her on her toes, at least. And her fingers still tingled with the memory of his touch.

Hayden was not so amused. "So you eat at other people's tables?"

"Did you bring a picnic lunch this evening…I'm sorry, you have the advantage of me, sir." The sarcasm in the words was clear. Thorne didn't think much of Hayden.

But Cordelia thought she should level the field. "Lord Thorne, this is Mr Theodore Hayden. Mr Hayden, as you already know, this is the Earl of Thornebury."

The two men exchanged a look so hostile it made Cordelia glance heavenward.

Then Thorne said, "Well?"

"Well, what?" asked Hayden, irritation in his voice.

"Did you bring a picnic lunch…sir?"

Before Hayden could do something rash like call Thorne out, Cordelia said, "I think we will all enjoy Mrs Albert's fine supper…if we make it to the dining room without doing battle."

Thorne accepted her warning with a suspicious alacrity. "Certainly, Miss Bering. As it happens, though, I did have another purpose in coming here tonight."

"And that is?"

"Merely to ascertain that you and your household have suffered no more acts of burglary or other things of that nature."

"I thank you for your concern. There has been no re-peat of the event."

"Once ought to have been quite enough," Hayden agreed. "Imagine the distress Miss Bering felt on finding her father's work missing!"

"It was alarming, " Cordelia said, though she looked at Hayden in puzzlement. She didn't recall telling him about the theft in the short time they'd been talking. "I'd rather not discuss it anymore."

"Let's forget it ever happened," Hayden said, putting a hand on her arm with what seemed like paternalistic fer-vor.

"Indeed," Thorne said, looking harder at the man.

At that moment, Mrs Albert called out that the meal was served. Thorne offered his arm, and Cordelia accept-ed it before she fully comprehended what it meant.

Hayden, however, noticed immediately, and objected. "I had the honor of escorting Miss Bering in to dinner."

"Oh, I told Mrs Albert I didn't mind in the least." Thorne's deliberately casual response left Hayden floun-dering for a suitable reply.

Cordelia, realizing she would sit next to Thorne instead of Hayden, felt a moment of giddy relief. "No doubt there is another lady in need of your charming company," she told Hayden.

Thorne walked Cordelia through to the dining room. He murmured, "So quick to rid yourself of an ardent suitor."

"It will take far more than that to get rid of Hayden. He is persistent."

"When did you meet him, if I may ask?"

"Last November. He was presented to me at some function at the Athenaeum. Why?"

"Curiosity."

"Well, yes, I assumed as much, or you would not have asked," Cordelia replied in a more acerbic tone.

They had reached the dining room, and Thorne held out the chair for Cordelia, then seated himself before replying.

"You shouldn't assume too much about me, Miss Bering. But since I have the honor of sitting beside you, I have another question having nothing to do with Hayden."

"Excellent. What is it?"

"Who is Mr Lear?" he asked.

Her heart skipped a beat. "Excuse me?"

His tone was too nonchalant. "Your friend Mr Jay mentioned him yesterday. Who is he?"

Cordelia bit her lip. She didn't want to discuss the existence of Lear in public. She would be far happier if no one connected her with the name at all. At least none of the other guests appeared to have overheard the remark in the bustle of sitting down.

"A friend of the family," she said shortly. "I keep in touch with him. Mr Jay knows him as well."

"An engineer like your father?"

"Yes," she said unwillingly.

"I'd like to meet him," Thorne pressed. "Perhaps you could arrange an introduction."

"He is extremely shy. I don't know that he'd welcome a new acquaintance," Cordelia said, hoping to put him off.

"As an acquaintance, I can be rather charming."

"I'll take your word for that."

"You haven't found me so, Miss Bering?" He leaned back, the picture of a confident lord.

She restrained herself from rolling her eyes. What arrogance. "If one judges an acquaintance by how much happier one becomes after starting it, I must admit that I find yours less than satisfying," she said, reflecting on how much he had unsettled her brain since she met him.

"Most women find me quite satisfying," he said in a lower voice.

Cordelia flushed instantly. She couldn't believe he would say something so suggestive at a dinner table, in the presence of others. "Have some sense," she hissed.

"I offended you," he said, contrite.

"Yes," she whispered, staring at her plate.

"It's possible we got off on the wrong foot."

Cordelia arched an eyebrow at him. "Possible?"

"Certain. Would you accept a sincere and abject apology?" he asked.

"Are you offering one?"

"Yes."

Cordelia looked at the man, her insides in turmoil. She ought to ignore him, but something inside drew her to him. "Will you behave *like* a gentleman, then?"

"To the best of my ability." He smiled as charmingly as possible.

"Then I accept your apology."

Once the first course was served, Thorne ceased his

difficult questions, and Cordelia breathed a bit more easi-ly. The talk turned to more general topics as guests bandied gossip and jokes around the table.

* * * *

Aware that he'd been too aggressive, Sebastien re-treated a bit as dinner began. He now knew he couldn't come on too strongly to Miss Bering. He glanced at the other people around the table. His eye grazed Hayden, who was chatting with the woman next to him. She ap-peared to be amused.

Sebastien wasn't. He experienced an instant and hearty dislike of Hayden. As soon as he saw the man dancing attendance on Cordelia Bering, he wanted to grab him and toss him out onto the street. There was no reason for Hayden to stand so close to her. Then again, any man who didn't notice how very well that evening dress fit her figure was either blind or dead. The curve of her breasts was damn distracting, and the unusual jade pendant she wore only drew more attention to that part of her body. Thorne had never actually envied a piece of jewelry until tonight.

So Sebastien had ordered himself to look only at her face, which carried dangers of its own. Her green eyes were alight with intelligence. She had understood the lay-ers of meanings in his words, while Hayden appeared to struggle along the surface.

And now, dinner brought new challenges. The lively conversation around the table amused her, and he heard her laugh for the first time. God, even her laughter was alluring. And her smile… He only once caught himself staring at her mouth, but that was enough to send a shock down his spine.

Her embarrassment at his earlier innuendo was unmistakable. Clearly, she wasn't as experienced as he'd assumed. Perhaps she was even innocent, in every sense of the word. That would make his seduction of her a bit more difficult, and far less justifiable.

But that didn't mean he wouldn't do it.

* * * *

Ignorant of the musings of her neighbor, Cordelia listened to the end of a story told by a gentleman who had just returned from a trip to America. "…and I said to the man at my left, 'Can you imagine going through life with the name of Barnacle?' Well, he looked sympathetic and said, 'Indeed! I am grateful to be Mr Cheerybabble!'"

Everyone laughed, even though some suspected the details might have been embellished.

"But Americans are so odd anyway!" one woman said.

The sentiment found a general consensus around the table. Then Thorne cleared his throat. "Speaking of odd names, I heard a strange one just the other day: Andraste. Mean anything to anyone?"

A silence fell around the table. Cordelia looked sharply at Thorne.

"Anyone?" Thorne asked blandly. "Miss Bering?"

Before Cordelia could answer, the blonde woman across the table spoke up. "Andraste is the name of an ancient British goddess," Miss Brecknell said. "I thought everyone knew that."

"Not everyone reads Tacitus after dinner," one of the other guests noted with asperity.

Miss Brecknell looked unfazed. "I refer to the work by Dio Cassius. But it's true all the same. In his history, Queen Boudicca is described as praying to Andraste for aid in her battle against the Romans."

"She didn't pray hard enough," Thorne noted, getting a general laugh. Cordelia was grateful the bluestocking Sarah Brecknell was so clever. She didn't want to discuss the name at all.

"A vicar would say that she prayed to the wrong god," Miss Brecknell added. "Of course, anyone going against the might of the Roman army would probably pray to anything and everything that presented itself."

"Truly ecumenical," Cordelia said quietly. She tried to laugh a little, and was helped by Sarah Brecknell joining in.

"Indeed, Miss Bering!" the other lady said. "The desperate will ally themselves with almost anyone."

"I hope to never be that desperate," Cordelia returned, glancing at both Hayden and Thorne. Where had Thorne heard the name of her ship?

"I also hope you'll never be that desperate," Hayden said, holding his wineglass up to her in salute. Though the words were supportive, his tone made her nervous. She wished that she had some pretense to stop him from paying his attentions to her. Of course, she could simply tell him to leave her alone. But something in her quailed at that idea. Hayden was frequently charming, attentive, and polite. But there was a look in his eyes sometimes, almost cold. Somehow she knew he would not react well to being told to go away.

She glanced toward Lord Thorne again. She was deeply conscious of his presence. She noted the shifts of his body, the slight variations in his tone when he spoke. Why could she not treat him as she did any other man? He offered compliments to her and jibes to Hayden with equal measure, but he also seemed to know more than he said. Or was she imagining everything, overwrought from an odd series of events? By the time the dessert course was served, Cordelia was ready to climb the walls in an effort to escape.

Afterward, the ladies went to the drawing room. The gentlemen, of course, all stood as the women filed out. They would linger briefly for a drink and smoke before following the women. Hayden winked at her as she left, clearly suggesting that he couldn't wait to rejoin her. She felt a slither down her spine at the idea of it.

Cordelia knew that Elly would want to speak to her about both Hayden and Lord Thorne, but she needed a moment of peace. As the ladies passed through the hall, Cordelia murmured an excuse and turned down a narrow hallway, ducking into the first open room she found.

The room was lined with books on one wall, with a reading desk set near the far end. A single light burned on the desk, leaving the room quite dim. She disliked intruding, but she would need only a moment to recover her equilibrium. She really must tell Hayden she would no longer see him. For the first time in years, Cordelia regretted not having a male relative she could trust. If her father were alive, he would have dealt with this nonsense. Of course, if her father were alive, she would not be in this situation.

She had been in the room for less than three minutes when she heard a voice behind her, shattering her nerves.

"Miss Bering, I hoped to have a moment alone with you."

She whirled around. Hayden stood there, his eyes fixed on her, his smile charming but out of place.

"Now is not the time, sir," she said.

"You fly like a bird, when I only want to be near you," Hayden said. "Must you tease me so?"

She stood up straighter, anger overtaking fear. "*Tease?*

How dare you follow me and then accuse me of leading you here. I wanted a moment alone!"

"And here we are. Alone." He stepped nearer.

"I didn't mean alone together. Leave me," she ordered.

"You don't mean that."

"I do. Leave me," she repeated.

But he only moved closer. "I wish I could, Miss Bering. Cordelia. You must let me say Cordelia."

"Do not call me that. I am serious. If you will not leave, I will."

She stepped toward the door.

The sudden appearance of a knife in his hand stopped her cold. "You won't leave, Cordelia. Not until you have told me everything I want to know about the rest of the *Andraste* plans, including how you'll give them over to me."

Fear zinged through her. All the months she had let him near her, as he pretended interest in her, he had been after the plans! Hoping to delay him, she asked, "The what?"

"Don't pretend. You know exactly what I'm talking about, and it's no secret, because you must have told that earl as well, or why would he say the name at the dinner table?"

"I told him nothing of the kind," Cordelia said, taking a deep breath. "And I assure you that our conversation—and our acquaintance—is at an end."

SHE TRIED TO LUNGE PAST him.

He darted toward her and grabbed her arm, twisting it painfully. "Don't be coy. I must have the remaining plans. And now I can't wait any longer." His eyes gleamed bright in the glow of the table lamp.

She asked, "How did you even know where they were? How did you know *what* they were?"

"There are always men interested in acquiring knowledge like the ship designs your sainted father made. And as for where they were, you told me yourself."

"I did not!"

"Remember when I asked about your father's study a few months ago? You took me there and showed me several things, but you never went near that locked cabinet. I even asked about it, and you tried to distract me. Knowing how clever you are, I backed off. Now what would be important enough to lock up and keep secret? I made a guess, and waited long enough that you wouldn't connect my tour with the theft."

"You courted me just so you could steal the papers and sell them?"

"Sell them? No, we intend to build the *Andraste*. Or rather, a more useful version of it. So give me the rest of the plans, and you'll never see me again. You'll be safe."

She frowned, caught by his words. "What do you mean, a more useful version?"

"Your father's little boat has no guns. The real *Andraste* will."

"You can't do that," she said, aghast.

"Of course we can. Adding guns to it will let the captain sink whole navies. You should be flattered, really. In fact, I might name the real ship after you. How does that sound? The *Cordelia*? Seems appropriate that it's ironclad and unyielding." He gave a nasty laugh.

Cordelia tried to twist out of his grasp, but he was stronger than her. She warned him, "I'll scream."

"Then I'll say you asked me here," he retorted. "Everyone will believe me, especially if they find us in the dark." With those words, he reached across the desk with one arm and knocked the lamp over, dousing the only light in the room.

Cordelia renewed her struggle to get free. "Let me go, you…bastard!"

"Such language! Tell me where the remainder of the papers are, and I'll let you go as soon as I have them."

Cordelia felt his hand move away from her body. She breathed in relief, but then gasped. He was now holding something very sharp at her back. She had forgotten the dagger. Cordelia started to shake, real terror creeping up her spine. "You can't get the papers if you kill me."

Hayden withdrew the knife, and the sharp pricking sensation near her spine eased. But he forced her around so she had to back up against the desk. Then he held the knife to her throat. "You mean I can't get them if I kill you *first*."

"How do you think you can build a ship like *Andraste* in England without someone noticing?" she asked to distract him. "Who are you working for?"

Hayden sneered. "Why would I tell you, you idiot woman?"

"Insulting me is hardly going to help your cause," she said, wondering if she could kick him and run out before he recovered.

"That's what the knife is for." Eyes narrowing, he pressed the cold metal against her neck.

She almost screamed, but in that moment, Hayden was abruptly pulled off her. She felt a streak of heat as the blade slid across her skin.

Another man had come into the room! The struggle was a short one, and nearly silent. The darkness made everything difficult to discern, but a sickening thud signaled the moment when the stranger's fist connected with Hayden's head.

As Cordelia's would-be suitor slid to the floor, moonlight streamed through the window, and she saw the face of Sebastien Thorne, looking deadly dangerous, with something like fury in his eyes.

When he focused on her, the expression changed. "You're all right?" he asked.

Cordelia nodded, then realized he might not be able to see her move. "He was going to…I didn't ask him to…" It seemed very important that Thorne understood that Cordelia hadn't invited Hayden's attentions.

He looked around at the disturbed furniture, carpeting, and the now knocked-over lamp. "It's quite obvious you didn't ask him to," he said wryly. Stepping over the prone body, he took her by the shoulders. "Did he hurt you?"

Cordelia inhaled when Thorne laid one finger on her throat and traced a line, from her ear to just below her chin. She turned her head so he could see better. "There's not a mark, is there?" she asked.

"This will be hard to explain away," he muttered. "It's

not deep, but it will be red and bleeding."

Cordelia turned back to look at him. "I can perhaps wrap my shawl to hide it…"

"You're not wearing one," he pointed out.

"It must have fallen off." Cordelia searched the floor where Hayden had first grabbed her. In the pale light through the windows, she saw the pile of fabric in a heap. Just as she began to pick it up, she felt his hand on her back.

Thorne said, "He tore your dress."

She twisted to assess the damage, grumbling, "He was quite free with the knife, once he decided to use it."

"I should have hit him harder," said Thorne.

"I'm only sad that I didn't get to hit him myself."

"It's not too late," he returned with unexpected humor. At least, she hoped it was humor.

Contemplating the helpless man at their feet, she shivered. "I'd actually just like to get out of here."

"Excellent notion. Wait one moment." He grabbed Hayden's arms and dragged the unconscious man over to an ottoman, heaving the body up onto it. Then he straightened Hayden's clothes a bit. "There. Obviously, he passed out from too much drink."

"No one will believe that," said Cordelia, wrapping her shawl around her shoulders.

"They also won't believe he's a spy after the *Andraste* designs."

"So you do know about them," she said, newly anxious.

"Yes, and believe me, Miss Bering, that's something we're going to talk about very soon. But first, we must address this slightly awkward situation."

"You mean us being alone in a dark room? Or that we're standing over a body?"

"Both." He paused. "You seem to be taking this all rather well. So I'd like to suggest something scandalous."

"Trust each other?" Cordelia asked.

He was clearly pleased that she guessed his intention. "Do you think you could you trust me?"

She looked again at the figure sprawled across the ottoman. "I trust you more than *him*, at any rate." Which wasn't saying much.

Thorne nodded. "Good. What matters now is getting you out of this room in such a way that no one ever dreams you were in it. I can do that, but you must follow me and do exactly what I say. I promise I'll keep you safe and, God willing, uncompromised."

With no other option, Cordelia accepted his word. She followed him through a series of darkened, deserted rooms and corridors. "How do you know your way around this house?" she whispered.

He gave her a half smile. "I went through most of those rooms as I was looking for you, or more accurately, for the bastard who was also looking for you."

"Oh." She really was lucky Thorne was so observant. "And where are we going?"

"The garden. From there, you can reenter the house through a different door and say you stepped out for a moment because you needed a breath of air. That shouldn't raise too many eyebrows. You seem to enjoy hiding in gardens anyway."

"And you seem to enjoy finding me in them," she noted, unable to stop a smile.

His answering grin was far too knowing. "You didn't protest too harshly."

She raised her chin and looked away, trying to look prim. "You forgot the part where I left you."

"As you will need to do again, sadly," he said. "I want

you back with the other guests within three minutes. You can't afford to be connected to the unconscious man that someone will eventually find in the library."

Yes, it would be extremely awkward if anyone discovered she'd ever been in a room alone with either Hayden or Thorne. She would be drummed out of society.

Finally, they found a room with large windows overlooking the garden. "This will do," said Thorne, pushing the sash of one window up. "Out you go."

Cordelia was flustered. "That's not a door."

"It's the best I can do at the moment." He frowned. "What's the problem?"

"I shall have to…lift my skirt hem to climb over the sill."

He shook his head in exasperation. "I promise I won't look." He took a step back and closed his eyes.

Alert to the fact that being seen climbing out a window would be as bad as being seen alone with Sebastien Thorne, Cordelia wasted no more time. She picked up the hem of her dress, sat on the ledge, and swung herself around so she could place her feet in the garden bed. Fortunately, the window was low to the ground. She straightened up and allowed the dress to fall back down to her ankles.

"I'm outside." She leaned over the sill and peered into the shadowy room. "You can open your eyes, my lord."

"I already did," Thorne said. He stepped over to the window, leaning down so his face was level with her own. "Make your way through the garden and enter though the parlor doors. If you have to explain yourself to anyone, claim you just stepped out."

"What will you do?" she asked.

"I'm closing this window and then wandering back to rejoin the men."

"And your explanation for going missing?"

He smiled arrogantly. "I'm an earl. I don't give explanations."

"I see."

"Miss Bering?" he asked in a more serious tone. "I need to speak to you. You understand that?"

She nodded. "About the plans, I know."

"It's vital. And our talk must be private."

"What do you suggest?"

He paused for half a second, considering. "When you get back inside, plead a headache. Call for your carriage. And for God's sake, don't let anyone see your neck."

"Wait, I don't have a carriage," Cordelia said. "I came with Mr and Mrs Ramsay."

He waved a hand to dismiss her objection. "Even better. Tell the footman to hail a hired carriage for you."

"And then?"

"And then you get in it, Miss Bering." He grinned. "Leave the rest to me." Without warning, he reached out to cup the back of her neck in his hand, then kissed her swiftly on the lips.

Cordelia was too startled to stop him, and then she was too mesmerized by the feel of his lips on hers—hot but somehow gentle. A fanciful part of her hoped that he was imparting some of his strength to her. She breathed in deeply when he pulled away, feeling as if her night acquired a whole new meaning. "What was that for?"

"Luck." He smiled at her. "Now go, Miss Bering. And be careful."

Luck was with her. Cordelia managed to slip inside the house again with no one the wiser. She found a large mirror on one wall and looked for signs of the disturbances of the last several minutes: first Hayden's mishandling of her, then Thorne's well-timed but exasperating rescue, and finally a walk through darkened garden beds and a dance to avoid a host of thorny rosebushes.

Fortunately, save for her shoes, which were destroyed, her outfit survived mostly intact. The rip at the back of the dress was a problem. She draped her shawl to cover the hole, and prayed that the dim light of the candles would keep her secret for her. Cordelia patted her hair back into place, and then pulled a few locks loose, drawing them down to at least partially conceal her neck. Then she heard a voice behind her.

"Cordelia, where have you been?" It was Elly.

"I just stepped out to get a breath of air," Cordelia said, proud of the way her voice didn't shake.

"It is warm in here, isn't it? You're quite flushed!"

Cordelia seized the opportunity. "Yes. And my head aches quite badly, in fact." She let her hand flutter up to her forehead, hoping she wasn't overdoing it. "I think I should call it a night."

Elly made sympathetic noises. "I'll have our carriage brought round and take you myself. Mr Ramsay can find his own way home."

"Oh, I couldn't do that," Cordelia said, thinking quickly. "You have been enjoying your husband's company this evening. How rarely you can go to an event with him! The footman can hail a carriage for me. It's a short ride, and I shall be quite safe." Strange words for someone who had just been threatened at knifepoint, but Cordelia knew that Lord Thorne wanted her to get into a hired carriage... and she trusted him, at least in this.

She asked Elly to retrieve the reticule she'd left behind, while she waited in the dim hallway. Elly returned with Mrs Albert on her heels. Cordelia apologized for her imaginary headache and said a quick good night.

Mrs Albert said, "You were a good sport about letting

Lord Thorne escort you in to dinner and sit next to you, by the way. I can't imagine forgetting that I issued an invitation!"

"Quite a turn of events," Cordelia murmured, not trusting herself to say more.

"He seemed quite taken with you, Miss Bering."

"We had a most interesting conversation at dinner," said Cordelia.

"Perhaps the beginning of several conversations," her hostess added, plainly delighted with the idea that her seating arrangements might lead to a match.

"Oh, I doubt that. We move in quite different circles." Cordelia tried to put an end to any speculation that she had an interest in Thorne…or that he had any in her.

Elly accompanied Cordelia to the door, where the footman hurried out to fetch a carriage to hire.

"Are you sure you're quite all right?" her friend asked with concern.

"Oh, yes, it's just a headache."

"Hmph. I will call on you tomorrow for more details! You may have fooled our hostess, but you haven't fooled me. There's *something* between you and Lord Thorne."

"Nonsense."

"We shall see," Elly said cheekily. "I saw him watching you. He was mesmerized."

The footman returned and escorted Cordelia out to the street. She climbed up into the carriage and heard the footman issue her street direction to the driver. She sat back, exhaling as she suddenly felt all the nervous energy run out of her.

"You were prompt getting out of there. Well done," a man's voice said. Sebastien Thorne leaned forward out of the shadows. He'd been sitting on the other side.

Cordelia practically jumped off the bench. "How did

you manage to get in here? You told me to ride home alone!"

"I told you to get in the carriage alone," he corrected her.

"This is hardly proper."

"Only if we're seen. Which we won't be. Besides, I've already seen you in quite an improper situation, Miss Bering."

She flushed, remembering his kiss at the window tonight, and the gardens before. "I shouldn't have let you do that."

"Let me what? Stop Hayden from stabbing you?" Then he stopped, guessing her train of thought. "Oh, I wasn't referring to that little diversion."

"Good." She cleared her throat. "In fact, I'd appreciate it if you never refer to it. Or, in fact, ever think of it again."

"I promise not to refer to it, if that's what you request." He gave her a look that could be described only as devilish. "But I can't promise not to *think* of it."

"Enough, sir. I believe any foolish transgressions on my part are *not* the reason you took such pains to meet me in this carriage," she hinted, remembering the more alarming part of Hayden's demands.

He sobered instantly. "You're right, Miss Bering. I do need to ask you something. Now that we trust each other, what if we tried something *truly* scandalous?"

His question stirred up heat in her belly, in a way she'd never experienced before. Lord Thorne was dashing, dangerous, and two feet away from her.

"What do you have in mind?"

He reached forward and laid his hand over hers, catching her gaze. "We tell each other the truth."

CORDELIA FELT A JOLT THROUGH her body, both from Thorne's proximity and from the words themselves. The truth was not something she was prepared to part with.

"Where are we going?" she asked first.

"I'm taking you home, where you'll be safe. But not until we understand each other." He arched one eyebrow at her. "When it comes to talking, am I not preferable to Hayden?"

She muttered, "A dead rat is preferable to Hayden," which earned her a surprised laugh from Thorne. He looked almost innocent when he laughed.

Then he leaned forward. "Hayden played his hand and lost. You can take a breath now."

Cordelia exhaled, barely aware that she'd been so tense. "Did you hurt him badly?"

"He'll wake up with his head pounding," he said. "But no worse."

"I thought you meant to kill him."

"I try not to do that, as a general rule. Would the loss of Hayden distress you?"

She raised her chin defiantly. "Not nearly as much as the loss of this outfit would. I pray it can be salvaged."

He laughed again, softly. "You keep your head, Miss Bering, I'll give you that."

She unconsciously tightened her grip on her reticule. "I thought I could protect myself if I simply acted sensibly."

"I did warn you that the people after you would not be civilized."

"I see that now." She paused. "You are also after the plans, and you didn't attack me."

"I prefer to use other methods to get what I want," he told her, and she only then became aware of how he'd been circling his thumb over her palm, and how soothing the feeling was.

She withdrew her hand, thinking that it was another line she ought not to have crossed. Sighing, Cordelia sat back, but then winced.

Without waiting for permission, he moved across the carriage so that he sat next to Cordelia. "Turn around. Let me see. He must have done more than simply tear your dress."

"That's not necessary."

"It is," he insisted.

Cordelia half turned away from him, allowing him to look at her back. Her hand drifted to where the pain was worst, but he caught it in his own, stopping her.

"Don't touch," he warned.

Cordelia waited, one hand in his, while his other probed her back gently through the fine fabric. "Well?" she asked.

"Be patient, I'm looking. Does it hurt here?" He barely touched a spot near her spine, low on her back.

"Yes," she hissed, surprised at the pain.

"There's a little blood." Thorne shifted, and Cordelia felt him press something against her back, over the cut, and hold it there.

"What are you doing?" she asked, trying to look over

her shoulder.

"I only have a handkerchief, but it will have to do until you get home."

Now that the cut was covered, she let both hands settle in her lap, wondering what a proper lady would do in this situation. Oh, yes. A proper lady would never, ever permit herself to get into such a situation. The fact that his hand was resting inches north of her bottom made it virtually impossible for her to think clearly. "I can hold it myself," she said.

"I like to be useful." He delivered his refusal in such a deadpan tone that she had to laugh.

Thorne urged her to settle against his side, a pose that she would never allow if she were not so preoccupied. "Just sit quietly," he advised, still holding the handker-chief against her back. "It's not a long ride."

It was difficult to relax when Thorne was pressed next to her with one arm around her body. The seriousness of the situation suddenly became very clear. Someone broke into her house, then someone threatened her life, and now she had put her life and reputation in the hands of a man she barely knew.

Cordelia looked over her shoulder and was caught by his eyes, dark and sensual in the half-light. He'd kissed her twice before. This was about to be the third, and she did nothing to discourage him. In fact, she lifted her head to meet his mouth.

Before she could do more, he bent his head to kiss her throat. Cordelia breathed in when his lips touched her skin. This kiss was somehow more intimate than the ones he'd given her before. His mouth lingered on her neck, moving slowly down next to the line the knife had traced earlier.

Reveling in the sensation, she didn't tell him to stop.

Heat seemed to rise off her skin. He reached the hollow at the base of her throat, and Cordelia murmured a warning when his tongue flicked out and tasted her there.

At the sound, he paused long enough to catch his own breath and, she realized, to give her the opportunity to say something. She didn't even have the words to ask for what she might want. Before she could say anything she would regret, he pulled back.

He smiled, completely disarming her. "Does it still sting?"

"No," she breathed.

"Good. I do like to make myself useful."

"Useful," she echoed, thinking that *useful* was not a term she'd match with the dissolute and maddeningly attractive Earl of Thornebury. Then she frowned, remembering what had brought them here. "Why are you so interested in my father's work?"

"It's not the only thing I'm interested in, Miss Bering," he told her with a wicked light in his eyes. "But if I'm to get the plans back for you, I need to know everything I can about the *Andraste* designs. Do you know anything about them?"

"Of course! That is…yes, a little." Cordelia reverted to the image of a dutiful daughter, only slightly aware of her father's genius. "What do you need to know?"

"Everything you can tell me." He glanced out the carriage window, looking concerned. "Yet we're close to Quince Street already, and I can't keep you out all night… appealing as that notion is."

"I could tell you about them tomorrow, but you must not call at my home again," she warned him. "It would be far too difficult to explain your continued presence. You're an earl, I'm nobody. People will talk."

"What do you suggest, Miss Bering?"

She considered the issue for a long moment. Finally, she hit on an idea. "Can you be at the East India Docks at two o'clock tomorrow? If you walk to the quay where the packet ships dock, I'll find you there and we can talk with no one to overhear."

"You can't go there alone," he objected.

Cordelia shook her head. "I won't be. I shall have a chaperone. Not Aunt Leona, of course. Don't worry, I know how to conduct myself in public."

"That sounds like a bit of a censure toward me."

She glanced at him. "And why not? I already have some idea of how you conduct yourself in private."

"Miss Bering, you have no idea how I conduct myself in private," he said with a slow smile that threatened to unhinge her. When his mouth quirked up at the corner, something seemed to heat up in her core.

Thankfully, at that moment the carriage pulled up the drive to her home. She sighed in relief. "I'm home."

He said nothing, but lowered his mouth to hers once more. Cordelia didn't even think to protest. The kiss was brief, but she was still shaken at the end of it. "Why did you do that? Not to make yourself useful this time, and not for luck."

"I don't know if you're good luck or bad luck, Miss Bering," he said, looking at her intently. "But I do know that you fascinate me."

He moved away from her, before she could make a fool of herself. "Are you strong enough to walk up your steps?"

"Yes, of course."

"Then forgive me for not helping you out. I'd think you'd prefer me to remain as unobtrusive as possible."

"I'm grateful for your discretion."

"See? I can be a gentleman…sometimes." He touched

her hand. "Have one of your people care for those cuts immediately."

"I will." She climbed out of the carriage. "Tomorrow at two," she reminded him, looking back.

"I'll be there."

Cordelia hurried into the house as the carriage rolled away behind her. Jem was playing footman tonight, and he frowned when he saw a hired carriage leaving the scene, instead of the Ramsays'.

"Anything we should know, my lady?" he asked bluntly.

"Yes," she replied. "You will be driving Bond and me to the harbor tomorrow afternoon. No questions and no comments."

"Yes, my lady," he said. He shut the door behind her, bolting it securely.

"Oh, and send Bond up to my room as soon as possible, with some clean cloths, hot water, and alcohol. Someone tried to stab me earlier tonight." A part of her enjoyed Jem's stunned expression as she said it.

Upstairs, she caused a certain amount of trouble for her maid as well.

"Oh, my lady!" Bond wailed. "What did you *do*? I don't know if I can save these shoes!" The young woman showed far more distress over the state of Cordelia's evening wear than she had over either knife wound, which Cordelia took as a good sign.

"Try your best. If they can't be saved, then give them to Ivy. We're of a size, and the shoes will still keep feet dry."

"I shall endeavor to clean them, my lady." Bond grimaced. Then she put the shoes down and turned her attention back to her mistress. "Are you quite comfortable?"

"I'm well enough."

Bond had already cleaned the wounds and bandaged them well, assuring Cordelia that both would heal swiftly. "And I can sew the dress as good as new. But that's not the half of it! You were *attacked*, my lady."

"Fortunately, I was rescued."

"By that *man*. The one in the house yesterday."

"Lord Thorne, yes." Cordelia paused. "He not only saved my life, he saved my reputation as well."

"Let's hope he doesn't hold it over you," the maid groused.

"A gentleman wouldn't do such a thing." Cordelia considered the possibility that Sebastien Thorne might use his knowledge against her. If he wanted to, he could easily blackmail her…for the portion of the *Andraste* designs still in her possession, for example. Was that the real reason for his sudden attention and the kisses she couldn't seem to forget?

Bond, meanwhile, was unaware of her turn of thought. "You don't know much of men, begging your pardon."

"You don't trust Thorne?"

"Does a lamb trust a wolf?"

Despite herself, Cordelia smiled at her maid's characterization. "To tell the truth, I know there's something about him that doesn't add up. So it's just as well that you'll accompany me when I happen to run into him tomorrow at the harbor."

"I'll not let you out of my sight, my lady."

Bond settled Cordelia into her bed, then turned down the light and closed the door. However, sleep was the furthest thing from Cordelia's mind. She relived nearly every moment of the evening, from the terror of discovering Hayden's treachery to the moment when Thorne kissed her nearly senseless in the darkened coach. She closed her eyes, remembering the feel of his lips on her skin.

It had been a daring, scandalous, and perhaps insulting thing to do. What kind of woman did he take her for?

The kind who wanted him to do it. She admitted to herself that she had given him plenty of leave. She should have been icy to him. Heartless. And yet, she loved the feelings he'd stirred in her. She knew that she would let him kiss her again. She might let him do more than kiss her. Being still unmarried at her age left her quite curious about some things. When she finally drifted off, her dreams were filled with images of Sebastien Thorne, a man she didn't yet understand, but couldn't ignore.

PRIVATELY, CORDELIA HAD DOUBTS ABOUT the wisdom of meeting Sebastien at the harbor. But she didn't see any alternatives. She couldn't let him keep coming into her home, whether he claimed to be visiting Leona Wharton or not! Furthermore, she didn't want her aunt to learn too much of her own activities surrounding shipbuilding. The less Leona knew, the less danger to her.

Cordelia admitted to herself that she had rather taken advantage of her aunt's trust over the years. She told her nothing about her secret work as Lear, for instance. And Leona was blissfully ignorant of the servants' shady pasts.

So Cordelia couldn't let Lord Thorne get further involved in her household. She also couldn't risk any gossip about them circulating among the *ton*. His first visit she could explain away by mentioning his connection to Aunt Leona. More than that and he'd have to be courting her, which was outside the realm of plausibility. The newest Earl of Thornebury must select a young, titled, and wealthy bride. She was none of those. For him to pretend that she was a candidate for countess was laughable.

So why did she spend so much time dressing for the meeting with him? Bond endured three costume changes and her mistress's doubts as to her hairstyle.

"You must pull it back, ma'am," she said finally.

"That raven hair is a beacon, even under a hat. Not to mention the wind!" The maid expertly twisted Cordelia's hair into a low knot and secured the style with several pins. "There now. You will not blow apart in a breeze."

Dressed in a pale cream walking gown covered with a green pelisse, Cordelia finally descended the stairs.

"Will you be out long, my lady?" Stiles asked. He, of course, had been apprised of the events of last night (and was full of opinions about the matter).

"A few hours at most, Stiles," she assured him.

"Just as long as it takes to get that lord off our backs," Bond added.

The butler glanced at her. "A servant does not speak of her betters in that fashion."

Cordelia intervened. "She's not wrong, Stiles. Once Lord Thorne is satisfied that he's learned…whatever he needs to learn, our household will return to normal."

"I pray that's the case, my lady." He opened the door for them and shook a warning finger at Bond as she followed Cordelia out.

Jem drove toward the harbor. Bond was playing the role of chaperone, and she looked the part, dressed in one of Cordelia's old gowns. Despite her humble origins, Bond's height and fine features gave her the air of a lady, and she had used her recent weeks of gainful employment to study and imitate her mistress; when she wanted to, she could mimic tones and gestures with uncanny accuracy.

Of course, Bond wasn't *all* lady. She took her duty seriously enough that she concealed a knife on her person. "He may be a lord or whatever, but if he so much as touches you, my lady, I'll gut 'im like a fish."

"Bond, that is not how ladies' maids talk."

"Aye, but I'm a very special lady's maid, ain't I?" Bond said, deliberately using her rougher accent.

Giving up on lecturing, Cordelia smiled. "Yes, I would say you are."

* * * *

Cordelia wasn't the only person feeling dubious about the meeting. Thorne couldn't stop debating whether Miss Bering could be trusted. Despite Forester's theory that it was some sort of trick, he could tell she was truly distressed about the theft, just as she had been shocked (and physically hurt) by Hayden's actions the night before. But there were many aspects that didn't add up.

He reviewed all the intelligence he'd gathered. Miss Bering was a spinster, but she had no difficulty funding her home and maintaining an uncommonly large staff of uncommonly conscientious servants. She had to get that money from somewhere. The easy answer was that she was selling something of value…and could that be but the work of her late father?

He didn't want to think of her as a traitor. In fact, he was uncomfortably aware that he wanted to be her protector…when he didn't want to seduce her for the pure excitement of it.

His musings were cut short by more urgent matters. His sister, Adele, cornered him at the breakfast table and asked him several uncomfortable questions regarding his activities the previous few nights. Though younger than he, she showed remarkable maturity…and very little deference to him.

"Did you stay out at your club? I sent a message there."

"You did? Why?" he asked.

"Because I needed to know where you would be today, dear brother. I thought you might want to know that

Mama has been plotting to get you to meet some more eligible ladies."

He groaned. "That's the last thing on my mind right now. Can't she just let me alone?"

"You'd best be gone by noon, unless you want to get snared."

"I'll be gone as long as necessary. Tell Mama you have no idea where I am."

"We hardly ever know where you are. You are not getting ensnared in your old vices, are you?" Adele paused. "I'd hate to see you…regress."

"You don't have to worry, Adele."

"Just be careful," she warned. "I do love you, Sebastien, and I'd hate to lose you."

Heeding his sister's advice, Sebastien kept a low profile for the day, and found his way to the docks at the appointed time. He'd dressed carefully, choosing clothes that suggested he was a gentleman, but which were nondescript enough that he shouldn't be noticed. His jacket was a fog grey, worn over a simple white shirt and darker pants. Plain black shoes made him look much like any other man, and a black hat gave a measure of anonymity. Not that he expected anyone he knew to be walking the quay. Cordelia had been clever to think of it. But then, she was a clever woman.

He began to stroll toward the end of the quay. Though it was spring, a stiff breeze off the river kept people from being too idle, and the level of activity around him gave him the comfortable feeling of being alone in a crowd.

But he was not alone for long. Two women approached him. The tall one, obviously the subordinate, addressed him first. To an observer, it would have appeared that she was asking directions, perhaps to a particular ship. But Thorne heard something quite different.

"Good morning, my lord," she began. "I am given to understand that you will be walking with my lady for a short time." Her voice was cool and proper, and several classes above where he suspected she came from.

"That's correct."

"Then know that I am watching you," she said simply, the threat in her voice unmistakable.

Before he could respond, the other woman joined them. Cordelia wore her raven hair bound tightly under her wide-brimmed hat, protected from both the wind and prying eyes. "That will do, Bond. Lord Thorne and I will walk. Please follow at a distance."

"Yes, ma'am," the maid said.

Sebastien offered his arm, which Cordelia took.

"You're not afraid to be seen walking with a man at the harbor," he said.

"People see what they expect to see." She shrugged. "No one here knows our identities. We could be family, or a married couple."

"So we could," he agreed, rather liking the suggestion.

She said, more hesitantly, "I suppose, if we are to trust each other, then we are…friends?"

He gave her a long, considering glance. "I certainly wouldn't want you for an enemy. So yes, friends."

"Then please call me Cordelia," she asked in a rush, with those green eyes wide and appealing.

"But only when no one else is around," he added, sensing her unspoken thought.

"It would raise questions if you used my Christian name in the presence of others," she admitted. "But I should like you to, when you may."

He nodded, unaccountably flattered by the offer. He'd had other women offer much more, only to feel much less affected. "And will you do the same for me, Cordelia?"

He spoke her name slowly, savoring the taste of it.

"Yes, of course," she said.

"Of course…"

"Sebastien," she finished. It came out a bit breathily, as if she felt too bold using his name like that, in the open air.

He enjoyed the sound of her saying his name. "That didn't tax your sensibilities, did it?"

"Less than certain other liberties you have taken," she said.

"I'm not sorry that I kissed you."

"I understand why you did it," she told him, her glance narrowing.

"You do, do you?"

"Yes." She swallowed. "I'm not completely naive. You said last night that you preferred to use methods other than force. Seduction can be as effective as violence to get information. You thought to expose my weakness by appealing to my baser instincts."

Sebastien was a little shaken by her blunt assessment. He said, "I thought ladies such as yourself had no base instincts."

"Apparently, a well-executed kiss can summon them."

"Oh, really." He smiled lazily, pleased by her inadvertent confession.

"That wasn't an invitation," she said hastily.

"But it sounded so inviting."

Cordelia looked down, her cheeks pink. She was obviously embarrassed by the turn the conversation was taking. "Fortunately, I did not succumb to your ploy."

"Maybe I just gave up too soon."

Behind them, Bond coughed loudly.

"Your chaperone has sharp ears," he noted.

Cordelia turned and gave a look to the maid, who

grudgingly slowed down a few paces. "She's very dedicated."

"I'll be a perfect gentleman," he promised, remembering the maid's challenge.

"Good. Now, you proved last night that you value my life slightly higher than some others do, like Hayden. I suppose you saved my life, and certainly my reputation."

"You're welcome," he said dryly.

"I thank you. And I will try to trust you. You have questions. Ask me."

"Let's start with the plans everyone wants. What are they for, exactly?"

"You don't know?" She gave him a quick, anxious glance.

No, he didn't, but he had no desire to look like an idiot. "I want to hear it from you."

Cordelia took a deep breath. "They are for a new type of ship. The prototype is called the *Andraste*."

"Before a few days ago, I'd never heard of it."

She said, "Almost no one has. If and when it is built, the *Andraste* will be the first of its kind. My father designed it." She paused, then added, "However, I did choose the name."

"After the goddess."

"Yes, a goddess of Britain, who a British-born queen turned to for help and protection during her battle. It seemed appropriate."

"Why should that name be so fitting? What kind of ship is it?"

Cordelia pointed to a frigate in the harbor, sweeping her hand in a grand gesture to encompass the whole ship. "Look. That ship over there is well made. The hull is built to withstand ocean swells and storms. The masts are strong. Yet, as you know, even a perfectly built wooden ship is vulnerable to cannon, or to fire…even lightning in a storm."

"Yes, of course. But what can a ship be made of, if not wood?"

She smiled then. "Imagine a ship made of steel, strong enough to withstand a blast from a sixty-eight-pound gun."

Sebastien tried, and was immediately horrified by the implications. "Made of steel? How is that even possible?"

Cordelia made a slightly disappointed sound. "Well, it's not made entirely of steel, of course. Not yet. The *Andraste* would be the first step, the first…iteration. The hull is wooden, like a regular ship. But plates of steel are hammered to that hull, both above and partly below the waterline. The plates are treated to be resistant to salt water, so there's no worry about rust or corrosion—in theory. And steel is fireproof as well. Thus the ship would be safe from cannon or even a chemical substance…you know, like Greek fire."

"But it would be too heavy to float," Sebastien protested.

"The weight is a significant factor. But by balancing the internal volume of the ship against the surface area of the hull, one can determine a safe range of size and weight." As Cordelia spoke, she used her hands to illustrate the points, her enthusiasm growing with every word. "The *Andraste* isn't meant to be a cargo ship. It would protect other ships by sailing where they can't. She would be used for running messages from point to point, or ferrying passengers."

"Or soldiers."

"Well, yes," she admitted. "Though that wasn't the intent when…my father first designed it."

"I had been under the impression that it was a weapon

of some sort," said Sebastien, though he knew it was very possible the information had been garbled somehow before the Zodiac got hold of it.

Cordelia shook her head, upset. "That was never the intent. But that *is* Hayden's idea. He mentioned adding guns to the prototype. I don't know how many he could add, considering the issue of weight." She looked like she was working out a calculation in her head, but didn't announce any solution.

"You have to tell me a little more about it," Sebastien said, more urgently. "How big is it? How many men could it carry?"

"The prototype is fairly small. It should be capable of carrying about twenty people comfortably, including the crew, allowing for some excess weight. Obviously, theory is all well and good, but until a working prototype can sail —or steam—through a few successful journeys, we won't know if all the specifications are correct. Did I mention that the *Andraste* will be propelled by steam as well as sail?"

"You didn't."

"Yes," she said proudly. "No more fear of getting becalmed. Or losing a sail. The ship will be able to travel without impediments, even through a battle. Of course, improvements will need to be made, following a successful launch…" She trailed off, noticing that Sebastien had stopped walking. "What is it?" she asked, turning to look back at him.

"You know a lot about this," he noted, watching her narrowly.

Cordelia flushed, her green eyes going wide. "I've had to learn, haven't I? When it became obvious that unscrupulous people were after the plans, it behooved me to know everything about it…everything I could, I mean," she added hastily.

He nodded, accepting her explanation for now. "Why didn't you destroy the plans immediately?" he asked. "You could have burned them."

She flinched. "I probably should have, but…it would have felt like burning a book."

Sebastien considered the woman walking beside him. If she were coldly practical, she would have gotten rid of the plans as soon as she realized someone else wanted them. Then he never would have been assigned to get them himself. And he never would have met her. "I understand your reluctance to dispose of something your father created," he said slowly.

"Do you?" she asked.

"My own father died only a little more than two years ago," he explained. "And while he never created a thing like the *Andraste*, I would be loath to get rid of anything he owned that was more valuable than a tiepin."

Cordelia beamed at him. "You do understand what I'm trying to say."

"Well, to a point. For instance, my father's tiepins wouldn't be much use in a war."

"No," she admitted, her worry returning. "So we are back where we started."

"Maybe not."

"How so?"

"Last night, Hayden cornered you because he still wanted something. I heard him say something about the remainder of the papers."

"You heard that?" she asked, her expression troubled.

"Yes. Did you have any intention of telling me the whole truth, *friend*?"

"I have not spoken my piece yet."

"Then do so, Cordelia. The burglar didn't get everything."

She shook her head. "No. He got the designs that relate to the hull. That is, someone could build the outer shell of the ship now. But they're missing an essential component." She stopped talking, biting her lower lip.

"What component?" he prompted, trying hard not to think about her lips. He'd gotten a few tastes…he wanted more.

She glanced sidelong at him, then said, "The propeller screw. Without it, the ship would be virtually impossible to sail capably, making it little more than an armored island."

"Not a bad thing to have," Sebastien said.

"Perhaps not. But they're after the whole ship. And you're right. They won't stop till they get the rest of the designs in my possession." Unconsciously, she began to nibble her lip again, which was something he'd really prefer to do himself. *Focus*, he thought.

"So you have something you are both afraid to keep and afraid to destroy. You trust me a little, I hope," said Sebastien. "Would you allow me to keep the designs safe for you?"

"How do I know that you could?"

"You didn't ask whether I *would*."

Cordelia shook her head. "For some reason, I do trust you. I spoke to a friend about you. She told me…I heard you served in the army. You were wounded during the War in the Vendée, correct?"

"It wasn't a serious wound." He waved it off.

"But you understand that war isn't a game."

"God, yes." He knew that all too well.

"So you see why my father was reluctant to offer the designs to just anyone. He did know that some of his work had military applications."

"And you also wish to keep those plans from being used in that way," he said, finally feeling as if he was beginning to understand the woman.

"Precisely. I would need some…assurance that the plans were in good hands," Cordelia said. Then she turned to her maid, who had somehow managed to follow them quite closely again. "Bond, give us a moment alone."

The maid reluctantly slowed her pace once more, dropping out of earshot. Cordelia shot her a warning glance before telling Sebastien to continue. "This is the moment when you tell me some truth…Sebastien."

He couldn't tell Cordelia about the Zodiac. He couldn't admit that he was an agent, even if he was on her side. But she demanded some kind of guarantee.

"You named the ship *Andraste*," he began.

"Yes." She looked at him, expectant.

"A British name, for a British ship, created by a British man," he went on.

"Yes."

"So you naturally want it to stay British. Safe, here on this island."

"Indeed I do."

He tried to speak as carefully as he could. "I can tell you that I share your concerns. Remember I too am a British citizen, who fought for a British king, and I hold a British title. Beyond that, all I can tell you is that I am in a better position than anyone I know to keep *Andraste* safe, here on this island. And I have some powerful friends. Do you understand?"

Cordelia watched him as he spoke, her green eyes all too alert. She saw how precisely he chose his words. She nodded slowly. "I believe so."

Sebastien didn't want to press the issue of the remaining designs yet, and he still had many questions for

Cordelia, more than this simple walk could answer. "Did you think this theft was a possibility? Is that why you separated the plans?"

"I wish I was so forward thinking." Cordelia shook her head sadly. "It was a matter of luck. The propeller screw necessary to run the ship was successfully designed only last year. Thus, it was never in the same box with the older plans."

"Last year? Then who did it? Not your father, obviously."

She looked away suddenly, her expression closing. "His colleague. Lear."

"And you know he wouldn't sell the plans?"

"He is as trustworthy as I am," she said.

But just how trustworthy was Cordelia? Sebastien dearly wished that he knew. "And you would rely on Lear more than me?"

Cordelia looked extremely nervous now. She was so evasive whenever the subject of Lear came up. "You don't understand. We are friends. Quite intimate friends."

How intimate? Sebastien was aware of a sudden urge to hunt the man down. "Then you can arrange a meeting," he said. *A meeting where I'll beat the man bloody if he confesses he's your lover.*

"That would be difficult." She looked out over the water, resolutely not facing him. "He's a retiring individual," she said. "Virtually a hermit."

"I'll be brief. You can't pretend that this isn't important."

An indefinable look crossed her face. "I'll bring it up with him," she promised.

They had reached the end of the quay. Thorne paused for a moment, looking out at the river. "We should head back," he said.

"I thought you'd demand the papers by now. That's all you want, yes? The meeting with Lear is…ancillary."

Sebastien still looked over the water. "I do need the papers. But I wanted to give you until the other end of the quay to get used to the idea."

"I already know that the sooner they are in a safe place, the safer I'll be."

He sighed. "I am glad you admit that, Cordelia. Can you at least promise me they are safe for the moment?"

"Yes."

"Good. Now I have to ensure Hayden won't try for them again. I'm going to find him."

"You must be careful," she said, putting her hand on his arm and squeezing.

"Heartless Miss Bering, are you worried about me?" he quipped to hide how much he liked her impulsive gesture.

"Of course I am, Sebastien." Those green eyes matched the water now, deep and dangerous.

Her declaration troubled him. He didn't want Cordelia to worry about him. He didn't want her to care about him. He wanted only to keep her attention long enough to get what he needed. Didn't he?

The rest of the walk was silent.

Cordelia and her fierce chaperone left him at the end of the docks, returning to the carriage they arrived in. Thorne caught a challenging look from the driver, the same lanky young man he'd seen before.

Thorne watched the carriage roll away. Cordelia Bering seemed designed to infuriate and intrigue him. For every scrap of truth he pried from her, more questions emerged. She pretended ignorance about her father's work, but she obviously understood both the details and the import of the designs. And this Mr Lear seemed to be a phantom, though she considered him an *intimate* friend. And her maid! The woman all but threatened him physically, and what was more, she nearly convinced him she could follow through. The Bering house must be utter madness.

But before he could tease out the layers of secrets that Cordelia was hiding, he had other work to do. First, he'd return to the Kingston China Company and find Dodd. The weasel he'd caught the night of the robbery was only that—a weasel, a hired thief who knew nothing about what he was supposed to steal. Thorne had to keep climbing this ladder until he got the real prize. In the international game Thorne played, even Dodd would be only a low-level rat, with a dim idea of the importance of the papers he was after. What Cordelia had shared about the plans frankly scared him. The little information he knew was already enough to make some guesses as to who might be working hardest to get the plans. He just had to use those scraps of knowledge to fool Dodd into revealing more. But first he had to find the man.

He headed for his private home near St James. When he was working for the Zodiac, the place was his only safe haven. Once again dressed in clothing most inappropriate for a man of his station, Thorne headed back to the poorer, working district of the city. He wasn't known to the residents of this neighborhood, but a few were happy enough to talk once he passed out some small coins. He got the name of the building where Dodd usually spent his time, not far from the supposed china company.

He let himself into the building and found his way to a cramped office that might have doubled as a junk room. A portly man was inside, facing away from the door as he rifled through a box of odds and ends.

"Gerald Dodd," Thorne guessed.

The man's back stiffened. He lurched suddenly, but Thorne moved like a cat and caught hold of his shoulder as he spun around. Dodd had half drawn a knife, but Thorne was faster. "So you are Dodd." He pried the knife from Dodd's grip.

Dodd watched the knife vanish with keen disappointment. "Sure. Who does that make you?"

"No one you need to remember."

"Then what do you want?"

"You're after some ship designs. I want you to tell me about them."

Dodd's eyes widened, but then he let out a blustery laugh. "Where'd you get that idea? I look like a clerk?"

"You look like a man who knows something I want to know. And I'm not feeling very patient."

"I'm not telling you anything."

"You already have, actually."

"That so?" Dodd sneered.

"You regret getting involved, for one. You thought it would be easy. The one who hired you seemed to know where the papers would be. He described the address, the room, even the box they were in. But you're lazy, so you got a smaller rat to do the dirty work. Bailey tried and failed to get all the papers. You tried to silence Bailey, but he got away."

"How do you know all that?" Dodd asked, looking much less sure of himself.

Thorne gave him a nasty grin. "I'm the one who let Bailey get away. You see, I also want the papers."

"Tough luck. I don't have the Andrews papers, or whatever they're called," Dodd pointed out, growing more nervous.

"Because Hayden already took them from you?"

"Yeah. Wait, how do you know about him?"

Thorne laughed. "Never mind. You have something else I want. The name of the other person who wants them. Not Hayden. Tell me who he works for."

"I can't tell you that!"

"How good a thief will you be once I cut off your right hand?" Thorne asked quietly.

Dodd jerked, trying to escape. Thorne sighed. Slamming Dodd's hand against the wall, he pressed Dodd's own knife against his wrist. "I hope you keep this sharp."

Feeling the blade bite into his flesh, Dodd choked off a scream. "Stop!"

"Tell me a name." Thorne pressed the blade in.

"Wait!"

"Why?"

"I don't know who he works for. But I can tell you something you don't know."

"Which is what?"

"What his boss looks like."

Thorne pulled the blade back. "Impress me."

"I saw the two talking from my window. Hayden was taking orders from the man. He never got out of his carriage. He looked like he was shorter than you. And all white hair. A gentleman, he was. Very posh. Not that you'd know a thing about what makes a gentleman, you dog!"

The gentleman in laborer's clothes gave that bit of insight exactly the weight it was due. "And what precisely did Hayden tell you?"

"Just what you said. He wanted the box of papers. Didn't say why. Just that he couldn't be seen taking them because he was in the middle of a long con. I was to get them from the house for him. He offered a pretty sum."

"How much?"

"A pony."

Thorne almost burst out laughing. Twenty-five quid? He suspected the *Andraste* designs were worth a thousand times that amount. "What was he planning to do with them?"

"Sell them, I think."

"Why let him? Once you had the papers, you could sell them yourself."

Dodd shuffled. "Not me. Wouldn't know who'd be interested." That part was probably true. Dodd would typically fence far more mundane things.

"Did he mention anyone as a customer?"

"No. All I know is that it sounds like something I don't want to be tangled in."

"Then why agree to do it at all?"

Dodd paused. "He was persuasive. Polite, like a gentleman. But some men got a way about them. I didn't want him to get angry. I saw him angry after Bailey bungled it. He was furious that not all of the them were there, but…"

"Tell me." Thorne's eyes narrowed.

"He let something slip while he was screaming. Seems the papers Hayden was after weren't all in the one swell's house. There were others."

"Where?" Thorne felt a sudden rush of excitement, but he was careful to hide it from the other man.

"At this place called the Atheneum. A sort of club for inventors, I think. Hayden thought he might need something from there."

"Is that so?"

"He tried to hire me to get them too. But after Bailey messed up the first job, I told him to shove off. I don't want any more to do with this. It stinks of politics."

"That's the first sensible thing you've said. Trust me when I say you want no part of this," Thorne assured him.

He left Dodd in his rubbish heap of an office. Dodd was too greedy and scared to stop entirely, but he hoped that his appearance would jolt someone into doing something without thinking first. A rash move would give Thorne an opportunity to strike at his real adversary.

And as it happened, someone did do something quite rash.

CORDELIA RETURNED TO THE HOUSE more pensive than before. Bond's silence hinted that the maid was lost in her own thoughts. Perversely, Cordelia wished the younger woman would say something, even if it was only another tart comment about Sebastien Thorne.

The man couldn't be motivated by simple concern for her. She guessed that he was using her, though in a slightly different way than Hayden had. Could she take advantage of that somehow, in order to protect herself and her household for certain? Cordelia drifted into her study, though she had no head for working right now. Instead, she stared at all the items on the shelves. That was where Stiles found her.

He cleared his throat. "My lady? Someone has been asking questions about this house, about everyone who lives here."

She looked up, her stomach suddenly lurching. "You mean the burglar asked about the people who work here to learn our habits?"

"Not just him. This morning, a neighbor's footman was asked about how long Jem has worked here. And not because they wanted to hire him away from you! No, someone is trying to find out about us. Also, I suspect the house is being watched."

Every worker at Quince Street had a secret to keep. If someone was snooping around, they would all pay. Jem and Bond would likely end up in prison again, or possibly transported to New South Wales. Even Cordelia, as their employer, would face serious consequences for hiring people of such dubious reputations. Stiles would certainly be sentenced to die by hanging for his previous crimes. He had cheated death before. It was unlikely he could do it again.

"Do not tell me you're all leaving," she said sharply. She wondered who was watching. Hayden? Thorne? Both?

He shook his head. "You took us in when no one else would. We won't abandon you."

"There must be something we can *do*."

"You have an enemy who wants something of yours. As long as you have it here, we're all in danger. It must be moved and hidden more securely."

"If you really think the house is being watched, then I have another idea," said Cordelia, suddenly excited. "Let's take away their reason for watching."

She'd thought that hiding the plans would be enough to keep them safe. It was now clear that powers far larger than her were involved. Hiding them was no longer an option. But maybe she could exploit her watcher, or watchers, to solve her own difficulty. Though her idea was impulsive, she knew it would work. It would hurt, but not as much as losing her reputation and all her household.

Cordelia stood up. "It's time I did what I should have done long ago. And we can't wait a moment longer."

She summoned Bond. Together, the women went up to Cordelia's room, where she instructed the maid to pull out her plainest outfit and help her dress.

"What are you planning to do, madam?" Bond asked.

"I'm going to set several things on fire," Cordelia said airily. Her heart, though, was quaking. "Follow me. I need to gather fuel."

To Bond's credit, she had learned enough of her new role to know that asking questions at this point would do no good at all. Stiles joined the two women in the study, where Cordelia sorted through things and put several notebooks, folded papers, and rolled diagrams aside.

"Those must all be burned," Cordelia instructed, pointing to the pile. "Jem keeps a barrel by the stables, doesn't he?"

Bond nodded. The trio gathered up all the papers and books. Stiles frowned at the idea of Cordelia doing the dirty chore, but he knew better than to object. He appreciated the need to see a job done personally.

In the small courtyard by the stables, Jem, who had been tending to the horses, quickly turned his attention to the new task. He lit a fire in the wide barrel he used to burn rubbish. Slowly, Cordelia fed each scrap of paper into the fire, watching as the paper caught, the ink darkened, and everything turned to ash.

"Hope they see *this*," Jem murmured to Bond.

"Not every day the lady of the house does the burning," she whispered back. "Look, the neighbors' servants are watching. That's good."

Cordelia kept feeding the fire. She was startled when the butler offered her a handkerchief, because she didn't even realize that tears were running down her face.

"You should go inside, my lady," Stiles said quietly. "It's all gone now."

Cordelia blinked, seeing that the last of the papers were burning, and that Bond's hands were empty. "Well," she said, an empty feeling settling in her chest. "That's that."

Stiles nodded to Bond. "Take the mistress inside and bring her something to drink. She needs to rest."

Bond took Cordelia by the arm. "I could ask Mrs Wharton to join you in the drawing room after she returns home, if you would like. I bet she has some stories of your father as a young boy that you haven't heard yet."

"Aye," said Stiles. "My lady, you'll need happier memories to replace…this." He gestured to the smoking barrel.

Cordelia nodded. Stiles could tell that the dark thoughts were still swirling in her head. Bond's suggestion was a sweet one. How many people would understand that, and offer a solution? Cordelia had gathered a very rare family in this house. A motley collection of disgraced souls and outcasts had found a harbor. And she'd do anything to keep them safe.

Inside, Cordelia washed the soot from her face and changed into a more suitable outfit for the evening. Ivy brought tea and a small plate of fruit to the drawing room. Cordelia sipped from a teacup without tasting anything. She'd never felt more self-doubt in her life than over the past week.

Leona, who had been out visiting friends, returned a half hour later. "Cordelia? Bond said you were feeling poorly." She sat down next to her niece.

"I am just melancholy," Cordelia said. "I feel as though life has become…" She trailed off.

"Tiring?"

"Complicated. I'm not sure I have the wherewithal to deal with it alone."

"You are not alone, dear."

"I know I have you, Aunt," Cordelia said. "I just mean…oh, I don't know. I want to be in charge of my life, but should I be?"

"Your father knew you would be capable, my dear. He left everything to you, with no clauses or catches. If nothing else, that act shows his faith."

"Thank you," Cordelia said, tears pricking her eyes. "You're right, of course."

"I'm worried seeing you so pale and drawn. That robbery upset you, even if you try to pretend it hasn't. But you must forget it. It's over now."

The warm feeling in Cordelia's heart vanished again, although she kept the smile on her face. Her aunt didn't know that things were far from over. Until the papers were truly safe, until Sebastien Thorne could be persuaded to forget about Lear, Cordelia couldn't rest easy. But how could she produce a phantom? She picked up the teacup again.

Meanwhile, Leona had moved on to other subjects. "You'll never guess who I ran into today," she said. "I called on my friend Mrs Martin, and who should be there but the Countess of Thornebury. It turns out both ladies tried to buy the same horse years ago and nearly came to blows over it," she said, no doubt exaggerating the conflict. "But they're now good friends. Anyway, I told her that her son had just kindly called on me. She was rather pleased with the boy, I think, for remembering an old acquaintance." Leona leaned forward, even though they were alone. She whispered, "I think she feared he was returning to gambling."

"Maybe he has," said Cordelia, feeling that everything Thorne did seemed to hold an element of risk.

"Oh, my, we should not speculate. But the point is that, as she left, she said she would send an invitation round to a party she is holding this Friday evening. Isn't that lovely? She is looking forward to meeting you."

Cordelia recoiled. She wasn't sure she'd be up to the challenge of conversing and dancing as if she had no cares in the world. Sebastien would likely be there. Could she act like a mere acquaintance toward him? "That may not be an altogether sound idea."

"Why should it not be? You'll enjoy yourself."

"But Lord Thorne…"

"Seemed most attentive to you when he called. Why, would you prefer not to see him again?" Leona asked rather impishly.

"It's just…last week these people didn't know I existed. And now we're invited to their parties?"

"They may have titles, but your blood is every bit as noble as theirs. Don't forget that your mother was the daughter of a lord."

"But I am not," Cordelia pointed out.

"You are the daughter of a lady and a gentleman. You have nothing to be ashamed of in front of the Thornes."

Cordelia looked at her aunt. "I still can't believe that you recognized Sebastien Thorne after all these years."

Leona blushed slightly. "Well, the truth is that I didn't. Ivy told me he was in the room before I joined you. I enjoy playing at surprise sometimes."

"Auntie!" Cordelia gasped. "That's dreadfully deceptive of you."

"I know it." The older lady preened. "But deception is so invigorating. You must try it sometime."

Cordelia looked down. Her aunt could not possibly know the extent of her own deceptions. Could she?

* * * *

"I'm not attending a party," Thorne said flatly. It was hours after Cordelia had met with him at the docks, and he could still remember the way the wind played with the few free strands of her hair. He'd recounted their conversation in his head several times, and admitted that one of his reasons for doing so had more to do with the way he remembered Cordelia's luscious mouth moving, rather than any need to memorize what he'd learned.

In contrast, the thought of enduring another party thrown by his mother nearly caused him to wince in real pain. He was now ensconced in his family home, waiting for his mother to see reason. She did not appear to want to do so. "I'm not attending a party," he repeated.

"Yes, you are. You may be the earl, but I'm still your mother, and you will do this for me."

"I have a host of things to attend to," he protested. Unfortunately, he couldn't talk about most of them. "I certainly don't have time for inane conversations with potential wives. That's what this is about, isn't it?"

"There may be a few suitable young ladies present," his mother admitted. "I want you to meet Lady Mary, who is the Marquess of Bromley's daughter. But there will also be old friends coming. It won't be painful, Sebastien. You must step more into the role of earl. Our family has held the honor for so long, and I know you shouldn't wish to tarnish the luster of our name now."

She turned to the housekeeper, who was jotting notes down on a pad. "Oh, that reminds me. Add Leona Wharton and her niece to the list of dinner guests. I'll have to find two more gentlemen for the list then..." she muttered. "Or perhaps someone will not attend..."

Sebastien went still. Had his mother somehow managed to independently invite Cordelia? What trick of the gods brought that about? He'd have a chance to see her again without subterfuge. He could ask her about Lear, if he hadn't tracked the man down by then.

"Very well," he said suddenly. "I'll be there. But don't think you can assign all my dance partners on my behalf." He'd be damned if he got stuck with a vapid miss while Cordelia danced with someone else.

An expression of triumph and relief settled on his mother's features. "Just behave yourself. That's all I ask."

He nodded, not trusting himself to speak. But first, he had much more to learn about Lear and the plans for the *Andraste*. The business of not tarnishing the title would simply have to wait.

He had to know what was in the Atheneum, which Dodd had been so sure was another target of Hayden and his group. Unfortunately, it would be odd for a man with Sebastien's past reputation to show a sudden interest in such scholarly things; he couldn't just walk in the next day. So he did the sensible thing: he broke into the building that night.

The Athenaeum stood at the corner of Adam and Manchester Streets: a tall, narrow building with a granite facade. Carved faces of learned men stared out from underneath the roof. The building housed the library and meeting rooms of the Britannic Society for the Advancement of Scientific Learning, which was founded years ago with the ambition to collect and preserve the scientific works of citizens, and to promote the cause of progress. Alfred Bering had apparently been quite active in the society during his lifetime.

Dressed entirely in black, Thorne found it surprisingly easy to gain entry to the Atheneum. The society didn't even hire a guard to watch the building.

But then, he thought, who would think the contents were so valuable? The society's members were those sheltered types who never dreamed of anyone taking advantage of their intellectual pursuits.

Thorne found the reading room and, soon after, the adjacent stacks, where boxes of loose papers, roughly bound manuscripts, and the occasional slim volume in leather lay in state along the shelves. He whispered a prayer of thanks when he saw that the library's contents were sensibly arrayed by the name of the author. He went to the *B*s, and at the shelf labeled *Bering, A.* he saw an impressive amount of material. The entries stopped abruptly in March of 1802, which must have marked his death.

As Cordelia suggested, nearly everything had something to do with shipbuilding, either specific parts or whole ships. But none of the pages he saw were marked with the name of *Andraste*. So either those plans never made it to the society, or they had already been stolen. But how could he be certain which was right? The sheer weight of paper was intimidating. Even if he broke in every night, he could spend weeks going through all of the papers, and he did not have weeks.

He moved on to *Jay, W.*, where he found a far more modest contribution. He surveyed the titles and dates. Several early papers thanked Alfred Bering in the first few lines, making the younger man's link to his teacher clear. Looking further, Thorne saw that a few more recent papers mentioned another name: *Lear*. The men seemed to have written at least a few things together. Jay must also know where Lear lived and how to approach him. Thorne might be able to persuade him if he could not convince Cordelia to help.

Eager to find some hint to the coveted plans, Thorne moved to another bookshelf, where the *L*s resided. Lear's contributions were more numerous than Jay's, even though the oldest one was dated fairly recently, in late 1802. Thorn leafed through them, reading titles.

"'New Methods to Prevent Breakage of Sheerline.' 'Why the *Maid of Kent* Sank.' 'Employing Steam in Propulsion Over Distance,'" he muttered aloud. Lear appeared to know his stuff. But Thorne didn't, and he had to admit that he was lost in the Atheneum. He couldn't begin to guess which of these things, if any, might be the one Hayden sought.

Then his eyes fell on something tucked among the articles: an invitation asking society members to contact Lear regarding an engineering problem he was working on. A street direction was listed. Thorne felt a wave of relief. The night was not a failure. He memorized the address, vowing that he'd go there first thing the next day.

He stood up. His mind was racing. Bering, Jay, and Lear were all connected. Something about the years of their work nagged at him, but the more important question was how to identify the all-important papers that Hayden wanted. It looked like only Lear could do that.

Thorne slipped out of the Atheneum and disappeared into the undergrowth around the building. Perhaps he could convince Lear to simply tell him, if he could find the man. And if he was not as scrupulous as Cordelia thought, Thorne could offer to buy the plans himself. He grinned, thinking of the bill he'd then send to Neville.

Of course, he could act on behalf of the Zodiac, go back inside, and simply *take* all the Atheneum's papers by Lear. Neville wouldn't like it—such a move would be indiscreet and provoke questions, and the Zodiac hated questions—but at least the papers would be safe. Of course, they still wouldn't know which paper was the key. Thorne shook his head as he emerged along the street.

The only real answer was to find Lear. At least he had a way to do that now. With luck, he could meet the man tomorrow and discover everything. He'd wrap up the mission in a day or two more.

And then do what? he suddenly asked himself. Wait for the next crisis? Focus on being earl? Marry a woman he barely knew to secure an heir? Lie to her about his other life? Leave her a widow if something went wrong? The questions rolled on. He tried not to think about the fact that his imagined wife had raven hair and green eyes.

Thorne had accepted his role in the Zodiac because at the time he didn't have to make those choices. Years later, his life had changed dramatically, and he was being pulled in very different directions. Sooner or later, he'd have to choose one path.

THE NEXT MORNING, THORNE WOKE early and made his way to the address listed as Lear's. He surveyed the building and the street, and felt cheated. It was a tobacco shop. But then he noticed the floors above. Perhaps the man rented rooms there.

He went into the shop, where a young woman was dusting the counter, and asked to see the proprietor. A matron came out of a small back room. "Yes, sir. How may I help you?"

"I am looking for a Mr Lear. I was given this address. Does he live here?"

"None but my family do, sir. Just above the shop, all seven of us."

The young woman spoke up. "I think he means the gentleman who has his mail delivered here." She looked shyly over at Thorne, to see if her guess was correct.

"Oh, of course. Lear!" the mother exclaimed. "Yes, he pays us a small sum to have his mail held."

"And he picks it up?" Thorne asked hopefully.

"He comes round every week or so," the young lady explained. "Usually in the mornings, just after I open the shop. That's why my mother doesn't often see him."

"And you give him whatever mail has come."

"Yes, sir. He usually gives us a penny per piece,

though he'll still leave a penny even if there's nothing for him. He's a very thoughtful gentleman, sir."

"Could you describe him to me?"

"Yes, sir." From her sudden blush, Thorne guessed that she quite looked forward to the man's visits. "He has brown hair, and he's rather tall, and is lean for his height."

"Middle-aged?"

"Oh, no." She giggled. "He couldn't be over five and twenty. And he always carries a very thin leather case."

Thorne had assumed that Lear must be of an age with the late Alfred Bering. But this girl was describing someone closer to William Jay's age. No, he suddenly realized, she was describing William Jay *exactly*.

"When was the last time he came?" he asked, his mind racing.

"This Wednesday past, sir."

He offered a coin for the girl's information, which she accepted with a nod. Then he left, enlightened in one way but now with new questions. Why would Jay pick up Lear's mail, and why would it be delivered to a shop instead of a home?

Every time he thought he found something new, it always led back to Miss Bering and Mr Jay. He decided that his mother's party couldn't come quickly enough.

* * * *

That same evening, Cordelia attended a small dinner at the Ramsays' home. She fended off several questions from Elly regarding Lord Thorne, and begged her friend to drop the whole matter.

"I do not wish to even be mentioned in the same sentence as him, Elly. There is absolutely nothing between us." The lie stuck on her tongue. Thorne had made his specific interest in her very clear, and she wondered how long it would take for him to offer an arrangement that any true lady ought to refuse. Cordelia didn't know if she would refuse. Despite the dangers of a potential affair, he had an appeal she couldn't deny. Just thinking about what it would be like to be the sole object of his attention, even for a short while…it made her stomach flutter.

Fortunately, Elly relented on that line of questioning, and the rest of the dinner was pleasant. Topics ranged from the political, such as the threatened embargo of British ships from French-controlled ports, a topic that worried Mr Ramsay a great deal, to the smaller social issues of the Season. Cordelia heard more about the likely pairing off of young ladies in their coming-out Season, and—from one guest—speculation about the finances of certain grand families.

"Take the Thornes, for example," the man was saying. "The finest ancestors one could ask for, with an honor granted by the conqueror himself, yet now they're scarcely more than beggars."

Cordelia pricked up her ears, as she seemed to do whenever Sebastien Thorne was mentioned.

"I think you exaggerate," Elly said, glancing at Cordelia to see her reaction.

"Not by much," the other said. "Either the new earl or that young daughter must make a sterling match to restore the family's fortunes. I hear Lady Mary Marshall will bring a dowry of nearly thirty thousand pounds, and that the Countess of Thornebury has expectations in that direction."

Cordelia kept her eyes on her plate. A title and thirty thousand! If those were the qualifications necessary to get the attention of Sebastien Thorne, Cordelia might as well not exist.

When she left, Cordelia felt oddly drained by the occasion, despite the fact that it was merely dinner at her friend's home. Jem had waited this time. He saw her into the carriage and drove away. Looking back through the window, Cordelia's eye was caught by another carriage, this one with a lantern blown out on one side. She frowned, remembering seeing the same vehicle on her way to the Ramsay house. She gave up all pretense and watched it from the back window. Yes, it followed them until the moment Jem turned into the drive of the Quince Street home.

Jem jumped down to open the door when the carriage halted before the house. Cordelia stepped out. "Jem, that carriage behind us. It followed us the whole way."

He took one sidelong glance as it rattled past them. "Perhaps I'll follow it, then. Go on inside, my lady."

She hurried up the walk, where the front door was already opened by Ivy, who stood in the hall ready to take her wrap.

Stiles joined them. "Good evening, my lady. Do you plan to retire immediately, or shall I keep the study lamp on?"

"Stiles, check the locks on the doors and windows tonight."

"I check them every night," he said somewhat stiffly. Then Stiles looked at his mistress more carefully. "Has something happened to concern you, my lady?"

"It may be nothing," Cordelia said. "I saw something odd tonight. A carriage followed me all the way home. The left-hand lantern was blown out, which is why I could tell. I told Jem—he's going to see if he can follow *them*."

"Hayden," Stiles growled.

"But he knows where I live already," she protested.

"He wants to scare you. He didn't get the plans, he lost his opportunity to hurt you, and now he seeks another. You must not go anywhere unprotected, my lady."

A hard light glinted in Stiles's eyes, and it was suddenly much easier to picture him as the smuggler he used to be. "I'll personally check every door and window in the house. If anyone is fool enough to try to get into this house again, he'll regret it." Then, just as suddenly, the proper tone of a butler returned. "Bond will bring you up some chamomile tea. Sleep well."

THE EVENING OF THE COUNTESS of Thornebury's party arrived. Since Cordelia hadn't seen or heard from Hayden since the other night, she told herself that the storm was over…though she didn't believe it.

Bond dressed her in a gown of shell-pink silk. The cap sleeves were entirely Belgian lace, dyed the same shade as the dress. The contrast between the light gown and her midnight hair was striking enough that Bond didn't want to distract from it, so Cordelia's headdress was restrained, little more than a wide ribbon and a few long ivory feathers. She allowed Cordelia to wear only a simple silver locket and a coral ring of her mother's.

"There you are," Bond said proudly, putting finishing touches to her hair. "Done up like a princess."

Cordelia laughed. "Then should I not be draped with diamonds or some such?"

Bond shook her head. "All the jewels in the world can't make a plain woman beautiful. Only God's grace can do that."

"Well, I shall try to be as graceful as I can."

Leona was waiting for her downstairs in the drawing room. The older woman was perfectly attired in a slim gown of stormy grey. Her gloves were black, and she wore a ruby at her throat. The colors ought to have made her look somber, but her impish smile belied the outfit. "Are we prepared?" she asked.

"As much as one can be," Cordelia said.

"Then let's be off!"

* * * *

Standing in the main ballroom of the townhouse, Sebastien Thorne plastered a smile on his face and endured a series of interminable encounters. His mother had, quite frankly, tricked him. The "few eligible ladies" she mentioned actually numbered over a dozen, and the one who campaigned the hardest was Lady Mary Marshall. She hovered at the edge of his vision, and just when he tried to escape, it was time to partner her in a dance.

To be fair, Lady Mary was a lovely young woman, with wide blue eyes and thick waves of brown hair cast over one shoulder. She was witty for nineteen, but that meant little to Thorne, who was used to older, more worldly companions. The idea of marrying her would have made him laugh if he were in a better mood. As it was, he found himself eager for the end of the dance.

Before the music concluded, though, another figure appeared in the corner of his eye. The glimpse of black hair was enough to make him turn, and then he nearly forgot the next steps in the dance.

From the entrance to the ballroom, Cordelia Bering watched him with a cool expression. Her eyes took in the whole scene, and whether she was impressed or not he wouldn't dare guess. But she herself was impressive, and he knew he wasn't the only man who noticed. The pastel silk she wore hinted at the perfection of the flesh it concealed, and it highlighted the darker pout of her mouth. He wanted to reach out and touch her from across the room.

Lady Mary said something, and he was forced back into the moment. "Excuse me?" he said.

"You are somewhere else, sir," she said, her voice smooth and teasing.

"Pardon me. I did not mean to be." With an effort, he finished the set and led Mary off the floor. He returned her to her chaperone, who was ensconced against the wall with several other matrons, and turned around, hoping to see Cordelia again.

* * * *

Cordelia waited to be introduced to the countess. Had the dress been a poor choice? She worried it made her look as if she were trying to appear young, like that gorgeous butterfly who had been fluttering near Sebastien. She felt out of place, despite Aunt Leona's assurance that she looked perfect.

Then an older blonde woman in a stunning gown of sapphire blue approached them. "Mrs Wharton," said the blonde lady. "How delightful to see you."

"The pleasure is mine," Leona said easily. "May I present my dear niece, Miss Cordelia Bering?"

"Of course," the countess said, focusing on Cordelia. Eyes accustomed to assessing now assessed her.

Cordelia curtseyed briefly. "I am so glad to meet you, Lady Thorne. You were most kind to include me in your invitation."

"Well, the Season would dull quickly if we never met anyone new," the countess said with a smile. Then she turned and gestured imperiously.

Cordelia looked over. Thorne was walking toward them, looking exactly like an earl should, and a girl as blonde as the countess accompanied him.

"There you are, my lord," his mother said when Sebastien met them. "I expected you to vanish halfway through the evening."

"If I had, I would have missed reacquainting myself with these two ladies," he returned, bowing extravagantly. He gave Cordelia a little secret smile as he spoke.

She felt a rush of heat in her chest. Whether she trusted him or not, she was undeniably attracted to him.

The blonde girl was watching Cordelia with avid curiosity. "You are Miss Bering," she said. "I'm Sebastien's sister, you know." By her youth, the modest cut of her dress, and the excitement in her eyes, Cordelia guessed that she had not yet had her first Season, so being allowed to join the party was an indulgence on the part of the family.

Sebastien gave his sister a stern look, then said to Cordelia, "Please let me introduce you to Lady Adele, though she has already introduced herself."

The young lady blushed at her gaffe, but wasn't silenced. "I've not seen you around before."

"I don't think either of us spend much time in society, but I am pleased to meet you," Cordelia said.

Sebastien's mother was a bit more subtle. "I am always keen to meet my son's acquaintances. Although I don't know precisely how you are acquainted..."

He interjected, "I met Miss Bering when I called on Mrs Wharton a while ago."

Cordelia shot a glance at Aunt Leona, who'd raised one eyebrow, but kindly didn't expose his blatant falsehood, considering Cordelia had pretended they'd already been properly introduced before then.

The countess surveyed Cordelia top to toe. "So you live here in town?"

"During the Season, ma'am," Cordelia said. "I also have a house in Bristol, where we sometimes spend our summers."

"Bristol!"

Cordelia smiled at the lady's reaction. "Yes, near the shore. My father, Alfred Bering, sailed before he married my mother."

"Your mother," the woman echoed with a clear question in her eyes.

"The Honorable Rosamund Russell. The only daughter of Lord Russell."

"Indeed." This intelligence marked a visible change in Lady Thorne's attitude.

Meanwhile, Adele was surveying Cordelia's ensemble. "That's a marvelous gown. Is it French silk?"

"I think so, and thus I may not have another like it for a while," Cordelia said, referring to Bonaparte's determination to block French goods from being sold in Britain.

"Reason enough to stop a war," Sebastien said quietly. Adele's eyes widened. Perhaps her brother was not usually so obvious in his attentions, or she was simply unused to hearing such exchanges. He went on, "I should like the honor of escorting Miss Bering for the next set, unless you have need of her, Mrs Wharton?"

Leona waved a hand. "Goodness, it's a party. I am content to watch you young people enjoy yourselves."

"Miss Bering?" Sebastien offered his hand.

She wasn't much of a dancer, but putting her hand in his felt natural, as if they had danced together many times before.

He led her to the floor, where they took their places in the lines of ladies and gentlemen. "I must thank you sincerely for agreeing to dance," he whispered on the way.

"Am I aiding you on some matter, my lord?" She was

reminded of the first time she saw him, ducking into her shadowed grotto in the garden…utterly upending her peaceful existence.

"Yes, you are." He looked around. "I'd like to disappoint some people. And dancing with a beautiful and mysterious woman will destroy some dreams, I hope."

She warmed at his comment, though she knew it was flattery. "I don't get asked to destroy a dream every day. If I can be your diversion, I am happy to do so." The dance began, taking her away from him for a moment.

When they reunited, he said, "You're hardly a diversion, Miss Bering."

"Except in the tactical sense."

"Not even then."

"Come, now. Once people realize that Lord Thorne's dance partner is merely Miss Bering of Quince Street, your pursuers will redouble their efforts."

Another circling away and back around. Cordelia's skirts swirled around her ankles, and she realized she was having a good time.

When he could, Sebastien said, "They had better not, if they have any sense." He looked down at her and grinned. "But never mind that. Divert me with your intelligence, Miss Bering."

She could think of one piece of intelligence important enough to divert him. "I am being followed." she said, as though merely noting a change in the weather.

He raised an eyebrow. "I won't ask if you're certain."

She appreciated his belief in her judgment. And when the pattern of the dance separated them for another moment, she missed his nearness.

They both met again, following the steps, and she smiled when he took her hand. Thorne returned the smile, but asked in a low voice, "Will you be followed from here?"

"Undoubtedly. Jem tried to track the person down a couple of nights ago, but he lost the trail."

"But no one has approached you, or spoken to you?"

"Not since Hayden revealed his true nature," she said. Cordelia spun and found herself temporarily partnered with an older gentleman to whom she had been introduced once before, but didn't much remember. Her thoughts were too far away for her to engage in anything but the most superficial pleasantries.

A few seconds later, she returned to Thorne. "Your opinion?" she asked, as if she wanted to know his thoughts on her dress.

"Either he wants to frighten you…though you don't seem easily frightened," he added. "Or he's following you for a more practical reason."

"Such as?"

"He thinks you'll meet someone. Or go somewhere in particular."

"He'll be disappointed, then," Cordelia said.

A separation, and then the rejoining. Thorne reached for her hand and held it rather tighter than the dance dictated. "What do you mean?"

"I burned all my father's papers."

His eyes flashed once, but then a sympathetic expression settled on his face. "Was it painful for you?"

"Yes," she said. "But I know it had to be done. I think Hayden had someone watching my house. So I burned the papers outside, where people could see. I hope he'll realize there's nothing left to find."

"That leaves only Lear's work, and what lies in the Atheneum."

She glanced over at him, startled. "You know about the Atheneum?"

"You'd be shocked at the things I know. But I wonder—" The dance concluded before he could continue his question. She sighed in frustration. People would notice if he spent too much time with any particular woman tonight, but how else were they to have a useful conversation?

Obviously trying to conceal his own irritation at the social strictures, he dutifully walked her back toward her aunt. But Cordelia told him that she wanted to sit by an open window, so he changed direction to secure her a seat.

"We're not done yet," he warned. "Don't think to run away before we talk again."

"I know we need to talk more. You need not chase me," she said.

He leaned over and murmured, "I would chase you even if you knew nothing, Cordelia." His breath stirred the few loose locks of her hair, and she was exquisitely aware of how close his mouth was to her skin. And using her given name in a room full of people…it was reckless, and she loved it.

He left her, and Cordelia waited for her heart to return to its normal pace. Adele came up to her. "May we chat, Miss Bering?" she asked rather shyly.

"Of course." Cordelia smiled at the girl. "To be honest, I expected to be a wallflower."

Adele laughed. "You? Mama says you never lack for admirers, even if you refuse to marry them. The Heartless Miss Bering."

Cordelia raised an eyebrow, and the girl blushed. "Oh, I should not have said that."

"It's not a secret. But tell me, what do you think of the party tonight?"

"Mama always puts on excellent to-dos," Adele said.

"When I was a child, I used to peek at the guests arriving from the top of the stairs. I'm so happy to be allowed to attend properly this time. But tonight, you know, it's all for my brother's benefit."

"Is that so?"

"She wants him to marry. Most of the ladies here have just been invited because they are eligible. Too bad they bore him to death. They always do. Even that French emigree from last Season…do you remember her? Covered in diamonds half the time. She set her cap at him. But he couldn't be bothered to see her after a few weeks."

"Maybe the language barrier was a problem." Many of the aristocratic refugees from the Terror hadn't learned English before they were forced to flee.

"Oh, Sebastien speaks French like he was born there. Good at Italian too. I'm terrible at languages. Drove my tutor to tears. Anyway, the way he cast that lady off upset Mama quite a bit."

Cordelia felt an odd little pang in her heart. How close had the pair gotten before he ended things? But she put on a brave face. "It's natural for your mother to care about the family line."

"*She* does, but Sebastien doesn't care in the least. I think that's why he runs away with his old army cronies all the time. He says he's going to Cheshire, but I know he's not there. He just despises being roped into things."

Interesting, Cordelia thought. So he sometimes lied about his whereabouts. "But he's here tonight."

"Well, Mama can be…insistent." Adele looked speculatively at Cordelia. "He certainly rushed over to greet you."

"For which I was grateful, seeing as he is almost the only one I know here."

"Perhaps it's more than that."

Since Adele couldn't possibly know about Sebastien's interest in the *Andraste* plans, she must think he was romantically interested in her. But that was equally absurd—a daughter of a peer would surely know who was considered appropriate to marry an earl...and who was not.

At the end of the evening, the coaches were brought around for all the guests. Thorne appeared by Cordelia's side to let her know the carriage had arrived.

"I'll escort you both out," he offered.

Cordelia nodded, but Leona, who was standing by, waved one hand in a distracted fashion. "I must ask Lady Thorne a question. I shall be along in a moment."

So the couple moved slowly down the wide stairs to the foyer. Cordelia enjoyed Sebastien's proximity, and she recognized that this was an opportunity to speak more or less privately.

"You want more from me," she said softly.

He arched one eyebrow.

"More information," she clarified.

"Oh. Yes." He blinked. "More than you can tell me in these few minutes. I'll have to find a way..."

"How did you know about the Atheneum?"

He gave her a quick smile that sparked a tiny flame in her heart. "I broke into the building a few nights ago."

At this point, Cordelia didn't even think to be surprised. "You're not going to break into my house, are you?"

"Would you like me to?"

She breathed in, trying to repress the blood rushing to her cheeks. Why did he keep flirting with her? "One might consider that an improper question."

"One might be correct," he said, his expression at odds with the teasing voice. "But it is an honest one."

"There is nothing honest about burglary," she said, deliberately misinterpreting his words.

"Has anyone ever told you that you're too clever for your own good?"

"Yes," she said. "Though I didn't believe it until lately."

"Would you believe me if I said that I think you're still in danger, despite burning those papers?"

"I know that, but I don't know how else to convince Hayden—or anyone—that there is nothing of interest left to get."

"You could send your pursuers to Lear," he suggested.

Cordelia closed her eyes. This was the one thing she could never do. Oh, why had she gone down this path?

He saw her expression, and leaned in closer. "Cordelia? What's wrong?"

"How could I save myself from danger by putting someone else in that same peril?" she asked.

"That's a noble thought, but not very practical. You don't have the ability to counter the threats against you. Why the *hell* can you not trust another who can deal with it?"

His vehemence was strangely touching. "You mean I should trust Lear?"

"You should trust *me*. Please, Cordelia." His eyes were dark, but she saw fire in them. And felt an answering fire in herself. An idea formed in her mind, all at once.

Cordelia considered the man in front of her. "I will give you a chance. Do you still want to meet Lear?" she asked.

"*Yes*," he said, exhaling in relief.

"Then give me an address where there can be a private meeting."

"My club is—"

"*Completely* private," she said, heat rising in her cheeks as she considered her plan.

He paused for a moment, glancing back to Leona, who would soon reach the carriage. He said, "I maintain a small residence near St James. There are no servants there, and no one to notice anything. You cannot mention this place to anyone other than Lear himself. It is a secret."

"Believe me, I won't breathe a word. Will eleven o'clock tomorrow night be suitable?"

"I'll be waiting."

THE NEXT DAY, CORDELIA WORKED feverishly to make a new version of the plans for the *Andraste*'s steering drive and propeller screw. The drafting took hours, and she had to ensure that every aspect looked correct, which required immense concentration. She was not at home to anyone, no matter who they were. Ivy brought in a few cards, but Cordelia didn't even glance at them. "I must keep working" was all she said.

At the end of the afternoon, she examined the papers spread on the drafting table with a critical eye. The drive was a complex system, and it would surely confuse anyone not familiar with steam technology. But she was satisfied that the most important aspect of the plans was invisible. A person would almost have to build the whole ship engine before he would discover the unpleasant truth—the drive itself was unworkable.

She sprinkled a bit of pounce over the paper to fix up any remaining ink spots. As she carefully dusted off the papers and rolled them up, she thought of what she intended to do…and of the potential consequences.

"If he proves trustworthy, I will have a chance to explain later, and if he is not, I will have averted a catastrophe," she said to herself, knowing that she was rationalizing. She had her own suspicions about Thorne's interest in the designs. But until she could verify them, she had to tread carefully.

Plus, Cordelia knew that it would not be enough to simply give the plans to Thorne. She had to convince him that he no longer needed Lear. She thought she could do that, although her heartbeat fluttered wildly when she considered how she intended to distract him. "It will work," she said, trying to convince herself. "It will work."

Bond was the only person she took into her confidence. Though she had known the young lady only a short time, Bond had already proven her intelligence and loyalty.

When Bond heard Cordelia's idea, she closed her eyes. "Oh, no," she said. "No, no, no. You mustn't. It's far too dangerous."

"I am not worried for myself, Bond. There is a larger issue at stake."

"But ma'am, if he should betray you…"

Cordelia swallowed, knowing exactly what Bond feared. But she had a counterargument. "He won't, Bond. You see, I know something about him that he can't afford to be aired publicly."

"It's not the same for a man, my lady."

"That's not what I meant," Cordelia said with a nervous laugh. "I know a sort of secret about him. One that has nothing to do with me, or any relationship we might have. It will be enough to keep me safe."

"As you wish," Bond said, capitulating. "I'll do what needs to be done."

What needed to be done first was prepare for the evening. Bond took out the golden-yellow gown, the one that Cordelia wore the first night she met Thorne.

"Oh, but he's seen that one."

"And he liked what he saw," Bond argued. "Trust me.

You must wear this."

Cordelia put on the gown, wondering inwardly if it looked appropriate for a scandal. Bond said nothing as she put a voluminous black velvet cloak over Cordelia's shoulders. It should render her almost invisible to casual onlookers once she put the hood up. Bond got her out of the house through the back, and convinced a carriage to stop at the entrance to the mews behind the property. (They'd agreed that not even Jem could be brought into this endeavor.)

Cordelia, her face hidden, got in the vehicle. The papers were in a leather case beside her. Bond looked to see that she had everything, and said, "When you come back, use the study door. I'll be awake. You have the key?"

"I do." Cordelia touched the key, tied to a ribbon around her neck. "It may be a few hours, or it may be… longer."

Bond bobbed her head in comprehension, if not approval. "And if Mrs Wharton, or anyone else inquires as to where you are…"

"You will not recall."

* * * *

As the hour hand crawled toward eleven, Thorne waited in his St James residence, wondering if Lear would appear. The place was ominously quiet. Once again, he worried that this was all some trap. Cordelia couldn't hide her nervousness when she told him of Lear's sudden reversal. He probably should have told Forester or Neville that the man would be surfacing. But it was too late now.

She had gotten under his skin. She wasn't an agent trained to seduce, she didn't have any of the skills of a courtesan, and yet every time he saw her, he nearly forgot about everything else.

"I have made no promises," he muttered aloud. He said the words to reassure himself that he hadn't come to any understanding with Cordelia, but immediately realized he was lying. He had made promises. He promised his family he would behave as a proper son should. He promised the Zodiac he would let nothing get in the way of his work. And he promised Cordelia he would protect her from harm. What was he to do when keeping one promise meant breaking another?

He had all but agreed to seduce Cordelia in order to get her to give him the plans. Yet his promise to protect her hadn't been a lie. It hadn't been part of the seduction. And if he allowed himself to care for Cordelia, would that get in the way of his duty to his family? He couldn't imagine marrying another woman while he had Cordelia.

But you don't have her, a cold voice reminded him. Sebastien realized then just how much he wanted her. And it had nothing to do with what she knew. He stifled the thoughts. This was no time to become obsessed with a woman. She was part of his assignment. Nothing more.

He went still as the sound of a carriage wheeled up on the street near the house. It slowed and then stopped. Light footsteps echoed on the stones of the path up to the door. And then came a hesitant knock.

Calming himself, Thorne stood and walked quickly to the door. As he pulled it open, he was startled at the image before him. No gentleman, but a woman dressed in a floor-length cape, the hood pulled up over her head and face. She tipped her head up, and green eyes gazed up at him.

"May I come in?" Cordelia asked.

Speechless, he stood aside to allow her to enter. He shut the door and whirled to face her. "Cordelia! What the hell are you doing here?"

"I have the papers you want." She held out the case.

He took it, but laid it aside on a table without even looking inside. "Where's Lear?"

"He…couldn't come. But I wanted to be sure that they were delivered into your hands. You'll take care of them, won't you?"

"Yes, of course. Cordelia, you can't *be* here. You shouldn't be alone with me."

She smiled, her gaze locked on his. "But I've been before." She unclasped the cloak, revealing the wonderful golden dress that she'd worn the first time he saw her. He suddenly had trouble breathing. And thinking.

"I still have to speak to Lear," he said, trying to stay on task.

Cordelia took a step closer, putting herself within arm's reach. "You have the designs. What more do you want?"

"You already know," he said.

"Yes." She paused, then said, "I want it too."

God, yes. Without waiting any longer, Sebastien drew her to him and tasted the mouth that just told him exactly what he wanted to hear.

She returned the kiss with mesmerizing zeal. Heartless, perhaps, but she certainly wasn't cold. He felt the heat of her body through her gown.

As if reading his mind, she took his hands in hers and guided them to her waist, to her breasts. With that unequivocal invitation, he abandoned restraint and took what he wanted. Cordelia gasped at the touch of his hands on her breasts. Her head fell back, and Sebastien took the opportunity to taste her throat.

She responded instinctively to his caresses, and it encouraged him to move ever lower down her heated body.

Without apparent guile, she moved against him with her hips, causing him to groan softly as she pressed against a part of him that was growing harder by the second.

He murmured, "Cordelia, you're going to drive me mad." He loved saying her name out loud.

"I want to drive you mad," she said, tossing aside all societal pretense. "I want you to drive me mad."

Sebastien pulled away to look at her face in the darkened hall, trying to judge if she meant it. "Do you know what you're asking?"

"I'm not *asking*, Sebastien." Having discovered what effect it seemed to have on him, she moved her body into him again. "I want to know what it's like. And I want you to be the man to show me."

He was supposed to be talking to Mr Lear now—but somehow it didn't seem to matter as much when this gorgeous woman was telling him *he* was who she wanted.

Cordelia glanced toward the case she'd brought over, and something flashed across her face, an almost furtive look. She said, "I gave you what you asked for. Why can you not give me something in return?"

"I'd just be taking something else from you," he said, though not with much conviction.

"No, Sebastien. You'd be giving me the one experience I never thought I would have. Can you not just give this to me, as a gift? Please. One night?"

Sebastien had never heard a sweeter or more maddening offer. He inhaled. "As a gift, then," he said, and swung her up into his arms.

He carried her up the darkened stairs, through the doorway of his bedroom. He was pleased that the moonlight was already shining into the room. He wanted to see all of her, every inch. He laid her on the bed, leaning down over her.

She looked up at him with wide eyes, the green faded to grey in the moonlight.

Was he really going to compromise this woman because she asked him to? Wasn't that still taking advantage of her, in a way? Would she hate him afterward, when the light of day made things look very different?

"Cordelia, you can walk down those stairs and just go home if you want," he said, the words dropping like stones. Inside, his mind was howling at him to shut up, to take exactly what she offered. But he couldn't not give her the choice. "I'll regret it, but I won't think less of you if you reconsider and leave."

She was silent a moment, then said, in a more vulnerable tone than he'd ever heard from her, "Will you think less of me if I stay?"

"*No.* Hell, no," he said instantly, drawing his fingers gently along her cheek. "I'd never judge you for choosing this…even if you didn't ask me for the honor."

A slow, sweet smile lit her face. "Well, I did ask you. So please, let's begin, shall we? The night won't last forever."

* * * *

Cordelia sensed the very instant he finally accepted her request—yes, he'd agreed with words before, but he didn't believe her until this moment.

And she had no intention of wasting time or being a passive observer. Curious, she raised her hands to his chest, pushing the jacket aside, then she helped him tug his shirt off. She stared at the devilishly handsome man revealed. She'd dreamed about him often enough, but this sight was far beyond her innocent little fantasies. Broad shoulders, rippling muscles, olive skin that seemed to burn under her touch. Possessed by something she didn't understand, she stroked her hands down his back, and he sighed with satisfaction. Then he pulled away.

"What's wrong?" Cordelia asked, anxious that she'd made a mistake.

"Not a thing," Sebastien told her. "But if we're going to have a night together, I want to see you too, darling."

With single-minded dedication, Sebastien took off every article of clothing she had on. Her slippers were the first to go. Then her stockings, expertly peeled off with one hand. His other hand rested on her thigh, an intimacy she found as tempting as it was shocking. Then he stroked upward, slowly, and she gasped as his hands reached her hips, caressed her skin. "Do that again," she whispered.

"Count on it." He laughed, a low, possessive sound. He loosened her gown and eased it off, followed by the stays, leaving only a thin chemise between his gaze and her skin. The nearly transparent cotton left little to the imagination. She felt his eyes travel every inch of her, and squirmed as an unfamiliar heat began building in her body.

"You're a goddess," he said quietly, and she trembled at his tone.

He bent down to kiss her throat. He trailed his mouth down to where the chemise began. Cordelia arched her back, instinctively pushing herself closer to him, giving him access to the flesh he desired.

He smiled at her reaction. Then he moved lower, worshipping her breasts, her belly, her waist. She tangled her hands in his hair, feeling the tension in her body rise with every touch. Her skin grew flushed, her breath came more quickly. He raised his head to look at her.

"What next?" she asked, curious.

"What comes next, darling, is that you enjoy everything I do to you." He slipped his hand under her chemise, which had bunched up to her hips by now. "As I will enjoy watching you."

"Watch me do what…ohh." She closed her eyes when he touched her between her thighs. Her head fell back into the pillow, even as her whole body arched in pleasure. He continued to stroke her gently, following her gasps and moans as he moved closer to what he sought. She cried out when he slipped one finger inside her tight warmth.

"Oh, darling, you're going to be my undoing," he murmured, even as he withdrew his hand.

"No," Cordelia protested softly, aching with newfound need.

"Patience," he said, perhaps as much to himself as to her. He swung off the bed, standing up to remove the rest of his clothing.

Cordelia also sat up. "Let me help," she said, putting her hands on his stomach, moving to the cord that would loosen his breeches. The offending clothes came off quickly, and Cordelia inhaled at the sight of his erection. Her daydreams about Sebastien would need significant revision.

"Do you truly want this?" she heard him ask through her dazed contemplation. "I can stop."

In answer, Cordelia stood up and moved to stand in front of him. "You said you would give me this night as a gift." She put her hand on his hardened length, circling her fingers around it, curious and surprised by how smooth he felt. And how hot.

He made a sound she'd never heard before, but definitely wanted to hear again. "It's all right for me to touch you like this?" she asked, fairly sure of the answer.

"If you want me to go mad, yes," he said in low tone. Then he took her chemise in his hands. "Why are you still wearing that?"

"Because you didn't take it off," she said, amused. "Please do it now."

He pulled it down so it fell at her feet, leaving them both completely naked and open to each other. He turned her around and held her close to him, cupping her breasts. Then he kissed the back of her neck, lifted her long black hair away, and ran his hands down her body, leaving her trembling.

"I've thought about doing this since I first saw you, darling," he confessed. Kneeling, he slowly spun her around once more, so his face was level with her stomach. "Sit on the edge of the bed," he commanded hoarsely. She did, reaching out to twine her fingers in his hair. "Now lie down, love."

Curious, she did, falling back among the covers, her feet still touching the floor. He put one hand on each knee, and slowly parted her legs. She inhaled, feeling exposed in a way she hadn't planned for.

"Trust me," he said, as if she'd told him her thoughts. Moving to her hips, he pulled her closer to the edge of the bed. Cordelia shook a little.

He calmed her, stroking her thighs with long, smooth moves. He laid his mouth on the heated skin of her inner thigh, kissing her lightly. She moaned, her hands touching him to make sure he was real. He found every sensitive, hot place, and made it hotter. It was shameless, and she loved it. Then he licked her core, and she almost cried out at the intensity of the pleasure she felt. Those sensual lips and his wicked tongue wreaked havoc with her body, drawing ever more heat to her center, until she hit the crest of a wave, arching her back as she gasped at the strength of her orgasm, and then felt her body ease.

Sebastien lifted her to lie fully on the bed, since she

was weak and trembling with the aftermath of his tongue. "Did you like that?" he asked. The smugness in his tone would have been annoying if that same mouth hadn't just destroyed her.

"Yes," she admitted, her voice breathy. "It feels different to when I've done it for myself."

"Mmmm. There's a thought to keep me warm through future nights," he murmured. He moved over her, kissing her with devotion, and she saw that he was still stiff with desire. Her legs fell open even more as she thought of taking him inside her. She was conscious of a deep yearning to move with this man and make their bodies one.

But he didn't take her, not yet. First he touched her again, his fingers quick and clever, making her gasp with need and wonder why he was delaying what they both wanted.

"I don't want to rush," he said between kisses. "You are marvelously wet, darling, but you're also very tight."

"Too tight?" she fretted. "Or you're too big for me."

"You'll be perfect. We'll be perfect. Trust me."

"I do. But please don't make me wait any longer."

"Yes, my insistent goddess."

He settled himself between her legs, pressing her into the bed. By inches, Sebastien moved into her, withdrawing and then returning, each time a little deeper. She realized that he was using this cautious entry as a way to arouse her. So she gave herself up to the sensations, and didn't try to hold back her little sounds of pleasure.

The coil started tightening in Cordelia's body again, ratcheting up with every powerful thrust. Her breath became ragged, just like the man's above her. She looked up, and caught his dark gaze raking her shoulders, her breasts, her skin. "Don't stop," she told him.

"I'd rather die than stop now, love," he said, and

obliged her by moving again.

When she cried out in delight, he smiled savagely and repeated that thrust, bringing her ever closer to the brink. He released one hip to cup her breast, the nipple rosy and hard under his touch. She didn't know how much more of this exquisite torment she could take, how much deeper she could hold him.

"Come undone for me, love," he ordered in a rough voice. He slid his hand down between her legs. Her muscles tightened around his cock when he grazed the nub at her center, making her whole body contract and then expand in waves of pleasure as the coil unsprung once more.

Sebastien growled, his gaze hot. Then he withdrew with a low curse, and finished in the sheets. He moaned with his release, his eyes closed and his back stiff. Then he sighed, saying, "It's safer that way, but God I wish it wasn't necessary."

Wordlessly, she held out her arms to him, and was delighted when he moved beside her again. She stroked his back, cradling him, giving him soft little kisses, uninhibited in her desire to touch him.

"Thank you," she whispered.

He lifted his head and smiled at her. "Don't thank me yet. The night isn't over."

Her heart skipped. "There's more?"

"Oh, yes. I'm far from finished with you, beauty. Satisfied, yes. Finished? Not a chance."

He showed her how much more there was. He praised her willingness to play, to let him do the things he thought would make her most pleased. He told her bluntly that so many other women, even the most worldly, had restrained him, had stopped him from pleasuring them, as if it were a sin to feel good.

"Well, I was taught that doing this unmarried is a sin

no matter what. So I may as well feel as good as I can while doing it."

He laughed at that, and then proceeded to make her feel very, very good in a few new ways.

The moon's light shifted from the bed to the carpeting to the wall before they were willing to slip into a doze for the few remaining hours of the night. Cordelia didn't let herself think about tomorrow. She curled up on him as sleep took her, robbing her of her waking thoughts and sending tantalizing dreams where she walked safely with Sebastien by her side, and he brought her to ecstasy every night.

Early morning light spoiled her dreams. Cordelia awoke, still languid with remembered passion. She sat up as she recalled that she was in a man's bed, and realized that Sebastien was not beside her. Surely he would not have left her there with no words at all!

Her heart jumped when she heard a footstep in the hall, but it was Sebastien who opened the door, bearing a tray.

"Good morning," he said, smiling at her in a way that made her insides warm. He put the tray down on a low table. "I don't really have the makings of a chef, but I thought you might be hungry."

Cordelia's stomach rumbled on cue. He had made coffee—strong, by the smell of it—and cut up a loaf of bread, smothering the slices with jam and butter. Cordelia devoured everything.

Food wasn't the only thing she craved this morning, but last night was over, and it would be unwise to continue what they had started. It was best to think of their affair as a singular event. Her supposedly absent heart ached at the thought.

Noting Sebastien's intense silence, she asked, "What are you thinking of?"

"I am sorry I can't stop the sun," he replied. "One

night with you wasn't enough."

Cordelia opened her mouth, but he silenced her with a look. "Don't worry. You wanted one night." He paused. "If you need anything, however, know that you can ask me. Anything."

"What time is it?" she asked.

"Well, that wasn't too demanding." He gave her an exaggerated, exasperated look. "A little after five."

"Is it? I must go soon, before…" Cordelia bit her tongue to stop herself from telling him how much she wanted to stay. It would be beneath her dignity, but oh, how she wanted him still. But she knew he was used to different, more experienced women. She would hold no fascination for him now, despite his words.

In tacit agreement, neither of them spoke further about what happened between them, either the reasons for it or the possible consequences. Cordelia didn't want to hear anything more. Her dalliance with him satisfied her curiosity regarding exactly what occurred behind a couple's bedroom door. And she knew he would be utterly discreet about their one encounter. Considering how short a time she had known him, Cordelia was sure that, at least regarding some things, she could trust Sebastien more than anyone else in the world.

He offered to take her back home himself, but she reassured him that it was unnecessary…and indeed foolish. "I'll return the way I came, alone and anonymously. That's safest for both of us."

He nodded, accepting her argument with a slight expression of surprise. Perhaps he expected her to break down, or beg him for something more after all. Cordelia would rather die before that happened.

She left the house as unobtrusively as she entered it. With her hood up, Cordelia hired a carriage to take her home. She paid the man well enough to lose any curiosity he might have had, not that he seemed to care at all who his fare was. Back at Quince Street, she slipped in the study door. She reached her own bedroom before anyone saw her. Bond appeared moments later, looking like she had not slept at all.

"It's over, Bond. Everything went well. He has the plans he's interested in, and no one should look at this house or my work again."

"That's good news, for certain." The maid did not ask about the other aspect of Cordelia's night. She helped her mistress undress and put her into bed.

At the door, Bond paused. "Ma'am? I…"

"Don't worry about me," Cordelia said. "I'm not sorry. I did it for myself and my home. But nothing like it will happen again. I know how foolish that would be, no matter how much I…" She stopped speaking, ducking her head before Bond saw the tender smile spread across her features.

Bond gave a small curtsey and left the room, with Cordelia's dress and cloak in hand. Cordelia sank back in the bed. What she told Bond was the truth…partly. She wasn't sorry she did it, but the whole truth was that she was profoundly happy she had. She would never do such a mad thing again, of course. But every moment with him had been wonderful, and she would never forget it.

* * * *

After Cordelia left, Sebastien locked up the St James house and roamed the early morning streets in a daze. His mind was full of the green-eyed beauty. Far from satisfying him, last evening only sharpened his need.

Her cool demeanor that morning threw him, to say the

least. He knew she had enjoyed their encounter, but she appeared to be perfectly willing to forget it now that it was done. Heartless, indeed.

That should be a comfort to him. Hadn't he just been worrying about the entanglements of a real affair? But nature was perverse, and he found himself aggrieved by her attitude. One night. At the time, it seemed perfect. Now he knew that it wasn't.

He had more than enough to give her carte blanche. He could see her when he was in England, and she could live anywhere she wished in the meantime. It was not an unheard of arrangement. But in his heart, he knew Cordelia would reject such an offer just as surely as she'd rejected all those marriage proposals, though for different reasons. She was gently bred, and had certainly never contemplated life as some man's mistress.

Then too, there was the nagging thought that he did not want her as mistress either. He wanted her, fully and completely. He was startled by the certainty of the feelings she aroused in him, but he knew himself better than to question them.

Eventually, he returned to his family's townhouse. Despite the early hour, he didn't even get inside before he was sighted. Adele was already in the street on her horse, about to leave on her morning ride. She was too young to keep late hours. A pair of grooms followed her.

On seeing Sebastien, she pulled up the reins. "Is this a good time to use the phrase 'look what the cat dragged in'?" she asked, dimples showing in her cheeks.

"Probably," he said in a tired, distracted voice.

"I say, are you feeling quite well?" Adele dismounted. "Have you even slept?"

"Barely," he admitted.

"Off at one of your gaming hells or some such," Adele

guessed. Though young, she was observant, and she understood far more than most girls her age, having seen Sebastien's earlier poor choices at close range.

"If I was, it's not your concern. Go on your ride."

"No," she said, determined. "We need to talk."

"This isn't the best time."

"Mama's still fast asleep, so it's a fine time," she insisted. "Do you want to go inside and get some coffee to pry your eyes open? Are you hungry?"

"I want sleep."

"You can have it after we talk."

He shrugged. "Then let's move to the garden."

Adele walked around the side of the house with Sebastien. The garden was filled with sunlight that filtered through the trees. Sebastien sat down on a stone bench. Adele paced in front of him, flipping her riding crop.

"Very well," he said. "What are we talking about that's of such import?"

"Your marriage prospects."

"What?" He blinked, his mind conjuring an image of Cordelia. "Why should you care?"

Adele looked at him as though *he* were the child. "Sebastien, it would be most helpful to me if you were married and well settled in Thorne Hall by the beginning of next Season. I will come out then, and Mama needs to be focused on that event. However, she is currently obsessed with your courtship…or rather the lack of any."

"One has nothing to do with the other."

"Of course it does. I will be judged based on my family. What sounds like more of a catch? The younger sister of a dissolute gambler who vanishes from polite society for weeks at a time, and then stumbles home drunk in the morning?"

He opened his mouth to protest, but Adele brandished

the crop meaningfully. "Or," she went on, "the younger sister of the esteemed Lord Thorne, Earl of Thornebury, who is well married, reformed, and the head of our newly solvent estate?"

"I think I can guess which one you prefer," he said.

"It's the second one!" she exclaimed with mock cheer. Then her eyes narrowed. "I don't want to field questions about your behavior during my first Season. I certainly don't want the world to doubt our finances or our family prospects. So you settling down will help me settle down."

"Next Season is months away."

"Which is why I raise the issue now. Courtship does take some time."

He reserved a moment's pity for the man who would end up in Adele's sights. Whoever he might be, he wouldn't stand a chance. "I promise to consider your concerns."

"You had better," Adele swore, slapping the riding crop against her boot. "Ow!" she yelped, suddenly sounding much more like the young person she was.

"Are you sure you know how to use that?"

"I'm an excellent rider," she sniffed.

"Are we done here? I think I need coffee after all."

"Not quite. Tell me about Miss Bering."

He went still. "What?"

She rolled her eyes. "Miss Cordelia Bering. You told Mama you were auditioning ladies for the part of countess! And you danced with her at the party," Adele reminded him impatiently. "I thought she was very kind. Mama says she's got good blood. Is she important?"

"There are different kinds of importance," he said. How could he explain Cordelia's importance without revealing too much? "She has neither a title, nor great wealth."

"What, then, is her appeal?" Adele asked. "I admit that she's a beauty. Do you think it unfortunate that I'm fair-haired? I worry that I should be faded by the time I reach Miss Bering's advanced age."

"Advanced? The lady is younger than I am!" he snapped. "Am I decrepit?"

"No, you're family." Adele put on her charming, dimpled smile. "Now tell me why you like her so."

"She's…intriguing," he said carefully. Lord, that didn't begin to describe her. He remembered the feel of her beneath him and actually began to shake a little.

"Do you love her?" Adele asked curiously.

He paused, unprepared for that question, even to himself. Love? Lust, oh, yes. But then why the dream of marrying her, keeping her with him? "It's not that. It's far too early…"

"I think you love her," his sister pronounced. "And does she love you?"

She left him that morning, refusing even an escort home. "I am sure she doesn't."

Adele's eyes widened. "Have you kissed her? I hear that's the best way to tell if one loves you."

"Stop your romantic driveling right now," Sebastien said, standing up so that he towered over her, hoping to remind her that he was the elder. "You think you understand the world because you read a few books and listen in on adults' conversations from the stairs. You think that one simply ranks potential spouses as if they're horses at the market? It's more complex than that, as you'll discover soon enough, *little* sister."

Adele was not cowed. She merely ducked around him and jumped up on the stone bench he just vacated. "You love her!" she whispered triumphantly.

"I don't," he denied flatly. "And even if I did, that is hardly the only consideration for a marriage."

"Oh, to be sure," Adele said, pacing the bench excitedly. "You can go get your breakfast now. I shall take my ride as usual."

"You're done with me?"

"Yes, indeed." Adele smiled. "Everything is well in hand."

He frowned. "I don't like that at all. What are you planning?"

"Absolutely nothing, my dear *older* brother." She pranced away toward the drive again. He let her go, unwilling to wade further into a discussion about romance at this hour. His mind in a tumult, he gave up and lay down on the wide bench. Adele's inquisition had set off far too many warning bells in his brain.

Cordelia was strange, secretive, and maddening. Even after last night, when she literally offered herself to him, he knew she was still hiding something from him, and he was sure that he didn't trust her any more than she trusted him. But he also knew that he'd happily destroy anything that threatened her. Then she asked him to ruin her, and he did it without a second thought. How was that for irony?

All he knew for certain was that she had become very important to him, and the thought of her vanishing from his life made his hands shake. Good God, was Adele right? Had he somehow, and long before last night, fallen in love with the heartless Cordelia Bering?

* * * *

Cordelia's day proved to be as off-kilter as Sebastien's. She slept late, rising only at Bond's insistence. The maid's worried look and fussing subsided only when

Cordelia quietly reassured her that she was not pining for Thorne or her lost innocence.

But she was certainly not the same woman as before. She was adrift, dazed by the experience of the previous night. Had it been worth the possibility of being discovered and disgraced? She thought it might be. Still, she knew that she had done the sensible thing in not trying to continue the affair.

She went to her study, determined to reassert her routine. Her mind cleared as she lost herself in the details of the various problems people sent in their letters to Lear. She was herself again.

And wasn't that just what she wanted? Now she knew what married life might offer. It was no longer a mystery, and she need not fear that she was going to miss out, because surely she would never meet another man like Sebastien Thorne. Any other potential husband would be… disappointing.

She was annoyed to discover that her thoughts had drifted from her work to the memory of last night, and she redoubled her efforts, responding to several queries.

A few hours later, Ivy rapped lightly on the door. "Mr Jay is here," the maid said.

"Oh, show him through!"

Jay was ushered in a minute later. He sat down when Cordelia indicated the seat across from her.

"What brings you here, Mr Jay?"

"I heard something I thought you should know," he said. His expression was serious, and his eyes raked her nervously.

Her heart lurched. Had she been recognized either last night or this morning? She'd be ruined. Cordelia realized she was not sanguine about that possibility after all.

But Jay was already speaking of another subject. "I

was at the Atheneum yesterday, and was asked if I had been contacted regarding either Mr Bering's or Mr Lear's papers held at the society. I said I had not, and the gentleman told me that I would be soon, since he'd given my name to the one who inquired. I don't like this sudden interest. Miss Bering, is there something I ought to know about what you're doing under Lear's name?"

She shook her head. "You know more than anyone else, believe me. Has Mr Hayden ever been to see you?"

"Hayden? The man who's been courting you?" Jay frowned. "No. I would not have thought that man had the slightest interest in these matters."

"Neither did I, but it has come to my attention that he has, let's say, a financial stake in my father's work…and Lear's, though thankfully he doesn't understand what *that* means. And he is most definitely no longer courting me," she added with finality. She gave him a limited account of what happened.

Jay's expression grew alarmed, then disapproving, then furious. "Hayden is a fraud, then. I am sorry you had to endure that offense. Should I bring this to the attention of the authorities?"

"No, I couldn't risk you getting involved."

"Miss Bering, I *am* involved. I do wish you could trust me."

"I trust you more than anyone I know! But I don't think there is anything you can do at this point." She inhaled. If Jay knew that she'd given the plans to Sebastien, and where and how it happened, he'd never associate with her again. Who was she to speak of trust?

Jay said, "What if someone asks me about Lear?"

"Be as unhelpful as you can without antagonizing him. Tell him that you've met Lear, but you aren't friends. If anyone asks why you visit me, tell them…oh, I don't know. Tell them you hope to court me."

"Not a difficult thing to believe," Jay said, a faint smile finally lighting his features. Then he stood up. "I must be going. Please take care of yourself, Miss Bering. If I may be so bold as to speak with such intimacy, you look as if you need rest."

"Good advice, Mr Jay. I will avail myself of it."

After he left, Cordelia did try to rest, sitting out in the gardens with Aunt Leona. But when her aunt retired for an afternoon nap, Cordelia stayed outside alone, lost in thought. She was consumed about the fate of the *Andraste* designs, not to mention the possibility that Lear's identity would be revealed if this fiasco continued. Then Cordelia would have no means of supporting her household, and their poverty would be on her head.

She might have to marry simply to keep herself and Aunt Leona fed. How miserable, to have turned down so many sincere proposals over the years, only to have to chase a husband out of desperation. She couldn't imagine marrying anyone. Well, she couldn't imagine marrying anyone who wasn't Sebastien. And after last night…how could she imagine sharing another man's bed?

In retrospect, last night had been most unwise. She'd only wanted to experience something she thought she'd never have. But by losing her innocence, she also lost her ignorance. Ironically, she would miss that far more.

"What was I thinking?" she muttered, even as she remembered the bliss she'd felt. *If you need anything…* Thorne had said. Yes, he'd been referring obliquely to the possibility that she might bear a child. But what if she asked him for more…such as marriage? No, she could never do that to him, and he'd resent having to marry her out of obligation. She had to continue on as before. Alone.

THORNE'S LIFE HADN'T GOTTEN SIMPLER, even though he now had the coveted *Andraste* designs. He could not make heads or tails of them, and he still had loose ends. He'd been busy with other things, but it occurred to him that it would be useful to find Hayden. The man was an opportunist only interested in money, but whoever employed him had grander ambitions. If Hayden was an agent of a foreign power, Thorne had to find out which one.

But no matter what, Thorne had the designs. He could deliver them to the Zodiac and they could be assured that at least no enemy of England would be building an armored steamship to destroy their navy. And that was his assignment. It was essentially done.

So why was he still so restless?

The next day, Forester called, asking for Thorne as if on a routine matter. He even joked with the countess and Adele for a few minutes. But when the two men reached the study, Forester lost his easy manner. "You have problems."

"You have no idea," Thorne muttered. "What ones are you referring to?"

"Miss Bering's servants."

"I knew there was something off about them. What did

you find?"

"Several things, and absolutely nothing good." Forester cleared his throat. "First, discovering all this took rather longer than usual because that household, for all its faults, does not gossip. At one point, I had to fool a neighbor's hostler into thinking I was a down-on-my-luck ex-soldier looking for any job that came my way."

Sebastien grinned despite his worry. "Isn't that the truth?"

"Be kind. I managed to find out the names of all the servants. Butler, housekeeper, lady's maid, two parlor-maids—the one named Ivy also acts as lady's maid to the older woman—a cook and her assistant, a gardener, and a lad who seems to be footman, hostler, and driver by turns."

"All for two rather retiring ladies. How does she afford it?" Thorne asked.

His friend shrugged. "That's a separate question. The better one is how did these wastrels find their way into her house in the first place?"

"Wastrels? What do you mean?"

"Not all of them are suspect," Forester clarified. "The older parlormaid seems upstanding, and I've nothing on the cook. But the others... The lad-of-all-work is a bad egg for sure. James Harper, or Jem as he's called, has a history with several local magistrates. He's been brought in for pickpocketing and housebreaking, but always managed to cast enough doubt that he didn't go to prison. He's not been seen by the authorities for a couple years, and the assumption was that he'd either died or left the city."

"But that's clearly not the case." Thorne was ready to go over and throttle the lad if he was taking advantage of Cordelia in any way.

Forester went on, "Housekeeper, Mrs Landry. Arrested

for operating a distillery without a license."

"Could be worse," Thorne commented.

"Oh, it will be. Next is the so-called lady's maid. Lucy Bond by name, though that's not her real name."

"I met her," Thorne said, remembering the flinty-eyed girl. "Miss Bering's most recent hire, she told me."

"Hired from Bridewell, apparently. Lucia Bonacchi is a jewel thief, specializing in robbing city homes. She was included on a list of female prisoners to be transported to New South Wales from Bridewell. The ship manifest indicates that she never got on board."

"But how did she end up getting a position? She wouldn't have had a reference!"

"Good question. However, the worst I've saved for last."

"I'm waiting."

"The butler. I checked with a few people who keep records of this sort of thing, just to make myself believe it. Including," he added significantly, "one of the administrators of Newgate." Forester's eyes were serious. "About ten years ago, there was a leader of a gang of wharf-side…wait for it…smugglers. The gang was famous for creating false compartments in the various ships they used to fool the law. Truly inventive stuff. The head of the gang was a vicious man who used violence to eliminate any sort of threat. He got sent to Newgate for murder."

"And?"

"The murderer is described as a short, stocky man with pale blue eyes and a scar along his right cheek," Forester said.

Thorne shook his head, unwilling to accept such a premise. "No. It must be a coincidence that Cordelia's butler has similar features. Surely that criminal was executed."

"He escaped from Newgate right before his scheduled execution. That was over six years ago. He changed his last name and hid where no one thought to look for him. I'm telling you, Hugo Morgan is now Hugo Stiles."

Thorne stood up. "And he's in Cordelia's house now. The same man. The murderer."

"Yes, along with a known housebreaker and a jewel thief. They're all there with Miss Bering and all her father's useful work on ships."

"You'll excuse me," Sebastien said, even as he started striding out of the room.

"Want company?" Forester asked, matching his pace.

When Thorne got to the street, he called for a carriage, unwilling to wait for anything to be brought from the stable. "Thanks, but I'll handle this myself."

It took far too long for Thorne's taste to reach Cordelia's home. He ordered the cab to stop in the street, and then strode quickly up the drive. The footman who opened the door was the lanky one Thorne matched to Forester's description. The pickpocket. He glared at the boy, who looked back insolently.

"Miss Bering is not at home, sir," Jem said. "Do you wish to leave a card?"

"I don't wish," he growled. "Get me Stiles."

"The butler?"

"Do you have another Stiles tucked away here?" Thorne asked coldly.

The footman wasn't impressed. "No, sir. If you'll wait a moment, I'll fetch him."

The lad vanished toward the kitchens, and Thorne momentarily regretted letting him out of his sight. What if he was warning Stiles to flee right now? He breathed in, reminding himself that he hadn't given anything away.

The stocky butler appeared a second later, shadowed

by the footman.

"How may I help you, sir? As you know, Miss Bering is not available."

"It's you I came to see, Hugo Morgan."

The butler's eyes widened.

Thorne lowered his voice and leaned in. "I know you were in Newgate, and I know you skipped the short drop."

Stiles began to protest, but Sebastien, far past furious, reached out and grabbed him, twisting the shorter man around, bending his arm to an improbable angle. The young footman fled up the stairs. The curly-haired parlormaid peeked in, shrieked, and vanished again, leaving the two alone.

"Tell me the truth, Hugo," Thorne spat.

The man gasped at the strength in Sebastien's hand. "It's true. But I ain't done anything since."

"So? You were in for murder! How did you get a position in this house? Did you fake your references?"

Stiles grimaced in his distress. "The lady forgave my past. Why should it matter now?"

"What do you mean, the lady?"

He groaned as Sebastien tightened his grip. "Miss Bering!"

"Cordelia *knows*?"

"Of course she does!" Stiles fell to the ground as Sebastien abruptly released him. "It's her way, is all. We'd all do anything for her. She trusted us."

Thorne took a step back, stunned by the possibility that Cordelia was complicit in hiring criminals.

Stiles winced. His scar was white against his flushed skin. "I run a tight ship, and the lady won't stand for any scandal in her house. One lad went back to evil ways. He was gone in a flash. My lady is generous, not stupid."

An imperious voice broke in. "Exactly what is going

on here?"

* * * *

Cordelia stood at the top of the stairs, sick at the sight in front of her. Jem had rushed into her room and told her Thorne had appeared, looking like the devil himself. Not knowing what to think, Cordelia ran to the hall, only to find Thorne tussling with Stiles as if they were guttersnipes.

Both men stilled at her voice.

"It's nothing to concern you, my lady," Stiles said, despite the fact that he was still on the floor.

"I am concerned," she snapped back, hurrying down the staircase. She glared at Sebastien. "What are you doing here, my *lord*?"

"I had a question for your butler," he said, tugging at the sleeves of his jacket.

"And *this* is how you asked it?" She bent to help Stiles up off the floor. The older man accepted her assistance unwillingly, his pride more damaged than his body. "Your method of questioning people leaves something to be desired."

"It depends who I'm questioning," he replied blandly.

She blushed at the innuendo, but didn't forget the matter at hand. "What are you doing here? No. Wait." She held up her hand, then turned to her butler. "Stiles, show Lord Thorne to the parlor and then return to me."

"No," said Sebastien.

"Excuse me?" Cordelia asked in a tone colder than ice. "Am I not mistress in my own house? Do you have some authority to tell me how to direct my servants?" She stared at him, daring him to refute her.

He stared back, unwilling to give ground. "Your butler

is not what he seems."

"Who is, my lord?" she returned with a thin smile. "Stiles, do as I say."

Stiles bowed. "This way, my lord."

Cordelia watched narrowly as Sebastien followed the stocky man to the parlor across the hall.

Stiles must have exchanged words with Thorne behind the closed doors, for when he came back, his face was even redder. "That man isn't fit to be in this house." He quickly explained what happened before she arrived.

"I will talk with him," she reassured Stiles.

Cordelia moved into the drawing room, her face carefully composed. "My lord, I demand an explanation."

"Your butler just threatened me," he said.

"Imagine that." Cordelia looked at him. "Considering you attacked him in the foyer, I'm surprised at his restraint. Which brings me back to the question of what you thought you were doing."

"Stiles is an escaped convict," he said, his tone careful and, to Cordelia's ears, condescending. "His real name is Morgan."

"Yes," she acknowledged. "What of it?"

He gaped. "So you do know about his past?"

"You seem to think that I am incapable of noticing the world around me." She frowned at him. "Is it perhaps because I'm a mere woman? Must I remind you that I am not like the other women you are familiar with?"

"You're like no woman I've ever known," he said, making her knees weak with a look.

"Nevertheless, you have no right to accost my servants in my own home!" she retorted, refusing to be distracted from her anger.

"Was Stiles telling the truth? You know that all your servants are criminals?"

"*None* of my employees are criminals now. Whatever happened in the past belongs to the past. I trust each of my employees with my life. I think of them as family. If my method of hiring them is unconventional, that's my concern. Not yours."

"Unconventional!" Sebastien sat down on the sofa, staring at her. "How did you even manage to find such people, let alone hire them?"

"It's none of your business." Cordelia began to pace the room, too worked up to stay still.

"You're right," he said. "But will you please tell me how such a thing came to pass? When I learned about Stiles's past, I assumed the worst. I thought you were in physical danger."

She whirled toward him, suddenly putting two puzzle pieces together. "It was you asking questions about the servants! Stiles informed me that someone was snooping around. And you let me assume it was Hayden. We know how he views other people's secrets: as a commodity. They were frightened to death, you know!"

"I had to know who was in this house. I had to know who was being trusted around the designs."

"So why did you not *ask* me?"

"I did ask you, Cordelia," he reminded her. "And you did your best to hide it from me until it was almost too late. So I did what I thought best."

She flushed. Despite all they had shared, he still did not know the whole truth, not yet. "You had no right," she hissed. His arrogant manner infuriated her.

"Cordelia..." He got up and crossed to where she stood. Reaching out to her, he said, "Forgive me. I did it out of concern for you."

She watched his expression for signs of duplicity, but then found herself simply gazing at him, remembering all too clearly how he'd made her feel like the only woman in the world for one night.

He smiled at her. "If you kiss me, I'll take it as forgiveness."

"Don't try to distract me," she warned.

He didn't listen. The distraction lasted for some time. Cordelia melted under his talented mouth, forgetting momentarily why he had come to her house. She only knew she would soon be addicted to the feelings he summoned up in her.

"Is that better?" he asked softly when he ended the kiss.

She blinked at him, now pressed against his body, supported only by his arms. "I told you not to distract me," she whispered. Then her eyes narrowed. "You can't do this, Sebastien!" She stepped back out of his embrace. "You cannot simply come into my home and…and take over! You have no *right*."

"Yes, you keep saying that. But you were going to tell me how you found your servants."

"Was I?"

"Unless you want me to distract you again." He smiled lazily.

"Sit down and at least act like a gentleman," she said, pointing to the sofa. He returned to his seat.

Cordelia's breath was still quick from the kiss. She debated how much to tell him. "Years ago, while my father was still alive, it came to my attention that one of our servants had a sister who badly needed employment. She couldn't find work in any respectable establishment because she had been convicted of theft and sent to prison. She was without references, and for a servant, there is nothing more important than a good reference.

"Naturally, she went to her family when she was released, but they were unable to provide for her. When I discovered this, I asked if the woman was a good worker in spite of her past. She'd been convicted of stealing a shilling's worth of food, you see, and only because she could barely keep herself fed on what some tavern owner declared to be a decent wage. When I was assured that I could trust the woman, I interviewed her and hired her as a kitchen maid.

"As the years went by, other positions needed to be filled as well, and even before my father passed, he left such decisions up to me, for I was the lady of the house by then. I saw no reason not to trust my own employees when they found someone in need of a position. It's in their interest as much as mine that everyone in this house behaves well."

"I can't believe this," Sebastien said slowly.

She raised her chin. "What's so unbelievable? I have the chance to give someone a new life, off the streets where such unfortunates usually end up. How could I turn someone away?"

"And you have no cause to regret it?"

"Only once. There was a young man who couldn't seem to stay away from silver—I called for the magistrate to take him." She paused, thinking. "But everyone else has been perfectly satisfactory. My friends have told me that the servants I recommend are among the best they have."

"Wait! You send these people to *other houses*?" he burst out.

"Occasionally," she replied. "What is it that troubles you so? The fact that some housemaids in London have an unsavory past? Or that you suddenly realize that servants can have a past at all?"

"That's not what I mean, Cordelia, and you know it."

"Then what do you mean, Sebastien? There's no point in telling anyone about this, you realize. I admit Stiles evaded his sentence, but he has shown his loyalty to me over and over again."

"What would you do if I did bring the authorities here?"

She stared at him for a very long moment. What could she do? Sebastien Thorne was an earl, an officer, and a man...and she suspected something more as well. She could never oppose him and win, not in any sort of public fight. So what did that leave her with? "The only thing I can promise, my lord, is that you would never see me or speak to me again." She doubted whether that was an adequate threat.

His expression was unreadable. "I'd like to speak to Stiles again. And the others."

She stiffened again. "You seem to have mistaken my house for your own. I refuse to allow you to interrogate my staff."

"They might have seen or heard something, but not known it was significant," he explained. "I want to protect you, Cordelia."

Ugh, why did he refuse to understand? "I have protected myself for years."

"You have no idea who is behind this, who Hayden is working with," he warned her, once again standing up. "I think I might. Please let me help you. Let me talk to them."

"You won't threaten any of them, or remind them of their pasts, is that clear?" she ground out unwillingly.

"You can sit in, if you like."

She shook her head. "They'll be more forthcoming if only you are present." She walked to the bell pull. "I'll explain that everyone should cooperate with you, and then let you work."

"Thank you," he said, suddenly subdued. "Cordelia—
"

"Don't say anything. I can't wait for this to end," she said, even as Stiles materialized at the door.

"My lady?" Stiles inquired deferentially, ignoring Thorne entirely.

Cordelia smiled at him, still feeling unmoored. "Stiles, I regret the bit of unpleasantness before. Lord Thorne has a few words to say about that, I'm sure." She paused and leveled her gaze directly at Sebastien.

He stood there for a moment, until it dawned on him what she expected from him. Then he said slowly, "My apologies, Stiles. I was unaware of the situation, and Miss Bering has corrected my mistake. You have nothing to fear concerning unwarranted character attacks from myself or anyone else."

"I am very glad to hear that," Stiles said, his eyes wide, perhaps at the novelty of receiving an apology from a noble. "I should not like to think that anything would disrupt my lady's household or peace of mind."

Cordelia sighed, satisfied. She instructed Stiles to have the staff answer any of Thorne's questions, and then fled back to her bedroom, knowing every minute she spent near Sebastien Thorne brought her closer to disaster.

THORNE WAS FRUSTRATED. HE ASKED Cordelia's people about Hayden and the robbery, but he wasn't much further along in tracking down Hayden, despite everything he'd tried. He had set a watch on Hayden's rooms beginning the day after the man attacked Cordelia. But so far, his underlings had nothing to report. The man had disappeared from society. A tip had to surface eventually. Meanwhile, he delved into the man's past.

What he found was troubling. Hayden was a member of the gentry. He attended Oxford (though more for the sporting life than the scholastic one), and had resided in London for several years. Judging by his habits and his wardrobe, his income was substantial. Thorne suspected that it came from blackmail.

The more Thorne learned about Hayden, the worse he appeared to be. He hovered at the edges of several scandals, but nothing could be linked to him with certainty. Through circumspect conversations at Thorne's clubs, he heard about ladies who had either been ruined after Hayden got hold of indiscreet letters, or others who were crippled by debt in attempting to get their letters back.

Hayden had left London for a while. He'd gone *somewhere* for two years. Some rumors suggested America, some thought the Continent. He returned last year, and had been living a much quieter life.

Thorne could guess what happened. Hayden fled London when one of his schemes went awry. Perhaps he attempted to blackmail the wrong person, or got too greedy. So he traveled the Continent to escape, and there met someone who knew about the potential of the *Andraste*. Sensing an opportunity, he joined forces with whoever it was. Hayden had the ability and lack of character to get such papers. The method would likely not be much different from how he procured his old blackmailing material from compromised ladies.

Only this time, he was to gain the confidence of an innocent woman, intending to get her to hand over her father's and Lear's papers. But Cordelia wasn't as empty-headed as he presumed, and when Thorne joined the chase, Hayden lost control of his scheme. Apparently, he'd gone to ground, to wait out Thorne and plot a new way to get the papers for his employer.

But where was he now? And was he still after the plans? Cordelia had given them to Thorne, and swore she burned the rest. If she was telling the truth, the only possible way for Hayden to succeed would be to reach Lear himself.

And no one seemed to be able to do that.

Except Cordelia.

Despite having the *Andraste* plans safe with the Zodiac, the mission wasn't over. He had to make Cordelia lead him to Lear. He remembered how coy she had been about Lear before, and prayed that she wasn't hiding something else, something worse.

But first, he had to go to the theater. His mother, quietly furious at his recent evasions, took revenge by preemptively arranging for him to join Lady Mary at *the* public event of the Season, the premiere performance of celebrated actress Mrs Siddons's turn as Lady Macbeth at the Theatre Royal.

"You will go, my son. *Everyone* is going," she said, closing her fan with the snap of a guillotine blade. "You will enjoy yourself or die trying."

He groused, but didn't oppose his mother's maneuver. If everyone was going, perhaps Cordelia would be there. And that might draw out Hayden. What better place to try to contact Cordelia again, if that's what the man had in mind? And if it turned out that Cordelia was selling secrets after all, she was going to be sorry.

* * * *

Cordelia was already sorry. Weeks ago, she had agreed to join Mr Jay and Aunt Leona for a theater performance. Unfortunately, she hadn't realized then that this evening's performance was to be a huge event—some of the royal family were rumored to be in attendance.

Yet it was far too late to cry off, so she now was attired in her fanciest gown, an empire-waisted watered-silk confection in ivory, flounced dramatically all along the bottom hem. She was flanked by Aunt Leona and Mr Jay, ready to see and be seen at the magnificent Theatre Royal.

The place was a madhouse, with folks from all classes milling about in the finest clothing they could afford, all chattering at the top of their lungs. The first performance was already in progress by the time Cordelia's party arrived. This was not unusual—theater was viewed as a rather casual pastime, and the audience came, went, and commented throughout the evening.

Jay's family reserved a private box, fortunately, and the young man escorted the ladies there immediately. The box, which held chairs for about ten people, looked out onto the main pit of the theater, and provided a view of the boxes on the opposite side as well. Cordelia sank into a red velvet chair near the rail, where everyone could see her. That was the point. For most patrons at the theater, the audience *was* the show. Leona sat down as well, and Jay left to order refreshments. They expected a few of his family members to join them shortly.

Cordelia gazed out over the mass of attendees. It felt as though a thousand eyes were on her.

"Anyone we know?" Leona asked as she also scanned the audience. "Ah, there is Mrs Martin and her family! And is that Lord Thorne?"

Cordelia followed her aunt's gaze, striving to not appear too intent. Yes, it was Lord Thorne in a box across the way. She feared he would be looking back at her, but in fact, his attention was occupied by the same young lady she had seen with him once before. Lady Mary something-or-other. Sebastien was smiling at the woman like she was the only person in the world.

A surge of jealousy brought heat to Cordelia's cheeks. Had he forgotten their encounter so readily? Then she breathed in, trying to reason with herself. Why should he not court the beautiful Lady Mary? It wasn't as if he'd ever been courting Cordelia. Their liaison had been as secret as it had been singular. She didn't *want* to be linked to Thorne. Really, Lady Mary was doing her a favor, if she took Thorne's attention away from her.

So why did she feel sick to her stomach?

When Jay returned, Cordelia made a special effort to be as engaged and lively as she could, going out of her way to ask questions about his family and to bring Leona into the conversation.

A wave of applause suddenly burst out. The legendary Sarah Siddons had taken the stage for her first scene as

Lady Macbeth, and the audience was briefly united in its attention. Cordelia chanced a look back toward Thorne's box. Lady Mary was watching the performance, but Thorne caught Cordelia's look and held it. She didn't know how to describe his expression, but it was not reassuring.

Before she could turn back to the performance, she saw someone else watching her. A shock went through her. Hayden stood in a box directly below Thorne's, gazing up at Cordelia with a knowing smile.

She couldn't believe his nerve. He'd almost killed her, and now he appeared at the theater like any other gentleman! When Cordelia would have turned her head, he actually beckoned her, making it clear that he wanted Cordelia to meet him.

She glared at him, then ducked her head. Jay noticed her distress, but she put him off, trying to focus on the performance. She certainly wasn't leaving. Hayden had to be mad to think that she would come close to him after what he had done.

Or he knew something.

Cordelia glanced back. Hayden was still staring intently at her. If he continued, it might cause comment. When he crooked a finger, she knew she didn't dare ignore him —if this kind of behavior continued in full sight of everyone, it could cause a scandal.

"Mr Jay," she whispered. "Hayden is here."

"What?" he asked, startled. "He wouldn't dare."

"He did dare. He wants to speak to me."

"I can't allow it. He's a scoundrel." Jay's voice was as low as hers, but Cordelia heard the outrage.

"He's a scoundrel who may have something important to say. I'm afraid I must go find him." She put her hand on his arm. "Will you do me the favor of finding the theater manager? Perhaps he'll know how we can hold Hayden until the authorities can be called."

"Of course." Jay nodded. "But I don't like you going alone to meet Hayden."

"I won't be alone. Half of London is here tonight. I shall never be out of someone's sight."

She rose to leave, warning Jay to wait a moment before following so Hayden wouldn't suspect anything.

The hallways and foyers of the building were just as crowded as the theater itself. People chatted, displayed their finery, and watched the parade of society. Cordelia hurried through the throng. She reached the ground floor and was almost to the large doorway to the street when a voice stopped her cold. "My dear Miss Bering."

She turned and surveyed him. Hayden was dressed perfectly, playing the role of carefree gentleman to the hilt. His eyes sparkled, and the charm of manner that had gotten him so far was still there. Even now, Cordelia found it difficult to believe this man had been willing to kill her.

"Mr Hayden," she said, hoping her voice didn't shake, "I see you are back on your feet."

His smile didn't waver, but the skin around his eyes tightened. "I am delighted beyond words that you are here tonight, Miss Bering. *Cordelia*," he added under his breath.

She stiffened at the insulting familiarity, but said only, "Am I to think it was a coincidence?"

He said, "Our last encounter ended far too soon."

"A matter of opinion, Mr Hayden. I thought it rather tedious," she said, looking around the lobby in the hope that she would see Jay appear with the manager.

"My replacement must be more to your liking," he said, too casually.

Cordelia looked at him. "Replacement?"

"Lord Thorne. A sudden but no doubt *satisfying* companionship."

"I do not understand your meaning, sir," she snapped. But she understood all too well. If Hayden had even the slightest shred of evidence to prove an affair… "I will leave you now."

"You won't." He moved into her path. "I think my price for the rest of the *Andraste* papers is clear. The designs for the drive will buy my silence."

She considered running, no matter what scene she might cause. "Even if I were to indulge your mad notion that you have something to hold over me—I note you offer nothing of substance to back your insult—it would not matter. The designs you are so keen to acquire are beyond all men."

He grinned. "You mean your little bonfire? Oh, I'm certain you didn't burn all of it. If those designs meant so little, you wouldn't have kept them locked up for so long."

"There isn't a scrap of paper related to the *Andraste* in my home. I would take you on a tour to prove it, but my housekeeper kills all rats on sight."

"You'll prove it now." Hayden pushed her toward the great doors. Cordelia protested, but as he got her to the top of the steps outside, he saw something behind them. He suddenly released her and took off running.

* * * *

Thorne saw Cordelia leave the box, and he saw Jay leave a moment later. Suspicious, he excused himself and went off in search of the pair. He didn't know how close Cordelia and Jay were, but he knew something must be in the wind.

He moved through the passages of the damnably popular theater, looking for either the young man or the unfairly alluring woman. He saw neither, but others saw him and innocently attempted to draw him away from his search. He ignored as many as he plausibly could, and was short with those he couldn't.

Finally, he reached the main lobby. He spied Cordelia first—his eyes were drawn to her black hair as if it were a beacon. She was talking not to Jay, but to *Hayden*.

Thorne was instantly furious. Cordelia had played him for a fool. She had no trouble finding the elusive Hayden. But even as he prepared to storm through the crowd, he saw Cordelia's expression, a mixture of fear and revulsion. Perhaps Hayden forced her to come to him.

He moved forward just in time to see Hayden steer an unwilling Cordelia through the entrance. The man glanced back once at the theater-goers. His eyes widened when he caught sight of Thorne. He abruptly turned and dashed through the crowd. With an inward roar, Thorne followed him.

* * * *

Cordelia stumbled when Hayden dropped his grip on her arm and rushed down the steps. She would have tripped if a pair of hands hadn't grabbed her around her waist and steadied her. She turned to thank her rescuer, and got a second shock.

"Sebastien!" she gasped. Her heartbeat accelerated, and it wasn't just due to the surprise. "What are you doing here?"

"Oh, I'm a fan of Shakespeare," he said.

"Are you *joking* about this?"

He shook his head. "Shakespeare's got a gift for language. Weren't you listening to Mrs Siddons's soliloquy in there?"

"Sebastien! Hayden just accosted me!"

"I know." He let the banter fade, looking at her with real concern. "What happened? What did he say?"

"He just…I told him I burned…" She couldn't put the words together.

"Get back inside," he said. "I'll handle this."

"I don't think so," she snapped back without thinking. "What right—"

She was silenced by his expression as he looked back at her. "Stop going on about rights, Cordelia. Let me do this, if only because I'll have an easier time chasing him since I'm not wearing skirts." And then he was gone, running down the street at a dangerous pace. She stared after him, wondering why she let him pursue Hayden. Not that she could have stopped him, she thought with a sudden laugh.

"Miss Bering!" Jay rushed out of the door with a man at his heels. "Where's Hayden?"

"He got away, I'm afraid. After he nearly twisted my arm off." Cordelia nodded to the second man, guessing him to be the manager. The man apologized profusely on behalf of the theater that an attendee should assault her. Cordelia, feeling rather guilty for misleading him, told him not to concern himself, as there was no lasting harm done.

"Shall I try to find him?" Jay stared down the street with little hope.

"No. Lord Thorne is already seeking him."

"Thorne? He came out here as well? Quite the coincidence," Jay said in a different tone.

"He is not in league with Hayden," she assured him.

"What makes you so sure?"

"He once hit Hayden in the face in front of me."

"And that's an endorsement, is it?" The two turned back toward the theater. Cordelia cast a look down the street where Sebastien had disappeared. She worried that, whether Sebastien found Hayden or not, the consequences would be bad for her. If Hayden suspected an illicit relationship, what better way to confirm it than by having the gentleman in question appear and give chase?

* * * *

Thorne raced down the street, but Hayden had a substantial head start. The scoundrel jumped into a hired carriage, at which point the driver whipped his horse to get the vehicle moving. Thorne ran as fast as he could, but the horse was moving at a trot and soon disappeared into the gloom of an unlit street.

He slowed to a stop, not caring about the curious looks sent his way. An enterprising boy came up to him and offered to chase the carriage down for a tanner. Thorne shook his head. "I've a counter offer. I'll pay you the tanner to go to the white house on Hanover Square. Find the boy watching the house and ask if he's seen the owner today. Come find me at the Theatre Royal with the answer, and I'll give you a shilling too."

The boy barely waited for his coin. He hopped onto the back of a moving carriage and rode toward his destination, eager for an even better payday.

Sebastien strolled slowly back toward the theater, knowing he could do little but wait for some clue as to where Hayden would be, either back in his rooms, or in a different hideout.

In the meantime, he tried to stifle his new concerns for

Cordelia. If Hayden got her to speak to him, the man knew something that could hurt her, such as her indiscretion with Sebastien. Or he offered something she needed, such as money. In either case, it boded ill. Cordelia was an intensely private person, and she could never endure the treatment of society if her relationship with him ever became public knowledge…no matter how he handled it.

But the other possibility was chilling too. Perhaps Cordelia had saved some documents from the fire, and perhaps she needed funds badly enough to accept Hayden's terms. Sebastien had to discover what he could about Cordelia's true financial situation.

In any case, he could do nothing now but return to the theater and watch the last performance of the evening. Fittingly, the playbill announced it would be a farce.

IMMEDIATELY AFTER HE'D SPOKEN WITH Cordelia at the quay, Sebastien had begun several threads of investigation, and one of his inquiries suddenly appeared more relevant. It was part of his plan to out more about Hayden's dealings in London.

Since the ship Cordelia named *Andraste* required large amounts of steel, Sebastien wanted to use the Zodiac's connections to find out whether Hayden (or anyone else) had tried to purchase steel in that quantity. He let Neville know about his idea, and that morning, a terse note arrived at the Thorne family home. The coded message, innocuous to any reader but a Zodiac agent, purported to be an invitation to a game of cards. To Sebastien, it revealed that someone had information on the steel he'd been looking for.

He hurried to the location that Neville had listed in the note. It was a pub not far from the docks. A young man sat at one table near the window. He had a drink in front of him, but he hadn't touched it. He was dressed in the uniform of a Royal Naval junior officer. By his ramrod-straight spine and closed expression, he was nervous. Yet his face also showed a level of curiosity that marked him as more intelligent than the average sailor.

Sebastien ambled over to him. "You're Ensign Hartley," he guessed. That was the name given on the encoded note.

The young man nodded. His skin showed a permanent tan, probably from serving in warmer climes than England. "Yes, Logan Hartley. I doubt you're going to tell me your name."

Thorne smiled. "A little confused?"

"No confusion, sir. I got orders from my superior officer's superior officer to come here and have a drink at eleven o'clock in the morning today. So here I am."

"Thank you for coming."

Hartley shrugged. "As I said, orders. From the meeting place, I guess this probably isn't quite official." He looked more closely at Thorne. "Is it safe to assume that something in one of my regular reports attracted the attention of the War Department?"

Thorne nodded. "Something like that. Do you remember offering any information about a large amount of steel?"

That was not what Hartley had expected to hear. He frowned for a moment, then his face cleared. "Steel. Yes, of course. What do you need to know about it?"

"Whatever you can tell me."

"Not much more than I put in my report, actually. I serve on the *Providence*. Our current assignment is to patrol the channel and keep watch on the French and Breton coasts. It's been quieter work since Trafalgar, so we've been able to explore the shoreline more, and even venture a bit into Bonaparte's territory."

Thorne detected traces of an accent he couldn't identify in the young man's voice. He said, "Go on."

"A few weeks ago, using one of the rowboats from the ship, we found a small harbor that's extremely well hidden. It's a river mouth, in fact. Though the river is supposedly non-navigable for ocean-going vessels, we found it to be significantly larger than initial reports indicated. The *Providence* hove to near the river mouth, and we began to row up it."

"And what did you find?"

"A shipyard. Small. Very well concealed. But in use, and not for commerce. It must be part of the French plan to rebuild their navy without our seeing what they come up with."

"There was steel there?"

Hartley nodded. "We found an unusual amount of metal plating. Definitely some sort of iron or steel. A funny color, though, as if it was coated with something."

Thorne inhaled. Exactly what any builder of the *Andraste* would need. Cordelia had been absolutely right about all sides wanting to try to get her father's plans. He remembered how Cordelia described the construction of the ship. "How much metal would you say was there? Enough to entirely cover a ship's hull?"

Hartley nodded slowly. "If it was a smaller vessel. Maybe a ship with twenty hands or so? Whether it would actually float with all that weight on the hull is another concern. We couldn't decide if that was truly their intention."

"How many men were in this contingent? Who saw the shipyard?"

For the first time, Hartley looked away. "Well…in fact, I went alone."

"Alone? Why?" Thorne asked.

"Because I could. I was curious."

"You violated orders?" Thorne sensed that some side of Hartley didn't care for rules. He still couldn't place the young man's accent.

Hartley looked uncomfortable. "Not exactly. I was

instructed to scout the perimeter, mostly to ensure the *Providence* wouldn't be sighted by anyone. There were no orders to go inside the shipyard itself. But neither was I under orders to leave immediately." He rushed on, "I knew I could get in and out unseen, and that the chance might not come up again. If anyone knew we were there, they might have closed it and moved it elsewhere. If the Royal Navy does this the right way, we can keep an eye on the place with no one the wiser."

"You're telling the Royal Navy what to do?"

"Who'd care what an ensign thinks?" Hartley shook his head, then looked directly at Thorne. "But you could suggest it, sir. They'll listen to you…whoever you are."

"Maybe I will." Thorne stood up. "I expect that your discretion about this meeting will match your perception."

"Certainly, sir." Hartley nodded curtly. It was obvious that he was a little offended by the suggestion that he would talk.

"Thank you for your information. You may return to your ship. After you finish your drink, of course." Thorne turned to leave, then said, "Oh, Hartley."

The young man looked up. "Sir?"

"The next time you want to storm one of the enemy's secret materiel dumps, perhaps you should take a comrade."

For the first time, Hartley allowed himself a faint grin. "I should have thought of that, sir."

Thorne left, laughing inside. Hartley reminded him of himself, years ago.

Hartley's news gave Thorne more to think over, and more to worry about.

Someone was trying to build the ship Bering and Lear designed. But they had not got the essential component. That implied that Cordelia was telling him the truth. She had every opportunity to give or sell the designs to Hayden. She hadn't.

He went to Neville's office to report.

Neville was pleased to hear that the meeting with Hartley was useful. "New idea that the Zodiac has been trying. Too often, intelligence gets trapped in routine paperwork in different channels. Crucial information never gets shared. We've been working to fix that. Your question about steel was ideal to test our work. We never would have found Hartley's report if you hadn't thought to consider steel purchases."

Thorne nodded. "Of course, we still have to link the shipyard to Hayden."

"We'll get there. The primary concern is that we hold all the necessary plans for the *Andraste*." Neville picked up a piece of paper from his desk. "That reminds me. Here's something else you wanted to know."

"What's this?"

"You asked for the name of Miss Bering's bank. She uses Child's."

"Excellent." Thorne had to learn more about the true state of Cordelia's finances. More subterfuge and lying, just as he'd done for years, when he worked with the military to learn troop movements and discover secret alliances. England was beginning to feel more and more familiar.

As soon as he could, Thorne headed to the city, where the bankers and businessmen congregated. He chose his clothing to be as nondescript as possible, all grey and black, and a plain white cravat over a plain white shirt. He even thought bland thoughts on his way. He wanted to vanish behind his facade.

When he stepped into Child's Bank on Fleet Street, he went to the nearest teller. He explained that he needed to speak to the officer who had charge of Miss Cordelia Bering's accounts there. Thorne apologized for not having the officer's name at hand.

The teller nodded as if this was not unexpected. He left to look up the name, and returned a few minutes later.

"You will wish to speak to Mr Abbott. What name should I give him?" the teller asked.

"Jackson Bourne," Thorne replied.

Moments later, another man appeared. "Mr Bourne, is it?"

"Good afternoon," Thorne said, offering a hand. "You must be Mr Abbott."

"I am. I was not aware Miss Bering had decided to relinquish control of her accounts. I have received no communications to that effect," he said, nervous that he had let something slip by.

Thorne smiled inwardly. He knew exactly how to play this man. "If we can speak in your office?"

"Of course, of course." He led the way.

After sitting down, Thorne took a moment to start speaking, knowing that the man was worried. He wanted to exploit that. "There is no need for alarm. Miss Bering is as satisfied as ever with Child's." Abbott sighed in relief, and Thorne knew he had him. "But I am her new man of business, and I wish to verify all accounts and figures."

"Certainly, certainly. Only…I don't recall Miss Bering having a man of business before. She was always most insistent on conducting all transactions herself." Abbott wrinkled his nose just slightly, unable to keep his distaste for her preferences totally concealed.

Thorne used Abbott's prejudice against him. "As you say. When I said I was her new man, I meant precisely that. Since she had no previous man of business, I could not consult with anyone but the lady. She is, you might have noticed, rather independent on some matters."

Abbott nodded. "To say the least. If I may say, I am glad that she has seen fit to engage you, Mr Bourne. Women should *not* take on such burdens themselves. They do not have the minds for facts and figures."

He thought that Cordelia was smarter than twenty Mr Abbotts, but he merely nodded as if he agreed. "I knew you would understand. Now, what I'd like is her records so that I may verify everything against her own notes."

Thorne spent a few more minutes buttering the man up, promising to submit all formal paperwork within days. And when he left the bank, he had gained not only Mr Abbott's esteem, but also copies of all Miss Bering's finances for the last decade.

He took the materials straight to his St James flat. It made for fascinating reading. He learned about the details of Alfred Bering's will, the deeds to the two houses Cordelia now owned outright, and her bank records from before her father's death to the present.

As he read, a picture emerged that he didn't like. According to the will, Cordelia ought to have an income of about three thousand a year. Not a pittance by any means, but not enough to support the lifestyle she appeared to live. Either she wasn't paying for some of those expenses—in which case, someone else was—or she had some sort of income the bank was unaware of.

In any case, there was more to her than what appeared on the surface. She'd burned papers, yes, but who could ever confirm exactly what she burned? Maybe she burned useless items, and kept others to sell. Sebastien's guts went cold. He didn't want to believe it, but what other conclusion could he reach?

He invited Cordelia over to explain the matter herself. For both their sakes, he hoped she was convincing.

THAT EVENING, CORDELIA READ AND reread the short letter in her hand. *I must see you tonight. Please come as before.* It wasn't signed, but the bold handwriting might as well have been a portrait of Sebastien.

She folded the note and slowly tore it up. No one watching her would have known that her heartbeat had accelerated sharply. At the memory of the last time she'd gone to see him, her skin flushed.

And now, he wanted to see her again. No explanation, no request. Just this…order.

She was not his mistress, she reminded herself. They had made no promises to each other, and certainly had not come to any sort of arrangement. He surely didn't think she'd fly to him just because he called her.

And besides, she had no intention of repeating the events of that one night. She had enjoyed it, yes. But un-married ladies like Cordelia did not conduct affairs. To even consider it would be madness.

Aunt Leona swept into the drawing room, wearing a gown of ice blue. "What do you think of this, dear? I bought it from Madame Eugenie in Bruton Street last week and the alterations were just completed."

Cordelia hurriedly dropped the scraps of the note into her teacup. "It's stunning. You should wear light colors more. But where do you intend to wear it? We have no parties to attend for a week, I think."

"Mr Dunham has invited me to join him at the opera this evening."

"Is that so?" Cordelia asked. She straightened up in her chair. If her aunt was gone…

"Yes. The opera, and then probably a late supper. You must think me quite silly for getting so excited."

"I think that you have every right to enjoy yourself," Cordelia responded easily, then caught herself wondering why she did not seem to have that right. She'd be thirty years old in a few years. When could she expect to enjoy herself? Of course, Aunt Leona was a widow, not an unmarried woman, and as such, her status was entirely different.

Leona smiled. "Well, Mr Dunham is a charming companion, so I expect the evening will fly by."

"I will probably be in bed by the time you return," Cordelia said. Not her own bed, perhaps, but it wasn't a complete lie.

When Leona left the room, Cordelia summoned Bond and told her she was going out as before. Bond plainly disapproved of Cordelia's decision this night. "He's turned your head," she worried. "Oh, I knew this would happen."

"My head is the same as always, Bond," she insisted.

"Then what of your heart?"

"My heart?" asked Cordelia.

Bond looked earnestly at her. "I know it's not my place to say, ma'am. But I see how you look at him whenever he's around. You must know that he never intends to court you, or offer any respectable arrangement. He's been after those plans since the day he met you."

"And I gave them to him, or at least a version of

them," Cordelia argued. "He certainly could have cut me off since."

"Oh, but the business is not concluded. And won't be till he's satisfied. Do you think he suspects the plans are flawed?"

Cordelia frowned. If he did, he might want to punish her for deceiving him. Luring her to a house and compromising her would be an excellent way to do it. But she didn't want to believe that. "What if he has learned about Hayden's whereabouts or his intentions?"

"Then he could inform you via a letter."

Cordelia shook her head, knowing that Bond was being rational…and she was not. "I will go. I feel I must. And…I want to."

"He has seduced you, then," Bond said.

"Perhaps. But why should I not enjoy the fall?"

Once again, she arrived at Thorne's secret home in the dark. Feeling like an incognita, she rapped lightly on the door. It was opened instantly, and she slipped through.

Sebastien closed the door behind her, then helped her off with her cloak, very properly. "I wasn't sure you would come."

"You implied that it was vital."

"It is," he said, but didn't add more. He looked her over. "You're beautiful, Cordelia." For some reason, he sounded sad.

Confused, she asked, "Why am I here?"

"I need you to look at something upstairs. There are papers on the desk."

"I should go up alone?"

"I must lock up. I'll follow you in a moment," he said, his words either a promise or a warning.

She went up. The desk was large, but it was clear of everything except a small pile of ledger papers. She had expected to see designs, or an engineer's notes, so she picked up the pages in some perplexity.

She gazed at the numbers for a moment before realizing what they represented. Then she felt like the very floor shifted below her. How had Sebastien gotten this information?

"Are those figures correct?" His cool voice came from the doorway behind her.

Cordelia turned, the papers still clutched in her hand. "Why do you have these? How did you get them?"

"So you know what they are," he said.

"No. No." She was flustered. She did know, of course, but he should not have these documents.

"They're your finances." His voice was flat, cold. The predator was back.

"You've no right—" she said, then stopped, her emotions too rocky to sort through. He was a man. He had all the rights. And did it matter how he'd gotten hold of her private records?

He stalked toward her, moving so he stood behind her at the desk. He leaned over, and said in a voice that was far too smooth, "According to those numbers, you have a lot more money than you should have. My guess? You've been selling your father's work to whoever will pay."

"No! I haven't," she protested. He could not believe *that*.

"Then where is the rest of your money coming from?" Leaning over, he pinned her to the spot without so much as putting a hand on her. She was conscious of just how much of him there was, utterly surrounding her, able to do anything he wanted to her.

"It's nothing underhanded," she said quickly.

"Then why do you hide it?"

"I'm not hiding..." She trailed off before she could

finish the lie.

"Did you think that by sleeping with me, you'd protect yourself? That I'd turn a blind eye after finding out what you really were?" His voice was tight, angry, and she wished she could see his expression.

"No," she said desperately, twisting around to face him. "I came here the other night…because I wanted to. Because you made me want you. I craved you."

"Very pretty words," he said, his eyes dark. Cold. "And a pleasurable night. But I can't help remembering that you also happened to use that occasion to distract me from the fact that I was denied a meeting with Lear. That was your real intention, wasn't it?"

She squeezed her eyes shut. "Ugh, Lear again. Can't you forget about Lear? *Please*, Sebastien. I haven't done what you're accusing me of!"

"Then what have you done, Cordelia?" He put one hand out, cupping her face and making her look at him. He then kissed her, drawing it out until she was whimpering with need. He pulled away, saying in a quiet tone, "Tell me, beautiful. I should warn you that I'm getting just a bit annoyed at your deviousness."

"There's no point in telling you," she whispered, her head spinning from the disconnect of his gentle, sensual kiss and the cold words he uttered. "You won't believe anything I say at this point anyway."

"Damn it, Cordelia. Do you think I'm blind? After all we've been through, after you claim to trust me, you're still holding out on me! What's more, you're still scared of something. Tell me what it is." He reached up to tuck a loose curl back behind her ear, but she turned her head away, actually ashamed of the tenderness in the gesture. "Please, Cordelia. I want to help you."

"Not even you can help me."

He pounced on her words. "So you do need help."

She shook her head. "Once this is over…this madness over the *Andraste*…no one will care. And you don't need to know. Trust me."

"How can I trust you when you've already admitted that you deceived me?" he asked, keeping his voice level.

"It's complicated." She looked up at him, willing him to understand her dilemma. She saw only his hardened gaze, and then snapped, "Oh, why should I explain? I was just an inconvenience to your search, wasn't I? You had to waste time on me. Hoping I'd give in easily, fall for your *charm*. And I did, didn't I? Fell like a ripe fruit into your lap. And you had to pretend I mattered. That you cared about me…"

She didn't have a chance to finish her diatribe.

Sebastien leaned in, his eyes locked on hers. "I wasn't pretending."

Once his lips touched hers, Cordelia almost believed it. She reveled in the sensations, feeling her body relax against him and then grow tense in anticipation of more.

His hands were on her hips, and then he lifted her up so she was sitting on the desk, her head level with his. She leaned forward, kissed him hard, thinking only that it felt right to do so.

Sebastien growled low in his throat as he slid her skirts up over her thighs. He pushed her knees apart and pulled her close. She clung to him, her legs spread as he pressed his hardened length against her core.

Cordelia was torn. She wanted this, but she knew he was only teasing her to get the information he was after. "What do you want?"

"I want you to tell me what you're hiding, sweetheart." He had somehow managed to loosen the top of her gown.

"And if I don't?"

He kissed her neck, and ran his tongue along the edge of her breasts exposed with the gaping neckline. "I'll stop."

She did not want him to stop. But that meant…she wasn't sure. She knew only that she wanted him to need her. She tugged at his shirt, yanked it loose, and slid her hands underneath, over his muscled torso.

That was enough to stop his questions for a moment, but when she moved her hands lower, he stepped back.

"You want my cock?" he asked, his voice low but scorching.

She flushed, because yes, she did.

"You've lied to me and you're keeping secrets from me, but you still want me to play with you. Is that it?"

"That's not it. But I do want this. You're making me want it. You confuse me," she whispered.

"You're the one who can end all the confusion, Cor," he said softly, rejoining her, using one hand to tilt her face so she had to look at him. "Tell me the truth, and there's nothing left to hide. Yes?" He didn't wait for her to reply. He just lowered his lips to hers and drew out a moan from her as he tugged on her lower lip with his teeth.

She leaned into him, craving his heat. She whispered, "Please, Sebastien, I can't have you hate me with your words and love me with your touch at the same time. You're breaking me in two."

He went still for an instant. He said clearly, "No more words, then."

She opened her mouth to ask what he meant by that, but from his breath against her skin, she knew exactly what he meant.

They clutched at each other, ripping fabric, discarding clothing until Sebastien was down to nothing, and

Cordelia wore only her thin chemise, pulled up over her hips and shoved down past her breasts. Beneath her, she felt the wooden desk and even the papers that he'd demanded she review. Hands pawed and stroked in an increasingly frantic rhythm, and their breathing grew ragged as passion drove them to the inevitable conclusion.

He reached between her legs and made a sound of pure masculine satisfaction at finding her so ready for him. She circled one hand around his cock and guided him into her, nearly crying out as he slid in so easily. He held himself there for a moment, his eyes half-lidded with lust.

Then he slowly moved his hands to her hips, and pulled her body sharply against his. He said nothing, but the implication was clear. He would be in the lead.

She inhaled, then nodded. He began to thrust, using what he'd learned about her to drive her to the edge. He didn't tease, he didn't hold back. Sweat broke out over her skin, and she felt even hotter inside. Her position on the desk seemed to give him whole new ways to find her most sensitive spots. The unyielding surface of the desk meant that she had nowhere to retreat, so she wrapped her legs around him and gave herself over to him, allowing every move and gesture, accepting his mastery.

The moment she did, she felt something unlock inside her. Yes, let him guide her body. Yes, let him tear down all her walls. Yes, let him undo her.

She hit her peak and crossed it all at once, crying out as bliss flooded through her core and out to her limbs. She closed her eyes, moaning as she felt him withdraw sharply and then press his erection against her belly. He finished with a groan that sounded like it came from the depths of his soul, and he had his arms around her, supporting her now-weak body. She sagged against his chest, putting her ear against him and listening to the drumming underneath. Whatever else he was, Sebastien Thorne was a man who did everything fully.

After a moment, she felt his lips on her forehead. He murmured, "You break me too, love."

Was that true? She couldn't imagine anyone breaking him. He was too committed, too completely passionate about the things he chose to believe in. Even if she couldn't ever fully know him, she knew that.

And what else did she need to know to trust him?

"I am…" she began to say.

"You're what, beautiful?" He kissed her again, on the neck, and she thought she might cry.

"Lear," she whispered.

"What about him?"

"I am Lear," she said, struggling to put the words together. "*Please*, Sebastien. Let me say this." What had happened to her? Hadn't she just been warning him to stop asking her? "I am Lear."

He leaned back to see her face. "What did you say?"

"You heard me." She sighed. "That's what I've been hiding. You know my secret. You win, my lord. Congratulations. You defeated me."

He wrapped her in his arms. "I don't want to defeat you, Cor. I want to understand you. Please tell me what the hell you mean by saying that you're Lear."

"I mean I use the name of Lear to make a living. And everything with Lear's name on it was actually done by me. Are you satisfied?"

He stood back, looking at her. Oddly, he smiled then, as if some burden had been lifted. "I knew it had to be something insane," he murmured. "But you have to tell me the whole story."

"All right. But perhaps not while still sitting on the

desk?"

He actually laughed, then swept her up in his arms and carried her to the high-backed settee near the fireplace. He put his arm around her, hoping to calm her. "Tell me. Whenever you're ready, love."

"I don't know where to begin."

"How about the beginning?"

She took a breath. "My father was an engineer, and since he had no sons, he taught me about his work. I loved it. It was like the best puzzle game in the world. By the time I was twelve, I could read any engineering schematic as well as a book."

"Which is more than I can," he admitted.

"That's not unusual. You never needed to learn," she said. She leaned against him. "But you can guess why I didn't tell people about my skill. I've kept my secret for years. It's the reason I've never wanted to marry. Husbands have too many rights, and wives too few. A husband would have access to all my things, all my father's work, all my work. He might have stopped me from pursuing my own interests, or worse, used it for his own purposes. That's exactly what Hayden was planning to do. I'm not a total fool. I knew that the ideas both my father and I came up with could be used to harm others. I couldn't take that chance."

"But what does all that have to do with Lear?"

Cordelia kept her head up, despite the turmoil she felt. "After Papa died, I needed an income to support Aunt Leona and my household. I had a talent, but who would trust a woman to answer questions about engineering? So I invented a man, because it would have been impossible to work under my own name. Lear was a useful fiction. The men and companies who hired Lear didn't know anything about him except that the work was satisfactory.

Which was how I wanted it."

"And of course you lied to me about Lear as well," he said, but not with anger.

"Yes. Until now," she admitted.

"Who else knows the truth?"

"Stiles and the other servants know about it, of course. It's a necessity, since they receive letters that come to this house—not everything comes to the location Mr Jay manages for me. And Mr Jay is integral to the subterfuge in another way. He's told others that he's met Lear, so there is no question of whether he is real…not that anyone has doubted it."

"Does your aunt know as well?"

"Oh, no. She wouldn't approve. And I don't want her to think that I couldn't support her!"

"Why did you choose the name Lear?"

"Shakespeare," she explained. "Cordelia is King Lear's daughter…and the one who should have inherited…oh, never mind. It was a foolish joke."

"But Lear wasn't a joke. It was your main income."

"Yes. I was doing quite well. Lear was one life. And I had my own quiet life at Quince Street. I didn't think the two should ever have to mix. Not too long ago, Hayden appeared, eager to court me, though I didn't realize why. And then you came along, asking all the wrong sorts of questions. And now it's all tangled up."

"I wish you had told me sooner."

"I was afraid. But I couldn't ignore you. You would have found out about Lear eventually, making it impossible for me to keep using the character. I hope you'll understand why I lied. It wasn't out of spite, believe me. I… think too much of you for that."

Thorne sighed. "Give me a moment. I need to adjust all the facts in my head to accommodate your little confession. So, this means you created the *Andraste*," he said slowly. "Not your father, and not Lear."

"Yes, I'm the only one who designed the ship," she said, watching him, seeing how he took the news. "Papa helped me with early versions, and I hid behind his name —and Lear's too. But it's mine."

"This changes things," he said, frowning. "It means you are just as valuable as the plans. Far more so, in fact." He kissed her gently, then added, "I don't mean your value is only in your knowledge."

Her heart eased a bit when he kissed her. "That's not all, Sebastien. You need to know about how my father died." Cordelia spoke softly. The pain of this secret would be harder to deal with.

His expression tightened with concern. "What do you mean? How did he die?"

"I think he was murdered."

↗

"Murdered?" Sebastien hadn't been prepared for that, and he felt the word *murdered* in his gut.

She was looking away from him now, her profile pondering and fragile in the light. "Yes. I can't prove it, but in my heart I'm sure of it."

"Tell me," he urged.

"Do you know that my father died abroad?"

"Yes." He remembered reading as much as he could about Bering when he was learning about the household.

Cordelia frowned, picking out her words. "At the time of my father's death, he was very frightened. He had gone to Paris some weeks prior to meet with some colleagues, or at least that's what he told me in his correspondence. He was very keen to share some of his new work with them. I gathered that if they thought it had merit, he would receive funding from a nobleman to bring his designs to reality."

He nodded. It made sense. "So what happened?"

"In the letters I received, the doctor said it was his heart, but I knew him. There was nothing wrong with his heart." Cordelia seemed to grow stronger as she spoke, finally letting her deepest fears out to another soul. To *him*

.

"In a letter he sent me before he died, my father wrote

that he was troubled by some of the things his colleagues had said, and that after learning more, he didn't trust the nobleman who was supposedly so keen on science. He was worried that they wanted his work, *our* work, for some sinister purpose. Fortunately, he never mentioned that he'd trained me, or that I had an interest in these things. But he *had* mentioned our ironclad ship by name."

"And they wanted it," he guessed.

"He was going to cut his trip short and return to England as soon as possible, according to the letter. It must have been the last thing he wrote. I think he died the very day that he announced he was leaving."

"But it could have been a coincidence," he argued.

Cordelia looked into his eyes. "Do you think anything surrounding the *Andraste* is coincidence?"

He looked back steadily. "No."

She gave a little sigh and continued. "In the last letter, he warned me to keep the papers safe until his return. I was not to let anyone look at them, no matter who they claimed to be. Of course, he was gone, so I could never ask him for more details. I did as he asked, though. I hid the most important papers and told several colleagues from the Athenaeum that I was planning to get rid of his work."

"Did any of them say you should give it to the society?"

She nodded. "Yes, of course. But I don't think any of those men were part of...I hate to say *conspiracy*."

He felt her pain pierce through her measured tone. "Did someone ask after the papers following the funeral?" he asked after a moment.

"A few written requests. I didn't respond to those. I was worried, but there was so much to think about after Papa died. First the mourning, and how to take care of

Aunt Leona. I suddenly had to deal with solicitors and bankers and the like. Life went on. I tried to find out more about my father's death, but it was so difficult to discover anything about what happened during his final journey to France. I didn't know who to trust."

She sighed, and leaned her head against his chest. He stroked her black hair, loving the feel of her head nestled on him.

She said, "When nothing more seemed to come of it, I thought the danger might be over. Yes, I kept the *Andraste* papers hidden, and I vowed to stay alert...but it seemed to be a memory. Nevertheless, I spoke to no one about it."

"Except for Mr Jay." He hoped there was no hint of jealousy in his voice.

"Who I have known for years," Cordelia noted. "And I had to trust him with some things. After several months, money was running low. I needed to devise some sort of income to keep the household together."

"So you invented Lear."

"Yes. You know now the other reason I didn't want to use the name of Bering for my own work. Lear was a necessary shield. And it worked. It worked for quite a long time."

"Until I swept in with my questions." He shook his head. He was so confident in his own abilities to uncover the truth that he ignored how much else he was uncovering, like Cordelia's carefully constructed protections.

"Yes. You wouldn't leave me alone."

"I had to keep at you. You were the only one who knew anything," Sebastien confessed. "Engineering wasn't part of my education."

"I thought spies were supposed to have very broad educations."

It was spoken in such a matter-of-fact tone that it took

him a beat to absorb the word. And what it meant.

"What did you say?" he asked in a low voice.

"I called you a spy." Cordelia didn't take her eyes from his, though her breath had quickened. "Do you deny it?"

Christ, why had she *said* it? He could dance around it, he could misdirect, he could pretend he didn't hear. But he'd demanded the truth from her. How could he lie now?

She was still watching him, challenging him, daring him to avoid her. "You don't think I'm stupid, do you? You have mysterious business on the Continent. Adele once mentioned that you speak French like you were born there. And despite the rumors that you're destitute, you always have the finest clothes and you spend money like it's water. You have some means of support, although I don't know who is paying you. Sounds familiar, doesn't it?"

"Cordelia…"

"And most importantly," she went on, "you stop at nothing to get the information you want, as you've just proven to me. Do you still want to pretend you're not a spy?"

Sebastien had never thought she was stupid, but he was troubled by just how much she had gleaned from their time together. Cordelia was well matched to him, he thought, in more ways than one. "Love, you can never tell anyone about this, do you understand?"

"Surely you know by now I can keep a secret!"

"His Majesty's government doesn't survive by being lenient. If anyone else knew you'd learned this, you'd be in grave danger. I wouldn't be able to stop it, darling, no matter how much I try."

"His Majesty's government? You work for the Crown?"

"Who else?"

"I don't know! I thought perhaps another group like Hayden's…"

He was angry at that suggestion. "Of course the Crown!"

"Well, how was I to know?" she asked, exasperation in her tone. "I didn't know a thing about you!"

"You know I did everything I could to keep you safe."

"Sometimes it's difficult to distinguish ulterior motives from common decency." She laughed then. "Not that anything you've done has been common."

"That applies to you as well." He kissed her, pleased that she kissed him back with no hesitation. Forgetting about secrets, they melted into each other, taking and giving as their breaths and limbs tangled.

"I need you," he said, need rushing over him. Christ, they'd just done this, and he was already wild for her again. "Please say you need me too."

Her eyes sparkled. "The answer is yes. But I must insist on the bed this time."

"Anything you wish," he promised.

Half fearing she would change her mind, he went slowly, inch by inch, driven to memorize every curve and hear every little sound she made. Afterward, they lay together on his bed, naked and unashamed, as if they'd been lovers for years.

The conversation eventually returned to graver matters. "You were wrong about one thing, Cor," he said lazily, wondering how he could stop time so Cordelia wouldn't ever have to leave his room.

"What's that?"

"I'm not destitute. Not even a little bit."

"But I thought…the *ton* says…" Cordelia was fumbling at the idea of repeating gossip to its subject, so proper despite being naked in his arms.

Sebastien laughed to see it. She never did what he expected, and he loved it. "The rumors are partly true. I did squander my personal fortune when I was young and reckless. Gambling, mostly. I was dissolute and the creditors were breathing down my neck. I had lands, but they barely kept me fed.

"That's when I chose the army over facing my creditors and the censure of the *ton* . It was in those years that…that my superior first found me and decided I had the makings of an agent. So I left the regular army and became what I am now."

"Why are you telling me this?"

"Because I trust you, sweetheart." He paused, remembering the past. "It was the time when I grew up, finally. Now I am wealthier than I was when I lost my first fortune. And when my brother, George, died, the title passed to me."

"But they say your father was quite impoverished as well."

"Also true…for a time. He invested poorly. George managed to turn the family finances around during his too-short tenure as Earl of Thornebury. Unfortunately, he also spent a large amount of money to restore the family estate in Cheshire. Much of the land had been neglected for a generation. I've been working hard to reinvest and build the family's finances back to what they should be."

"But how do people not realize your fortune was restored?"

"I choose not to enlighten them. My mother, who is no fool, understands why. She worries that fortune hunters will be after Adele when she's presented next Season. But the silence serves me too. The *ton* loves gossip, and a poor nobleman makes for a good story. If society thought

I was penniless, it helped to keep their damnable daughters away."

"Except for those who wanted you for your title," Cordelia guessed shrewdly.

"Indeed. Truth to tell, my time abroad is as much to escape England as it is for the good of England."

"So you had your secrets too."

"Yes. But if you'd told me yours earlier, you would not have had to hide so much." He kissed her lovingly to take the edge off his criticism.

She accepted his attention for a moment, but then said, "And what should I have told you? That a mere woman not only understands engineering, but actually drafts plans on her own? That I designed a ship that could forever change how war is fought on the water? Would you have believed that?"

"Not at first," he admitted. "But you should have told me all the same."

"Just as you should have told me you were working for the Crown." She paused. "Do we know everything about each other now?" she asked quietly.

Sebastien laughed. "Well, do you have any other secrets besides being the sole owner of some priceless weapon designs, a penchant for hiring felons as servants, and oh, yes…actually working as an engineer and creating an entirely fictional man as a shield?"

She nodded slowly. "I'm also having an affair."

He went cold. "With who?" he demanded furiously.

"With you, Sebastien." Cordelia rolled her eyes. "How many covert affairs do you think I could manage with all those other secrets?"

He shook his head, impressed at how easily she played his rawest fear. She'd make a good agent. "Your capacity for subterfuge never fails to amaze me."

"Impressive, considering your own talent for living lies." She ticked marks off on her fingers. "You are a spy for the Crown. You pretend that you're impoverished when you're rich. You pretend to be seeking a bride in your role as earl…"

"Enough," he said, putting one hand on hers. "We both learned to live two lives, each hidden from the other."

"Does your family know what you do?"

"Of course not. It would endanger them…and me."

Cordelia made a skeptical sound. "Adele knows that when you vanish for weeks on end, you're not really in Cheshire when you tell her you are."

"Adele is uncomfortably observant. I've done my best to misdirect her. She worries that I'm still gambling. Mother is occupied with many other matters, and she is easier to manage. But that's why I acquired this house. I needed someplace to hide."

"I can certainly understand that," she agreed. "Nearly everyone wants to hide at some point—" Then she broke off.

Sebastien shifted, attuned to her mood. "What is it? What are you thinking?"

She said, "I was thinking that Hayden is also good at hiding. So we need to get him into the light. To catch him, you need bait. Which, in fact, you already have."

"The plans you gave to me?" He shook his head. "It's far too dangerous. Should Hayden manage to steal them, we'd give our enemies the means to destroy our ships."

"Actually, the plans I gave you…"

"Yes?" He looked at her with narrowed eyes.

"They contain flaws. Very subtle ones—whoever tries to follow them will get quite far before he discovers that the ship's steering simply won't work."

He didn't say anything for a long moment, realizing that he'd just glimpsed *another* layer of Cordelia's mind. Then he said, "Well. I guess you did say you weren't sure who I worked for."

"I'm sorry. Truly. But I thought it was for the best. I'd rather no one built the *Andraste* than to have the wrong person build her."

"I can't argue against that," he admitted. "So you propose that we somehow get Hayden to steal these designs?"

"No, buy them."

"Even if we could find him, Hayden would never believe that you would sell him plans, after what he did to you."

Cordelia waved that off, clearly excited by her idea. "He wouldn't buy them from me, that's true. He'd suspect a trap. But he might be persuaded if the seller was someone who was close enough to me that he'd believe they could get them, especially if they had an axe to grind."

"And who would that be?"

"A disreputable former servant, of course. One with a criminal past."

He inhaled, realizing what she intended. "That is… perfect."

Cordelia laughed. "Jem can do it. He'll love it. And once Hayden gets the flawed plans, he'll want nothing more to do with me!"

Sebastien shook his head. "No, wait. It won't work."

"Why not?"

"Because Hayden may sell them to someone else. Some person we don't know. And he'll just find someone familiar with the technology who can fix the plans."

"The only person familiar with this technology is Lear," Cordelia noted, smiling impishly.

Sebastien suddenly understood. "Whoever asks Lear for assistance will be the man we want!"

"Precisely."

"You're a genius."

"How kind of you to notice."

"Are you sure you can do this?" he asked.

"Of course. But only if you let me get dressed so I can get back home."

"I knew there would be a flaw in this plan," he said with a half-mocking frown.

Cordelia opened her mouth to protest, then shook her head and winced dramatically. "My lord. That was appalling. Unworthy of the Crown. And…worst of all, it was funny."

He grinned, unrepentant. "I thought you'd like it."

It was time to return to Quince Street and enlist Jem, but Sebastien refused to allow Cordelia to travel alone any longer. "You're too valuable," he said.

She was impressed by the skills he used to bring them both back to Cordelia's home with no one the wiser. He even managed to slip past all of her alert servants, allowing himself to be seen only when Bond entered Cordelia's sitting room to attend her mistress.

Bond jumped when she saw him. "What is *he* doing here, my lady?"

"He is helping us, Bond," Cordelia said firmly. "We trust him."

The maid looked hard at Thorne, then offered a resigned sigh. "Very well, my lord. What can I do for you?"

"Find Jem and bring him back here, Bond," Thorne said in a respectful tone. "We have a task for him, if he's amenable."

Soon after, the footman appeared at Bond's heels. She must have told him everything, because he didn't bat an eyelash at finding the gentleman in Cordelia's rooms. "Put the bars on the windows for nothing, I see" was his only comment.

Thorne's lip quirked. "Not for nothing. You are protecting something quite precious." He glanced at

Cordelia, who blushed at the deeper meaning in his words.

Getting ahold of herself, she faced her servant. "Jem, I need to ask you a very great favor. Not just for me, but for our country."

Jem's eyebrows rose. "What is it, my lady?"

"Hayden, the man behind the burglary, is still convinced that I have something he wants."

"And is he right?" the young man asked.

"I want him to think he is." Cordelia pulled out the papers that had been in Sebastien's custody. "These plans contain what appears to be the necessary information to complete a ship. Hayden wants them. Once we find him, I want you to tell him that you stole these from me, and that you'll sell for the right price."

"Why would he believe me?"

"Let it slip out that I sacked you after learning of your criminal past. Out of spite and greed, you took something you knew to be valuable."

Jem was already nodding. "An easy story. He'll believe me when I'm done," he said. "But this is all to cut a sham, right?"

"Cut a sham?"

Jem clarified, "Trick him."

"Oh. Yes. I've drawn them just a bit wrong. But he'll have most of the ship built before he realizes that it won't work." She knew she didn't have to go into specifics.

Jem's only question was "How much should I ask for, my lady?"

Cordelia had no idea what amount Hayden would find believable. "My lord?" she asked Sebastien.

"Demand six hundred pounds, but accept five," he declared after a thoughtful pause.

Bond's eyes widened when she heard the number.

"He'll pay that?"

"Oh, he'd pay far more," Thorne said. "But not to a servant like Jem. Any higher price and he'll get suspicious."

Jem nodded. "All right. I'll do it."

"You must be very careful, Jem," Cordelia told him, already worrying about what might go wrong.

"Yes," Sebastien added. "Hayden will quite likely try to take the money back, or simply inform the local gang that you're a perfect target."

"Not worried, sir," Jem said.

Cordelia wished he *was* worried, and Bond's expression said the same.

Meanwhile, Sebastien said, "The only problem is finding him. I've put a watch on his rooms, but he must be living elsewhere. He could be anywhere in London."

Bond exchanged a look with Jem, then said, "If he's in London, we know folk who can find him."

"Who?" Cordelia asked.

Jem shook his head. "No one whose name we'll tell you, my lady. But trust me, for a bit of coin, *anyone* can be found if you ask in the right places."

"I've tried that already," said Sebastien.

"Begging your pardon, my lord, but you don't know the sort of people I know." Jem cast a significant look at Sebastien's fine clothes.

"Point taken," Sebastien said. "Do what needs to be done. I'll cover the cost of your work."

"Might take a few days," Jem said. "But I'll sell Hayden these plans, never fear."

* * * *

To keep up appearances, the supposedly sacked Jem

moved out, just in case Hayden was keeping tabs on the household. In the meantime, Sebastien funded the search for Hayden through the shady contacts of Cordelia's servants.

While waiting to hear the results of Jem's gambit, Cordelia went to a few minor functions, maintaining a demeanor of placid spinsterhood. Days dribbled by. To be at the mercy of events was not a new sensation—she was a woman, after all—but the waiting made her anxious.

She attended a musicale with Elly one evening, and was restless all night. While she waited for Elly to return from the retiring room before they left the event, she fancied—without any firm evidence—that several of the other attendees were watching her with judging eyes. Cordelia was never so glad to follow Elly out the door and into the dark night.

Then, the next afternoon, William Jay called at the house. They exchanged the usual pleasantries and some desultory chat about an upcoming lecture at the Atheneum. But he seemed out of sorts, a mood Cordelia could sympathize with.

"In fact, I have a specific question to ask you, Miss Bering."

"Oh?" She was surprised at his sudden formality. "Please go on, there's no need to stand on ceremony among friends."

Jay cleared his throat. "Miss Bering, it would gratify me considerably, and be a satisfactory arrangement for you, if we, that is…I am asking for…well, your hand in marriage."

Cordelia felt a moment of pure shock, then a wash of emotions poured over her. Jay's sincere proposal stabbed her through the heart. "Oh, Mr Jay. *William*," she began, appalled at how events could have led to this. "You are my dear friend…"

"I would continue to be that, I hope."

"I cannot marry you."

He looked upset. "I have about three thousand a year, which is more than enough to live comfortably. I know I will never be my older brother, whom you loved first and most deeply. But I thought you would welcome a certain level of protection, and…"

Protection! As if the darling boy could protect her from anything that threatened her right now. Not the *ton*, not Hayden, not the host of powers of Europe. "I do appreciate your desire to provide me a buffer against the world. But it is quite impossible."

He frowned. "Why? I don't care about your age."

"That's not what I mean, though you do deserve a younger lady by your side. You think marrying me would offer me protection. In fact, it would only bring pain to you. You must trust me. Believe me, turning down your kind proposal gives me no joy."

Mr Jay held still for a moment, as if frozen in place. "Has the earl proposed to you?" he asked in a low voice.

She blinked. "Lord Thorne?"

"Is there another earl with whom you have been spending time?" he asked, partly joking, partly worried.

She went still. She had thought she was imagining the glances of others over the past week or so. But if even Jay—not known for being out on the town—was concerned for her reputation because she was associating with Thorne too freely, then it meant that her actions were being more closely watched than she thought.

"Lord Thorne has not asked me to marry him, nor would I accept if he did," she assured him after she recovered her voice.

"I wonder," said the young man, speaking to the floor.

Cordelia wanted to reach out and comfort him, realizing her impulses toward him were exactly like that of a mother toward her child. "I am too old for you," she said softly. "Nor can I help you move up in society, or secure a better life for the children you should have."

"Sod all that! I know that you have been facing real trouble of some kind, and I know *he's* involved in it. I want to…save you."

She smiled, despite the painful situation. "How can you do more for me than what you already have, helping me create Lear and working with me on the projects I so enjoy? By being the one I could speak to when I was so raw with grief after Vincent died, because you knew him like no other person? Your friendship and trust have already saved me. I could not repay that by shackling you to an old maid with no prospects. You will find a bride that is a true match for you, I'm sure of it."

Jay straightened up, mastering himself once more. "I note that you haven't denied the essential fact. You are in danger."

"No. I *was* in danger," she said. "You—and yes, Lord Thorne as well, in his way—have helped me weather it. I am quite certain that the storm has passed and I will not have to worry anymore."

"So my offer is as unnecessary as it is unwelcome."

"Say rather undeserved. I could never use the word *unwelcome* in the same breath as your name."

Jay didn't respond for a long moment. Then, uncharacteristically, he bowed to her. "I do hope so, Miss Bering. I will not disturb you anymore. Good day."

"William, please wait."

But before she could stop him, Mr Jay left her and the house.

Cordelia paced the room, her slippers shuffling over

the carpet as she turned the conversation over and over in her mind. She fretted about the failed proposal. Had she encouraged Mr Jay to think of her in that way? In all their conversations, they had never spoken of marriage. But then she berated herself for being naive. She was a woman, and he was a man! It was as simple as that.

Cordelia put her hands to her temples. No, what was she thinking, to ascribe such unworthy thoughts to Mr Jay? Of all men, he at least appreciated what she wanted to do with her life. He never suggested she stop working, and he had endorsed the Lear plan with relish, like it was a grand schoolboy prank. He was a true friend. If she had any sense, she would have accepted him.

But she could not. And it was all because of Sebastien. She had let him into her life, and her heart, and now she would suffer for it. Jay's earnest proposal made it clear that she could not go on as she had been with Sebastien. Jay was too kind to think badly of her, but others would be quick to pounce on the most prurient (and in fact correct) interpretation. So she had to break it off…and soon. Or else she would lose everything.

She had played with fire in pursuing any association with Sebastien. For herself, she might reconcile with the idea of being frozen out. But she was not alone. She had family and a household to care for.

The answer came to her as she drifted off to sleep that night. She would leave London as soon as possible and go to Bristol, to the family cottage by the sea. She must get clear of gossip, but also of any possibility of running into Sebastien again. She doubted she could resist temptation if it arose.

The next morning, Jem appeared in the kitchen, flush with cash and the success of having gulled Hayden, who had bought the story and the designs all at once. Cordelia sent Jem to the Thorne townhouse, so he could report the news to Sebastien directly—and so she could avoid him.

Meanwhile, she mentioned her plan to go to Bristol casually to the household. Bond thought it such a fine idea that she started packing almost immediately. Even Leona approved the decision, though she did not understand Cordelia's true reason for it. She said, "The cottage ought to be opened up again. And the city air has not been good for your health, dear. You've got shadows under your eyes."

"Yes," Cordelia said, trying to keep her voice calm. "A change of scenery is what I need. I do hope that you'll come too, Aunt, unless you are enjoying London too much."

"Pah. The Season is almost done, and I too could use a rest. We'll go together, my dear. It will be like the old days, when I visited you and your father all of July and August. We had such lovely rambles along the water, didn't we?"

"Soon enough, we'll do that again," Cordelia promised. But would it be soon enough?

* * * *

In a room far away from the one in which Cordelia paced, the designs that had caused all her present troubles were laid out on a large, dark oak table. An unusual collection of objects held down the corners of the pages, which threatened to curl up if anyone so much as glanced at them wrong. A smooth granite stone, an ivory figurine of a Chinese beauty (holding an ivory fan demurely in front of her face), a heavy brass candlestick (sans candle), and even a fresh pineapple had been called into service. Finally pinned down, the papers could now be examined at leisure.

"I do not like this." The terse conclusion was voiced in French. "I have only scraps to work with. Clearly there was more to this design."

"She burned some things," another voice said apologetically. It was Hayden who spoke. "The lad confirmed it…he lit the fire. Perhaps this is all for nothing."

"No!" The other man at the table stood up, sweeping one hand across the desk. He struck the brass candlestick and it went flying, hitting a chair several feet away. "I have spent far too much money to give up now. Bering said it could be done, just before he died."

"But he's dead, and if she destroyed the remains…"

"I'll break her neck if she did! That minx of a woman, with her sharp-eyed servants! She never even knew what she had, yet every plan I made was thwarted…"

Hayden shrugged. "Cut your losses, then. Sell the metal. Start over with something else."

"No," the white-haired man snarled. "I want the *Andraste*. I want a flotilla of *Andrastes*, ready for battle by the end of the year!"

"But it can't be done. If Alfred Bering were still alive, we could force the answer out of him. But his old papers are all that's left."

"Old papers," the other echoed. He suddenly looked at the paper itself. "Old? You say these are what the servant sold you. And he stole them from the Bering woman, after she burned everything else?"

"Everything but these, yes."

The white-haired man's eyes glittered. "*Look.* If her father made these, they would not be so fresh! Look at this paper! Pristine! The ink is barely dry."

"The other one, then. Lear."

"If the hermit Lear made them, they would never have

been in Miss Bering's possession! Unless..."

"What is it?"

The other man nodded, then said, "I wish to meet Miss Bering."

"She'll never agree."

"Don't *ask* her." The white-haired man's grin was cruel now.

"I can bring the Bering bitch to you, sir." Hayden narrowed his eyes. "But it will cost you."

"Imagine the cost if you fail," the other man said.

"I meant the cost of the operation," Hayden amended, swallowing nervously. "I'll need to pay for a ship, and bribes for the crew... Once I have her, where do you want me to bring her? Straight here?"

"No. Let her see the progress of our *Andraste* first. Ask her how to complete the ship. And if she refuses, bring her back here, where she'll be well looked after." The older man smiled, unnerving even Hayden. "I look forward to meeting this lady."

$\nearrow$

THIS IS THE LAST TIME, Cordelia vowed. She took stock of herself in the mirror. The dark green dress complemented her skin, and Bond worked her usual magic to arrange Cordelia's black hair into a style worthy of an ancient Greek maiden. But to her own eyes, her face looked ashen, her lips pinched. She could not continue like this.

Since meeting Sebastien Thorne, she was swept from fear to bliss and back, over and over. He was by far the most fascinating man she had ever known. But his life was so unlike hers that there was simply no possibility of sharing it.

Sebastien had sent word via Jem that he had news for her, and that he knew she was attending the Rampling ball —one of the final events of the Season, and thus it would be a well-attended crush.

With luck, he'd know if Hayden left London, and perhaps where he had gone. If so, Cordelia intended to thank Sebastien for everything he'd done for her, and then to break off their affair. The whole exchange might take the span of a dance. And then it would be over.

Unless he didn't agree.

Cordelia shoved that thought aside. Sebastien would understand. He knew even better than Cordelia that his life had no place for her. In fact, he might be secretly grateful.

At the ball, she wandered among the crowd, wondering if he would even find her. She need not have worried. A touch on her arm, and there he was.

"Lord Thorne," she murmured, her heart lifting as soon as she saw him.

"Miss Bering," he returned with aristocratic cool. "Do you want the latest news?"

"What news is that?" she asked. One thing to be said for espionage, it was far more exciting than her usual life. She would miss the intrigue when it was over. She would miss Sebastien more.

He said in a low tone, "Come with me. I can't tell you here."

She didn't have to be convinced.

He found a quiet room on an upper floor. Once inside, he swiftly turned the key in the lock and yanked it out.

Cordelia waited anxiously for the news. "Well?"

He started pacing. "Hayden's been sighted. He boarded a ship bound for France a few days ago. He'll either meet with his employer, or try to sell the plans on his own there."

She sighed in relief. "He did believe Jem, then. He thinks he has it all. Wherever he went, whoever ends up with it, they'll spend months trying to work it out."

"Spending money all the while," he added smugly. "Funds which Bonaparte would surely like to spend elsewhere. This is the best outcome we could hope for. Your ship designs will confound them, and when they give up, they'll seek out Lear to discover the flaw." He smiled, turning to her. "As soon as you get that request, just hand the information to me and I'll take steps."

"Of course I'll get word to you as soon as that happens. But Sebastien..." Cordelia was about to launch into her carefully rehearsed explanation for why they must no longer associate.

Before she could, he stopped in front of her, cupped her chin in his hand, and turned her face toward him. "I have to tell you. I like your courage, Cor."

"My courage?"

"Yes. You've handled this whole endeavor with the bravery of a soldier and the grace of a princess. Of course, your courage isn't the only thing I like about you."

He lowered his mouth to hers, breaking down her resolve within a breath. His tongue teased her in ways she'd never dreamed of.

"You may do this all the time, but I cannot," she whispered, but then kissed him back as if her life depended on it.

"I never do this," he protested. "I've never lost my mind like this until I met you." Step by step, he backed her up until she felt the wall. His hands ran over her waist, her breasts, into her hair, as if he couldn't get enough. Then, in an undertone, he said, "I need to taste you. Pull up your skirt."

"*Here?* Standing up?" she asked, astonished and suddenly very curious.

"I can't wait," he growled. "Neither can you."

True. She was already wet, nearly mindless with desire for him, and she only faintly remembered a resolve to break things off for…well, there was some reason. She murmured, "Sebastien, this is wrong."

His mouth grazed hers, and he said, "Being with you is the only thing in my life that feels right, Cor. You were made for me. Please. Be with me."

Was he admitting that he wanted something from her simply because it made him happy? The way he was touching her seemed to prove it, because every little move turned her skin to fire. She kissed him back, no longer caring whether it was right or wrong.

She pulled up the skirts of her gown, and he knelt in front of her, his hands firm on her thighs, teasing her skin there. And his tongue…

She stifled a moan when he began to pleasure her with a few slow strokes of his tongue, a soft bite, then steadily more aggressive attention. Her legs were shaking by the time he rose to his feet, his erection bulging. She reached to undo the buttons of his falls, greedy for everything she shouldn't have.

Then he was inside her, filling her. Before she knew what she was saying, she heard herself begging him to do anything he wanted, to devastate her.

He was all too eager to oblige, and Cordelia came undone in that scandalous pose. His own climax followed instantly. The pair sank slowly to the floor, recovering. She could hear the blood rushing in her ears, and felt the thudding in her chest.

Sebastien reached out, tipping her face to his. His fingers traced her jawline, her brows, as if he wanted to memorize her. His expression was dazed, probably the mirror of hers. He said, "Believe me, I didn't intend this when we came into this room, sweetheart."

"I wanted it to happen," she whispered, her breathing still uneven. "I suppose it's just me being inexperienced, but you wake up my whole body."

"Experience has nothing to do with it. Sometimes, two people are meant for each other." He kissed her tenderly, and Cordelia nearly died as she lost herself in the feeling, so gentle after their desperate, almost violent lovemaking. "I've never met anyone like you, darling," he said, his lips still touching her own.

"I…I won't forget you," she said, her voice cracking.

He pulled away, staring at her in confusion. "What did

you say?"

"Sebastien, don't pretend you don't understand. This…exchange can't continue."

"You're labeling us as an exchange?" Now he sounded more than confused. He sounded incredulous.

"Affair, then. I never thought I'd be the sort of woman who conducts affairs. But here I am."

"Yes, you're here with me. And yes, I guess it's technically an affair. I tried not to name what we have," he added. "I wasn't ready to do that, not with everything else happening. My assignment, the plans, uncovering your role…"

"I'm sorry I hid the truth for so long," she said, looking at the floor. "I was afraid…but also, perhaps part of me wanted to keep you coming back to me."

Sebastien sighed. "I found every excuse to do just that. But Cor, I would never do anything to hurt you. You know that."

"Of course I know that. It's not what *you* would do…" How could she put into words all the emotions battering her heart? How could she tell him what she wanted when she barely knew what she wanted herself? All she knew was that she ached for a life with him in it, and that was the one thing she couldn't have if she was to maintain her reputation and protect those she cared about. She shook her head, then moved to stand up. "I have to go."

"I'll escort you home," he said, also standing.

"I think not," she retorted. "We can't be seen together."

"Why? Has someone said something to you?" he demanded, looking much more like the alert spy, the soldier ready for some attack. "Tell me."

"No one has said anything directly. I've avoided that so far, and I would like to continue avoiding it. But there have been a few questions. And a few…looks across the room. You know what I mean."

He grimaced. "Yes, I know."

"We must not see each other again." It pained her to say the words, but she knew it was right. Besides, she was not meant to be part of his life.

"You're worrying over nothing," he countered, his dark eyes inscrutable.

"Maybe it's nothing to you. After all, what harm will fall on you if our affair became known? Whereas I would be shut out of society without another thought." She managed to put her appearance in some semblance of order.

"Don't make me into some soulless fiend," he said, putting his hands on her shoulders. "I would never let it come to such an extreme. Marriage would answer all that."

"Oh, a proposal to stave off the scandal? How very touching," Cordelia said, no longer looking at him.

His hands tightened on her shoulders. "Damn it, that's not why I would marry you!"

Cordelia shook herself free. "You assume you *could* marry me. But not if you're already married, sir. What if our relationship is revealed *after* you've acquired your countess? You're getting married to someone, and soon. Isn't that correct? After all, an earl must have an heir."

"I must have *you*," he said, his expression fierce. "That's all that matters."

"What about what matters to me? Be rational, Sebastien. You met me by chance, in the course of your secret work for a secret group. Soon you will have new things to worry about, something entirely different. Isn't that how it works? You won't have time for me, even if you might have an inclination for me."

"An *inclination* for you?" he repeated, incredulous.

"Cordelia, you don't understand."

She did not want to understand. "I should tell you that I intend to leave London. I'm going to spend the summer in Bristol. My absence from the city should dampen any possible rumors. And I trust that you will never speak of me to remind anyone. Not that you would—you are good at secrets, aren't you?"

"Stop talking about secrets. I'm sick of them. Cordelia, listen to me. There's another way," he protested.

"I don't see how. You already live two lives. Do you have room for yet another?" She walked to the table, looking back at him. "Don't worry. I'll get word to you if Lear is asked about the *Andraste*."

"I will not allow you to disappear on me, Cordelia!"

"You can't prevent it. The best solution is the one I've just proposed—we must end this. Now." She slid the key off the table and walked to the door. "Goodbye, Sebastien." She said his given name tenderly, cherishing her last opportunity to do so.

Before he could reach the door and stop her, Cordelia darted out into the hallway. He'd never run her down when there were others present, so she kept hurrying toward the ballroom, where she would be surrounded by people. She did not dare glance behind her, so she didn't know if he even tried to follow her.

Soon enough, she arrived in the front hall. She asked a footman, "Will you call a coach for me?"

The servant nodded and left through the great front doors, down to the street. Cordelia waited nervously, praying that Sebastien wouldn't find her before the footman returned. Several couples were filtering out of the ballroom, calling for their own carriages or, like Cordelia, for hired cabs.

"This way, ma'am," the footman said, returning. "He

had to park away from the door; it's crowded tonight."

"I can manage," she replied.

"Wait!" he cried suddenly. "He's driving away! I told him to wait!" He shouted in annoyance at a coach rolling slowly down the street.

"Never mind," she said. "There will be another in a moment."

And sure enough, another driver pulled his vehicle directly in front of the steps. "Got a fare?" the driver called out, directing his words to the footman, but looking at Cordelia.

"Yes, yes, the lady is your fare!" The footman ran to the door of the coach and opened it for Cordelia. "Here you are, ma'am. What address?"

"Forty-two Quince Street," she replied.

The footman called the address up to the driver. "Good night, ma'am." He shut the door, and the coach began to roll away from the house. Cordelia sagged against the seat, utterly exhausted.

She didn't know if breaking with Sebastien would truly work. Her heart ached at the thought of not seeing him again. But if she hadn't ended their affair, he would have done it soon enough. It would hurt less this way, she tried to reassure herself.

But what did that leave her? Recent weeks only high-lighted how at odds she was with polite society. If she had any sense, she would withdraw from it entirely. She did not want any of it. *Only Sebastien,* a little voice insisted before she could quash the thought. But that was over.

The coach wound through the streets of London, and Cordelia, lost in her own misery, didn't notice what path it took. But when she inhaled the sharp, salty tang of the Thames, she sat up suddenly. Had the driver gotten lost? They shouldn't be anywhere near the river.

Before she could call out the window to find out what was going on, the coach clattered to a halt so suddenly that she was thrown forward onto the floor of the cab. "Oh, for pity's sake," she hissed. Was it possible the driver was drunk?

As she tried to right herself, the door opened and the driver put a hand in. Rather than help her up, he grabbed her by the shoulder. "Come on," he growled. "Get moving."

"What are you *doing* ?" Cordelia tried to shrug him off, but his grip only tightened. "Where are we?"

"Makes no difference where we are, since you're not staying here long," he said, grinning foully. "You're going aboard."

The coach had pulled up at a small dock, where a sleek schooner was moored. Realizing that he meant to drag her onto the ship, she resisted. The man was far stronger than her, though, and he wrestled her out of the coach and held her tight. She kicked him, hitting his shin, but his hold did not loosen. "Stupid minx," he growled. "Should have brought a rope with me."

He dragged her along. Cordelia opened her mouth to scream, but he sensed her move and clapped a hand over her mouth. Then he called out to the ship, alerting them of their arrival.

Someone was evidently on watch, because two shapes appeared on the gangplank. The sailors were on the dock in a matter of seconds.

"So this is our cargo," one said, laughing. "I like it better than the usual."

The other didn't speak, but grabbed Cordelia from the driver, who warned, "Watch out for her, she'll give you trouble."

"She can try," the sailor replied, glancing at her. "But

we give trouble too."

She quailed at the threat in his tone.

"She's yours," the driver went on. "Where's my cut?"

The sailor produced a small pouch and tossed it to the driver.

The driver opened the bag to be sure, then closed it again and grinned, tucking it into his pocket. "Well, that's that." He turned and walked toward the coach without a care.

The sailors hauled her, still struggling, up the gangplank. On board, her heart sank when she heard a familiar voice.

"Miss Bering! How kind of you to join me." Hayden stood on deck, looking as pleased as a cat with fresh cream.

She glared at him. "You ordered me to be kidnapped?"

Hayden put on a mock frown for a moment. "It looks that way, doesn't it? Why waste time chasing after designs when we could have simply chased you?"

"There is nothing simple about it," she said.

"But it *is* simple. You help us build the *Andraste*, or you don't see your home again." He gestured to the men standing on either side of her. "Take her."

Hands tightened on her arms. She lost sight of Hayden as they moved her below deck. In despair, she realized that she was truly alone. No one knew where she was. Sebastien was the one person who might know how to find her…and she had told him she never wanted to see him again.

SEBASTIEN DIDN'T SLEEP WELL. HE couldn't forget Cordelia's words when she announced that he should no longer see her. Whether or not she was correct about the risk involved, the idea of losing her still made him turn cold. He was sickened at the thought of her shutting herself away in a sleepy seaside town to avoid gossip.

He had to convince Cordelia that she belonged with him, and marrying him wouldn't be the penance she seemed to consider it to be. He thought he had convinced her that some aspects of marriage could be enjoyable indeed. But Cordelia cherished her freedom more than anything else, and he didn't know how to make her believe she'd always be able to do what she wanted. Of course, all that convincing was dependent on her actually listening to him. And she had told him in no uncertain terms that she never intended to speak to him again.

In the morning, he glanced at his reflection in the mirror across his bedroom. The image he saw scarcely looked familiar. He'd been running ragged the last few weeks and it showed, at least to his critical eye. Whatever else was going on with the assignment, he had to settle the issue of Cordelia Bering's status in his life. And that meant swallowing his pride and going to her, despite the fact that she didn't want to see him.

He called for his valet. It didn't take long for him to dress, and soon he was in his two-wheeler, driving toward Quince Street. The morning was a fine one, nearly cloudless and already warm. He allowed himself to hope that, after he'd successfully persuaded her to listen to him, Cordelia might let him drive her to the park. After they became engaged, such an outing would be perfectly acceptable. And he'd love to show her off and devastate the social climbers at the same time.

When he arrived at Cordelia's home, however, all pleasant thoughts were driven from his mind. As soon as he pulled up, Jem appeared to take the reins. From the look in the young man's eyes, it was not the horse he was concerned about. "Morning, my lord," he said shortly. "Stiles was hoping you'd come."

"Stiles?" Sebastien frowned, but hurried up the steps. The door opened before he could knock, and the parlor-maid Ivy bobbed a careless curtsey, too distracted to do more. "If you'll go to the drawing room, my lord, I'll fetch Stiles immediately."

Stiles again. Sebastien couldn't imagine that the man was particularly eager to talk to him, considering their previous encounter. And why did no one mention Cordelia? Was she ill? But if she was not receiving, the maid would have surely said so.

He just stepped into the drawing room when he heard the deliberate footfalls of the stocky butler from behind him. He turned to see Stiles, his normally unshakeable air definitely disturbed this morning.

"My lord," he began, his gravelly voice pitched low, as if he didn't want anyone to overhear him. "It's very good you came."

"What happened? Where is Cordelia?" Sebastien demanded.

Stiles looked stricken. "We don't know."

"What?" he said in a dangerous voice.

"She never returned home last night. Bond waited up as long as she dared. Sometimes the parties go late. But at four in the morning, she roused me. I sent to the night watch to see if there was an accident, but they knew nothing. Jem went round to all the hospitals, just in case, but she's not in hospital either. I think it's the ones, sir. You know…"

Grimly, Sebastien nodded. "At this point, I don't believe in coincidences." He took Stiles by the arm. "Tell the other servants not to worry. There's someone I must see, but I'll return as soon as I can. In the meantime, keep the household running just as usual, and *don't* panic."

"Yes, sir," said Stiles.

Before Sebastien could leave the room, Leona appeared, looking pale and fragile in the bright light. "Stiles?" she asked, stepping into the room. "Did someone come with news—" She saw Sebastien and sighed. "Oh, it's you, my lord." She cast an uncertain glance at Stiles, who interpreted her wordless question.

"I have told him, madam," the butler said.

"Oh." Leona seemed relieved. "My lord, you were at the same ball last night, correct? When did you last see Cordelia?"

He remembered all too vividly his last moments with Cordelia. But he said only, "I saw her in the front hall shortly after midnight. She had just called for a carriage."

"Midnight! That's even earlier than I had thought!" Leona twisted her hands in frustration. "Oh, she could be anywhere! An accident to the carriage, or worse…"

Sebastien was sure it was much worse, but he said nothing.

"Please sit down, madam," Stiles begged his

mistress. She complied, wilting onto a chair. Ivy, who had peeked in, immediately left again to fetch tea. Stiles followed her, leaving the two alone. Leona looked again at Sebastien. "It has been an awful morning," she said candidly.

"It will be a bad day," he warned. "You can't let anyone outside the household know that she is gone. Not until I find her, Mrs Wharton."

"Mr Dunham already knows," Leona said quietly. "He escorted me home last night, and was here when the servants alerted me."

"He's trustworthy," Sebastien said. "He won't spread rumors. But if anyone else asks, you must have a story ready."

She looked up at him, considering. Her eyes gained a certain hard light. "I can tell any visitors that Cordelia has gone to Bristol already. She'd been talking about it, and no one will question it if I say she left town a little early."

"Send a servant or two to that house, in order to answer questions if they come up. No one who writes to her there should expect a quick answer, so a few days of silence won't attract comment."

Leona nodded, then said, "Oh, there is the matter of Mr Lear. I can only hope that the letters arriving for him are not terribly urgent. Cordelia is usually so prompt when she responds to them."

Given his distraction, Sebastien took a moment to register what the woman said. Then he stared at her. "Wait! You know that Cordelia is Lear?"

"Dear boy, I have eyes, do I not? My brother was a brilliant man, but not a rich one. His bequest to Cordelia would never have allowed us to live as comfortably as we do now. My niece has used the trick for years, not just to supplement her income but to distract herself from boredom. I knew she didn't tell me because she feared that I would think her pastime unseemly. But as it happens, I'm quite proud of her ingenuity." Leona paused, tilting her head in consideration. "But how did *you* learn about it?"

He cleared his throat uncomfortably. "We've had reason to have several discussions about her activities."

"Have you? Then you approve of her choices?"

"I don't know that it makes a jot of difference whether or not I approve. But I couldn't imagine her any other way."

Leona sighed. "You said that you will find her. Do you know how?"

"I think so. I promise you I'll do everything in my power." Which, to be honest, was rather a lot, even if he weren't a part of the Zodiac. Thorne was willing to spend thousands of pounds to recover Cordelia, and perhaps more to avenge her. He profoundly hoped it would not come to that.

Leona looked up at him. "That is heartening. I think you understand how much she means to me, to everyone who really knows her."

He stood up. "I do. Wish me luck." As he left, Sebastien turned the situation over in his mind. Whoever was after the plans must have discovered Cordelia knew more about them than she claimed. Taking her was a logical step, if one were ruthless. And if it was Hayden, then ruthlessness would certainly apply. He only hoped that Hayden didn't realize that she herself was the creator.

He went to see Forester first. His friend would understand the gravity of the situation.

"Cordelia…that is, Miss Bering…is missing. I have no proof yet, but I'm sure that she was taken by Hayden," he reported.

"But Hayden already bought the flawed designs," said

Forester. "Why would he want *her*?"

Sebastien inhaled. "Because she designed the *Andraste*."

The look on Forester's face was almost comical. "Designed…how?"

"Meaning she bloody *made* them. She thought up the ship. She learned what metals to use. She drafted the plans to construct the prototype!"

"But what about Lear?"

"There is no Lear. She created him too, as a shield to hide her own inventions. She used the name when she wanted to communicate with others."

"Well, that explains why the gentleman was so hard to find." Forester was watching him carefully, and said, "You look furious."

"I am furious. I should never have let her out of my sight."

"Am I right in thinking that Miss Bering has become a rather important person in your eyes?"

"She's not just a person. She's a vital asset. To the country, that is."

"And to you," Forester pushed.

"Yes." Thorne made a frustrated sound. "But I'm not exaggerating when I say she's vital to the war. We have to find her."

"When you say we…"

"I mean the Zodiac. But also, you and me, going all the way to Napoleon's camp if that's where they stashed her."

"I believe you," Forester said simply. "Shall we go tell Aries what's in the wind?"

Aries was easily found, still holed up in the Zodiac's office. When the two men entered, they found him speaking to a young woman who was recording every word, her hand flying over the notebook in her lap as she wrote in odd looping letters.

Neville stopped talking when he saw them both. "That will do, Miss Chattan. You may transcribe today's work, and send it out to the correct parties tomorrow morning."

"Very well, sir," she said, gathering up her materials into a tidy pile, capping her ink bottle, and stowing the pen. Blue ink stains spotted the fingers of her right hand, and several more blue spots decorated her dress. She did not so much as glance at Thorne or Forester as she left the room.

Thorne cleared his throat. "We've got news. And trouble." He explained the most recent developments in his assignment, including how valuable Cordelia really was, and the fact that she was now missing.

Neville didn't say a word until the end of Sebastien's explanation. Then he stood up slowly, considering. "So the woman herself is what the enemy needs?"

"Yes. We have to get her back."

"Any ideas?"

"Only one. Remember Ensign Hartley's shipyard? He mentioned that there was a large quantity of metal there, which is exactly what is needed to build the *Andraste*. It must be connected to Hayden. Doesn't it make sense to take the designer of the ship to where you intend to build it?"

"Possibly," Neville said, his eyes distant. He was obviously thinking rapidly. "Though they might have other ideas for her."

"Even if she's not there, we might discover something to go on."

"That's true." Neville nodded once. "We need to get you to the shipyard as soon as possible. Hartley knows where it is, so I'll put someone to work on locating him immediately. We'll annex him from his duties and promote him to captain for a little while. With a small, fast ship, he can sail you there himself."

"But he could be anywhere!"

Neville walked quickly to the door. Opening it, he called, "Chattan, are you still here?"

After a moment, the ash-blonde woman appeared in the doorway. "Yes, sir?"

"I need to find a man by the name of Logan Hartley. He's an ensign with the Royal Navy. Sails with the *Providence*. Find out where he is and issue an invitation, would you?"

The woman nodded coolly. "At once, sir."

Neville closed the door again. "Good." He turned back to the spies. "Chattan will find him and send him to you. In the meantime, you gentlemen prepare yourselves for a channel crossing. Trust no one. It will be up to you alone to find the lady in question."

CORDELIA DIDN'T KNOW WHERE THEY were going, only
that they'd been on the water for hours. The crew had
locked her in a tiny cabin, and no amount of yelling or
begging resulted in so much as a reprimand. Her stomach
was tight with hunger.

She still wore her evening dress, the lightweight fabric
and short sleeves unable to compete with the chilly sea air
that permeated the ship. She sat on the edge of the bunk,
huddled in a rough wool blanket that was probably left
over rather than provided for her. Her brain was too numb
to deal with the situation at hand. With every passing
moment she was being taken further from her home, from
her family, and from her lover.

She felt so weak. If someone opened the door that
instant and demanded the designs, she might tell them
everything. What did it matter to her? She wanted only
Sebastien. But at the thought of him, she drew in a steady-
ing breath. He would never give over information. In fact,
he'd begged her to give the information to him so he
could keep it safe. Of course, once he realized that the
Andraste designs also resided in her head, it wasn't just a
matter of keeping the papers safe. But he offered to keep
her safe too.

She'd always believed that she was better off alone,
but she'd never been alone like this before. Suddenly,

refusing Sebastien's offer of protection seemed nothing short of idiotic.

But she didn't want protection from Sebastien Thorne. She wanted something much more. By holding out for that intangible *more*, she allowed another danger in. And now she was paying for it.

As hours passed, she fell asleep despite her intention to stay vigilant. A subtle change in the ship's motion woke her. The constant rolling had ceased, and the sound of water rushing past the hull had quieted. Unfortunately, this cabin had no porthole, so she couldn't peek out and see the surroundings.

After a time, the ship must have dropped anchor. Footsteps preceded the sound of the key in the lock, and Cordelia stood up, tense with anticipation. Hayden appeared in the doorway. He looked her over, and made a mocking bow. "I see you haven't fainted dead away. Good. We're leaving the ship."

He didn't wait for her to obey. He leaned forward to grab her and haul her out of the tiny cabin. "Move."

"Where are we?" she asked.

"You'll see. Come on."

"I can walk," she protested.

"Then do so, Miss Bering." He released her arm, yet remained far too close to her.

On deck, only one sailor was visible, but she doubted that she could escape. Not to mention that she had no idea where to go even if she got free of her captors.

It was morning, but heavy clouds obscured the sun. As her eyes adjusted, she saw that the ship had docked along a river edge, and the pier led to a large, low building right along the shore. From the assorted materials and the skeleton of a structure rising in a dry dock, Cordelia knew what the place was. A shipyard.

Hayden herded her down the gangplank. Cordelia knew better than to struggle. He led her to the main yard, where the half-finished ship stood, with metal plates stacked nearby. The wooden hull was nearly complete, but work on it had stalled, and she knew precisely why. This was Hayden's version of the *Andraste*. He couldn't finish it.

She looked around curiously. "Where is everyone? Who's working on this?"

"They were told not to come today. I didn't want more eyes on you than necessary."

"Are you sure that's the reason? It looks to me as if you don't know what you're doing."

He glared at her. "We're going to finish it. Just as soon as you give us the final elements."

"I can't do that."

"You can," he said. "And the longer you wait, the more it will cost you."

"If you've learned anything about me over the course of your false friendship, you should know that I won't help you. My father wouldn't, and neither will I."

Hayden shook his head. "You keep going on about your father. As if it was his knowledge we need."

"Of course it is," she said, nervousness sparking in her heart.

"And what of his elusive co-conspirator?"

Cordelia closed her eyes, as if to stave off the inevitable. "Meaning?"

He grinned at her. "You are rather charming when you're coy, Miss Bering. I refer to Lear, of course."

"Then why didn't you kidnap him?"

"Because no one can find him," Hayden said. "But I'm not quite the fool I've been pretending to be. I researched all of the society's papers, and corresponded with nearly everyone who has worked with Lear in the past four years. So I know that his work is much closer to the innovations of the *Andraste* than anything your father completed."

"What of it?" she asked.

"I also know that Lear's mail ends up at your home, and the only person who refused to talk to me is also a close personal friend of yours, Mr William Jay. He wouldn't say a word. At least, he wouldn't at first," Hayden added.

His tone made Cordelia shake. "What do you mean?" she demanded. Mr Jay would never have knowingly revealed Cordelia's secret…unless he resented her refusal when he offered marriage.

"How do you think we knew to take you from that party, Miss Bering? It was Mr Jay who told us exactly where you'd be."

"He would never!"

"Not a strong man, that one," Hayden said, as if to himself. Then he went on, "But never mind that. I've brought you here for business. Survey the ship and the shipyard at your leisure."

"My leisure? Or yours?" she asked sharply.

"Well, if you get too leisurely, I will encourage you to hurry along. Tell me what materials or items this yard lacks in order to complete the ship."

"You didn't listen to me before. I'll *never* help you," she said. She didn't bother to hide her disgust.

Hayden put a hand on her arm and moved so he was standing in front of her. "Miss Bering, I really do admire your devotion and uprightness and all that." It was the first time he ever sounded sincere, and it troubled her. "But you would be smarter to forget all that for a little while. If you tell me what I need to know, I will send you back home immediately. In that little ship right there. You'll reboard, be treated well, and you'll sail home on the next tide. I promise."

"Your promise is worth precisely nothing," she said. "The last time you promised me something, you had a knife to my throat."

"I don't actually like killing women," said Hayden, more urgently. "But my employer has no such compunction. Trust me, you don't want to meet him."

She believed him. Who could scare a man like Hayden? He didn't seem to have a conscience, yet he was warning her about this other man. But then, she thought, it could just be another ploy. Cordelia looked away. "I will not help my enemy."

He sighed. "Well, I guessed you'd say that. So off we go." His old expression returned. Rather than spend more effort enticing her into compliance, he forced her toward a carriage that had been pulled up near the road on the other side of the building. The vehicle was old and musty-smelling, and the windows were all covered with heavy leather flaps. She did not want to get in. But when she struggled, he bound her hands and gagged her.

In short order, Hayden and Cordelia were riding down a bumpy road toward an unknown place. She tried to remain clam, but every passing mile brought her closer to the ugly truth of her likely destiny. She wouldn't find any friends on the way, and once she got to the final destination, she might never leave it again.

"Just think," Hayden was saying. "I was a few days away from proposing to you when this house of cards began to collapse. Just think if I had, and you said yes. Everything would have been so much simpler."

Cordelia was glad the gag prevented her from answering. Her response would not have been worthy of a lady.

THORNE'S MOOD TURNED BLACKER AS time passed and
no one could discover anything about Cordelia's whereabouts. No one had seen her or Hayden anywhere in London. There was no note, no demand, no communication at
all.

He snapped at everyone, ignored all the niceties of
social discourse, and spent his sleepless nights cursing his
mistakes. He was used to hiding his thoughts, but he'd
never had to endure something like this; guessing whether
Cordelia was even still alive was torture. Afraid he'd lose
his composure completely, he hid in his St James residence as much as possible. But that brought torture too,
because everywhere he looked—the desk, the couch, the
bed—he remembered Cordelia there. He remembered
how gorgeous she'd looked when she'd come undone in
his arms. When she told him exactly what she wanted,
and when she fell asleep next to him, her body tangled
with his, her head on his chest, a smile on her lips.

She'd taken his whole heart with her when she left
him the last time. And if she was lost to him, he'd do
something terrible. Because he was the heartless one now.

Unable to live with the ghost of her laughter and the
emptiness of the rooms, he went home. Unfortunately, the
townhouse of the Thorne family was filled with laughter

and feminine chatter, which drove Sebastien nearly mad as he waited—simply waited—for news from the Zodiac. His hands were tied. He could do nothing but hope that Hartley could be located. Only then could he advance. Hartley's fortuitous sighting of the shipyard might be the only thing that would lead them to Cordelia.

His family, of course, would not be put off forever. Adele was the first to brave his mood. It was afternoon, three days after Cordelia had vanished. He sat in his study, doing nothing but staring at a wall.

"I suppose you will not tell me what is going on," his sister said, entering on silent slippered feet. With worry on her young face, she came closer. "It's not about Lady Mary, is it? Mama may have been rather overbearing on that issue. She wouldn't be a good match for you. I thought her a bit dull, really."

"Lady Mary?" Sebastien asked distractedly. "No."

"Then what is it?" Adele asked. "Are we penniless again? Do I need to marry some tradesman for wealth? I don't mind if it comes to that, as long as he's not too ugly. Or I can become a governess."

He frowned at her. "You'll do no such thing. Our finances are more robust than they have been in a decade."

"Well, that's a relief. I'd make a miserable governess. So you're not gambling again?"

"I haven't gambled in years. I got some bad news a few days ago. That's all."

"Extremely bad news, I should guess."

"I'm waiting for more details," he explained. "I'll be insufferable until I hear something. I'm sorry."

"I think it's dreadful to wait alone." Adele took his arm. "Will you not come and sit with me and Mama? There are no guests at the moment. It's quite safe."

He allowed his sister to lead him out of the room, even

as he protested, "I'm not fit for human company."

"We're not company. We're family."

In the drawing room, his mother sat on a long couch, embroidery on her lap. She put it aside when he entered.

"Dear boy, I thought you were going to brood forever."

"I'm not brooding."

"Of course you are, dear. Don't contradict an elder."

"Yes, Mother."

"That's better." She smiled. "Shall I ring for tea?" She did so without waiting for an answer.

Sebastien sat down opposite her, apologizing for his mood.

She accepted the apology graciously. "I may have put a bit too much on your mind."

"Just stop hurling potential wives in my path," he begged.

"Lady Mary was seen with the Viscount Grenville yesterday in Rotten Row," his mother noted.

"I wish them joy," he said, indifferent to the news.

She noted his disinterest and tried another tack. "And when did you last see Miss Bering? After our party?"

"Yes," he said shortly. He saw her every time he closed his eyes.

"She is a very unusual woman, I must say."

"I liked her," Adele interjected. "She's a good deal cleverer than Lady Mary."

Sebastien shot his little sister a grateful look, then turned back to his mother. "Regardless if you found her to be unusual, the choice isn't yours to make."

"So you have made a choice?" she asked, her voice sharpening with interest.

He'd never said his intention out loud, but maybe doing so would make it more likely to happen. "I intend to make Cordelia Bering my wife. No matter what I have to do."

Adele, blissfully ignorant of the depths of the matter, merely raised one eyebrow. "You needn't sound so militant about it. Why should you expect the lady to refuse you?"

"Oh, she is famous for her refusals," her mother said. "She was considered touched in the head when she turned down that foreign prince three years ago!"

"Perhaps she didn't love the prince," Adele said with a knowing look.

"Love! She couldn't have made a better match than that."

"Mama," Adele said sharply. "Sebastien is sitting right in front of you!"

"Oh, I didn't mean…" his mother said, suddenly flustered.

But Sebastien only smiled wryly at his mother. "Your support is overwhelming, truly."

"She'd be mad to turn you down, dearest," his mother said. "She'll vault upward socially, and of course you're rather a good man, which is never guaranteed."

Before his family could pester him further about his potential marriage plans, the maid came in with a tray bearing one card. "An Ensign Hartley to see you, sir. He said it was urgent."

Hartley! At last. Sebastien exhaled in relief, then glanced at his curious family. "This isn't a social call. He's connected to the matter I'm dealing with. I'll see him alone in my study."

Adele asked, "You're not keeping an eligible bachelor away from me, are you?"

"This doesn't concern you, Adele. Try to imagine such a concept for a moment."

"I say, Sebastien!" she said, her eyes widening in dramatic offense.

Their mother intervened. "Hush, Adele. I know you're teasing, but your brother is quite right. You must remember that a lady never solicits acquaintance with a man, particularly one she has no connection to! It is most improper."

"Listen to your mama," he said, standing up. Avoiding any more discussion of propriety seemed prudent, considering his own recent behavior.

Thorne hurried to meet the tanned young man who had shown up at the door. He wore civilian clothes this time, but still with the bearing of an officer. Thorne extended a hand. "Hartley. You can't imagine how grateful I am to see you."

"Sir," Hartley responded, his young face serious. "I was told to present myself at this address."

"Follow me, please." Thorne waited for the maid to take Hartley's things, then led him down the hall to his private study. Closing the door, he said, "You can speak freely here. Did they tell you anything about what happened?"

"No, sir. I was merely contacted and told my presence was required for a matter of the gravest urgency. Am I correct in thinking it involves the shipyard you were so interested in?"

"I must go there," Sebastien confided. "Something of very great value has been taken. I suspect that it may be at that shipyard…or that I may find a clue there."

"You intend to go alone?"

"I will be joined by one other man. You know the way. Can you get us there with no one knowing?"

"I can bloody well try." He added, "I don't know who you work for, but whoever it is, they've got clout. I was given leave for as long as you say it's necessary."

Thorne asked, "Can you get access to a ship?"

The young man smiled mysteriously. "Done and done. My own private vessel, with a small and trustworthy crew. No one from the navy will need to be contacted, and no one on board will breathe a word. I can take you and your friend across the channel this evening."

"Thank God," Thorne said. "I'll tell you more along the way."

"Tell me only what I need to know, sir," Hartley warned. "I'm content to be a ferryman."

"Then let's find my friend and we'll be off." Thorne stood up.

"No sense in rushing, if I may say. Tide won't be out until nearly nine. And I wouldn't want to sail much earlier…this sounds like a moonlight mission."

Sebastien grated at the delay, but admitted that there was little he could do to speed up the tides.

At eight o'clock that evening, Thorne met Forester at the harbor. Both men were dressed for business in nondescript outfits and worn greatcoats. Forester looked particularly scruffy. No one would guess the tall, hulking man was a peer of the realm.

In the deepening twilight, the two agents found the small vessel they sought: the *Mistral*. Thorne didn't know much about ships, but he could tell this one had been designed for both speed and stealth.

As they approached the ship, a voice on board called out an alert, and Hartley appeared at the rail.

"Come aboard!" he called, his tone just loud enough to reach them.

They boarded and heard Hartley conversing with a crewmember. The sailor nodded in comprehension, saluted, and left, giving only a cursory look at the new passengers.

Hartley turned to them. "Welcome aboard the *Mistral*."

"Riding rather low in the water, isn't she?" Forester asked.

Hartley gave him a sharp look. "Aye, there's a full load of cargo in the hold."

"What kind of cargo?"

A ghost of a smile crossed Hartley's face. "'Them that asks no questions isn't told a lie.' I'm an ensign in the Royal Navy, but I'm captain of the *Mistral*. And as captain, you've got my permission to not think about this ship's primary purpose."

"A purpose the Royal Navy wouldn't approve of, I suspect," Forester muttered.

Hartley's smile took on a devilish air. "Maybe not, but if you want a discreet ship, the *Mistral* will answer. There's a small cabin aft. You can put your bags there."

Forester followed Thorne to the empty cabin. Four bunks, two on each side, occupied most of the space. Forester tossed his leather bag onto one of the lower ones. "Didn't know the navy was hiring smugglers."

"You think most sailors are saints?" Thorne asked.

"No, but he's an officer!"

"He's helping the Zodiac. That's all I need to know."

Forester grunted. "Let's go on deck. I like to get sick in the fresh sea breeze," he added sarcastically. (Forester wasn't the best sailor.)

On deck, Hartley informed them they would sail shortly. His demeanor had completely changed from how he'd acted on land. The diffident young ensign was gone; this was a man used to command. "It looks clear, but if weather—or something else—comes up, I may need to act fast. You'll follow what orders you're given."

"Aye, Captain," Thorne replied.

As it happened, the crossing was smooth. Once the *Mistral* cleared the Thames, Hartley barked out an order. The small crew immediately took down the main sail, rolling it neatly. Thorne was puzzled, until he saw that there was a second sail attached to the boom, this one dyed dark blue. He and Forester watched as the shadowy sail was hoisted and caught the wind, billowing out like a storm cloud. The smaller sails had similar replacements. In the nighttime, the dark sails rendered the ship all but invisible to anyone who wasn't practically alongside it.

"I can barely tell the sail from the sky," Forester said, gazing up at the top of the mast. "That's a brilliant idea."

Hartley said, "Isn't it? Thought of it myself. The *Mistral* is a shy and modest lady, you know, and doesn't like to be seen."

"You're protective of this ship."

"I helped build her," Hartley said proudly. "She'd based on the Bermuda sloop I grew up around…with a few improvements."

Thorne nodded, then said, "If this all ends well, there's someone I want you to meet. We could build a whole new navy with you two working at it."

Hartley smiled. "Any time. Always glad to talk to a man of sense when it comes to making sailing easier."

The *Mistral* slipped through the dark waters of the channel, neatly avoiding the faint signs of other ships appearing in their path. Hartley explained, "It takes a bit longer to do it this way, but I'd rather be safe than triumphant, if you take my meaning. Coming back, the *Mistral* can outrun nearly any ship of the line, given a head start."

"She'll be faster on the way back to England?" Thorne asked, thinking of how quickly he could get Cordelia back home.

Hartley nodded. "Lighter, and therefore faster."

"Because you sell your unnamed cargo."

"Do you really want to know what I do, sir?"

"In for a penny…"

Hartley nodded. "Fair enough. My family's as English as yours, my lord, but I grew up in Bermuda. It was an interesting childhood. My mother's side of the family hasn't always had the smoothest relationship with the law, you see. I learned the tides and the coastlines of dozens of islands by the age of ten, as well as a fair bit of the family trade."

"You're a smuggler."

Hartley gave a shrug. "Sometimes. First time I met you, I thought that's what you were going to harass me about! But we've always been loyal to the Crown. I joined the Royal Navy to serve as best I can. Nowadays, sometimes I carry letters…sometimes people. The fact that the *Mistral* also does 'honest' smuggling hides those special shipments."

"I think I know enough," Thorne said. "I trust that we all have secrets to keep."

Before dawn, the ship's progress slowed, her path now shadowing the foreign shoreline, barely visible in the wavering starlight.

"Do you know where we are?" Thorne asked Hartley, who was at the helm.

"Of course."

"And you know where the river is?"

"I do. Isn't that why you wanted me to bring you across?"

"I just don't understand how you can see in the dark."

Hartley smiled. "To me, it isn't dark. I'm used to sailing at night."

"I expect you are," Thorne said drily.

The *Mistral* eventually sailed into the mouth of a small river. Hartley spoke again, his voice pitched low. "She's not a large vessel, but I don't know how deep the bottom of this river is with the current tide. I'll get you as close as I can."

"Can you wait once we're off the ship?"

"How long will your errand take?"

"If what we're looking for is there, much less than an hour."

"I can wait an hour. Longer than that…" Hartley was plainly curious now. "What if the thing you're looking for isn't there?"

"Then we'll have to scour the place for a hint as to where it might be. Can I send a signal to let you know not to wait?"

"Yes, I can arrange that."

It was still dark when the *Mistral* came abreast of a crude pier. Hartley ordered the ship moored. "We're here. Last time, there was one man who watched the place at night. You have to assume he's there now. You'd better find him before he can tell anyone that a ship docked here."

The two agents wasted no time. They jumped the rail to the pier, and entered the seemingly deserted shipyard.

Forester muttered, "They're not building much right now. Did you see that ship hull? Like a skeleton."

"She must not have told them what they need to know yet," Thorne replied. "That's good. But we have to find out where she is. Start searching for Miss Bering…or anyone who might be on watch."

It didn't take them long to find the man Hartley had noticed before. He didn't look like a guard, but rather a clerk who also kept an eye on the premises overnight. He must have had a long, boring night, because he'd nodded off in a chair by a desk.

Thorne wasn't too gentle waking him up.

The man's eyes flew open when he found himself upright and in the grip of a coldly angry stranger.

"Where is she?" he asked in French.

"Who?" the other man gasped out.

Thorne tightened his grip. "You know who I mean. The woman with Hayden. Where is she?"

"Are you a husband? Brother?" The man stopped caring when Thorne moved one hand to his throat. "Wait!" he begged in French. "They didn't stay here. They took her away!"

"Where to?" Thorne asked, loosening his grip.

"Calais, I think," the man said quickly. "Hayden has a house there. It's where he meets Ar—" He stopped.

"Meets who?"

The man's voice dropped. "Arceneau." He looked sick as he said the name.

"Who's that?" Forester asked, also in French.

"The one who pays for everything."

Thorne looked hard at the man. "Including Hayden's house in Calais?"

The man nodded. "But I don't know where it is. I only know who they pay for it."

"The landlord, you mean?"

The clerk wanted to be helpful. He tapped a book nearby. "Always a payment to M. Belrande, Rue de Parnasse, Calais, for each quarter's rent. I keep the books."

"I'm so glad you do," Thorne muttered in English. He nodded to his friend.

Ready for the silent order, Forester delivered a short, quick hit that ensured the man would snooze for a while.

"He's out," the tall man said. "But we haven't got long

until the morning work crew comes."

Fortuitously, Thorne found a bottle of brandy tucked in a drawer. He applied a liberal dash of alcohol to the unconscious man's clothes, then left the mostly empty bottle conveniently close to hand. "That might confuse the issue slightly."

"They'll be less inclined to believe what he says anyway. Though he might not say anything—he'll only get in trouble if he does."

Thorne and Forester returned to the ship.

On board, Hartley saw Thorne's expression. "You didn't find it," the young man noted.

"No, but we know where we go next. Calais."

Hartley nodded. "I'll take you there. It's not far."

Later that same day, the *Mistral* reached the Calais harbor.

"How long will it take for you to distribute your cargo?" Thorne asked Hartley.

"Three days at most. I usually finish my run in Calais, so I'll come back by Thursday."

"We'll find you then," Sebastien said.

Hartley nodded. "If you can't come yourselves for any reason, or if you need me to sail elsewhere, send a messenger to the Calais harbor master. It's safe to ask for the *Mistral*...I've greased a few palms in this town."

"If you hear nothing by Thursday night, return to England and report what you know to a Captain Julian Neville. He'll know what to do next."

Thorne retrieved their bags and disembarked again, watching just long enough to see Hartley turn the ship about. He hoped he would see it again. But for now, he had work to do. Cordelia needed him.

Thorne and Forester entered the city itself. "Let's get that address and get Cordelia."

"We'll find her," Forester said encouragingly.

Thorne was not so sanguine. "The man said it was the landlord's address, not Hayden's."

Forester grinned. "And how long do you think the landlord will hold out that information against the two of us?"

CORDELIA SAT BACK ON THE narrow bed, despairing. Her room was comfortable, with soft bedclothes, high-quality furniture, and clean floors. They had given her new clothes too. She now wore a comfortable though rather old-fashioned dressing gown in the continental style. Her own evening gown was gone, which was no great loss, considering the rips and stains it suffered during her kidnapping.

Even the food was good. But it was still a prison. She wasn't sure how long she'd been here, but she made a small mark on her room's little table with her fork whenever the sun slipped through the tiny window for a few hours. Four days, she thought. No one touched her, but she feared the main jailer more than she feared Hayden.

The jailer knew better than to harm her physically, but the way he looked at her made her blood run cold. When the door to her room was open, she could see a larger room just beyond, and multiple men were in it at all times. They usually kept her door open so they could keep an eye on her, though they never made much of a fuss if she asked for it to be closed when she needed privacy. But they locked her in then, and she didn't like it. Either way, she could hear them talking in French, either in conversation or sometimes over a card game.

Cordelia's French was sadly lacking, but she strained her ears anyway, hoping to put some meaning into their talk. It helped that they clearly thought she knew no French at all. They never lowered their voices, or spoke out of her hearing.

"Avez vous soif?" She heard a voice near the door. She looked over. A very young man stood there, looking in at her. "Are you thirsty?" he asked again in English, his accent thick.

"Yes," Cordelia answered.

"Water." The boy thrust a bottle at her. "Careful," he added softly. "Be sharp if the bottle broke."

It took her a moment to decipher his words. Then Cordelia took the bottle. She drank half of it down before she spoke again, finding the water surprisingly sweet and cool. "Thank you."

The boy did not reply, but continued to survey her. Cordelia sensed nothing untoward in his inspection, only intense interest. She hadn't seen this boy before. He was thin, tall for his age—if he was about fifteen as he seemed. He had a rather delicately featured face, framed by messy and unkempt hair. He looked almost elfin.

"Jacques! What are you doing, boy?" the jailer yelled in French.

The lad turned around and snapped something.

The man bickered back, a comment Jacques had no trouble responding to in kind. He seemed to have no fear of the jailer. Cordelia tried to follow the argument as best she could.

The lad, even if he wasn't on her side, had been decent. Cordelia nursed the rest of the water. The glass felt cool in her hand. Then Cordelia realized what she held.

Glass. No one else had given her glass, because glass could be a weapon. If she had to, she could break the bottle and have something sharp to defend herself with. And the boy had known what he was doing, though he'd spoken obliquely.

Cordelia carefully tucked the bottle away in the corner of her room, hidden by the edge of the bed. She felt infinitesimally better. She wondered what Sebastien would do in this situation. Would he have already worked out an escape plan? Would he fight his way out?

Despite everything, she prayed he was looking for her. She was certain he wouldn't stop until he found her. He must come soon.

* * * *

The landlord's address proved to be easy to find. The two Zodiac spies discussed how best to approach him. Forester was all for simple bullying. His athletic frame and wide shoulders naturally encouraged cooperation from most people, and he often relied on sheer size to intimidate.

Thorne feared making a scene. "I don't want him to alert anyone that we're looking. Let's try something more subtle."

"Such as?"

"Calais is a market town. We'll say we're here to do business with Arceneau and Hayden. The landlord won't want to get in the way of business."

"But we forgot the address?"

"Something like that."

They entered the landlord's shop, and Thorne fell easily into a persona he'd played before in his work with the Zodiac: the unscrupulous trader who didn't let national pride get in the way of profit. He guessed it would fit right in with Hayden's approach.

It worked with the landlord too. Calais had a long history of English traders in the city, and the man didn't blink when Thorne asked if a man named Hayden or Arceneau was a tenant. Thorne deliberately kept his story vague, only hinting at the need to contact Hayden quickly. With a minimal amount of bribery, the landlord offered up the location of the house.

When they left, Thorne was ready to do battle.

"Wait, you're not thinking clearly," Forester warned him. "We might know where she is, but we still need a plan to get her out safely."

Thorne growled, "I hate waiting. If they've hurt her, I swear…"

"Calm down, man." Forester steadied him. "If the lady is in anything less than pristine condition when we find her, I'll help you dissect the offenders myself. What are friends for, after all?"

The Zodiac spies found the house on Rue Auber with little difficulty—it was stone, with a blue painted door. It was in a rather modest neighborhood in the quarter of the city west of the Place d'Armes, the square that held the main market.

Across the street from the building in question, Thorne saw a house that advertised a room to let. He went in and learned it was the front garret on the top floor. Secretly elated, he nevertheless haggled fiercely with the owner of the house to rent it, starting immediately.

The men took turns watching the street from the grimy window, trying to decide the best way in. The house with the blue door was a popular one. Men came and went regularly. Soon they knew the face of each man who passed through the door. Thorne was more and more convinced that the house was indeed where Cordelia was being kept.

"All those men, though," Forester grunted. "They must always have two or more guards watching her, undoubtably armed. We won't be able to stroll in and simply overpower them."

"Perhaps we can trick them into leaving all at once?"

"Short of setting the house on fire, which I wouldn't risk, I doubt they'll all go. They know they've got something valuable."

The pair continued to watch. One of the most active residents of the house was a skinny young man who appeared to be some sort of errand boy. He brought in food, he brought in coal. He carried out letters and came back bearing newspapers and yet more food.

"Watch out," Forester cautioned at one point. "Don't lean too close to the glass. They might see you."

"No one will look up here."

"The boy might. He's got eyes," Forester muttered. At that moment, the lad in question paused on the doorstep, facing their hiding place across the street. The boy raised his head, adjusting his cap. Thorne had the sudden, uncomfortable notion that the boy was tipping his cap in recognition. But then he turned and headed up the street, whistling a jaunty tune.

Forester must have got the same impression, because he said, "He's gone. I don't like that boy. He's too sharp."

"What makes you say that?"

"Just *look* at him."

Sebastien looked, but saw the same thing as before: the now-retreating figure of a narrow-framed, dark-haired boy. His face did have a certain sharpness about it, with a long, narrow nose and dark eyes. But Thorne didn't see anything special there. "What am I missing?"

"I don't know. I just don't like him. He's altogether too…cheerful." His friend grimaced, clearly groping for another word but not finding it.

"I'll take your word for it." Thorne sat back, trying to relax. He *had* to think of a way to get Cordelia safely out of that house.

"We could sneak in the back way? Or even over the roof," Forester suggested, though without enthusiasm.

Thorne shook his head. "They'll see us coming. What we need is leverage."

"How so?"

"Hayden. When he shows up, we'll follow. But we'll grab *him*, and then bargain for Cordelia."

"Will that work?"

"Do you have a better idea?"

"Sadly, no."

"Then we wait for Hayden."

IT WAS LATE AT NIGHT. The room had been warm enough during the day, but a chill had set in with the evening. The stove in the front room didn't put out enough heat to reach Cordelia. She wrapped herself up tightly in a blanket and lay down on the bed, facing the door.

She didn't know if she could sleep, but eventually she fell to dozing, her body worn out from days of constant anxiety. She dreamed Sebastien was with her, beside her. She dreamed that he was holding her, and her coldness seemed to melt away. Cordelia clung to him in her dream, not out of passion, but from pure joy at being able to touch him and be with him. Why had she ever told him that they shouldn't be together?

"Mademoiselle?" a low voice came to her.

She opened her eyes, but it was still dark. "Who's there?" she whispered.

The voice returned, "Jacques."

"What is it? What's happening?" Cordelia sat up, pulling the blanket with her. She got up off the bed and hurried to the door, which opened a crack.

"Be calm for now." Jacques stood on the other side, his eyes large in the dimness. Only one lantern on the far wall was lit. He looked over his shoulder, then continued, striving to keep his English clear. "But you will have a visitor soon. Arceneau. Our real employer."

"What will he do?"

"He wants you to tell him about the ship. Why it's broken."

"How do you know this?"

Jacques waved an impatient hand. He muttered something in French and then went on. "Listen. Don't be noble. Don't play dumb—he knows you understand this work."

"Why are you telling me this?"

"Never mind. He's going to make you an offer. Give him a good plan for the *Andraste*, and he'll send you home. He'll even offer money."

"I wouldn't take it," Cordelia snapped.

"So you say now." Jaques looked at her in a pitying way. "If you want to get out of here alive, you do as I say. Refuse Arceneau's offer at first, but not too heartily. Act scared. Give in after a little while. Make him think that he's won."

"He will have won."

"Not quite. Appear to cooperate, but do whatever you can think of to keep him from using the designs right away. Be *slow*."

"Stall him, you mean? For how long? I can't get out of here." Cordelia curled her hands around the handle of the door, as if willing it to dissolve. "Can't you help me escape?"

Jacques raised an eyebrow. "I'm helping you now, cherie."

"But what can I do once Arceneau gets here?"

"Don't lose hope," Jacques whispered. "I probably won't see you again—I can't be here when Arceneau arrives. But I think you have angels coming for you."

"Why are you helping me? I'm not on your side."

The young man looked at her steadily. "I don't like

Arceneau. But I do like you," Jacques whispered. Without warning, he leaned forward and laid a swift kiss on Cordelia's lips. She was startled, but not scared. Jacques pulled away and gave her a sudden, wild grin. "Bon chance." And then he was gone.

* * * *

The two Zodiac spies slept in fits, trading watches. It was late at night when Thorne cautiously approached the window, alerted by a sound in the street. They had not dared to light a lamp or candle, lest someone see their position, so his eyes were already adjusted to the darkness.

After several minutes, he sucked in a breath. "Hayden's coming! And he's not alone."

The man they were waiting for was walking alongside another man, whose hair was completely white under his hat. The two reached the house with the blue door and were admitted instantly.

Forester made a satisfied noise. "Well, our bird is in his nest. Odd companion he's got. Did you notice his hair? Completely white. Think it's a wig?"

"We can find out when I scalp him." Thorne clenched one hand into a fist. He had never felt any sort of battle lust during his time in the army, but he felt it now. Here was the man who was keeping the one person Thorne wanted. And he was finally within reach.

* * * *

The hours passed with agonizing slowness. Cordelia's stomach was tied up in knots. She could barely eat any of the food they gave her. Jacques hinted at angels, but Cordelia hadn't seen any, and miracles felt impossible.

She kept thinking a storm was about to break in the atmosphere above them. And perhaps it was. If she ever got out of this place, nothing would be the same for her.

Having been forewarned by the now-vanished Jacques, Cordelia was ready when an unknown gentleman entered her room after her supper dishes had been taken away.

"Mademoiselle Bering?" the gentleman asked in cultured tones. He was slender, with fine clothes that nevertheless looked slightly garish. His hair was startlingly white, considering that he was not old.

"You have the advantage of me." She stood up quickly, divining that this man craved respect. She even managed a little curtsey.

"Ah, Mademoiselle Bering, it is you who has the advantage. Call me Monsieur Arceneau, if you please. Unlock this door, man. Let the lady out."

The jailer rushed to do the man's bidding, but Cordelia was under no illusions. She was still a prisoner.

"Mademoiselle, if you will come with me?" He offered his arm to her.

Grimly accepting that her captivity would last a little longer, Cordelia allowed him to escort her to a room on the top floor. It contained a small fireplace that blazed merrily. The walls had been painted not too long ago, and the ornate furniture looked like it might have once sat in Versailles. The overall effect was rather jarring. She suspected Arceneau wanted to impress her. But the only thing in the room that she truly noticed was the large table covered with schematics and papers.

Arceneau said, "Your advantage, I hope, is clear now. All I wish is for you to aid me in deciphering these trifles."

Cordelia walked slowly toward the table. "What

makes you think I can do any such thing?"

His eyes narrowed. "Do not play innocent. Your creation of Mr Lear was very clever. You have a gift for subterfuge, Mademoiselle Bering. But you lacked the means to make your trick perfect. I studied the designs made by your father and Lear. I saw certain similarities in the style. So I knew someone was lying. When Lear proved an illusion, I realized the glorious truth. The daughter was the source! It was very well done, Mademoiselle Bering. Who would think of a woman?"

"No one," she said, a bit sourly.

"Until me!" he said, pleased with himself. "So you have nothing more to hide. You will find that I know all your secrets. But I am not your enemy. All I ask is that you explain the trick of these designs. You see, we both know they are wrong."

Cordelia asked, "Why should I? It would be a betrayal."

"To whom? Your father? He has passed on, and would surely wish you to live anyway."

"Not to my father. To my country."

"Your country!" He laughed, genuinely amused. "Your country does not care about you, Mademoiselle Bering. If they knew what I know, they would have acted to steal your work for themselves. Perhaps they have already tried."

Yes, and their efforts brought her Sebastien, who proceeded to upend her life and ravage her heart. If only he were here. She said, "I have no reason to help you, in any case."

"You have several reasons, Mademoiselle Bering." He examined her with an appraising eye.

She looked away. "I can't think of any. Let me go. I will not help you." She was following the plan given to her by the French lad. She would stand strong—but not too strong—at first.

"I am surprised at you, Mademoiselle Bering. So steadfast, even though no one is on your side." He walked closer. "Consider this, then. If you continue to refuse to aid me, your honor will be destroyed."

She hated the way he smiled at her. She lifted her chin, and said, "I am willing to accept that shame. If you think I am so fragile—"

He held up an aristocratic hand, stopping her. "And I will have one of your servants killed."

"What?" Cordelia cried, her shock unexaggerated.

"Oh, so you *do* care about something more than yourself."

"You would not! They've done nothing to you!"

"They work for someone determined to stand in my way." Arceneau regarded Cordelia, his eyes flat. "Do I seem like a person who would let the death of a housemaid trouble my sleep?"

He did not. This was what Jacques warned her about. She could refuse Arceneau for a little while, but giving in was inevitable. But she could do her best to convince him that she had given up hope of rescue. "Please…" she said, her voice shaking all too realistically. "They're innocent. Leave them be, and I promise…"

"Promise what, mon amie?"

"I'll draft you a new version of the *Andraste*. Complete and correct. You have my word."

He was all smiles again. "You warm my heart, Mademoiselle Bering. Do this for me, and you will be rewarded. I will see that your honor is untouched and that your finances are replenished."

"And my household kept safe. Just don't hurt anyone," she pleaded.

"Their safety is in your hands, Mademoiselle Bering."

She didn't have to pretend to look defeated, but she also felt a little triumph deep inside. He thought she was completely in his power. "I don't have much choice, do I?"

"No," he said, almost kindly.

Remembering more of Jacques's advice, Cordelia moved slowly to the table, thinking of the glass bottle she had left behind in the cell. How she wished for some kind of weapon! Then she had an idea.

"Could you spare me a glass of wine?" she asked. "I feel a bit parched, and I haven't been eating well this week, for some reason."

He laughed at that, and ordered the man standing outside the door to bring some food and drink.

She sat down at the table, aware the man was surveying her intently from behind. She tried to ignore him, and bent to study the drawings. In spite of herself, she became instantly absorbed. Someone had tried to make sense of the puzzle Cordelia left in the schematics. Comments and alternative drawings littered the pages.

Cordelia jumped at the touch of Arceneau's hand on her shoulder, but he merely handed her a glass of ruby-red wine. Still, his touch lingered longer than was proper. "Thank you," she said frostily.

He only smiled at that. "You can do this, yes?"

"Yes. But I need fresh paper. And space. And a little time. These aren't simple drawings."

"Certainly. Take as long as you need. I shall be delighted to remain at your side." Cordelia glanced up, and saw the glint in his eyes as he appraised her. His gaze hovered at her chest, and she resisted the urge to shrink back.

With an effort, she dragged her attention back to the

papers. She called Sebastien's name silently, sending out a message from her heart, willing him to sense where she was. To cover her frustration, she took a sip of her drink.

"You like the wine?" Arceneau asked, interrupting her thoughts.

"It's very good," she allowed.

"If you have a taste for such things, Mademoiselle, you might consider working for me permanently. I promise you that it has its rewards."

"I doubt I should like the work you offer," said Cordelia.

His voice remained smooth. "What do you think I offer you? You have skills, but as a woman, you have little option to pursue your talents. I do not value women cheaply, I assure you. Your contributions should be as dear to me as that of any man."

"And what is your ultimate aim for those contributions, sir? I have no wish to help kill men more efficiently, and from everything I've learned, your interest is war."

"Not at all!" Arceneau smiled, his teeth flashing in the light. "My interest is money. You think I work for France, for the Emperor? Why should I, when the government may change next month, next year? No, I work for myself. I will sell to the highest bidder—or better still, to anyone who meets my price. Then they are all equal, eh? Let the nations of Europe slaughter their men on the battlefield in glorious combat! I do not kill. I am merely a businessman."

Cordelia shook her head. "Forgive me if I do not share your interest."

"The interest in money? Perhaps not. But we may share another interest." He reached out to touch her cheek, ran his finger along her jawline.

She shivered in revulsion. "I thought your interest in

me was my ability to re-create this design. I can do it, but only if you let me alone."

Arceneau dropped his hand. "As you wish."

The man relented when she told him to…this time. She doubted he would do so again. How much longer did she have left?

"Oh, look! Miss Bering has finally seen reason!" The voice belonged to Hayden, who'd just walked into the room.

She hadn't seen him since he brought her to the house on the first day. She thought that he had returned to England.

"Has our lovely lady been hard at work?" he asked.

"She has." Arceneau surveyed the new schematic she had begun to draft. "These plans are correct, mon amie?"

"Yes." She prayed her voice held steady.

"For your sake, I hope so," he said. "I want to trust you, of course, but you've proven to be quite subtle before. I'll let you go when the prototype is successfully built."

She was horrified at the implication. "That would keep me a prisoner for months! You promised me you'd release me."

By the fire, Hayden laughed at her naiveté.

Arceneau only smiled. "Too bad you did not consider the costs before attempting to thwart me. I always win, Mademoiselle Bering." He paused. "But if you are telling the truth, and these plans do work, I will see that you can begin a new life under my protection."

"Forgive me if I have extreme doubts about your protection," she spat out.

Arceneau lost his smile. "Be careful, cherie. Who else is looking out for you now?"

Sebastien. Her heart called out to him.

Arceneau turned his head suddenly. "Did you hear that?" he asked.

Hayden frowned. "Hear what?"

The white-haired man moved toward the door. "Some sound…I will look. You stay here and watch Mademoiselle Bering."

Arceneau shut the door behind him. But he didn't lock it, and she ached to run and yank it open.

Hayden saw her gaze, and guessed her thoughts. "Don't try it."

"Try what?"

"You wouldn't even get to the stairs. Besides, I would never let a thing as beautiful as you get away." He snaked out an arm and drew her tight to him. "I admit, you get more appealing each time I see you. I am pleased you fell into my lap."

"Fell into your lap? You kidnapped me!"

"It's all in the phrasing." He shrugged. "I won't hurt you, beautiful. Not unless you want me to," he said, grinning foully.

Cordelia wrenched herself free of his grasp and ran to the door.

"Maybe I will hurt you, you little vixen." He was faster than she was, and pinned her to the wall next to the door before she could open it. "I bet you taste good," he leered and reached to kiss her.

"Get away from me!" Cordelia used all her strength to push him off. He still had hold of her, though, and they both tumbled to the floor, hitting the table on the way.

A wineglass shattered, and a shout came from the

hallway. The guard must have heard the fight.

Cordelia tried to sit up, but Hayden crawled on top of her, grabbing her arms to hold her down. Throwing caution to the winds, she screamed at the top of her lungs, hoping someone in this house had a shred of human decency.

Hayden slapped her hard across the jaw, snapping her head to the side. "Don't scream."

If he knocks me unconscious, at least I won't know what happens, she thought, dazed.

Then, through a haze of stars across her vision, Cordelia saw the door open. Miraculously, Sebastien stepped through it. His clothes were rough, and his expression was pure fury, his eyes burning. Her avenging angel. *He hit me harder than I thought.* That was all Cordelia could come up with to justify seeing her beloved in this place.

But that didn't explain why Hayden howled in rage, or why he suddenly tried to grab Cordelia again, sputtering something about *ransom*.

Sebastien rushed forward, grabbed Hayden by the hair, and dragged him upward, off the still-prone Cordelia. Hayden dangled almost comically, held up by the enraged Sebastien.

"Cordelia, are you all right?" Sebastien asked.

"Now I am," she breathed.

Staring for a long moment into Hayden's face, Sebastien curled his lip in disgust, then asked his companion, "Take care of this trash for me."

He tossed Hayden into the none-too-gentle grip of the hulking man who accompanied him. "Won't you step outside the room with me, sir?" the man asked. "I have some things to discuss with you. And let's see if your white-haired friend can join us."

He dragged the screaming Hayden through the doorway as if he weighed no more than a sack of flour, and then both disappeared.

Cordelia was disheveled and dirty on the floor, but she still smiled at Sebastien through her tears. "Hello," she said.

Falling to his knees in front of her, he gathered her up and held her as if he would never release her. "I've been looking for you since the morning after you were taken. I thought I'd never see you again," he said, his voice raw.

"I knew you would find me," Cordelia breathed into his ear.

"Are you hurt, love?" He tightened his arms around her, as if trying to protect her from the world.

"Nothing to speak of. I'm glad you got here when you did, though." She shuddered. "How *did* you find me? Here, in this house?"

"We had a hint, and then I followed the trail. Did you think I'd let anyone keep you away from me?"

He kissed her. It had barely been a week since their last kiss, but Cordelia felt like she was drowning in a sea of love when Sebastien put his lips on hers. She hardly wanted to breathe.

A voice from the doorway interrupted them. It was Sebastien's companion. "Sorry to interrupt, but I'm not sure how much time we have. Arceneau must have snuck out when he heard us. I don't know if he'll come back with reinforcements."

"And Hayden?"

"I'm a little upset about that," the black-haired man said flatly. "I barely got to ask him anything when he suddenly keeled over and stiffened up like a plank. His face was purple within a minute. Am I that frightening?"

I expect you are, Cordelia thought, *when you want to*

be .

"He poisoned himself?" Sebastien asked.

"I'm afraid so. Wouldn't have thought he had the guts. Oh, well." He looked around the room. "But as I said, we'd best move on."

Sebastien nodded at his words, reluctantly letting go of Cordelia and helping her stand up. "Oh," he said. "Cor, this is a good friend of mine. He tagged along."

"It was very good of you to come and help retrieve me. I'm afraid I've inconvenienced a lot of people. I'm Cordelia Bering." By habit, she offered her hand as if they were at just another party of the *ton*. Not that this man looked like he spent much time among the *ton*.

The other man's lip quirked. He appreciated the absurdity as well. He bowed over her hand, saying, "Bruce Allander. Lord Forester, actually. I'm pleased to meet you, but we really should get out of here."

"Wait." Cordelia nodded weakly toward the table. "The plans."

"Take them?" Forester asked, moving to gather them up.

"No. Burn them."

"She's right." Sebastien nodded, putting his arm around Cordelia to help support her. "We don't want to be caught with them."

Forester swept all the papers into the fire, which suddenly flared with sooty orange flames. The trio watched it all disappear into smoke.

"Farewell, *Andraste*," Cordelia whispered.

CORDELIA'S ORDEAL WASN'T OVER—THEY were still far from a safe haven. Before the trio left the house, Sebastien picked up a cloth bundle he'd brought along, telling her, "You'll need to be unremarkable if we're to get you out of Calais. Hayden might not have been working for France, but this town is crawling with soldiers who do."

He draped a lightweight wool cloak around her, the fabric dyed a forest green. "Keep the hood up," he warned. "I don't want anyone to see your face or remember who you are."

She nodded, pausing only to bind her hair back with a strip of cloth. "Where are we going?"

"The harbor. A friend awaits us there. I hope." He glanced at her, and then over to Forester, saying to him, "You both have black hair. If anyone asks, she's your sister."

"I've always wanted a sister," Forester quipped. "Perhaps I could trade my brother in."

"Who would take Ash in trade?" Sebastien asked.

"No one I know," Forester growled, frowning.

She didn't get a chance to ask who they were talking about, as Forester urged them to hurry. "We don't know if someone heard something and will get nosy," he warned.

The hour was late, but the main thoroughfares were still active. Not wanting to risk even a half hour in plain view, the men hired a coach to drive them to the harbor. The driver was paid well, but Cordelia imagined the looming threat in Forester's stony expression was just as important in getting the man to agree. Ever alert to the subtleties of such situations, Forester stated that he would ride beside the coachman. "Just in case the man gets any ideas," he muttered.

Sebastien gave him a grateful nod, then helped Cordelia into the carriage. She huddled in Sebastien's arms, not quite trusting that she wasn't dreaming. He was silent, and she could feel the tension in his body. When she looked up at him, he was watching her with an inscrutable expression.

"Are you really here?" she asked.

"Yes, love. I found you."

"How will we get home?"

"We're going to get a ship across the channel. A friend is the captain, and we can trust him. Soon you'll be back where you belong."

At the harbor, Forester hunted down the location of the *Mistral*, while Sebastien kept Cordelia in the carriage. "I'm not going to risk anything at this point," he told her.

Forester returned soon. "Follow me. We cut it fine—the tide's in less than half an hour."

The couple scrambled out of the vehicle, and they all raced down the quay until they stood at the gangplank of the *Mistral*.

Sebastien paused, giving a final glance around, then called out, "Permission to come aboard?"

"Permission granted," a tenor voice responded.

Cordelia caught sight of a youthful-looking man in civilian clothes standing on the deck, though he bore himself with the confidence of a naval captain.

"Let me," Sebastien murmured to Cordelia, picking her up. He carried her up the gangplank and onto the deck. Forester followed, looking behind them to see if they were pursued. The night was undisturbed.

Looking at Cordelia, the man made no attempt to hide his surprise. "That's what we came for?"

Forester grinned. "Yes. You can see why my friend wanted to get her back."

"No argument here," the young man said. He bowed to Cordelia, who had just regained her footing after Sebastien set her down. "Captain Logan Hartley at your service. Welcome aboard the *Mistral*."

"She's beautiful," Cordelia said, looking up at the mast and sails. "I've never seen a sloop quite like her. What's her draw? And is the keel a bit unusually shaped? Is it elm? It must be elm, yes?"

Before Hartley could reply, Sebastien gently hinted that the discussion could wait. Hartley nodded and ordered his crew to begin to ready the ship to sail. He looked at Forester. "Were you followed?"

"We don't think so. And I trust your business is done?" Forester asked casually. "He's a smuggler," he told Cordelia.

"Oh, am I being smuggled now?" she replied, feeling rather giddy.

"Right back to England, Miss Bering," the captain replied.

"How long will the crossing take? I'd love to see your ship in the daylight."

"Time enough for that," Sebastien interjected. "You need to rest, Cordelia."

"Are you injured?" Hartley asked, concerned.

"Just exhausted," she explained. "I had a rather difficult few days…wait, what day is it?"

"Thursday. Soon to be Friday."

"Oh, no. My absence will be awkward to explain."

"It's already being addressed. Come, I'll explain in the cabin." He glanced at Hartley. "Same one?"

"It's all yours," Hartley responded, "though it's not quite up to a lady's standards. Call out if you need anything."

In the small cabin below, Sebastien laid Cordelia on a bunk that was tucked into the wall, a nook that not even the worst storm could shake. She looked around. A lantern hung from the ceiling, swinging slightly on the chain. The light cast from the yellowed glass made the room seem warm and cozy, though the cold sea air belied the image. Sebastien tucked a blanket around her.

He surveyed her carefully, checking for damage that he might have missed in his initial fury. "You must be starving."

"They fed me. Though my appetite wasn't strong. I would like water."

"In that bottle there," he said, pointing. "Do you need anything else?"

She needed him. Cordelia finally felt safe again, now that Sebastien was with her. She couldn't stand the thought of losing him. "Nothing at the moment. Just don't leave me alone."

"I'm here as long as you need me." He knelt by the bed, his eyes vulnerable and looking oddly young. He took her hands in his own. "I need to tell you something, Cor. When you disappeared, I thought I would go mad. I couldn't sleep, wondering where you were. And it was my fault."

"How?"

"Because I didn't explain myself before, and I made

you think that leaving me was the only option you had. I should have said it earlier. I need you."

"You have me," she said wonderingly. "I'm right here."

"I mean that I need you forever. Not as a lover or a mistress, but as my wife. I bungled it before, and I didn't tell you what I really meant to say. I love you, Cor. I've never loved anyone the way I love you. Please let me care for you for the rest of our lives. Marry me. Not to protect your reputation, or for protection of any kind, but because you *want* to be with me, and my equal in all things."

"Oh," she said, her heartbeat suddenly fluttering. She'd received so many proposals before, but none like this. "Oh. Sebastien."

"I mean it. I love you, Cordelia," he said, his eyes on hers. "I wish I could say it in a more poetic way, but all I have is the truth. I love you."

She breathed in very slowly, aware of how much that speech had exposed him, the noble, the spy, the man used to knowing more than anyone else in the room. "If we're being truthful...I love you as well."

A smile lit his face. "Then you'll marry me?"

"I...I do want to." More than anything.

"But what?" he asked, his eyes darkening.

"My life...my work..."

"Your life is always yours to live, Cordelia. And I would never dream of asking you to stop pursuing your work," he vowed. Then he added, "Though you must promise to inform me if there will be an international incident over a design."

She bit her lip. "Of course I will keep you apprised. But be serious, Sebastien. My household is...unusual..."

"You needn't fear for your reformed disreputable servants," he told her. "We'll keep them all, I promise."

"Truly?"

"Truly. I know they're as good as family to you. And to be honest, they're rather growing on me."

With a sigh, she threw her arms around him, holding him as if she'd never let go. "Oh, Sebastien. What about *your* family? I'm sure I'm not what they expect in a countess."

"Expectations are traps," he said. "You've destroyed every expectation I've had about you. Besides, I know that you've charmed both my mother and my little sister—no mean feat, that."

"Society has expectations too, though."

"You'll find that one of the advantages of being a countess will be that you can ignore virtually anything or anyone you choose," he countered. "And you'll have me to back you up."

"That's true, I suppose." Then she raised her face to his. "What are you waiting for? Kiss me."

He kissed her, and more. He showed her how much he needed her, and her desire matched his. They fell into each other, into a dance they would never tire of no matter how long they were together. Then both lay entwined on the narrow bed, their breathing slowly returning to normal.

Sebastien ran a finger along her jawline, and then traced her lips. "I won't let you go this time, you know."

"I should never have tried to convince myself I didn't need you." She smiled at him. "We've got hours to cross the channel. Kiss me again."

"I love you," he breathed. "I should have told you long before."

"No matter, as long as you keep telling me from now on." Cordelia smiled at him. "And you'll have to bear me telling you the same."

"Awful fate," he murmured.

Then his mouth touched hers, and she forgot everything else.

* * * *

The *Mistral* crossed the channel as if a hurricane were at her back. The wind favored the midnight enterprise, filling the sails so that the ship seemed to fly through the darkness.

As dawn approached, Cordelia emerged from the cabin looking much more alive than when she boarded the night before. Part of the reason may have been the way Sebastien hovered by her side, his arm firmly around her waist.

The ship sailed up the Thames and came to dock. Once again, she kept the hood of her cloak up to conceal her identity. She was profoundly grateful that the day was too young for many people to have arisen. The streets were still largely empty, with the exception of some hurrying to work and street hawkers setting up for the day. They were all too busy at their tasks to notice anything else.

Sebastien left Forester with Hartley and hired a closed carriage to take Cordelia the last leg home. He gave the driver the name of Quince Street, and bundled Cordelia inside the carriage. He sat next to her and cradled her against his body.

She recalled the first time he'd done so, after Hayden had attacked her. "Do you remember when you used that paltry excuse of a knife wound to put your arm around me, on that first night you showed up in my carriage?"

"You saw through that, did you?" He smiled down at her.

"Eventually." She cuddled closer to him, and whispered, "But if I had avoided that maneuver, I'm sure you would have thought of something else."

"When it came to capturing your eye, Cor, I have almost limitless determination."

"I'm glad," she said, her eyelids closing. "You kept me up most of the night, Sebastien. Wake me when we get there."

"Anything you say, my love." He kissed the top of her head, and his arm tightened around her. Cordelia fell into a doze, feeling she was already home.

THE HIRED CARRIAGE ROLLED UP to the house at 42 Quince Street. Sebastien nudged Cordelia awake. "It's time, love."

She sat up just as Jem ran to the door of the conveyance and flung it open without asking. "Very glad to see you home again, my lady!"

Sebastien leaned forward. "Please tell a maid to wake Mrs Wharton. Miss Bering will need assistance."

Jem's expression turned serious. "Are you ill, ma'am? Injured?"

She shook her head. "I'm fine, Jem, but I am tired, and Aunt Leona ought to know I'm back."

Sebastien helped Cordelia out of the carriage. Jem ran ahead, opened the doors of the house, and alerted nearly everyone with one shout.

Cordelia walked into the house on her own feet—it was important to her that she do that—but then it seemed she was not allowed to do a thing for herself. Bond actually burst into tears of joy on seeing her mistress back, and even Stiles had suspiciously glassy eyes. Sebastien stayed near Cordelia the whole time, forgoing all previous subterfuge. Evidently, he intended to make his place very clear.

When Aunt Leona entered the drawing room, Cordelia thought the older woman might faint. "Please sit, Aunt. I am quite safe and well, you will see."

"I'm so happy," Leona said, sinking into a chair next to Cordelia. "I knew Lord Thorne was doing his best, but…oh, my dear, I thought something terrible had happened to you! I couldn't sleep. If Edward…that is, if Mr Dunham hadn't been there to lean on, I don't know what I would have done."

"Well, I am back, and all will be well."

Leona nodded. "I've done my best to keep your disappearance quiet, but a few people asked after you. I said you were at the house in Bristol. There might be…consequences."

Thorne cleared his throat. "I suppose this is as good a time as any to make a small announcement."

Cordelia looked at Sebastien, who was waiting for her approval to speak further. "Go on, Sebastien," she said, using his given name quite deliberately.

He smiled at her, and said to Leona, "I'm happy to say that Cordelia has accepted my offer of marriage, and the wedding will happen as soon as humanly possible."

Leona clapped her hands together once. "Oh, how wonderful!"

A while later, Bond took Cordelia upstairs and insisted on giving her a scorching-hot bath. "You need to scrub out the past, my lady," she said. Cordelia couldn't disagree.

While in the hot water, she drank a glass of brandy, a remedy also insisted on by Bond, and then was tucked into her bed like a child.

She slept a blessedly dreamless sleep until hunger awoke her in the evening. Bond dressed her in a lovely, loose-fitting gown and draped the jade pendant around her neck.

"There's a bit of a celebration planned," the maid explained.

Downstairs, she found that both Sebastien and Mr Dunham were in the parlor, along with Leona. Everyone was dressed for dinner. The only guest who had not yet arrived was Mr Jay, who had been notified of Cordelia's return.

Dunham lifted his glass to Cordelia when she appeared. "The prodigal returns," he said. "But now that you're back, I find myself at a loss. I was able to offer comfort and diversion to Leona in your absence. Perhaps I have overstayed my welcome."

Her aunt smiled like a schoolgirl. "Your jests will never cease, will they?"

"I see that he has been a true companion to you," Cordelia said, a wry edge to her voice.

Leona moved to stand quite close to Mr Dunham. "Well, we have reached an understanding."

"Mr Dunham has finally proposed to you," Cordelia guessed.

"A second marriage may not have the thrill of the first, but I managed to convince this charming lady that it might be better than she expects." The stately Dunham looked very pleased with himself. And Leona had a glow about her that made her look many years younger.

"Congratulations," Sebastien said, moving so that Cordelia could feel the heat of him next to her.

Then Ivy knocked on the drawing room door. "Mr Jay," she announced.

As Ivy moved aside, Sebastien leaned down. In a low voice, he said, "You should prepare yourself, Cor. Mr Jay may not look his best."

She looked at him, puzzled. "What do you mean?"

He didn't have the chance to explain before footsteps sounded in the hall, accompanied by an odd clicking. Mr Jay appeared in the doorway.

Cordelia gasped, and Aunt Leona cried out in dismay.

"William!" Cordelia was so shocked that she let his given name slip out. Her own ordeal forgotten, she rushed over to her friend.

She surveyed his injuries. He was walking with the aid of a cane. One foot was bandaged. Worse than that, his face bore the marks of slowly healing bruises, and gloves couldn't conceal the damage to his hands. Cordelia helped Jay to a seat. "I don't know what to say. What *happened* to you?"

Mr Jay looked at the floor. "I hesitate to relate the details to a lady, Miss Bering."

Sebastien interjected quietly, "He had an encounter with some of Hayden's gang. From what he told me earlier, I expect Hayden himself was responsible for much of the damage."

Jay looked devastated. "It's true. It happened the night of…the night you were taken, Miss Bering. I was at my club. Someone found me and told me you had sent an urgent message for me. Of course, like a fool, I followed him out into the street. There I was manhandled and taken to an alley where four other men were hiding. They set on me. They made me tell them about the *Andraste* plans. About Lear. About you, Miss Bering. I'm so sorry."

"Oh, William, *look* at you. They almost killed you!"

"They might have if I'd kept silent," he agreed. "But still, it was unconscionable that I told them anything. I betrayed you, and it nearly resulted in your death."

Sebastien said, "I called at your house the following morning and found out that you weren't here. I started by looking for anyone who might know your whereabouts. I found Mr Jay at home, abed, recovering from the injuries Hayden's men gave him."

"I feel dreadfully responsible," Jay said. "Miss Bering,

I beg your forgiveness."

She shook her head. "No. I refuse to forgive you when you did nothing wrong."

"Miss Bering…"

"Fine, then! I forgive you! I forgive you for telling men who were beating you to death what they wanted to know, and for being human and for loving life. But now you must forgive me for making *you* a party to my ill-advised Lear persona. I forced you to lie, and I put you in danger."

"I didn't mind in the least." He winced as he moved. "Well, not till this week."

"In any case, Lear is retiring," she informed him. "I've learned my folly regarding living a lie such as that. Henceforth, there will be no more secrets."

Beside her, Sebastien smiled. "Well, there will still be a few secrets."

Across the room, Cordelia caught the eye of Stiles, standing unobtrusively in one corner. He didn't smile, but she knew he was laughing inside.

Then the butler announced that dinner was served.

* * * *

Late that night, after he bid good night to Cordelia, Sebastien Thorne once again headed to the discreet offices of the Zodiac. He knocked on the outer door, and it was instantly opened by the woman named Chattan.

"Good evening, sir," she said, stepping aside to allow him in. This time she was less covered in ink, though her light hair was messily bound and she still exhibited no regard for the niceties of ladies' fashion. She opened Neville's door without knocking and announced, "Sagittarius is here."

At Neville's invitation, Thorne came inside. Chattan closed the door behind him.

Neville looked Thorne over. "Allow me to congratulate you on your coming nuptials."

"That just happened. Is there *anything* you don't know?"

Neville paused. "No. At least not that I know of."

That rare flash of humor let Sebastien know that Aries was in a good mood. "Speaking of weddings, I have something of a gift to give you, sir."

"How so?" Neville asked.

"My frighteningly clever fiancée wants to offer this to His Majesty's government." He placed a roll of papers on Neville's desk. They were the final and correct plans for the *Andraste*. "I think you'll find them interesting."

Neville picked up the papers, unrolled them, and began to look them over. His eyes widened. "Is this feasible?"

"In theory, yes. Cordelia incorporated several innovations into this design. She thinks it can be built, though only as a prototype. The cost will be significant, and some of the processes need refinement. Still, if a ship like the *Andraste* can be made, it will change the face of battle."

"Indeed."

"If the Astronomer agrees, perhaps these can be sent to the right department in the navy…through the proper channels, of course."

Neville said, "You managed to find quite an asset, didn't you?"

Thorne recognized *that* tone, and headed it off. "Don't think you can count her as an agent, Aries! My soon-to-be wife is quite done with international espionage."

"Let's hope so." Neville smiled, but his air was a bit distant.

Thorne frowned. "Something on your mind about the assignment?"

"No. This one has concluded brilliantly."

Something in Neville's choice of words disturbed him. "There have been others that haven't ended as well?"

"Too many. Good agents have been lost. Information has been wrong. We like to think we're smarter than the other side, but that's an efficient way to die. The Emperor has someone like me working for him, and whoever he is, he's doing an excellent job. This conflict won't end soon. It will get worse."

"It is a war. We will have losses."

"Losses like *these* are unacceptable. Suspicious."

"Someone sold us out?"

Neville looked up. "If someone has, I will bloody well find him and kill him with my bare hands."

Thorne didn't doubt that for a moment. Neville only looked harmless.

The other man sighed, shaking off his mood. "Speaking of that, I want to tell you something, Thorne. I'm taking you out of the field."

"What?" Thorne sat up in his chair, outraged. "After what you just told me?"

"Never think that I'm not proud of what you've accomplished. But the time has come for a change, and I'm sure you'll agree with me...after you've had a chance to think it over." Neville held up one hand to prevent Thorne from interrupting. "I have a new assignment for you: I want you to take over the recruitment and training of the Zodiac's agents."

Thorne blinked, stunned. "But...I don't have any experience doing that."

"You didn't have experience being a spy when I met you either. But you learned."

"You think I can do this?"

"I can't think of anyone better. And you'll be able to stay here in England with your new wife, and better act the part of the earl, which I know has been a difficulty so far. What do you say?"

"I'd be honored."

"Good." Neville smiled. "Your first student has already been chosen, and I expect he'll leap at the chance to join us."

"Who's that?" asked Thorne.

"Young Ensign Hartley."

Thorne laughed. "He does seem to have the personality for it."

"Brash, daring, stupid, and smart," Neville said. "And a smuggler to boot. He has potential."

Thorne returned to the main issue. "The most important thing to realize is that Hayden and his employer Arceneau weren't working for the Emperor, or the government of France. Arceneau told Cordelia he worked for himself. I made the mistake of thinking that the Emperor was aware of the *Andraste*, but it seems he doesn't know about it. Arceneau is a rogue. We must devote more attention to finding out about the man."

Neville nodded. "Absolutely. You'll submit your report on what happened tomorrow, of course. As a wedding gift, I shall not ask you to start your new duties until after you return from your honeymoon. You *are* taking her on a honeymoon, yes?"

"We haven't discussed it yet," Thorne said. "If we do, wherever it is, it will be somewhere extremely boring and safe." In fact, he decided that *boring* and *safe* were two words he was becoming quite enamored with.

↗

HUMID SUMMER HAD TAKEN HOLD of London, the Season was over, and the city had already begun to empty out. The wedding of Lord Thorne and Miss Bering would be a small one, which suited nearly everyone involved.

Their engagement was announced to polite society, and the countess endured many well-meant condolences on the folly of the next Earl of Thornebury, marrying a woman with few connections and no prospects, especially considering the state of the Thorne family's finances. To those people, she admitted only that her son was most determined on the match, and she had no power to change it. But she said it with a smile.

Cordelia herself was set upon by an unexpectedly high number of callers. Most of them simply left their cards, because Cordelia was understandably busy preparing for her unexpected change in fortune. However, she received a few guests in the drawing room, where she entertained them with mostly fabricated accounts of her courtship, since the truth would have been frankly unbelievable. (Elly proved quite adept at making up utter nonsense about Cordelia and Sebastien's early conversations, while making it sound as though Cordelia had been chaperoned the entire time.) She endured several cautionary tales about the dangers of marrying impoverished noblemen, no matter how handsome they were. Cordelia listened to all this advice graciously and did not care in the slightest.

Sebastien called on her nearly every day. Following the announcement of the engagement, his privileges in seeing her, both in public and in private, were considerably expanded. They were able to walk, dine, and drive where they liked. Cordelia reveled in the novelty of performing such non-clandestine activities. When she confessed that to Sebastien, he laughed out loud.

"I'd almost forgotten how!" he said. Then he took her hand in his. "Marrying you might well save my sanity, Cordelia. You'll keep me anchored."

"You'll find plenty to anchor you at Thorne Hall, from what I've heard about the place," she warned him. "And if you carry out your plans for a…school there, we'll have plenty of intrigue ahead."

"Oh, our life together will never lack interest," he said, his tone full of promise.

Cordelia blushed, believing every word.

Aided by his mother and the shrewd young Adele, Sebastien continued to keep accurate news of the state of the Thorne fortunes as quiet as he could. His solicitors drew up several legal documents before the marriage, some of them quite odd. Cordelia was permitted to keep ownership of all papers in her home that had belonged to her father and his colleagues, including those of a man known as Mr Lear. The solicitors didn't understand that one at all, but Lord Thorne was most insistent, and when an earl insists, the matter is done.

For her part, Cordelia laughed at the annual amount of pin money Sebastien settled on her. "What could I possibly do with that much?"

"I'm sure you'll think of something," he said smugly. "Besides, I have to compete with Lear's old income, don't I?"

"You have no competition, my dear."

About one week before the wedding, Cordelia and Sebastien called all of the servants together. Though events had kept everyone busy, there was an underlying concern about what would happen after the marriage.

Cordelia looked over the faces of her household.

"Good morning," she said. "It would be an understatement to say that two months ago, I would not have expected any of this to be happening. I can't tell you how much I appreciate the steadiness of your support. I only hope that I can someday repay the trust you have shown."

Stiles cleared his throat. "My lady, it is your trust *we* have been repaying." A murmur from the others confirmed his words.

Cordelia smiled fondly at her butler, then went on. "As you know, I will be moving to Thorne Hall in Cheshire following the wedding. And Mrs Wharton will be marrying Mr Dunham at the end of the summer, so she will of course join his household."

A sniff from Mrs Landry was loud enough to be heard throughout the room. "Won't ever be the same, my lady, after we shut up this house and go our separate ways."

Sebastien broke in before the maids could start crying en masse. "That is the issue we wish to discuss," he said. "Miss Bering has made it quite clear to me that she regards you all as her family. And family does not get cast aside when situations change, no matter how drastic that change is."

He looked around the room, having captured everyone's attention. "Cheshire is a long way from here, but we have space for everyone. However, it is my intention that those of you who join us at Thorne Hall will not just be regular servants. I have an idea which will require people with a very particular background. Ordinary servants will simply not do."

A mild babble broke out, but Cordelia soon calmed everyone. "What my fiancé is saying is that those who wish to can join a…sort of school for servants. A special school, where people we trust will learn not only the usual tasks of serving, but also a few extra skills." She smiled. "And you may use some of the more unusual skills you gained in previous lives."

Jem half raised his hand. "My lady, are you saying I can be a footman *and* a thief?"

"I'm saying, dear Jem, that you'll be a man who can play at being a footman in order to catch thieves…and others who would harm the people and the country we love."

"Oh, well, then. I think I'd fancy that," he responded with a grin.

"So would I," Lucy Bond echoed, twining her hand in Jem's.

* * * *

On the day of the wedding, Cordelia woke up early. Bond entered with a breakfast tray. "Last morning you'll be breakfasting alone, my lady," she said with a knowing smile. "Eat up. You wouldn't want to faint in church!"

Cordelia ate a little bread and butter with her tea, then Bond dressed her in her wedding finery. The ivory gown was extravagant, the delicate lace worked in rosettes all along the length of the skirt. Bond carefully curled her hair, and held the locks in place with a circlet of green-tinged roses, created especially by Aunt Leona. Cordelia's gloves were light green as well. At her throat, she wore Sebastien's wedding gift, an emerald necklace of stunning deep green stones. Bond treated the stones with the sort of reverence that only a jewel thief could.

Cordelia walked down the stairs with Bond following faithfully behind her, watching the slight train of her dress so it would not get torn.

She entered the drawing room, where Elly and Leona waited. Upon hearing about the engagement, Elly had instantly agreed to attend her for the ceremony. In order to keep Cordelia the center of attention, she dressed in simple pale blue lawn. She wore pearls and her light hair was coiffed into an elegant knot.

"Oh, you are a perfect bride!" Elly exclaimed. "Just looking at you makes me want to get married all over again."

"I think the Church has rather firm rules about that, so long as you still have Mr Ramsay," Leona commented. Then she gazed happily at her niece. "You are a vision, Cordelia. I always knew you would become a bride."

"Despite my many protests to the contrary?" Cordelia looked indulgently at her aunt.

"Oh, yes. You are made for loving, my dear. Such a heart as yours needs to have someone to love."

"I would have been happy living with you till we were two old ladies."

"Before you met your match, perhaps. But once Lord Thorne crossed your path…that was that!" Aunt Leona shrugged, consigning everything to Fate.

"And I am not the only one in love today," Cordelia noted slyly.

"Yes, well." Leona looked down, smiling. "Edward is a good man."

"It is a good match," Cordelia insisted.

"I think so," a male voice said from the hallway. The ladies saw Mr Dunham standing there, grinning without a trace of compunction. Since Cordelia had no close male relative to give her away, she had rather shyly asked Mr Dunham to perform the service, seeing as they would soon be nearly related anyway. The gentleman had accepted the offer graciously, and so it was he who rode with her to the parish church.

When the carriage stopped in front of the church steps, he jumped out and helped her, paying careful attention to the dress. "Your maid will have my head if I allow anything to happen to it," he said.

At a signal, they entered the church and walked down the aisle to where the party had gathered, all watching her advance on Dunham's arm.

She saw Sebastien standing on the dais, and her heart nearly stopped on seeing him—the man who snuck into her life as a spy, and found a home in her heart. Cordelia glowed with a happiness she'd never felt before. She felt as innocent and as radiant as, well, a bride.

She beamed at Sebastien when he took her hand.

Neither Cordelia nor Sebastien remembered a word of the ceremony.

Afterward, everyone returned to the Quince Street house for the celebration. Stiles and Mrs Landry had outdone themselves in preparing the house for visitors. The dining room was filled with flowers, and the best dishes were laid out with a precision that the great houses of England couldn't best.

Sebastien's mother looked around and gave her approval. "Very lovely. And on such short notice! You run a house well, Cordelia."

"I have been extremely lucky with my help," she replied, straight-faced.

The meal was lively. Mr Ramsay looked as besotted with his wife as if they were the newlyweds, and young Adele demonstrated her ability to capture a man's attention in the way that she effortlessly snared Jay with her innocent laugh.

Dunham showered all the ladies with compliments,

saving the most ridiculous ones for Leona, sparking laughter around the table. Even Sebastien's laconic best man, Lord Forester, seemed amused.

Cordelia looked around and decided that if this was the path her life took, she had no cause for complaint. And when she caught her husband's gaze, she knew that she was destined for happiness.

After the final toasts, Cordelia invited the guests to join her in the gardens, where cake and tea would be served. The gardens were in marvelous form and filled with the timeless scent of summer, the roses at the height of their season. The gazebo had been draped with pale green bunting, and rose petals were strewn all over the paths.

Adele, normally so convinced of her own taste, was quite impressed by the overall effect, and got a speculative look in her eye as she surveyed the gardens.

The happy couple stood under a tree with Sebastien's mother. His arm around Cordelia's shoulders, Sebastien watched his sister's antics and said, "Best take notes, Mother dear. I think my little sister is getting ideas for her own wedding."

Lady Thorne smiled. "She'll have ten thousand ideas for her wedding before the real thing occurs. I only pray she doesn't make me wait as long as you did!"

"It was worth the wait. Don't you think I found a perfect bride?" He smiled down at Cordelia.

"She's not what I would have expected," his mother noted. "But sensible and intelligent. She's a good match for you, and she'll be an excellent mistress of Thorne Hall." She paused, smiling at Cordelia. "Now, you two wander off into a bower or something. It's the beginning of your life together. You must make this day memorable!"

"I couldn't agree more," Sebastien said.

He led Cordelia to a stone bench in a secluded part of the grounds. It was surrounded by newly opened roses, making the air heady with their scent. He said, "Did I not meet you in a place just like this?"

She looked up to him, her heart in her eyes. "You forget that it was night, and that marriage was the furthest thing from your mind when you sought to kiss me."

"True. I suspected you were part of some heartless design to seduce me. But I very quickly realized that my attraction to you wouldn't ever fade."

She offered him her hand. "Well, go on and say it. I know what the gossip will be. 'Heartless' Cordelia Bering finally gave in."

He shook his head. "The gossips will never comprehend one-tenth of the truth. Let them talk." He took her hand in his, and kissed her palm gently. "I know you're not, and never have been, heartless."

"Of course I am," she said, laughing, even as her heart began to race. "I gave my heart to you."

He swept her up into his arms. "But you took mine in exchange."

"A fair trade, then." She smiled and kissed him. "Now, my heart, let's go and face the world together."

ABOUT THE AUTHOR

Elizabeth Cole is a romance writer with a penchant for history. Her stories draw upon her deep affection for the British Isles, action movies, medieval fantasies, and even science fiction. She now lives in a small house in a big city with a cat, a snake, and a rather charming gentleman. When not writing, she is usually curled in a corner reading...or watching costume dramas or things that explode. And yes, she believes in love at first sight.

Find out more at: elizabethcole.co